Wild in Montana

JULES BENNETT
& JOANNE ROCK

MILLS & BOON

First Published 2019
Second Australian Paperback Edition 2024
ISBN 978 1 038 90600 7

First Published 2021
Second Australian Paperback Edition 2024
ISBN 978 1 038 90600 7

MIX
Paper | Supporting responsible forestry
FSC® C001695
FSC www.fsc.org

Published by
Mills & Boon
An imprint of Harlequin Enterprises (Australia) Pty Limited (ABN 47 001 180 918), a subsidiary of HarperCollins Publishers Australia Pty Limited (ABN 36 009 913 517)
Level 19, 201 Elizabeth Street
SYDNEY NSW 2000
AUSTRALIA

Printed and bound in Australia by McPherson's Printing Group

CONTENTS

Montana Seduction

Jules Bennett

USA TODAY bestselling author **Jules Bennett** has published over sixty books and never tires of writing happy endings. Writing strong heroines and alpha heroes is Jules's favorite way to spend her workdays. Jules hosts weekly contests on her Facebook fan page and loves chatting with readers on Twitter, Facebook and via email through her website. Stay up-to-date by signing up for her newsletter at julesbennett.com.

Books by Jules Bennett

Harlequin Desire

The Rancher's Heirs

Twin Secrets
Claimed by the Rancher
Taming the Texan
A Texan for Christmas

Texas Cattleman's Club: Houston

Married in Name Only

Two Brothers

Montana Seduction

Visit her Author Profile page at millsandboon.com.au, or julesbennett.com, for more titles.

You can find Jules Bennett on Facebook, along with other Harlequin Desire authors, at Facebook.com/harlequindesireauthors!

Dear Reader,

I'm beyond thrilled to bring you two fun, sexy stories involving twin brothers Dane and Ethan. Up first is Dane, a recluse who just wants to gain back his late mother's property so he can go home to his ranch. Oh, but I have something much more exciting for him than a quick in and out. He won't sneak off that easily.

Stella wants this resort for herself and has no clue her competition is the late owner's son! Oops! This could get tricky, especially since they get along so well behind closed doors.

I'm a sucker for combining a multitude of tropes so I hope you enjoy the close proximity, stranded in a snowstorm, mistaken identity, twin combo in *Montana Seduction*. I'm also all for a strong shero who knows what she wants and gives the hero a good challenge. This was definitely one fun book to write!

I hope you all enjoy Dane and Stella and look forward to the next book featuring Ethan.

Happy reading!

Jules

To Lori Foster,
who spoke at the first writer's meeting
I ever attended *a few years ago* and
has turned into a great friend.
Thank you for everything!

One

Getting dumped only days before the wedding and spending the romantic mountain honeymoon at a fantasy adults-only resort by himself was humiliating. What could be worse than going on a honeymoon riding solo?

Or at least, that was the response Dane Michaels was counting on.

Sympathy could be a powerful tool, and he planned to use it in his favor. No one would have the slightest suspicion about the poor, abandoned man staying at Mirage Resort and Spa—and by a combination of laying on the charm and playing on everyone's solicitousness, he should be able to get all the information he needed.

So did it really matter that Dane had never actually had a fiancée—never intended to marry? The lie had embedded itself so deep in his head, he was more than ready to play the part of the jilted groom.

Dane pulled his truck to the front of the resort. The four-story lodge seemed suspended on the side of Gold Valley

Mountain and with each guest suite having one-way windows from floor to ceiling, nearly every angle offered a breathtaking view of the valley below.

Gold Valley, Montana, had been his mother's first choice when opening Mirage. She'd had a vision, a life plan. But before she could fulfill her dreams, she'd suffered a fatal stroke, and her bastard husband, Robert Anderson, had taken over the two Mirage resorts and left Dane and his brother, Ethan, penniless and alone.

Dane exited the vehicle before the valet could assist him with the door. Dane wasn't here for the amenities or the secret rooms designed to fulfill couples' fantasies. He was here for one purpose and one purpose only—to find his opening to get this resort back in his name where it belonged, so he could honor his mother's memory.

Slipping the attendant a couple of Benjamins, Dane headed up the stone steps leading to the grand entrance. Nostalgia threatened to suck the breath from his lungs, but he pushed on, determined to get exactly what he came here for.

He hadn't been back in so long for several reasons. Mainly because he didn't want to return until he was sure he could secure this place for himself. The time had come.

Ignoring the pain of being back nearly two decades after his mother's death, Dane steeled himself against any emotions. He hadn't gotten this far by being soft and sensitive. Dane had been smacked with a dose of reality at the age of eighteen and life had been a giant kick in the ass since.

Everything he'd done, he'd crawled and fought for until he got back the money, the power due to him…there was just one thing left.

Without a glance to any of the couples milling about in the open lobby, Dane headed straight to the front desk to check in, reminding himself to remain constantly aware of those around him. There was no room for error and no time to waste.

Dane had a nearly twenty-year-old promise to fulfill.

Mirage manager Stella Garcia had no clue who he was, had no idea her world was about to change. Mustering up charm and sex appeal wasn't exactly Dane's area of expertise anymore, he left that to his playboy brother. But right now, and for the foreseeable future, Dane would use every other tool in his arsenal to pull those family secrets from this stranger to get back what belonged to him.

Once upon a time, a seduction would have been Dane's method of choice for an operation like this. Back then, he didn't have to try to get a woman into bed, they were more than willing to follow.

Fighting overseas in Iraq had changed him, hardened him, made him even more hell-bent on getting what he deserved.

It had also left him scarred and horrendous.

Getting close to anyone, let alone being sexual, had been practically impossible ever since. He wasn't stupid or naive. He knew what he looked like, knew doctors said there was hope if he wanted to go through painful surgeries in an attempt to cover the scars.

He didn't need to cover them. They went far beneath the surface of his skin so some vain attempt at erasing the past was a moot point.

And that had been the sole reason as to why he'd been reluctant to follow through on this plan. But when he couldn't think of another way to get what he wanted, Dane realized this might be the only way to gain full control of Mirage.

Besides, he needed a distraction from his own mind, the prison he'd been trapped in since coming home from Iraq.

He'd thought getting his hands dirty and working from dusk till dawn at his ranch would exorcise the demons away, but they were still waiting every single night.

From the photos he'd seen of Stella, flirting with and charming her certainly wouldn't be a hardship. "Charming" wasn't his default mode, but he could turn it on if he needed to. And presenting himself as an abandoned groom seemed tailor-made to winning her sympathies and softening her reserve.

He sure as hell hoped his act of vulnerability and loneliness got her to trust him, to open up and give him a glimpse of exactly how he could use her to get to her father. Presenting himself as some woman's reject chafed at his pride, but he'd put up with it so he could gain the information he needed. Then he'd head back to his ranch, make this deal a legal thing and no one would even care about his initial plan.

Of course he'd have to hire someone to run the resort. That person would have to be trustworthy and loyal. Dane would accept nothing less than the best for his mother's place.

Dane kept his sunglasses firmly in place and quickly checked in, turning down the offer to have his bags taken to his room. He knew the way. There was nothing about this resort he didn't know. A few things may have changed—the decor, the staff—but the layout hadn't. He'd practically grown up here.

Dane had booked the largest luxury penthouse, the one he knew matched the owner's penthouse. They were the only two suites with a mini pool and oversize hot tub off the enclosed bedroom balcony. Lovers could literally take just a few steps from their bed and sink into the pool or hot tub while overlooking the beauty of the mountains and valleys.

All of the rooms were top-notch, but Dane wanted the

best. After all, wouldn't any groom plan the most romantic getaway and spare no expense?

As he stepped into the elevator, Dane removed his glasses and pocketed them. Once he put his things away, he had every intention of going out and "accidentally" running into Stella. He knew her schedule, knew every single thing about her thanks to the investigator he'd hired. Dane's knowledge of her schedule and her personality were the keys to gaining her trust.

Dane was well aware that her father treated her like shit and that he'd given her only six months to prove to him that she could run this place and show a profit—a mammoth undertaking after years of mismanagement had nearly run Mirage into bankruptcy.

Getting Mirage for himself was the main goal, but besting the arrogant bastard who treated his daughter like some bothersome employee was going to be icing on the proverbial cake. Victory was always sweet but victory over assholes was just plain fun. Dane was willing to admit he wasn't exactly an angel himself, but at least he was a smart and careful devil.

Dane left his bag in his suite, taking only a moment to admire the open view and spacious room. The wall of windows made it seem like he was suspended above Gold Valley. The curved pool was just as inviting as he recalled.

Later he would fully take in the beauty of the room his mother had designed. The stone fireplace, the balcony, the high beams stretching across the ceiling.

For now, though, memories would have to wait. He had a woman to find.

"What do you mean he didn't show up?"

Stella Garcia attempted to tamp down the migraine that

threatened to further sour her already stressful, overloaded day. She stared at one of the hostesses for their main dining area and Stella thought for sure the poor girl was going to burst into tears.

Tears solved nothing—a life lesson Stella had learned from the start. Her mother had died after complications giving birth, ultimately leaving Stella with the most unloving father.

For reasons Stella still tried to wrap her mind around, she wanted his approval—craved it even. Would do anything to earn it, even if that meant taking on impossible tasks.

Which was how she found herself in the current situation—running a top-tier resort with a crowd of hungry patrons about to descend for dinner…and no cook.

Maybe if she'd had her mother, maybe if she'd had just one parent who pretended to actually care…

"He called and said he quit, effective immediately," the hostess said, nervously tucking her short blond hair behind her ear. "He said something about moving back home to his wife in Oregon."

Stella pulled in a deep breath and wished she could fast-forward to midnight when she could go up to her suite, pop open the prosecco and unwind.

Unfortunately, at this rate, she didn't even know if she'd get to bed tonight. All-nighters were depressingly common with this job. Some days were certainly more difficult than others, but she had to keep reminding herself that she'd inherited a mess from the previous manager and her father thought her incapable of fixing it. Those were two highly motivational reasons to prove to the whole damn world that she could and would make Mirage the greatest, most talked about resort on the globe.

"Our guests will start rolling in within an hour," she stated, tapping her finger on her chin as she thought out loud. "I'll need to see if there's anything already prepped or if we have to start from scratch. I know zilch about cooking."

But she could make a spreadsheet on the financial analytics of nearly any type of business and never break a sweat. She actually loved business and numbers. Damn, she was such a nerd. Too bad her hobbies hadn't included donning an apron and sizzling steaks.

Her young hostess shook her head. "I burn Pop-Tarts, so don't look at me."

If Stella had the time, she'd call up her now ex-chef and verbally shred him. But using her energy to get angry wouldn't solve their problem. For now, she simply had to push that employee out of her mind because at this point, he was irrelevant.

Really, it was better that he was gone. She didn't want anyone working for her who wasn't loyal. There was no room for mistrust or laziness, especially when she was on the verge of getting Mirage back on its feet and finally taking charge of her own life.

"Maybe Martha could help," the girl suggested.

Stella shook her head. "No, she's off because her sister is getting married. Damn it. She would've been able to salvage this evening. She's an amazing chef. I don't even think Raul is coming in until Friday. I may have to call him in because we are in a bind. But I doubt he'd get here in time."

Employees' names raced through her mind. It was hard to think of any options. The kitchen staff had the perfect rhythm down and worked like clockwork…well, they did until someone decided to up and quit. But the synchronicity meant no one really stood out as someone who could be trusted to take over the kitchen, even just for one night.

"Okay," Stella stated as she tucked a wayward strand of hair behind her ear. "We can do this. There's a logical solution, I just have to figure it out."

"Excuse me?"

Stella jerked her attention to the double wooden doors leading to the bar and private seating area. She was about to say they weren't open yet, but her words died in her throat.

Hello, cowboy.

That charcoal-and-red-plaid shirt tucked into well-worn jeans did nothing to hide the beautifully muscled bulk of the mystery man in the doorway. Those shoulders stretched the material of his shirt and his silver belt buckle shone with some emblem she couldn't quite make out.

Well, she could if she wanted to get caught staring at his junk, which wouldn't really be the classiest move. Not to mention it would be totally unprofessional of her since he was a guest…and likely here with his significant other.

Shame, that. This man might be worth the risk of forgetting her duties and obligations, but she preferred her men to be available…unlike the jerk who thought she was his ticket into the family money—and that she was too dumb to uncover that he actually had a girlfriend with a kid on the way.

Yeah, no thanks, asshole.

Stella pulled her mind from the nauseating memory and opted to focus on the living fantasy standing in the doorway.

But that man would just have to stay a fantasy—along with every other man for the time being—because anything or anyone taking up her time would mean failing at her job, and her father was just waiting for one little slipup to sell this place out from under her. Her sole focus had to be on Mirage.

Smoothing down her button-up shirt-style dress, Stella took a step toward the striking man with dark eyes. "Our dining room doesn't open for another hour. Did you need to make a reservation?"

Which he totally should, because there was plenty of divine food prepared by an experienced chef. Part of Stella wanted to laugh at the snarky comment inside her head, because she'd realized over the past few months that if she didn't laugh, she'd have a nervous breakdown.

But at this moment, she worried that her laughter might border on manic or deranged. She was so, so close to getting what she wanted. There was no way she'd let a rogue chef thwart her plans.

"I couldn't help but overhear that you're in a bind."

That whiskey-soaked voice had her shivering and the vivid fantasy she'd tried to push to the back of her mind kept rushing to the front. Wasn't there some resort rule about lusting after a guest? After all, this was an adults-only resort so he probably wasn't here alone. A man who looked like that likely never slept alone…while she knew no other way.

Oh, she wasn't innocent, but she never stayed the night in someone's bed, and over the past year she'd barely dragged herself into hers. She'd been working her ass off for her father, wanting to gain his approval, wanting…hell, something from him other than disdain.

Getting Mirage running like a dream was her last chance at some type of parental nod.

"I might be able to help," the stranger added.

Stella crossed her arms and smiled. "Oh, well, that's not necessary, but thank you."

"Do you have someone else to cook?" he asked.

Oh, that dark arched brow that accompanied the question had her belly quivering with unwanted arousal. She must be sexually deprived if a brow and a voice turned her on. Well, the whole rough, manly-man exterior also gave a healthy punch of lust.

Maybe she should examine that belt buckle a little closer.

"Are you a chef, Mr...?"

"Michaels. Dane Michaels." In two strides he was in front of her and offering a half grin that drew her eyes down from his perfect teeth to the dark stubble covering his jawline. "I'm not a professional chef, but I'm a damn good cook. Ask any employee on my ranch."

His ranch. Of course someone this rugged and mysterious had a ranch. Montana had no shortage of cowboys, but this guy...he was the real deal and no doubt hands-on with his work if those weathered lines on his face were any indication. Likely the emblem on his buckle was that of his ranch.

"Mr. Michaels—"

"Dane," he corrected and had her toes curling in her boots with that full-fledged smile. "And you are?"

"Stella Garcia. I'm the manager of Mirage." Soon to be owner...she hoped. "Dane, I can't ask a guest to come into the kitchen where food is being prepared."

He propped his hands on his narrow hips and held her gaze. "You didn't ask and I don't see that you have many other options right now. Do you?"

Well, no, but that didn't mean this was a good idea. She couldn't let a stranger just come in and ride to her rescue. Good heavens, if her father heard of that, she'd definitely be reprimanded.

"Stella."

She turned to the Mia, the hostess Stella had completely forgotten was even in the room. "Yes?"

"We just got three more reservations and that booked us up for the night. That doesn't include the fantasy rooms and the room service." Mia chewed on her lip and stared over Stella's shoulder to the fantasy man. "I mean, you should at least think about his offer, but do it fast because in forty-five minutes, people will start coming in."

Stella rubbed her head and tried to remind herself that she wanted this job, that she loved Mirage. So far she'd had one headache after another, but for the most part she'd been cleaning up the mess left by the previous manager. Apparently he'd been a jerk to the employees and now Stella was paying the price of the resulting disloyalty. Loyal employees didn't leave without giving notice.

But she did want to own Mirage. True, she wanted her father to see her as a valuable businesswoman and a capable daughter…they were all the family each other had. But more so, she wanted this place because she'd heard of the woman who built it. A single mother who branched out to create something spectacular all on her own.

How could Stella not admire that and strive to be as strong as the original owner, Lara Anderson? When her father had acquired the resort, Stella had done her research on the place before her father let her in this position. She did that with each of his acquisitions, but this one had always stuck out to her and she'd had her sights set on it for years.

"I can't believe I'm considering this," Stella muttered as she spun back around to Dane.

Had he just been checking out her ass?

Well, well, well.

No. That should not excite her. She'd been in a relationship several years ago with a guy whose eyes, and other body parts, wandered a bit too much.

Stella cleared her throat. "I couldn't pull you away from your significant other."

"I'm actually here alone," he countered.

"Alone?"

"It's a long story," he added with another slight grin—this one looked a little pained. "I'll tell you about it while we prepare dinner. Deal?"

Stella shouldn't go along with this. The idea of letting a stranger, a *guest*, into the kitchen was preposterous, but at this point, she wasn't sure what other option she had. She needed help and she'd be in there the entire time watching to make sure nothing lawsuit-worthy happened, so what could go wrong?

The worst choice would be to do nothing and stand here and have a mental debate with herself. If her father happened to find out what she'd done, she'd be more than happy to defend herself and be proud that she'd pulled this ill-fated night out of despair…so long as this stranger could do all he'd promised.

Stella nodded toward the kitchen. "Follow me, Mr. Michaels."

"Dane, remember?"

As she led the way through the dining room, she felt very aware of the intriguing stranger following closely at her back. She worked with men every single day. Her father was one of the most powerful men in business and had a slew of minions in suits that worked for and with him. None had her in a fluster like this one.

There was certainly something to be said about a mysterious, attractive man riding to the rescue at the eleventh hour. It was like fate had planted him right in her path.

And the fact he was here alone had her even more intrigued. Stella couldn't imagine there wasn't a line of women with lingerie packed and ready for a getaway to a fantasy resort with this guy.

"There should be several starters made up in advance," Stella began as she pushed on the swinging kitchen door. "Let's hope that's the case tonight."

"Either way, it will all work out," he told her.

When that velvety voice washed over her, she wanted to believe him, but considering they were coming from two different positions, she wasn't sure she should be so quick to let her guard down.

"The menu is set up two weeks in advance so we can have enough supplies ordered in—that means we have a direction on where to go." Stella pointed toward the wooden board hanging outside the walk-in refrigerator. "I know we'll have everything for tonight's menu, it's just putting it all together like it should be that's the challenge. And well, I'm not known for my kitchen skills."

Dane stepped around her and placed a hand on her forearm. That warm, rough palm slid over her skin and had her wondering just how those hands would feel over other, more neglected parts of her body.

Now was not the time for her dormant hormones to come rushing back to the surface.

"I promised it would all work out, right?" he asked. Those dark eyes held her in place. "Trust me."

"That's a bit difficult since I don't know you," she stated as she stared into those midnight eyes framed with heavy black lashes. “But for now, I’m going to have to trust my instincts and roll with this plan.”

His thumb stroked over her arm. “I’ll make sure this all works out. For both of us.”

Suddenly, Stella wondered if he wasn’t just referring to dinner.

Two

Dane had originally thought his plan was going to be easy, but getting in the door had taken charm and a little flirting. He was usually so good at getting information he needed.

Both actions painfully outside of his comfort zone these days, but he'd taken a page from his younger, more social brother, Ethan.

For now, Dane would act like he was the most confident, suave man Stella had ever seen. There would be no cause for her to be suspicious. Soon, she'd trust him with all sorts of secrets, and after that, the resort would be his in no time. Finally, after all of these years.

And all he had to do was get close to a striking, sexy woman. Cooking was going to be the easy part, and hopefully this instant foot in the door would give him that extra boost he needed when it came to capturing her trust and attention.

She'd certainly captured *his* attention with no trouble at all. That first glimpse of Stella when she'd turned around had nearly rendered him speechless. Thankfully, he'd remembered why he was here and that any distraction, no matter how sexy, could cost him everything.

Just because he was here to get close to her, didn't mean he could lose sight of the prize.

But then the rest of the kitchen staff started milling in and Stella went to work and took charge. While Dane figured out what the hell he needed to do to create a dinner for one hundred–plus people coming in and out over the next few hours, he also managed to watch Stella in action, knowing that would give him insight as to how to handle his next steps with her.

Damn if she wasn't even sexier when she focused on her own goal. He knew she wanted this resort for herself, he also knew her father wouldn't let that happen. The old bastard was stringing her along and had no intention of giving his daughter anything.

While Dane had never met the man in person, watching him from a distance and hiring an investigator to dig up details had shown that Ruiz Garcia was the biggest male chauvinist jerk Dane had ever heard of.

But that was just one more weapon in his arsenal—a point of connection between them he could use to create sympathy and trust. They both had bastard father/stepfathers and they'd both lost their mothers.

Once all was said and done, and he'd secured Mirage, Stella would see that he'd actually done her a favor by getting her out from under the thumb of her controlling father.

Until then, well, Dane would have to do a little more socializing than he'd planned. The pleasure of spending time with a sultry, alluring woman would make up for the comfort zone he'd stepped so far from. She was responding to him nicely so far—he just had to make sure that he kept up the act…and that he didn't let her expose the ugly, scarred parts of him, whether they were visible or not.

There was one obstacle after another, but that end result…

Several hours and countless dishes of pork roast with mashed potatoes later, Dane worked on the cleanup. The rest of the staff had been dismissed and Stella was out in the dining room straightening everything.

Dane certainly wasn't a star chef, but being raised by a single mother had given him an edge in household tasks. Lara Anderson had been adamant that her boys do every bit of work deemed for "women" and she swore she'd make them good husband material. His mother wasn't here to see that neither of her sons had any intention of being a husband, but Dane was still thankful he'd paid attention when she'd shared her special recipes and guided him through basic preparation steps.

Most of the dishes were washed and put away. From the checklist, it looked like all Dane needed to do was prepare a few things for the breakfast crowd. The fruit needed to be cut and placed into separate bowls. The bread was all ready to go, it just had to be put out at room temperature.

The more Dane did, the more he missed his ranch. Being alone and feeding just one was more his speed. His cattle could fend mostly for themselves and the horses were like his best friends. Aside from his ranch hands, those animals were about the extent of anyone or anything he wanted to care for.

Soon, though. Soon he'd be out of here, with the property in his name and then he could figure out how much time to spend at the ranch and how much to spend here. The penthouse he'd gotten for this stay would be a perfect suite for him to keep, but he knew the owner's suite was even more spectacular. His mother had spared no expense when she had brought her dream to life.

"Well, you saved my ass."

He'd admired said ass quite a bit since first stepping through the dining room. The sway of her little dress as the hem hit the back of her knees. Those tiny buttons that ran down the middle of the front had teased him all night. He'd stared at the one just between her breasts as if willing it to slide right open.

Dane wondered what she wore beneath and opted to use his own imagination. He figured Stella to be a lace type of lady. Someone like her would want to be all business on the exterior yet all woman beneath.

His body responded instantly to the image of her with the dress stripped away, her dark hair around her shoulders and her breasts bound by lace.

Dane slid the sharp knife through the juicy strawberry, but didn't glance up at Stella. She came to stand on the other side of the stainless prep area and rested her palms on the flat surface. If Ethan were in his place he would've cleared off this island and had her beneath him in seconds.

Dane wasn't Ethan. Revealing his body by taking Stella to bed wouldn't seal the deal—it would sour it, once she saw what he was hiding under his clothes. No, there wouldn't be sex—just flirting. Teasing. Winning her trust slowly and carefully. Well, as slowly as his sanity would allow. He wanted Mirage in his name right now, but he knew he had to be patient.

"Happy I could help," he finally replied, attempting to get control over his hormones. He needed to pace himself.

"I'm just going to get this fruit cut up and set in the fridge. What time should I be here tomorrow?"

"Oh, no," Stella retorted. "You've more than helped. I called in our part-time chef and offered an exorbitant amount of money if she would cover for the next few weeks."

Dane stopped slicing and set the knife down as he lifted his gaze to hers. "That wasn't necessary. I would've helped while I was here."

Stella smiled. Not the flirty smile he often got from women when he ventured out, but the type of smile that contained a sense of…pity.

Damn it. He'd seen enough of that from his staff at the ranch when he'd get lost in his war nightmares. He'd let the majority of them go because he did not need sympathy and he didn't want anyone in his house hearing his cries. He refused to take pity from anybody and he sure as hell couldn't afford to have it from the woman he was trying to get close to.

But pity from Stella was a bit easier to handle. She didn't even know the real reason to pity him, so technically her emotions toward him right now were null.

"It's not like I had anything else to do," he replied. "Besides, it wasn't bad and I got to help a beautiful woman."

Stella pursed her lips, but she didn't even blush. He'd have to reconsider his verbiage. Clearly she was either used to compliments or she wasn't interested in them. Either way, he had to tread carefully and keep working to build a connection between them.

"I'm sure you could've done just fine on your own," he amended. "I can't imagine you would've let a rogue chef ruin the night."

Stella crossed her arms over her chest and cocked her

head. "I don't let anyone ruin my plans once I set them into motion."

Perhaps they had even more in common than he'd initially thought. Which would make this entire process that much easier...once they got over this initial get-to-know-you phase.

"That attitude is why this place is so successful." He flashed her a smile and picked up a strawberry, extending it across the island toward her. "You're an admirable woman."

She kept her eyes on his as she took the fruit from his hand. "I've already comped your room for the duration of your stay. Flattery isn't necessary."

Comped his room? Wasn't that adorable. He had enough money to buy this entire resort and not put a dent in his finances, but the fact she'd done so just proved she was sincere in her commitment to Mirage...and her father didn't deserve such loyalty.

"That wasn't necessary," he replied.

With a shrug, she bit into the strawberry. The second her lips closed around her fingers to clean away the juices, Dane was pretty damn thankful he had a barrier between his waist and her eyes.

Was she purposely taunting him? She'd been so all-business before, he'd thought he'd have to be the one to initiate all the flirting. Only one of them could take the lead and he'd already signed up for that position. No way was he going to be sidetracked.

On the other hand, if he'd already gotten her curiosity piqued, his work here could be over sooner than he'd planned.

"I believe you owe me a story," she told him after she finished licking each finger and driving him out of his mind with want. He wanted that mouth on him. "We got so busy you didn't get a chance to tell me how someone like you is at an adult resort all alone."

At least this part he'd rehearsed and prepared for. He didn't know how to hide his actual arousal because that sure as hell wasn't an act and not planned…at least not standing in the resort kitchen.

"I'm on my honeymoon."

Stella stared at him a moment before she let out a sharp laugh. "And you left your wife at home?"

"Actually, my fiancée opted to leave me a couple days before the wedding."

Her smile vanished as her brows shot up. "You're serious."

Dane nodded, pushing forward with the lie that rolled easily off his tongue. "Humiliating as this is to admit, yes. Apparently ranch life wasn't for her and she decided to reconnect with her ex. I thought about canceling the reservations, but I figured I deserved a getaway so here I am. I hope that's not against any house rules."

Stella pulled in a deep breath and made her way around the prep island. Dane shifted to face her as she came to stand before him.

"Not at all. We don't usually get singles, but there's no rule." Stella's dark eyes held him, captivated him. "Your fiancée is either a moron or undeserving. You're better off without her."

"You don't even know me. Perhaps she's the smart one."

Stella reached over and plucked a cut berry from the chopping board and held it out to him. "I realize we just met, but I'm a good judge of character. I'd say you're pretty noble and loyal."

Loyal? Hell yes, he was loyal—to a very select few. There

were only two people in this world he'd do anything for: his twin brother, even though their personalities were completely opposite and they rarely saw each other, and his mother.

His mother was the sole reason for this charade and his brother…well, they each had their own thing going in trying to track down the bastard who stole everything from them once their mother passed. Yes, he knew plenty about loyalty. But he was about as far from noble as he could get.

His plan to take her father down and reclaim what belonged to him might be devious; it might be cruel, even. He wasn't proud of that. For all his faults, he'd never been selfish, he'd never purposely been deceitful. But he was about to do a hell of a job now because the future of his mother's legacy was on the line. With honor on one side and loyalty on the other, his choice was clear. There were no rules for him.

"Looking back, we could best be described more as friends than anything," he added. He didn't want to come off as a complete prick for flirting with Stella right after ending an engagement. "I'd gotten used to the idea of not being alone and being a couple was more habit than anything. She found someone and they're in love. She's happier now."

"And you?" Her question came out in a slight whisper. "Are you happier now?"

Dane swallowed the strawberry and licked his lips. Her eyes darted to his mouth and he wondered if seduction really could be this easy. No wonder Ethan always had a new woman. Still, this wasn't Dane's typical behavior. There was no going back now, though.

Not with the chemistry crackling between them even though he hadn't even laid a finger on her. Damn…he wanted to get her into bed. Even though it wasn't in the plan—even though it might ruin everything—the temptation was growing stronger with every passing moment. Something shifted, something he couldn't quite place a finger on.

Lust. He hadn't expected this strong of a pull. He hadn't wanted a woman in so long. Well, he had natural urges, but to actually feel the desire and the ache…he couldn't recall the last time. Granted, avoiding people in general probably contributed to his lack of sex life. But sex or getting close to anyone would open the door to questions he wasn't ready to answer.

In the last several hours, Dane found he actually wanted to get closer to Stella. That could be the lack of sex in his life talking, though.

"I'm happy that the marriage didn't happen," he stated. "When I marry, I plan for it to be a one-time thing."

He nearly laughed at that statement because he rarely left his ranch, let alone dated anyone. Dodging people and any social activity had been his new normal since leaving the army, deepening the seclusion that had started with the untimely death of his mother, when he'd opted to keep to himself instead of talk to anyone—even Ethan.

So, no. Marrying was certainly off the table because he'd never let anyone get that close to him. Besides the fear of abandonment again, he wouldn't subject anyone to his nightmares.

"So you do want marriage?" she asked.

"Maybe. Eventually. I'm not in a hurry."

He leaned his hip against the edge of the stainless steel and reached out to push her long inky hair over her slender shoulder. There was no reason for him to try to avoid touching her.

He also needed to get away from this topic because the

last thing he wanted her to believe was that he was ready for some fictitious happily-ever-after. The attraction clearly had a place here and that's what he'd hone in on. Any sort of romance had to be left behind.

"You're staying for a week." She smiled and every nerve ending sizzled at that tiny dimple nestled against the corner of her mouth. "Consider every upgrade and meal on the house."

"I can't do that." He shook his head and laughed. "You've already settled the bill for my room. That's more than enough for just helping out over a few hours, though no thanks were necessary."

"Thanks was very necessary," she countered. "Considering I'm riding a thin line and I have someone waiting for me to fail… Well, that's a story for another time."

"So there will be another time?" he asked, not pressuring her on the topic of her father.

Her eyes held his and her smile remained. "As much as I'd like to, I work what seems like thirty hours a day."

"All the more reason to take a break."

"Breaks could cost me everything," she murmured as she glanced away. Then she adjusted her shoulders and returned her focus to him. "It's late and I'm sure you'd like to get to your room and relax."

Only if she came with him.

"I'd relax more if I had some bourbon. Pappy Van Winkle would do the trick, but that's not an option right now," he half joked. "What do you do to relax, Stella?"

Her lids fluttered just a second when he said her name. Good. He wanted her thrown off. He wanted her to be flustered and aroused, thrown off guard enough to let things slip.

"I don't even know what relaxing is," she stated, but he knew she wasn't joking.

"Have a glass of wine with me."

Stella raised a brow. "And what about breakfast prep?"

"I'll finish up afterward," he told her. "I've seen the list and once I get this in the fridge, the rest has to be done in the morning."

"I can't leave a stranger in my kitchen."

Fair enough. "Then help me and we'll get out of here and have that wine."

When she started to shake her head, Dane reached out and gripped her chin with his thumb and forefinger, pulling her gaze directly to his. Those dark eyes held so much emotion. He wondered if she even knew that the pain and the worry inside them was projected to anyone who looked closely.

Had anyone ever looked? Was there someone who took the time to care how much she ran herself ragged? Sure as hell not her father…and Dane wasn't volunteering for that position, either. But she deserved someone. People like Stella worked hard and had great aspirations, but they could get run over.

"Breaks can cost me everything, too," he told her, needing her to know they really weren't all that different, also silently warning himself that he needed to tread lightly for his own sanity. "But I'm willing to take the chance. Are you?"

Three

What was she doing here? Stella had more pressing things to do than to stare at the seam of the closed private elevator doors leading to Dane Michaels's penthouse suite…with a chilled bottle of prosecco in hand, no less.

Maybe she should've brought a nice cab instead? Or bourbon. Hadn't he mentioned a bourbon earlier?

"This is the most ridiculous thing I've ever done," she muttered.

What was she thinking? Just because one mysterious, sexy rancher sauntered in to rescue her, she got all excited and aroused and suddenly couldn't control her desires.

She didn't have time for desires or sexy attractions. Yet here she was heading straight toward both.

The faux wooden doors slid open with a soft whoosh. Stella immediately took in the fitted tee stretching across broad shoulders and well-worn jeans over narrow hips. Dane's hair was wet, making it seem even darker than before. He'd shed the plaid shirt and, mercy's sake, this rancher certainly did the whole hands-on thing. That body made it very clear that he didn't just stay in some office writing checks for his employees.

Clearly Dane had freshened up while she still looked like the haggard mess she'd been since this morning. She should've at least changed, but she hadn't even considered removing her dress and knee boots.

She'd been too busy arguing with herself over why she'd let this virtual stranger affect her so. Maybe she'd been smitten by his white knight routine, but she couldn't just dismiss how ridiculously handsome he was, nor could she ignore how her entire body seemed to tingle with a rush of arousal whenever he got close.

There was something rough and rugged about him. When he'd mentioned a ranch…well, toss her a set of chaps and mount up because that was just flat-out hot. Plus, she'd never ridden a cowboy.

Oh, ranchers and cowboys were all throughout Montana, but none had interested her and she spent most of her time with men in suits who only pretended to know the ranching lifestyle. They'd never do anything labor-related that might mess their suits or smudge their manicures.

Dane rested his hip on the back of the leather sofa in the living area and greeted her with a crooked grin. "So you are a risk taker."

Stella merely held out the bottle of wine and shrugged. "What can I say?"

"You can say that you'll stay awhile."

He didn't stand, didn't move toward her. He simply relaxed there like he was giving her total control, yet that leveled, dark gaze told her who really called the shots. Hadn't she come to him? How could he be so powerful, yet not a bit demanding or even making a move?

The way he stared at her…

Like a lion inviting his prey and she was positive she wouldn't mind being feasted on.

Stella stepped into the spacious penthouse suite. The views never got old, and even from the doorway she could see across the room and stare out the wall of windows. Even in the dark, there was a soft glow coming up from the valley and casting mysterious shadows all over the mountainside.

Lara Anderson had seriously thought of everything when she'd built Mirage on the side of the mountain. No expense had been spared and that's what made Mirage such a magical escape.

If all of these guests opted to come here and get away from their daily stresses, why couldn't she do the same… even if for a short time.

The high-beamed ceilings and dark wood floors made the space appear more like a glorified cabin than a room in a resort. The crackling fire called to her. The stunning feature of the fireplace with its stone surround extending to the high ceiling seemed so inviting…so romantic. No, that was the hot guy that seemed romantic. And she'd brought the wine.

This was too easy. Sex was easy. Seduction was easy. Giving in to hormones and not giving a damn about tomorrow or consequences would be so…liberating.

Unfortunately, she didn't have that luxury of a one-night stand. But flirting and unwinding with a sexy stranger was dangerous ground that she couldn't help but want to dance on tonight. Just one time. That wouldn't hurt anything, right?

"I didn't think you wanted to take a risk."

Stella offered Dane a smile. "I'd say this one is harmless."

Though she knew a man like Dane was anything but. Yes, this was taking a huge chance coming to his room, but, well, her father couldn't control every move she made. She didn't have to justify her personal life to him. All she had to do was prove herself worthy of keeping Mirage and having him sign the property over to her at the end of this six-month experiment. She had only three months to go.

"*Harmless* isn't a word people usually use to describe me," he countered, his dark eyes half-hidden behind lowered lids. That husky voice sent shivers racing through her.

Maybe they didn't use *harmless*, but the word that seemed to embody Dane Michaels was definitely potent. She hadn't even tried to rationalize the hows and whys of this man and her instant attraction to him. What would be the point? Nothing would come of this…whatever this was. Besides, this was fun. When was the last time she'd done something simply because she wanted to? Every move she made had a purpose and an end gain.

Dane crossed the space, keeping his gaze locked on hers. The snap of the fire behind her filled the silence and added to the allure of the moment. The mysterious man, the late hour…the sexual tension.

"Why don't you go have a seat," he murmured. "I'll take care of everything."

Everything? As in…

He slid the bottle from her grasp and she suddenly recalled why she was here. Wine. Not orgasms.

Relax, Stella. Don't make a fool of yourself.

One glass of wine and then she needed to go. Because if she stuck around much longer, she may come across as desperate and not the kick-ass, independent woman she'd fought so hard to be.

"What time will you start back to work in the morning?" he asked as he came over with two very generous glasses of wine.

She wasn't much of a drinker, so if she sucked down all of this she'd likely end up draped over the rug in front of the fire before long. And since "drunk Stella" lacked impulse control, she'd probably be posed in some "come and get me" style that would surely embarrass her once the buzz wore off.

"I'll go back down about five."

Dane settled next to her on the leather sofa and glanced to his watch. "That's in five hours. When do you sleep?"

"When I have time."

Which was rarely. If she could go through these next few months on no sleep, she totally would. There simply wasn't enough time in the day. She had to keep all these balls juggled in the air. Dropping even one could prove fatal for her goals.

"Have you always put so much pressure on yourself?" he asked, taking a drink and then putting his glass on the raw-edged table.

"I don't see it as pressure," she retorted. "There are things I want and failing isn't an option."

"You're the manager of a picturesque mountain resort. What other goals could you possibly have?"

Stella stared into her wineglass. "Not everything is as it seems."

Before she revealed too much, she took a sip and closed her eyes as the fruity flavors burst in her mouth. She couldn't suppress the sigh that escaped her. That was a great bottle she'd grabbed from the wine cellar.

When she lifted her lids, Dane's gaze had dropped to her mouth and…had he shifted closer?

Arousal churned through her and she couldn't even blame the wine considering she'd just taken her first sip. The seclusion at this late hour and the roaring fire might be impacting her, yes, but not the wine.

"Do you want something more than Mirage?" he asked.

Stella set her glass next to his. The intimate image had her biting on her lip for a just a second before shifting her focus back to him.

"Mirage is all I've ever wanted," she explained. "My father bought the resort several years ago and I'd heard the story of the lady who had built this, relentlessly pursuing her dream. A single mom who pushed through and built something so dynamic and spectacular just hit me, you know? I didn't grow up with my mother, but I just felt pulled toward this strong female, even though I'd never met her. I knew I wanted this business to be mine. My father has plenty of companies around the globe, but this is the one I want."

Dane's eyes seemed to grow even darker, his jaw clenched, but he remained silent. She'd started talking and hadn't even considered that he probably wanted a short, quick answer.

"Sorry," she said with a soft laugh. "I didn't mean to ramble."

"Never apologize for going after what you want."

Stella's smile faltered as she swallowed. "And what is it you want, Dane?"

"That's not so difficult to guess."

Oh, he wasn't subtle. And yet, something about the way he didn't quite come out and say it, but let the implication hang heavily in the air packed an even sexier punch.

"And do you think I came here for sex?" she asked.

"I think you came here because you wanted to know what would happen once we were alone."

"We were alone in the kitchen," she reminded him, clasping her hands in her lap to prevent them from trembling—or reaching for him.

"Not like this." He eased forward, never taking his eyes from hers. "You might not want to take risks, but you can't help yourself. The resort, me… You want to know what it's like to fully throw yourself into temptation and ride out the challenge."

How did he peg her so easily when she'd met him only hours ago? And why did her entire body stir with each low, rumbled word that slid through his lips?

Because she wanted those lips on hers, on her body. The need crashed through her and took hold like nothing she'd ever experienced.

"I try to have a little more control than that—I'm not as reckless as you make me sound." Or at least that's what she tried to tell herself. "And I'd never take a risk with this resort. Mirage is my life."

"You're quite the professional," he agreed. "But you still took a risk by taking it over. Business isn't for the faint of heart."

"You sound like my father," she murmured.

Dane placed his hand on her knee. "Does he also tell you what a stellar job you're doing?"

Stella eyed those tanned, rough fingers against her dark skin. The hem of her dress proved to be no barrier as the tip of his pinky slid beneath the fabric.

"He, um… No. No, he doesn't."

Mercy, how could Dane carry on a normal conversation? Her body was revved up and she was about to start begging. She really shouldn't deprive her body so long from such a basic, necessary need.

Stella reached for her glass and took another sip. “Let’s not bring my father into this.”

His hand inched a bit higher, then his thumb slid over the bottom button of her dress as if he would pop it open at any moment.

“Agreed. Everyone should stay out of this room except us.”

Stella took another sip and set her glass back down. “We’re not having sex.”

“Not yet.”

She couldn’t stop her smile. “At all,” she clarified. “I can’t afford to get caught up in anything but work right now.”

Dane’s eyes crinkled in the corners as he smiled. “Yet here you are.”

Well, he had her there. Stella laid her hand over his and for a split second—okay, maybe more—she wanted to slid it on up and show him exactly how he could alleviate her stress. But she held his hand firmly in place on her bare thigh.

“I don’t even know you,” she stated. “Clearly there’s chemistry, but I can’t get sidetracked by a sexy man who came to my rescue.”

“I obviously wasn’t looking to get sidetracked, either, but there’s nothing more I want than to lay you out in front of that fire and give you exactly what your body is aching for.”

The man knew all the right words to say. There should be some major red flags going up. A stranger coming in at the exact time she needed someone, the fact he knew precisely what to say and just how much to press without being a jerk…

No matter the flags, she honestly couldn’t find a flaw here.

Stella reached for her glass and tipped it back, taking

every last drop of her favorite wine. With a soft clink, she set the glass back down and came to her feet. Dane's hand fell away, and he rose, as well.

"I should get to my room and attempt a few hours of sleep."

Dane brushed her hair from her face, letting his fingertips feather across her jaw. Something flashed through his eyes a second before he curled those same fingers around the back of her neck and pulled her mouth to his.

Stella didn't even try to fight the kiss…why would she? They'd been building toward this moment since they met—did it matter that was only a few hours ago?

Besides, a kiss was harmless. Well, most of them were. A kiss from Dane Michaels was powerful, toe curling, panty melting, and instantly had her mind on sex. The way his body lined perfectly with hers, the way his lips coaxed hers apart, eager for more, only had her more than ready to take him up on his offer.

The wine had gotten to her just as she'd thought it might. She swayed against him, reaching up to clutch his bare biceps. Those were rancher arms. No sedentary job could produce muscles so firm, so…magnificent.

Dane eased back and Stella whimpered. Damn alcohol. She'd never whimpered or begged for any man, yet she'd just done the first and was closing in on the second.

"I'll check on you tomorrow," he told her. "If you need me, you know where to find me."

When he released her, Stella had to concentrate on staying upright. She hadn't had nearly enough time with him. She wanted more of that whiskey-soaked tone, that dark gaze, those lips and hands on her.

Straightening her dress, Stella pulled herself together and

crossed the suite to the elevator. Dane came up behind her, practically pressing her against the doors. Stella closed her eyes and inhaled that spicy, masculine scent.

"I'll see you tomorrow."

The whisper in her ear, the warmth of his breath on her skin had her shivering and with the way his chest was pressed to her back, there was no way he missed her body's reaction to him.

Stella risked a glance over her shoulder. "I look forward to it."

And then she fled back to her room where she replayed over and over the entire evening from the moment Dane stepped into the dining room to the moment he sent her entire body up in flames.

So why didn't she just give in and let him douse them?

No. The real question was, how long would she make them both wait?

Four

Dane sipped his morning coffee and relaxed in the Adirondack chair on the expansive enclosed balcony. He'd come out at sunrise to admire the breathtaking view. He'd had a restless night, thanks in part to one seductress who'd plastered her sweet body against his and left him wondering just who was playing whom.

He'd remained in control of the situation last night, but barely. He needed to have a better grasp of just how potent Stella was before their next encounter. Coming into this whole plan, he sure as hell hadn't planned on questioning his damn sanity regarding his hormones.

Stella had certainly surprised him last night by coming to his suite. He'd written off seeing her again until today after she'd seemed to reject his invitation. Dane wasn't often taken off guard and finding more reasons to admire Stella was not helping his cause.

He didn't want to admire her, he wanted to use her for her insight into her father's sharklike mind when it came to business. Yet each moment he spent with her, he found himself growing more and more captivated.

Dane had already sent an offer to buy Mirage outright that was more than reasonable, but Ruiz Garcia had turned it down without a counter.

There had to be a way…and Dane was using the method he felt would be the most effective. If the guy treated his daughter like a peasant employee, why the hold over this resort? Why not just sell it, take the money, and cut his daughter out of the business entirely? Why string her along?

So many questions, yet none of them really mattered. All Dane cared about was what it would take for Ruiz to sell Mirage. That was the bottom line.

Dane extended his legs and crossed his ankles. He'd give his brother another hour or so before he called. Ethan was not a morning person, pretty much because he was a nighttime partier. His current state likely involved being wrapped around at least one woman.

While Dane worked here in Gold Valley, Ethan was hoping to work his own magic at the second Mirage resort on Sunset Cove. The island off the coast of California was certainly more Ethan's lifestyle. Dane preferred his secluded ranch, he thrived in being alone where he didn't have to feed a relationship and had nobody depending on him.

The bond between Dane and his younger brother had been strained since the passing of their mother, but they were still brothers and had two goals binding them together: get back the Mirage resorts and take down Robert Anderson. That bastard had stolen too much from them when they'd been helpless, but now Dane and Ethan were powerful and even more so when they put their resources together. There wasn't a place Robert could hide, not anymore.

None of this was about the money. Both Dane and Ethan could buy any resort anywhere in the world. Hell, they could build something even bigger, better, but they deserved what their mother had created.

With the twentieth anniversary of her death approaching, Dane wanted, needed to feel closer to the only woman he'd ever loved.

Tamping down the ache resonating in the void in his heart, Dane came to his feet and rested his arms on the wrought iron railing. Clutching his coffee cup, he overlooked the valley and felt like a damn king. There was nothing more refreshing than mountain air that was so crisp, so raw.

Dane wouldn't have a difficult time coming off the ranch with picturesque views like this to tempt him. He'd worried about who would actually run the place in his absence once he got Mirage in his control, but the worry seemed less potent now that he realized how comfortable he still felt here. He would be a hands-on owner. This was his mother's place, his mother's dream, there was no way he could turn Mirage over to anybody else.

So long as he kept that in the forefront of his mind, Dane knew he could push through his doubts and fears. If anyone could get him to step back out into society on a regular basis, it was his mother. She deserved for him to step up and put his own issues aside and be the man she'd raised.

Dane pushed off the rail and took the last sip of his coffee. As he made his way through the double glass doors, he pulled his cell from the pocket of his jeans.

There was no time to waste. He needed to discuss things with his younger brother. If that meant disrupting his morning slumber and irritating his bedmates, so be it.

Dane set his coffee mug on the large raw-edged wood island between the kitchen and the dining area as he dialed. He waited for Ethan to pick up, but voice mail kicked in and Dane muttered a curse before clearing his throat and leaving a message.

They were closing in on Robert and Dane was chomping at the proverbial bit to serve a healthy dose of vengeance to his stepfather. Dane wanted to know where Ethan stood and what intel he'd uncovered since they spoke last.

Each day that went by was another day closer to the anniversary of their mother's death and another day that bastard was able to live his life as a free man. Those days were coming to an end and a new chapter in the Michaels brothers' story would begin. Maybe regaining their legacy would bring them back together, closer, like they used to be.

Dane pocketed his phone and headed toward the en suite to shower. While waiting to hear from his brother and plan their takedown, Dane had a lady to charm. And judging from her reaction last night, he wasn't too far from accomplishing all of his goals.

The vibration on the nightstand irritated the hell out of Ethan. Couldn't a guy get a good morning's sleep? If that damn thing kept going off, he'd throw it out the open patio door, not caring if it landed in the ocean.

He turned his face into the soft, warm pillow and blinked against the sunlight streaming in. He purposely kept that patio door open so he could hear the ocean crashing to the shore. Security wasn't an issue—unless a thief who could defy gravity decided to scale the high-rise penthouse. Ethan had confidence he was safe.

Besides, he thrived here. The beach, the ocean, the endless water views from his bed. He'd grown up in Montana and the mountains were fine for his brother, but the second Ethan had set foot on a beach, he knew exactly where he belonged. Everything about this atmosphere called to him and he couldn't imagine spending his life in the mountains like Dane.

The cell buzzed again and Ethan rolled over and smacked the damn thing before pulling it toward him. The screen lit up with a few texts from numbers he didn't recognize and a voice mail alert from Dane.

The texts could wait. Even though they were likely from the ladies he'd met last night and Ethan rarely kept a woman waiting—in bed or out—this business with Dane had to take top priority. They both had their own individual goals, but their joint goal had Ethan sitting up in bed, the sheet pooling around his waist as he dialed his brother.

"Did I interrupt anything?"

Dane's answer in lieu of hello had Ethan grunting and glancing to the other side of his king-size bed. The four-legged, furry feline hadn't stirred since crawling over his face to get to her spot in the middle of the night.

Not many people knew about the fur ball that he'd rescued. But damn it he'd seen the poor lethargic thing out in a storm and he simply couldn't leave it there. Ethan had had every intention of finding a new home for it.

Two years later, they were still together.

"I'm sandwiched between two redheads," Ethan replied, instead of mentioning the real pussy in his bed. "This better be good."

"I'm at Mirage in Gold Valley."

Ethan felt a swell of pride and anticipation, quickly followed by a dose of jealousy and longing. Dane had already pushed through to the next phase of their mission to gain back what belonged to them, but timing was everything and Ethan wasn't quite ready to make his presence known at Mirage in Sunset Cove.

"I've already gotten close with the manager—who also happens to be the owner's daughter—and it's just a matter of time before I can get the angle I need to get this location back in our family."

Our family. They hadn't been a true family since their mother died. When that happened, Dane had closed in on himself, their stepfather had shown his true, greedy self and Ethan…well, he'd turned to anyone who could make him forget, even if that was for just a night.

"You're moving fast." Ethan threw off the sheet and swung his legs over the side of the bed, taking a moment to enjoy the breathtaking view. "And here I thought I was the charming, irresistible brother."

"You're cocky. There's a difference," Dane retorted. "What have you found out about Robert?"

Ethan raked a hand over his bare chest as he came to his feet. "Right now he's comfortable in Hawaii. We're so damn close. I want to lure him in. I need him at Mirage in Sunset Cove."

"You're confident you can get him there?" Dane asked.

"He's never been able to turn down the idea of making millions." Ethan had formulated a rock-solid plan, but he needed his brother's help. "If he thinks he can get this resort back and flip it again to make money on it twice, he'll break records getting there."

"Don't make a move until you tell me," Dane stated. "I want to be there when you approach him. We're a team on this deal."

Right. A team. Ethan had hinged his entire life on that…

or at least the first eighteen years. But losing their mother had torn a hole through both of them, and they just hadn't been able to reach each other across the empty space. They'd stuck together until they'd both finished high school but then, motherless and penniless, they'd both joined the military and gone their separate ways.

They stayed in touch, calling and texting, randomly getting together, but nothing was the same. Ethan couldn't even blame their polar-opposite personalities. When they'd been growing up, they'd simply balanced each other.

While Dane was more studious, Ethan had been a jock. They could put down an extra-large pizza—covered with sausage of course—and one ate all the edges, the other ate the entire middle. Everything they'd done just seemed to jive.

As adults, well, they were more acquaintances than anything. Their main goal of taking back the resorts and annihilating Robert had always kept them bonded…but Ethan wanted more. He wanted his brother back. In the years since they'd split apart, no one had filled that void. He was always surrounded by people, but he was lonely for family.

"I'm hoping to lure him in within the next month," Ethan replied. "I'll keep you posted."

"I'll do the same from my end." Dane cleared his throat. "We're going to make this happen. For Mom."

The void in Ethan's heart throbbed. "For Mom," he repeated.

And for us.

Five

Stella stifled the urge to breath a sigh of relief at how smoothly the morning had gone with the part-time chef. Thankfully she'd agreed to step up full-time and save Stella's ass.

Considering it was only lunchtime on day one of the replacement, Stella wasn't about to pull out the confetti and celebrate just yet. But she did feel some of the weight ease from her shoulders.

Granted she should be relaxed after that wine and those kisses last night from a virtual stranger, but that sexual tension…

She'd had friends in college who had had one-night stands and Stella had never understood how someone could tumble into bed with a person they'd just met.

Well, now she knew exactly why they didn't let their inhibitions get in the way. Just the memory of that intimate moment had her body heated in ways she didn't think possible.

Unfortunately, as much as she wanted to replay the events

and tack on her own fantasies, there was too much work to be done.

Since the lunch rush seemed to be under control, Stella headed toward the front desk. Checkout time had passed an hour ago and they were due to get a new wave of couples. Every room was booked, which was always a good thing on a weeknight.

Since Stella had taken over, she'd been trying her hardest to make sure her marketing team kept pumping out information and waving the amenities around all over social media. The previous manager hadn't been interested in growing the business, but rather staying behind his desk and remaining stagnant. All he cared about was that he got paid.

Well, that had put a damper on her father's plans to watch cash just flood in, so Stella had jumped at the chance to not only manage this remarkable resort, but also show her father she was a worthy businesswoman.

She didn't need his approval. She didn't need his money. But she wanted his respect and she had a sickening feeling in her gut that she'd never get it. This was her last chance. She was done putting herself out there, basically waving around in his face all the ways that she was worthy to be in his world, his damn life. If he didn't acknowledge her or treat her the way she deserved, then she'd be done.

Even if that would leave her officially alone. Over time she had come to the realization that perhaps she'd be better off alone than begging for attention or love from her own father.

Stella passed through the wide-open, four-story lobby. She never tired of the beauty of this place. Not only had Mirage been built with wood from the forest where the building stood, the place had been built around some of the old trees. Literally, there was a large, live ponderosa pine growing straight up through the middle of the lobby. It was quite a focal point for newcomers looking for a place to take selfies.

Besides the live trees randomly found inside the resort, there were windows absolutely everywhere. A breathtaking view was never farther than a glance in one direction or the other. Mountain views were the main reason Stella loved not staying behind her desk. She'd taken the smallest office, though she had a feeling her father had a hand in doling that area out to her.

Even though she was rushing from one crisis to another, at least she was surrounded by breathtaking splendor, so she wasn't about to complain.

After Stella registered several people, she headed toward her office just to double-check on the couples currently on fantasy dates. No matter what the couple wanted, the discreet employees at Mirage worked overtime to make it happen.

In the short time she'd been there, she'd had some strange requests and some…risqué ones, as well. It was not her place to judge or try to understand people's fetishes, but she had to admit sometimes she was intrigued.

And that intrigue only intensified when the thought of Dane Michaels flooded her mind. She couldn't help but wonder what he'd think if she invited him to the Lumberjack Room or the Campfires and Corsets Room. No doubt she'd be in over her head, but part of her wanted to. She ached to get his hands on her.

But there would be no need for fantasy dates between her and the sexy rancher in the penthouse. That man was already like every single sexy dream she'd ever had come to life. If she wanted to try something daring, risky, adventurous, she had a feeling just sleeping with that man would embody all three.

Stella smoothed her hair behind her ears and let out a sigh as she rounded her desk. She didn't bother taking a seat, there was never any time for such things. She cross-referenced her lists of guests and their requests, feeling reassured in her certainty that her staff could handle every need that was requested and any additional ones coming in.

Well, food and fantasies were covered for the next twenty-four hours. Maybe she would get through this day without a complete meltdown or catastrophe. One could hope.

Stella rounded her desk to head back out, but Dane filled her doorway and she froze in place. Her hand rested on the mahogany desk and her toes curled in her boots.

"Didn't think you'd be someone stuck in an office."

He hooked his thumbs through his belt loops and steadied those dark eyes right on hers…right after he gave her a visual sampling. Perhaps the sampling he'd had last night hadn't been enough.

Her eyes were drawn to that belt buckle again. She'd ask him about the emblem sometime, though she already knew he'd tell her that it was his ranch. She found that she genuinely wanted to know more about it…about him.

"I'm rarely in here," Stella replied, attempting to get her heart rate and nerves to settle. "I had a few things to check on. How did you know where my office was?"

The offices and anything considered "behind the scenes" were discreetly hidden from guests. Lara had thought of everything when she'd designed the adult retreat. She'd wanted the guests to feel like they were truly in a magical place and reality didn't exist.

Dane shrugged and offered that sexy, borderline naughty half grin. “I can be persuasive when I want something.”

Wasn’t that the truth. She wasn’t naive enough to ask him what he wanted from her. He’d made that perfectly clear last night. In his defense, she’d also made her own wants quite apparent, even if she hadn’t fully acted on them.

“Dane—”

Her cell rang from inside the pocket of her button-up plaid dress. She held up a hand to Dane. “I need to take this.”

He nodded, but didn’t step out to give her privacy. Instead, he actually came on in and made himself at home by going straight to the window to look out over the back of the property.

Stella smiled at his audacity, but pulled her ringing phone out. One look at the screen and that smile vanished. She resisted the urge to groan or flat-out ignore the call, but she reminded herself that she wanted this. She wanted a relationship, so she swiped her finger across the screen.

“Dad,” she greeted. “I haven’t heard from you for a while. How are you?”

“I’ve been busy working.” The gruff reply wasn’t abnormal or unexpected. “Have you been keeping an eye on the weather? There’s a storm coming and they’re saying it could be quite substantial.”

Storms in Montana were always substantial. They were in the mountains so high, they were about one good stretch from touching clouds—or so it seemed most days. Snow and blizzards were nothing new here. And of course she kept her eye on the weather. Just like everything else around here. She had to stay sharp and know everything going on inside and out of her resort. Well…almost her resort.

“I’m aware,” she replied, risking a glance to Dane who

remained with his back to her. "Everything is under control, Dad. Our backup systems have never failed and all of our guests will remain comfortable and happy. We're actually booked up for the next month."

She couldn't help the pride that surged through her. When she'd come on board, they hadn't been completely booked up, which told her that her marketing team had tapped into something brilliant in a relatively short time.

"Only a month ahead?" he scoffed.

Stella gritted her teeth and turned to pace to the other end of the office. There was no way Dane wasn't hearing every word she said, but she couldn't focus on the handsome stranger right now.

"In comparison to last year, we're doing a remarkable job," she retorted. "It's been years since Mirage has been completely booked for more than a night at a time."

When her father had first purchased the resort, he'd had an amazing manager, but when that manager passed away suddenly, her father had scrambled to fill the spot. Unfortunately, the replacement lasted only a year and that had been enough time to see numbers start to decline.

So here she was cleaning up someone else's mess all while proving to her father that she was capable and deserved to have this property.

"One month of solid bookings won't make up for three years of dismal numbers," he replied.

"Yes, well, I'm working as hard as I can." If he was here, perhaps he'd see that. "I'm confident the numbers will continue to grow now that I'm in charge."

"And what have you done about the chef who quit?"

Of course he would know about that. He wasn't a ruthless businessman for nothing. He'd never let his investments go unsupervised—and he wouldn't consider his daughter to be supervision enough on her own. Stella had no doubt her father had spies strategically placed throughout the resort, either as employees or guests.

Dread curled through her. She'd just been half joking to herself, imaging the resort full of spies, but now that she thought about it, she realized she wouldn't put it past him. In fact, she was positive he'd done just that. There was no other way he would know about the chef less than twenty-four hours after the man quit.

"Like I said, I have everything under control," she told him.

On a sigh, she spun back around, only to lock eyes on Dane. She hadn't seen that look from him before…something akin to compassion or worry. But just as quick as she saw it, the look vanished.

"If you want to know more about what's going on here, you can ask me or maybe come check things out yourself. I think you'd be pleasantly surprised," she added. "But I don't appreciate being spied on."

Her breath caught in her throat as she continued to stare at Dane. "I have to go," she told her dad before disconnecting the call.

Without taking her eyes from Dane, she slid her phone back into her pocket then crossed her arms.

"How long have you been working for my father?"

Dane's dark brows rose toward his hairline. "Excuse me?"

"You were sent here to spy on me, right? See if I can actually do this job and not screw it up?"

She'd been such a fool to think a kind stranger just happened upon her and saved the day, then was suddenly attracted to her.

"Does he know you want to sleep with me or is that all part of his plan?" Stella asked, suddenly sickened at the idea. "How much is he paying you?"

Before she could draw her next breath, Dane had closed the distance between them. His fingers curled around her biceps and he hauled her against his chest. The motion had her tipping her head back to keep her focus on him.

"You think I'd whore myself out?" he demanded. "I don't work for anybody and I sure as hell wouldn't take money to have sex with you."

Oh, he was angry. She didn't know Dane, but after hearing the conviction in his voice, she had no doubt he was telling the truth. Beneath that anger, Stella saw pain.

"When I get you in my bed, it won't have anything to do with your father," he growled.

When.

Her entire body heated between the threatened promise of her in his bed and the way he'd plastered his body against hers from hip to chest, and Stella couldn't do a thing but hold on.

She gripped his arms and stared back into those dark eyes, now hard with fury. But she wasn't scared. Dane wouldn't hurt her. Someone who sacrificed his whole evening to help a complete stranger, expecting nothing in return, wasn't a person who should be feared.

But he was hurt by her accusation.

"I'm sorry." Stella closed her eyes and pulled in a shaky breath, trying to rein in her frustrations. "My father… It's all complicated, but I think he's spying on me and how I'm doing here. With the timing of you showing up, I just jumped to conclusions when I shouldn't have doubted you."

Dane's grip lessened, but he didn't let her go. He eased back slightly, the muscle in his jaw clenched.

"Your father doesn't trust you?" Dane asked, his brows drawn in.

"Apparently not. I never thought that was an issue," she replied, hurt spreading through her. "But it would seem that my loyalty is in question or at least my judgment." Stella shook her head and attempted a smile. "I don't know why I find you so easy to talk to. Sorry about all that."

Dane stroked his thumbs over the curve of her shoulders. "Don't apologize. I'd say I'm easy to talk to because I don't know the dynamics here. I'm just a stranger to you."

Yes, something she needed to remind herself of. She shouldn't get wrapped up in a stranger, emotionally or physically.

Yet here she was, doing a stellar job of both.

Everyone had a breaking point and apparently Dane Michaels was hers. She'd worked so hard for so long, putting her personal life on the back burner. No, her personal life wasn't even on the stove, let alone a burner.

Maybe she should take an hour a day just for herself… and whatever pleasantries came along.

"Come to my penthouse for dinner," she told him. "I'll have everything ready at eight."

Dane's brows shot up. "You live on-site full-time?"

Stella nodded. "There's no way I'd want to commute when I'm always needed. This resort is my life, my baby. I want to always be available."

"You really do love this place," he muttered.

"Of course I do." She stepped back, needing to distance herself from the man who had her reevaluating her priorities. "So, eight o'clock?"

"You don't need to feed me dinner."

Stella smoothed her hair away from her face and squared her shoulders. "I do, so don't argue. I'll apologize and you'll be a gentleman and accept my offerings."

Once again, he got that hungry look in his eyes. Being in such close proximity with Dane made it quite difficult to remain a professional.

"Do you really think you'll be back to your room by eight?"

"I'll make it happen if you promise to be there."

Dane flashed her that smile that had her stomach tightening with anticipation. "I'll be there."

He leaned forward, not reaching for her or even attempting to touch her. His breath on the curve of her ear sent shivers assaulting her every nerve ending.

"I'm counting down the hours until I touch you again," he murmured.

Before she could regain her mental balance, Dane had eased around her and walked out of her office. Stella remained in place, wondering how she was going to focus on work when her body was more than ready for Dane's promised touch.

And just how the hell was she supposed to concentrate on the potential storm heading toward the resort when her own storm was taking over her emotions?

Six

Damn. There was nothing sexier than an aggressive, confident woman. Stella not only embodied both of those qualities, she was so much more and Dane hadn't expected her to be the complete package.

What he had expected to be a little flirting with a vulnerable woman who would give him insight to her father was turning into so much more than he ever expected.

Dane had the flirting down and was well on his way to the seduction—a little *too* well, really. Whenever he was near her, he couldn't seem to remember why taking her to bed was anything other than an excellent idea. He was drawing her in, just as he'd intended, and yet the draw pulled just as strongly on him. This woman was a force all her own.

And as far as the insight to her father? Well, Dane's original assumptions were correct. The guy was a bastard in the same over-entitled category as his own stepfather.

It was no wonder those two had done a business deal. Sharks tended to swim together. But Dane had heard a rumor the reality was that Robert had lost the resort in a gambling bet gone bad.

Never in all of his plotting and scheming did he ever think she'd assume he worked for her father. Dane hadn't lied when he told her no. He hadn't lied when he said he wouldn't whore himself out or take money for sex.

But he would take the resort.

The guilt he'd tried to ignore, the guilt he'd told himself wasn't there, suddenly grew sharp teeth and clung tight to his soul.

He'd come this far. Nothing and no one would stop him… not even Stella. He hated with every ounce that she was going to get hurt by his takeover of the resort. There was no avoiding that. But perhaps once she moved on she would see that Dane had saved her from her father. Because that man would never be happy with her running any of his businesses. Dane wasn't sure of the issues that circulated between father and daughter. That wasn't Dane's business, but that didn't stop him from wondering.

Dane left his penthouse at exactly eight and headed toward Stella's rooms on the other side of the resort. Since leaving her earlier he'd done some exploring, taking in what had been changed since his mother's passing and the last time he'd been there.

But even the remodeling, the addition with more saunas and private movie rooms in the back, the suspended decks overlooking the valley…none of that had taken his mind off the scene in Stella's office. His mind just kept circling back to the phone call he'd overheard.

What the hell kind of game was her father playing? From what Dane knew, Stella had six months to turn this resort around and pull in more money than the previous manager had lost in the past year—a manager hired by Stella's father, and kept in the position despite obvious incompetence, when her father still didn't see her as fit for the job.

Well, here she was, doing a stellar job and Ruiz Garcia still didn't see what an amazing businesswoman she truly was. Dane hadn't missed the way she'd lowered her voice when he'd been present. He hadn't missed the disappointment and the hurt lacing each and every word. And he hadn't missed the pain in her eyes when she'd realized her father had likely planted a spy.

What really pissed him off was that she'd thought that was him. But he wasn't angry with her anymore—no, he was angry with himself. She had every reason to be suspicious, given the timing. But her suspicions were pointing her in the wrong direction. He *was* a spy, but the only person he worked for was himself. Dane would never work for a backstabbing mastermind like Ruiz, but could he really claim to be that much better when he was plotting against Stella even as he headed toward her for their date?

Dane made his way through the lobby and glanced out the doors into the darkened night. Snowflakes swirled around in the beams of light. The storm was rolling in and, if the forecast was correct, they were in for a hell of a blizzard.

Living in Montana had acclimated him to snow and cold. He loved the weather, actually. His ranch was postcard worthy all blanketed with snow. He longed to be back there now, to be in his den with a roaring fire and his two golden retrievers, Buck and Bronco, asleep on the rug in front of the crackling flames.

Thankfully his housekeeper was staying in the guest quarters and taking care of the dogs while his foreman oversaw everything ranch-related. Dane trusted very few people, but once they were in his inner circle, they were there for life.

As Dane passed the hallway toward the Sleepy Forest suites, he did a quick glance and spotted a couple in their midfifties, if he had to guess. They were hand in hand and staring at each other as if nobody else existed outside their happy little bubble.

Dane couldn't imagine ever letting someone that deeply into his heart. There was only so much brokenness a man could take and Dane truly felt he'd had his fair share over time. With the loss of his mother, the distance with his brother, the loss of friends in the war…

He didn't even want to pretend to play the game of feelings and emotions and hoping for a successful long-term relationship. Living on his own and worrying only about himself and his ranch was more than enough to make him happy in this life.

When he took the private elevator to Stella's penthouse, he forced himself to calm down and regain his focus. Getting wrapped up in her personal struggles with her father was definitely not Dane's place. The only reason he needed that information was to use it to obtain everything he wanted.

And the damn guilt? He couldn't get wrapped up in that, either. Not only was his brother counting on him, Dane owed this to his mother who never, ever had any intention of selling her businesses…let alone to the devil.

Stella may think she wanted to be here and manage Mirage, but until she was out from her father's thumb, would she truly be happy?

She was brilliant, she had a drive not many people had. Stella would go on to do greater things, on her own, without her father.

Ready to get this night going, Dane tapped his knuckles on the door and waited. He didn't have to wait long. The double doors swung open and Stella stood before him looking just as stunning as she'd been this morning. Even working herself ragged, somehow she managed to come across as in control and put together.

If it hadn't been for that brief moment in her office when she'd looked so hurt while on the phone with her father, Stella would have convinced him not a thing was wrong in her world. He knew better.

The nugget of guilt grew, taking root.

"Perfect timing," she stated with a smile as she gestured him in. "I just got everything set up and sent the cook away."

Dane stepped in and instantly fell back into his past. Nostalgia hit him hard as he scanned his eyes over the open space. He'd been a preteen when his mother had opened Mirage. This had been her on-site room and Dane and Ethan would take turns getting the fire going on cold, snowy nights…just like tonight.

He swept his gaze back across the spacious room, taking in all the familiarity and noting each change since he'd been here last. Little touches made the room all Stella. The pictures across the mantel, the bright red throw over the leather chair, a pair of worn boots next to the sofa.

But so much was still the same. That stone around the fireplace he'd helped choose with his mother, the dark kitchen cabinets and raw-edged countertops… The leather sofas were the same, the lamps were the same, the chocolate fur rug in front of the fire was the same.

So much reminded him of his mother, which only added to his steely structure and mental drive to finish the job he'd started.

Lara had loved her boys with her entire being. She'd done all of this for them, for their future. She'd taken the inheritance from her grandfather and invested every single penny first into this resort and then, just as soon as it started showing a profit, she'd opened her second Mirage location.

Nearly twenty years had gone by since Dane had seen her or even heard her voice, but she was still here. This room, this resort, they were all pieces of her and he wasn't going to stop until he got them all back…no matter who he had to use to serve his purpose.

"You didn't have to send up wine and flowers this afternoon."

Stella's sweet voice pulled him from the tunnel of thoughts. He turned to face her just as she closed the door and leaned back against it.

"And the basket of spa and bath items was too much," she added. "But that robe and those slippers feel like heaven, so thank you."

Dane nodded. "I figured you don't take the time to pamper yourself, so I thought you might need a reminder."

Stella pushed off the door and closed the distance between them. "I don't even know how you managed to get everything delivered to my penthouse because I know you didn't purchase the flowers from the gift shop and those lotions in the basket are from France."

"And how do you know that?" he asked.

"Because that is my favorite brand, right down to the scent." Stella crossed her arms and tipped her head. "Apparently you have some incredible resources if you could manage all of this in a short amount of time."

She didn't need to know that it took only one phone call to make all of this happen. He'd spared no expense on the items themselves and had paid another hefty sum to get everything delivered without Stella sensing a thing.

And yet he got the oddest sense that it was the fact that he'd made an effort, that he'd tried to treat her, to spoil her a little, that pleased her the most. Did she ever have anyone do something just for her? Or was she too busy worrying how to please everyone else and still reach her goals?

Ignoring her statement, because she didn't need to know just how far his reaches were, Dane took a step back and glanced toward the fireplace where a table had been set up.

"Did you order all of this or did you have them send up some leftovers?" he asked, turning his focus back to her.

Stella's dark eyes narrowed as she swatted at him. "Leftovers? You think I invited you to my room for leftovers?"

Dane reached for her hand and had her tumbling against his chest, earning him a small squeak from her lips. She tipped her head back and met his gaze.

"What *did* you invite me here for?" he murmured, mesmerized by the thick black lashes framing her expressive eyes.

Damn it. If he wasn't careful he'd find himself lost in Stella and ignoring all the things he actually should be doing.

Like getting her to open up and trust him…

"I wanted to see you," she whispered. "To…talk."

Dane couldn't stop the twitch of his lips. "Talk? When I kissed you earlier you didn't seem so eager to talk."

"Maybe that kiss affected you more than it did me."

Dane didn't even think before he crushed his lips to hers. Like hell she wasn't affected. And so was he, whether he wanted to be or not. He'd been waiting too long for another sample. Nine whole hours and every minute that went by, he could still taste her. Well, now he didn't have to fantasize because she was in his arms.

Or more like plastered against him, which was exactly where he wanted her. He hadn't expected to physically ache for her. Never once did he consider that he would have an issue with self-control. Dane was always in control—except when the nightmares came. But with women? When he'd gone to bed with the few women he'd had since coming home scarred and broken, he'd never relinquished his power or felt out of control.

Dane wrapped his arms around her, settling his hands over her round backside and urging her hips to align with his.

Stella let out a little moan as he coaxed her lips apart and thrust his tongue against hers. There was no hesitation on her end, and much to his surprise, she reached up with her free hand and threaded her fingers through his unruly hair. That slight tug had even more arousal pumping through him.

He turned her toward the back of the leather sofa and lifted her to sit on the top of the cushions. Dane stepped between her spread legs and raked his hands up her bare thighs and beneath the hem of her skirt.

Pulling her hand from between their bodies and out of his grip, Stella reached for the buckle on his belt and gave a swift jerk.

Dane pulled away and worked on taking deep breaths and getting this situation back under his control. He still needed information and it was damn difficult to think with her mouth all over his.

"Why don't we eat?" he suggested.

Stella blinked and dropped her hands. "Right…um, that is the reason I invited you."

"And to talk," he reminded her, because hearing all about her life with her father was of the utmost importance… despite his arousal.

Stella slid off the couch and straightened her dress. Every part of Dane wanted to finish what they'd started—but that just proved that he needed to back away. He had to stay in control, had to keep his eye on the prize and not get distracted by how good she looked. And smelled. And tasted…

Everything about Stella had become more complicated than he'd initially thought. Each moment had to be assessed and plotted.

Dane followed the sway of Stella's hips as she led the way toward the table for two set up in front of the fireplace. But when she just stood there, looking down at the setting, Dane came up beside her.

"Something wrong?"

Her eyes shifted to him and she smiled. "Let's take dinner onto the balcony."

The climate-controlled, glassed-in balcony off the bedroom would be less intimate.

"Sounds good to me."

They both filled their plates and grabbed their wineglasses before heading out to the cozy, spacious area high above the valley. This was just another area he and Ethan had enjoyed when they came to stay with their mother. They'd pretend they were military spies looking over enemy territory.

Dane glanced to the L-shaped sofa and pushed aside the memories of when the space had three plaid upholstered chairs for Ethan, their mother and Dane. Their stepfather was often out doing business, leaving the three of them alone, which had been just fine with Dane. From day one he'd had an odd feeling about the guy his mother had married, but it hadn't been until after his mother's death that that feeling had grown into full-fledged hatred.

Stella took a seat in the corner of the sofa and extended her legs out, propping her plate on her lap. Dane sat on the other end and balanced his plate on one leg and sat his wineglass on the maple table before him.

"Is this the first time this week you've made it back to your room at a reasonable time?" he asked, stabbing the steak with his fork.

"Yes." She took a sip of her wine and leaned to the side to put her glass next to his. "The first time in a lot longer than a week, actually. I've never had a reason to get back to my room by a certain time. Nothing seemed as important as being with my staff and ensuring all the guests' needs were attended to."

"I'm flattered I ranked above that," he commented.

"Oh, if I get a call, I'm heading back down," she stated with a laugh. "Nothing comes between me and my goals."

Dane shot her a side glance and found her looking back at him. Apparently he'd been added to her goal list, which was fine with him. But then the scars would come up and that wasn't exactly a point he wanted to discuss.

And yet another niggling speared at him. She had no clue why he was here, what he was capable of doing…what he would ultimately take from her.

Guilt could be all-consuming, but he had to remain focused. He had to see this through.

Dane forced his eyes back to his plate and focused on the meal. Guilt had no place here, not if he wanted to complete this mission. It wasn't his fault that she'd ended up in this situation, nor was it his duty to protect innocent people.

Dane had been innocent, too, but his life had still been ruined and he'd been left to his own devices.

None of this was what his mother would've wanted. She'd had her own plan of passing these resorts to her boys and Dane and Ethan were going to see that plan through…no matter the cost.

"This place is rather remarkable," he said after a while. "You've got to be proud of what you've done."

"I am, but it's not my opinion that matters."

"Your opinion should be the only one that matters," he countered, trying to rein in his anger. "If your father can't see how amazing you are, then maybe he's not worthy of your loyalty."

Stella set her plate on the table and grabbed her wineglass. "I'm not sure anything can impress my father, to be honest. He sets a level of standards that no one could possibly reach."

Dane finished his meal and set his plate next to hers. He reached for his own glass and scooted down to sit next to her. Stella took another drink, then let out a clipped laugh.

"I should've learned my lesson when I was nineteen. I got the silver medal in a national competition for cross-country skiing and he was angry that I hadn't lived up to his expectations and placed first."

Dane recalled her medal mention in the background check he'd had done. He shouldn't be surprised at her father's lack of enthusiasm or praise. He didn't deserve her loyalty.

Dane knew all too well what it was like to be alone like Stella was. Having a bastard father was the same as going through life without one. While he had his brother, he and Ethan had never been the same since their mother passed, and he knew that emotional gap was partly his fault.

When he came to Mirage, Dane never expected to have

so much in common with Stella, yet he found himself drawing closer to her in ways that could and would get him into trouble if he didn't stay emotionally detached.

Dane set his glass down before plucking hers from her hand and placing it back on the table. He shifted toward her, placing one hand on the cushion beside her head and the other near her hip.

"Maybe for the next several hours we forget everything outside of this room," he suggested.

Stella's eyes widened as she eased farther back onto the cushions. "Hours? You think quite a lot of yourself."

"When I get your clothes off, I intend to take my time," he promised.

He very deliberately said nothing about shedding his own clothes. Maybe there was a way they could make this work without him baring too much—of his skin or anything else. There were so many ways to make a woman feel good. Stella deserved every single one of them.

Stella's chest rose and fell with each breath. The little button at the top of her dress strained against her chest and Dane didn't take his eyes off her as he reached for the closure and freed her.

When she smiled, he slid his hand down to the next button and slid it through the slit. A flash of red lace teased him, mesmerized him. That was exactly the lingerie he'd imagined she'd be wearing. Nothing plain or simple for this bold, assertive woman. Of course she'd have red. The power color suited her.

"Are you starting that time now?" she asked, her voice breathless with want.

Dane ignored her question and slid a finger between her breasts. Such silky skin against his rough, ranch-hardened hands. He'd always been a hands-on guy—in and out of the bedroom. And he couldn't remember the last time he'd wanted to get his hands on someone this badly.

He knew he should resist. But she made it so damn hard… in all the best ways. He needed to slow this down. Regain control. Focus on what she needed, rather than what the craving in his blood demanded.

"I'm still exploring." Up, down. He continued to let his fingertip glide over her. "Trust me, you'll know when I get started."

Stella covered his hand with hers and pushed down. "I still have more buttons."

Yeah, he'd noticed. The damn dress had little buttons that went from chest to just above her knees. She'd looked like an adorable little package just waiting to be unwrapped.

He placed her hand on the next button and let go, silently urging her to continue. With a naughty smile to match the gleam in her eyes, Stella kept her focus on him as she finished revealing the rest of her curvy body.

And then a shrill ring pierced the moment.

With a groan, Stella sat up, forcing Dane back.

"I have to get that," she stated with an apologetic tone.

Dane let her up and watched as she covered her body and made her way back into the penthouse. A large part of him wanted to take that phone and smash the hell out of it, but the other part of him, the businessman in him, understood her commitment to her work.

He'd fallen into his ranch by sheer luck. He'd purchased it during a foreclosure and made one wise investment and purchase after another. He'd worked damn hard to get where he was today.

Honestly, Dane hadn't known just how much he would

appreciate Stella until he arrived and saw her in action. He'd never taken into account just how much she did for Mirage. Because of her, his mother's business was back to thriving. The resort was moving into a stronger year of sales and coming back from the brink of near financial ruin.

Dane went to the window and shoved his hands into his pockets as he looked out onto the fat flakes coming down. The storm was going to hit hard and fast. People accustomed to Montana weather wouldn't be fazed by this blizzard, but those who had traveled in from places that didn't measure snow by the foot might be in for a surprise.

The mountain would be cut off to all traffic if the storm came in as wild and ferocious as predicted.

Dane blew out a sigh and cocked his neck from side to side. Even analyzing the damn weather did nothing to squelch his arousal. He'd had Stella spread out before him, arching against his touch, and—

"I have to go."

Dane turned to see Stella pulling her hair back into a low ponytail, her dress now all buttoned back up as if nothing had ever happened. His heart rate was still accelerated and now that he knew exactly what she hid beneath that dress, he couldn't shut down quite so quickly.

"What's wrong?" he asked.

Stella turned and headed through the penthouse, pocketing her cell and charging toward the door. Dane followed behind her. "Emergency with one of the rooms. I'll tell you more later. Stay and have more to eat or…whatever."

And then she was gone.

Dane could search her entire penthouse if he wanted, but he knew there would be no hidden secrets kept here. Everything he hoped to learn would come from the tidbits he picked up from Stella herself.

And from the little time he'd spent with her, he'd learned a good bit about her father. Other than the fact Ruiz was a bastard, something Dane already knew, he also discovered there were very likely spies in place throughout Mirage, which meant Dane had to be careful.

Ruiz was stringing his daughter along, making her do his grunt work at this resort, all while waiting to bring in the extra cash.

Dane was willing to up his offer, but there had to be something he was missing. A man like Ruiz Garcia let his entire life revolve around money. The first amount Dane proposed had been turned down flat without so much as a counter. What was it that Ruiz was holding on to? And why?

That was what Dane needed to find out and he wasn't done with Stella until he did.

Seven

After three hours of trying to calm down the newlywed couple in the Summit Suite, Stella was beyond exhausted.

She'd run out so fast on Dane that she was a little embarrassed—but she'd been nothing less than honest with him about how married she was to this place. Everything fell in line behind keeping Mirage in the best standings with each guest that came through.

Good thing she wasn't looking for a relationship because she was not the prize any man would want. Every man she knew had an ego that was too large for him to stand behind her career. That was fine with her.

Stella stepped off the elevator and crossed the hall toward her penthouse. Once she was inside, she closed her eyes and leaned back against the door. She wasn't sure what time it was, but she knew she was dead on her feet. She also was well aware the storm outside was raging and come morning, the mountain road would likely be shut down.

One worry at a time.

"You look worn-out."

Stella startled and blinked as she focused on the man across the room. Oh, what that man could do to a simple tee and a pair of jeans.

"Dane." She pushed off the door and bent down to pull off her knee boots. "I never thought you'd still be here."

Dane remained across the room near the fireplace. Clearly he'd made himself at home because he held a tumbler of the bourbon she knew had been tucked away in a cabinet when she'd left. Stella didn't care for the stuff, but when her father came, she tried to have his favorite brand on hand.

"I wanted to make sure you were taken care of," Dane replied. He tipped back the last of his drink and crossed the room to her. "Go soak in the bath and I'll bring you a glass of wine."

Stella dropped her boots next to the door and laughed. "It's after midnight. I don't have time to sit in the tub no matter how amazing that sounds."

When he came to stand in front of her, Stella let out a sigh and that pretty much stole the little bit of energy she had left.

"Dane, if you came for—"

He framed her face with hands that held her so very gently, all while looking at her like she was made of glass. Right now, that wasn't too far from the truth. The days were catching up with her and she was starting to worry maybe she did need help and couldn't do this all by herself. But if she admitted any type of weakness, her father would immediately deem her unsuitable to run his business.

It would be the national championship all over again. Never coming in first, always falling short.

"I knew you'd argue."

Dane's words barely registered before he bent and picked

her up. With one arm behind her back and the other behind her knees, he headed toward the master bath. Stella laid her head against his chest and closed her eyes.

"You should go," she murmured. "I'll take a quick bath to relax, but you should already be in your room sleeping like the rest of the guests."

Dane eased her onto the edge of the Jacuzzi tub. "If I left, you'd fall asleep in the bathtub and drown. Now get your clothes off."

He started the water, testing it with his hand and completely ignoring her as she started working on each button.

"You really didn't stay for sex?" she asked, shrugging out of her dress.

Dane's focus turned to her, his dark eyes raking over her bare skin. The hunger just as apparent as when he'd been touching her earlier.

"You'll be wide-awake when I have you."

He stood straight up and glanced around the spacious bath. He went to the vanity and searched through the basket he'd had delivered, pulling out products before settling on one. He flicked the top, sniffed, seemed to nod in agreement with himself and dumped the entire bottle into the bath.

Stella laughed. "That's a bit much and one hell of an expensive bath."

He set the empty bottle back on the vanity. "I'll buy you more."

Stella couldn't wrap her mind around this guy. Who was he? Other than a perfect stranger who'd swept into her life just as fiercely as the storm threatening the mountain.

But...was Dane a threat? He hadn't shown any sign of that and she truly didn't believe he worked for her father. That idea had popped into her head due to stress and exhaustion from dealing with, well, everything.

Stella removed her bra and panties and slid into the warm bath. She didn't even try to suppress the moan as she let the heat and fragrant bubbles envelop her. She leaned back against the cushioned bath pillow and closed her eyes.

"Don't let me drown," she muttered.

Dane's chuckle carried from the room, as did his footsteps over the hardwood floor. Maybe if she just relaxed for a few minutes and let someone else take care of her she could revive herself.

Letting someone else have control certainly wasn't the norm for her. Since her mother passed during childbirth, Stella had spent her whole life figuring out how to take care of herself.

Her father often blamed her for her mother's death. He punished her with a strict childhood that always kept Stella in line. By the time she was a teen, she realized that he was an angry, bitter man, lashing out over the loss of his wife. Being left with a daughter when he'd wanted a son hadn't helped matters.

Still, he was the only parent she knew and she wanted… something. At first she wanted acceptance, then she wanted acknowledgment. Now…

Stella opened her eyes and blinked against the burn. She hadn't cried in so long and she certainly didn't like feeling so vulnerable. But was it too much to ask to just be loved by a parent? Was she that hard to accept and let in?

"Here you go." Dane strode back into the room and set the stemless wineglass on the edge of the garden tub. "Oh, no."

He stared down at her as he took a seat next to her glass. "Why the tears?"

Dane reached out and swiped the pad of his thumb over her cheeks and Stella's heart thumped. She'd known him such a short time, yet she felt some strange connection to him, yet she truly didn't know him all that well.

"It's just been a long day," she replied, offering a smile. "The bath does help and the wine is a definite perk."

"I'm not sure how much this is helping if you're upset." He cocked his head and continued to look at her with worry etched over his ruggedly handsome face. "I only stepped out for a minute."

Stella curled her fingers around her wineglass and lifted it to her lips. Bubbles slid down her arm and dripped back into the water. She let the cool, crisp, fruity blend calm her and make her think of happier times. There were happy times…weren't there?

"Have you ever wanted something so badly, living your whole life for that moment when you'd get it, but once you got there, you realized maybe you're just a fool and it was never in your reach at all?"

She was babbling, she knew, but she risked a glance at Dane and noted the sympathy had turned to understanding and maybe a dose of anger. The muscle in his jaw clenched and he merely offered a clipped nod.

"I don't know that I'll ever be what my father wants," she went on. "I'm not sure *I* want to be, honestly. I'll never understand how he couldn't just love me for me. Why we can't just be father and daughter. But after all this time, it's just not going to happen. Is it?"

She shouldn't have tacked on that question, but part of her wanted him to counter and tell her she was mistaken. She wanted someone on her team, in her corner, cheering her on. Damn it. When did she get so wimpy and weak?

"I don't know your father," Dane stated slowly as if choosing his words carefully. "But I do know we don't always get great parents. My mother was the best. She raised my brother and me as a single mom and we were always her top priority. Then she remarried and my stepfather was…well, he wasn't parent material. When she passed, we were stuck with him and that's when we realized what a true bastard he was."

Stella set her glass on the edge and sat up in the water. Dane's eyes instantly went to her chest and her body immediately responded.

"Sounds like we both had to pave our own way."

Dane reached into the water, keeping his eyes on hers the entire time. "You're not relaxing."

His hand found her thigh. That firm grip held her for a moment before he trailed his fingers up. Stella instinctively spread her legs and let her head fall back against the bath pillow.

"Drink your wine," he demanded in that husky tone dripping with arousal. "I've got this."

Stella reached for her glass, but had to hold it with two hands to prevent herself from dropping it into the bubbles as those clever fingers parted her. Stella took a sip, her eyes locking on Dane's over the top of her glass.

That dark unruly hair, the heavy-lidded gaze, the black stubble along his jawline all joined together to give him that mysterious, alluring factor. She'd never been reckless with anything in her life, let alone with her body. She'd been too focused on work, on moving forward to prove herself.

Letting a near stranger touch her this way felt wrong… yet oh so right.

Dane slid one finger into her and Stella arched her back, biting her lip to keep from crying out. As wave after wave of pleasure slid over her, she closed her eyes and let the moment capture every bit of her.

Nothing existed but Dane's touch. She gripped her glass and clutched it against her bare chest. Water rippled, almost providing soft music to frame the intimate moment. She hadn't expected this, hadn't known he'd still be here when she came home.

As her body jerked, the wine sloshed from the glass and over her chest.

Suddenly the glass disappeared from her hands and Stella focused her attention to Dane. He'd leaned down, his free hand resting on the ledge beside her head. His other hand continued to work her and her hips rose to meet each pump.

Dane dipped his head and ran his tongue along the trail of wine. He made a satisfied purring noise low in his throat. "I never thought I'd crave white wine, but damn. That's good."

He slid his lips along the path again and took his time, quite the opposite of the frantic movement of his hand beneath the bubbles.

Once the wine was gone, he lifted his head and simply watched her. Watched her as if this would be enough to satisfy him.

Stella had never been on display like this, never realized how arousing it could be to have someone watch you so intently with such determination and fixation in their eyes.

The touch, the stare, the intensity of being utterly consumed by a man she barely knew…it all became too much.

Stella reached up and curled her fingers around Dane's biceps, her other hand went to his wrist beneath the water. She didn't know if she wanted to help him or if she just didn't know where else to put her hand, but the way his muscles and tendons were flexing beneath her touch, working so hard at bringing her pleasure, had her body spiraling out of control.

Bursts of euphoria pulsed through her, her entire body tightened around him, and he murmured something as he leaned down and captured her lips. Every part of her continued to quiver as the release flowed.

Dane consumed her, but still, she wanted more.

Stella's body started to settle, leaving her sated, exhausted, and most definitely relaxed.

When she regained control of her breathing and returned to reality, Stella opened her eyes. Dane's hand rested on her thigh and that cockeyed smile matched the hunger in his eyes.

"Ready for bed?"

Stella started to sit up.

"Not sex," he added. "I already told you that's not why I'm here."

Confused, she stood, her legs trembling more than she'd expected. "Then what do you call this?"

In that slow, easy manner of his, Dane rose to his feet and reached toward the heated towel bar. He pulled off a fluffy white towel and with an expert flick, he wrapped it around her.

"I call this getting you to relax and maybe being a bit selfish in taking what I want, too." He shrugged and clutched the towel together between her breasts. "I'm human."

Her eyes darted down to just below his silver belt buckle. "I see that and you're also miserable."

"After what I just saw?" He smiled even wider and shook his head as he scooped her up and out of the tub. "I'm far from miserable. Turned on and aroused? Absolutely. But watching you like that is something I'll never forget."

Yeah, she wouldn't forget it, either. Dane had a touch like none other…at least none she'd ever had. Those rough hands could certainly do more than run a ranch—or whatever it was he did.

Mercy's sake. She'd just let a man she barely knew pleasure her in such an erotic way. When did she become that woman?

Stella rested her head against his shoulder. Perhaps she'd always been that woman—the type who deserved more than she allowed herself to have, the type who should take more of what she wanted out of life and not work herself to death, and the type who knew when a fling was too good to turn down.

"I really can't sleep long," she murmured.

As he carried her, a wave of dizziness overcame her. The hours on her feet, the warmth from the bath, the lethargy from the greatest orgasm she'd ever had…everything made her feel as if she was caught in that world between being asleep and awake.

"Stay." The single word slipped from her mouth before she could stop herself. "I don't want to be alone."

She cringed at her own words. That sounded like begging and after coming undone all around him a moment ago, she'd better watch out or he'd think she was getting attached. There was no room in her life for attachments.

Honestly, she wouldn't know how to do a relationship or commitment anyway. It wasn't as if she'd grown up with a good example. Stella wasn't sure she could ever have a normal or real relationship. Most little girls dreamed of their wedding day, but she'd only dreamed of the day her father wrapped his arms around her and told her how proud he was of her.

Tears pricked her eyes again as Dane settled her onto her bed. Before she rolled over, she thought she felt a dip on the mattress behind her.

He'd stayed. After giving so freely of his passion, expecting nothing in return, and after she'd accused him of horrible things earlier…he'd stayed. For her.

Eight

Dane stared out into the darkness. Swirling snowflakes fluttered through the soft beam of light coming off the patio. He did his best thinking in the middle of the night, in this stretch of time when the world seemed to be calm.

After his years in the military, sleeping never came easy. Nightmares plagued him night after night, but he figured that would forever be an issue. In truth, it didn't seem to be as bad lately. He didn't know if his memories were getting better or if he'd just grown accustomed to living with the horror that was his new normal.

Dane glanced over his shoulder toward the king-size bed. The navy sheets and duvet were all twisted on one side where he'd tried to rest, but perfectly placed on the other where Stella slept beneath them.

And that sight right there perfectly summed up their differences. He was restless and edgy, never quite feeling settled with anything in his life…not since his mother's death. One would think after nearly twenty years he would find some calm center inside of himself, but one life event had rolled into another and Dane had never quite found his inner peace.

Now that Dane had a bit more insight to Stella, he had to assume she never had, either. Perhaps she didn't even know she was chasing a dream that would leave her only broken and angry.

Dane hadn't lied when he said he didn't know her father, but he was well aware the type of man Ruiz was. It didn't take much digging to find out the guy wasn't the most honest and loyal to his associates or with business deals. He looked out only for one person…himself.

So where would that leave Stella? Her father treated her like nothing more than a piece on a chessboard…and then Dane came along and did the same thing.

Guilt clawed at him as he turned his attention back to the blizzard raging outside. He caught his reflection in the darkened part of the window and muttered a curse.

How the hell did he obtain his ultimate goal and not run over Stella in the process? That's not what his mother would have wanted. She hadn't raised them to be selfish and scheming. Yet here he was, excelling at both.

He hadn't expected to care about what was going on with Stella's personal life. When he'd planned and plotted all of this to get Mirage back, he'd only had his family in mind. Somehow, he wanted to get back what he and his brother were supposed to have and if gaining back the two resorts pushed them closer together, then that was just another reason to keep moving forward.

No matter who stood in his way.

Rustling sheets had him glancing over his shoulder. Stella sat up, the duvet pooled at her waist, her breasts on display and her midnight-black hair all around her shoulders.

The crackling fire sent a glow throughout the open room, putting out a romantic ambience that shouldn't affect him, but had his body stirring as he made his way toward the bed.

Stella raked her gaze over his bare chest. When he'd gotten up, he'd removed his shirt, but kept his jeans on. He'd like to blame his lack of sleep on the confining garment, but the truth was that PTSD and the guilt over his current situation were gnawing at him.

When she eased the covers aside and swung her legs over the bed, Dane stopped. She came to her feet and without a care to her nakedness, she crossed to him. That curvy body approached him and had his arousal pumping.

Her bare feet left whispered sounds as she seemed to glide across the wood floor. There was something so mystifying, so captivating about this woman. That was the only explanation for why he kept allowing himself to be pulled in deeper.

He'd set out to seduce her, but somewhere along the way, the roles had reversed.

Without a word, Stella reached out as she came to stand before him. Her fingertip went to the tattoo of the eagle on his chest that crept over his shoulder. His muscles tensed beneath her touch and he clenched his fists at his sides to keep from picking her up and taking her back to bed, finally having what his body craved.

Those fingertips left the ink and started traveling downward. His abs tightened as he kept his eyes locked on hers.

"Stella," he growled in warning.

The warning was more for himself, though. If he ultimately went through with this seduction, he would be just as much of a bastard as the men he hated.

Her fingers went to the snap on his jeans, pulling it loose. The zipper slid down next.

Damn it. He was human with temptation staring him right in the face. He wanted her too badly to care if it made him a bastard.

Something snapped, likely his sanity, but he circled her waist with his hands and lifted her against him. Dane crushed his mouth to hers and Stella opened for him as she wrapped her arms around his shoulders and her legs around his waist.

Dane wanted to completely consume her, to strip away everything—the clothes, the lies. The damn world outside. He wanted every bit of it gone.

Taking long strides, he headed toward the bed. He wasn't waiting any longer. Guilt had no place in business…or the bedroom. Only desire belonged here. And he desired the hell out of her. From her pants and moans and the way her fingertips dug into him, she was just as achy.

When he reached the post at the end of the bed, Dane eased her down to her feet. She blinked up at him, but he took a step back. He continued to watch her as he rid himself of his jeans and boxer briefs.

Dane stepped out of his things and kicked them aside.

"Turn around," he demanded. He couldn't risk her seeing his back, but if she wanted to believe he just enjoyed this position, that was perfectly fine…because he did.

Stella quirked a brow before obeying. Dane shifted behind her and slid his hands down her arms until he reached her wrists. He circled her delicate skin and lifted her hands, wrapping them around the thick, wood bedpost.

Dane tucked his body up against hers as he trailed his lips across her shoulder, up her neck, to the curve of her ear.

"Hold on."

He quickly grabbed a condom from his wallet and covered himself as he stepped in behind her once again. With his hands gripping her hips, he pressed his body into hers.

"Spread your legs," he murmured.

Stella stepped wider and Dane used the opportunity to ease his hand to the front of her body, pleased to discover she was more than ready to take him. He slid the tips of his fingers through her, fighting the staggering need to take this final step.

"Dane."

His name coming off her lips in a cry of pleasure was all the motivation he needed. Dane slid into her and had her crying out once again. He, on the other hand, stilled.

She. Was. Perfect.

Closing his eyes against any emotions other than lust and raw, primal need, Dane concentrated on just how amazing they were together. For this night, and maybe the duration of his stay, he wanted to be here in her bed. And out of her bed? Well, that was a space he couldn't think about right now.

Stella's knuckles whitened as she gripped the post. Her head fell back against his shoulder. As Dane continued to pump his hips, he kept his hands firmly on her thighs, his fingertips digging in to keep her in place.

He leaned down and sucked on that curve of her neck, earning him another pleasure-filled groan. Damn if he didn't know her body already and that was one of the most powerful tools he had in his arsenal.

Stella reached up higher on the post and sank back against him even farther. Within seconds she was coming undone and panting his name. Dane couldn't hold back another second and he was done trying. He followed her release, pressing his forehead against her shoulder as he gritted his teeth.

He held on to her until both of their bodies ceased trembling and even then, he didn't let go.

"I think my legs are going to give out." Stella's breathless words broke the silence. "I don't know how we're still standing."

He nipped at that curve in her neck again, suddenly realizing he liked that spot because each time he touched her there, she trembled. He liked having that control over her, just that little kernel that was all his.

"We're still standing because I wasn't about to miss a second of this sweet body by falling down," he countered.

Dane spun her around and lifted her up before circling the bed and laying her back down on her side. He rested a hand on either side of her head and stared down at her dark eyes, that midnight hair spread all around her.

A sheen of sweat had broken out on her chest and Dane couldn't resist. He leaned down and took one breast into his mouth. How could he want her again when his body hadn't even recovered from the last time?

When she arched against him and let out something akin to a purr, he knew exactly how. Stella Garcia was magnetic and there was no way he could say no or deny either of them what they both needed.

"You're not going to get any more sleep."

She smiled up at him. "Is that a threat?"

He palmed the other breast. "No. That's a promise."

Nine

She didn't know how she was doing it, but somehow Stella was going from one part of the resort to another, checking on staff, guests, food, and anything else she could. She tried to stay calm and competent, but it was much more of a struggle than usual. This storm was raging like nothing she'd ever seen and she was running on next to no sleep.

And yet in spite of that, the memories from last night had her smiling as she made quick strides to one of the theater rooms. If the power went due to the blizzard, she knew her generators would kick in and there would be no worries. But she still wanted to make sure everything was in good shape and that all of her guests were as comfortable as possible. They'd likely be stuck beyond their projected date, so she planned on offering discounts and extras to make up for their inconvenience.

As much as she hated the idea of stranded guests, Stella couldn't help but feel a little giddy about one guest in particular.

Once she checked on the theater rooms and the fantasy suites, she breathed a sigh of relief. So far this day was going better than most. Each guest was quite understanding of the fact the mountain road would likely close. Each guest was also given the choice to check out now and get a discount on their next stay or continue their vacation at a lower rate. Everyone had decided to stay and she couldn't help but feel a burst of pride. Thankfully they had just enough rooms and they were full.

She was actually doing this. She was kicking ass at being the manager of Mirage, one of the most spectacular adult resorts in the world.

Stella hoped like hell whoever her father had planted here saw that. She only wished she knew who the culprit was, but she wasn't wasting her time trying to find out. Whoever it was, there was nothing she'd be doing any differently even if she knew. Her guests always came first and losing sleep, skipping meals, and having achy arches in her feet were all worth it to have happy guests.

Stella pulled her cell from her pocket to check the radar once again. Not that anything had changed since she looked at it thirty minutes ago, but she just wanted to see…just in case.

The bright blue blob right over Gold Valley stared back at her. Okay, well, she would get through this. Blizzards were expected in this part of the country and there wasn't much she could do to fight Mother Nature. If the mountain closed, at least her guests would be safe right here and she would play the dutiful host and make sure each need was met.

Perhaps she could include her own needs in that mix. Her cell vibrated in her hand and she glanced back down to see her father's number.

Quickly swiping the screen, she answered, "Hello."

"Stella. How are things with my resort?"

His resort. She didn't roll her eyes, but she just barely suppressed herself.

"Every room is still full and the guests are all staying through the storm."

"Of course they are. Why would they leave?"

No reason to give her any credit. Really, no problem.

"I will be arriving in two weeks to check things out," he went on. "I trust the penthouse will be ready for me."

Stella gripped the cell. "We are booked up. I wasn't aware you wanted a room."

"You don't think you should always have a handful of rooms at the ready for special clients or your own father?"

Stella smiled at a young couple strolling through the hallway. Once they passed, she still lowered her voice as she made her way toward her office.

"I think that every client deserves the same treatment no matter their financial status," she stated. "I wouldn't turn someone away in the hopes that some millionaire needed a room. I maximize on every profit possible."

"That line of thinking will get my doors closed," he growled. "If you're running my resort, then you'll do it my way."

Stella finally slipped into her office and closed the door at her back. Fury pumped through her.

"*Your* resort. *Your* way." The words slowly slipped through gritted teeth. "And here I was under the impression this resort would eventually be mine."

"That's my call and for now, Mirage is still mine. I'm sure in the next two weeks you will figure out a way to have my suite available."

"You can stay in mine," she offered. "I'll sleep on the sofa."

"Don't be absurd."

Stella took a seat in her chair and immediately realized her mistake. Now that she was down, she didn't want to get back up.

"If someone cancels, I'll be sure to put your name on that room," she promised. "But for now I need to go unless there's something else you needed."

"There is one more thing."

Stella's eyes scanned the security cameras at the front desk, the lobby, the public decks, and the front entrance. The security cameras in her office had all angles of the resort, save for the suites and the fantasy rooms.

"What's that?" she asked.

"I was offered a great deal of money to sell."

Stella's heart clenched, her breath caught in her throat and she stilled, afraid to move, desperately praying she'd heard wrong.

"I've turned the would-be buyer down," he added. There was something akin to gloating and arrogance to his tone. "But I've been wondering if you'd rather have a nest egg than a business. You could always take the money and invest, travel around the world, or even start up your own place."

Stella rested her elbows on her desk and rubbed her forehead as she pulled in a shaky breath. So that's what all of this was. Everything in his life was still about money. He'd never change, likely he never intended to give her this property. But that wouldn't stop her from pushing forward and making sure her reputation remained impeccable.

She owed that to the single mom who'd started this. A strong woman who had a vision, a passion. Stella might not have much in common with Lara as far as family life went, but she understood drive and determination.

"I don't want the money," she explained. "At the end of this six-month experiment, I want the resort. I know I'm not the son you wanted, or the perfect business partner, but I've never given up on us."

She bit her lip the second she realized it was quivering and she was close to losing it.

"I just want a chance," she stated, once she got control of her emotions. "I've tried for so long to please you. What will it take?"

Silence on the other end had her glancing to the screen to make sure they were still connected.

"I never said you didn't please me," her father finally said. "And rehashing the past won't change a thing."

"Rehashing the past? You mean discussing my mom? Because anytime I try to talk about her, you shut the topic down."

"Stella, I will not discuss this now," he reprimanded. "I believe you have things to do. I will see you in two weeks."

He disconnected the call, leaving her emotions in even more of a jumbled mess than before. She hadn't meant to bring up her mom, but sometimes it just happened. She'd always wondered about her, wanted to see photos of her, hear stories about what she'd been like. But there had been nothing. No photos, no stories. Ruiz had shut completely down.

How did the man deal with grief or pain if he never faced it?

Laying her phone down, Stella ran her hands over her face and took long, slow breaths to calm herself down. Leaving her office upset was not in keeping with the professional front she wanted anyone to see.

She smoothed her hair back from her face and started to stand, but stilled when she spotted Dane on the screen. He was actually outside on one of the covered patio areas. He wore a pair of jeans and a thick, wool coat. He was talking on his cell and staring out at the swirling snow. Whoever he was talking to had him shaking his head and gesturing with his free hand.

This was none of her business. She had no real ties to him, no reason to expect to be allowed some insight into his life. Yet she continued to stare. When he raked a hand over the back of his neck, Stella sank back into her chair and wondered who or what had him so upset. This wasn't the laid-back man who had pleasured her multiple times. This certainly wasn't the guy who had a life motto of "it will all work out."

She'd seen only the very sexy, very giving side of Dane Michaels. Who was he really? A rancher and ex-military, but that's all she knew.

On the screen she watched as he ended the call and pocketed his cell. Realizing she'd been staring for quite a while, Stella grabbed her own phone and came to her feet. Lunch had just passed and she hadn't grabbed a bite. She'd swing through the kitchen, make sure they were all set for dinner and the wine and cheese hour and pick something up for herself really quickly.

Maybe she should go ahead and plan a dinner for her room again. They had nowhere else to go and she wanted to take time for herself. If her father was seriously making a visit in a couple weeks, Stella was taking her reward now for the headache she'd have later.

Her cell chimed again, this time a text from the employee who kept the private hot tub areas maintained between guests.

Apparently the guests were requesting a special bottle of pinot noir and not the regular house white that was kept in that area.

Stella went to grab a bottle of the preferred wine. She of all people knew the importance of wine and a nice relaxing soak.

And once again, even in work, her mind circled back to Dane. What was she going to do when his time here came to an end?

Ten

Ethan stared at the phone and wondered what he'd said to make Dane so angry. His brother wasn't one to let his emotions drive him…or he never had been. Had that changed? Considering they hadn't spent too much time together in the past, oh, couple of decades, Ethan couldn't really consider himself an authority on his brother anymore.

All Ethan had said was that if Robert showed up at Mirage in Sunset Cove, then Ethan wasn't sure he could wait for Dane to tie up loose ends and get down there to join him. They'd waited all this time, years, to build up their resources, their finances, their power. The time to strike was now and there wasn't a chance in hell Ethan was going to let Robert slip out of their grasp again.

Ethan didn't mention that he happened to already be at Mirage. Dane thought he was just in California, but Ethan figured he should keep his plans to himself. He trusted his brother—even with the distance between them, there was no one he trusted more than Dane. They may have grown apart, but they would always have a bond like nothing else in the world. But that didn't mean his brother needed to know everything.

Shoving his cell back into the pocket of his shorts, Ethan strolled out of the open lobby area and straight toward the beach. While he was waiting on dear ol' stepdad to make his appearance, there was no reason he couldn't take in the sights while he waited…and by sights he meant that sexy, lush lady sporting a red bikini. Suddenly he had a new favorite color.

Who said he couldn't enjoy himself while on the hunt for Robert? Besides, Ethan planned on being at Mirage for a while—like forever.

As soon as he secured this place in his name, as his mother had originally intended, he planned on living right here where he belonged to manage the place and keep it prosperous. The beach, the ocean, they were home. Ethan may have grown up in Montana, but there was nothing like that salty breeze and the sand between his toes.

And the views. Had he mentioned that already? Because he never could understand why anyone would rather be bundled up around a fire when they could be showing off sun-kissed skin and enjoying their favorite beachside beverage.

The lady in red sprayed herself with sunscreen and tossed her bottle back in her striped beach bag. He glanced up and down the shoreline. With this as an adults-only resort, there was a peacefulness not many beaches had. There were no screaming, running children since this was a private island.

Family vacations were great, but Mirage was not that type of destination. His mother, a lifelong romantic, had built two stellar resorts all with couples in mind. Her sense of romance had led to her commercial success, but also her personal downfall. She'd wanted to marry for love, she'd wholeheartedly believed in it, and she had married…but Ethan highly doubted love had entered anywhere in that equation.

Her father had passed and Lara had been left raising two boys on her own. The scenario seemed to be tailor-made for Robert because he obviously preyed on the weak and vulnerable.

The Michaels boys were neither weak nor vulnerable now. They were angry, they were still hurt, and they were ready to fight back. There was nothing Ethan wouldn't do to honor his mother, and she'd raised strong boys. This was what she would've wanted.

Ethan slipped off his flip-flops and looped his fingers around the straps as he made his way across the warm sand.

Walking along the edge of the water always relaxed him, always helped him see a clearer picture. That was why he'd come out to Mirage instead of waiting. He needed to be here to sort through all the mess in his head, to figure out the precise steps he needed to take. He had to act fast, but he also had to be smart about it.

The sexy, curvaceous woman in red glanced his way and Ethan didn't even try to hide his smile…and he didn't move when she made her way over. A woman who knew what she wanted was one of the sexiest qualities.

Considering her smile widened as she crossed the sand toward him, well, apparently they wanted the same thing.

"I'm sorry, sir. Who did you say you were again?"

Dane didn't fault the young male for questioning the stranger who was in the midst of checking on the generators in the maintenance area. No guest should know where this room was, as rooms dedicated to the staff or the maintenance of the resort were hidden from the guests.

The entire resort had the illusion of running on fairy dust or some other magical oddity. That had been imperative to his mother who wanted couples who came here to only see the perfection, the fantasy, the beauty. "Real life" shouldn't exist on vacation, she'd always said. And she was correct. People wanted to get away from all cares and responsibilities, and she provided exactly what patrons wanted.

"Dane Michaels," he stated again as he settled his hands on his hips. "Miss Garcia asked me to check on this and she said you might be down as well since you're so thorough with your job."

The BS just rolled off his tongue, but hit the mark as the twentysomething puffed his chest with pride.

"I wasn't aware we had a new maintenance guy," the other man said. "But I checked on these yesterday."

Dane wasn't about to get into an argument or contradict the guy's mistaken assumption. But Dane would feel better if he checked on all of the "behind the scenes" things himself. After all, he had to keep up with all sides of his property.

"The storm closed the mountain." Dane purposely dodged the questioning stare from the other guy. "It's not going to let up for a few days. These generators will likely be put to use very soon."

The worker nodded. "That's what I was thinking, too."

The radio clipped to his hip crackled and a female voice came over the airwaves. He knew that voice and she may not like knowing he was in here checking things out. He listened as she requested any available hands to get to the dining area to set up for the lunch crowd.

With the storm, so many employees were unable to make

their shifts, which meant the ones stuck here were pulling overtime for the foreseeable future.

And that meant Stella would be running from one end of Mirage to the other, taking little time for herself—if any. He'd make sure his mother's resort was running just fine, the guests were happy, and Stella's needs were met…every single one.

The worker turned his radio down and started looking over the area with the generators. Dane stood back and crossed his arms over his chest, calculating and contemplating.

"These are all set to go," Dane assured him. "Aren't you going to the dining area to help?"

The boy shrugged. "Other workers will help out."

Dane stared at the back of the guy's head and clenched his jaw to keep from yelling at the boy for his lazy, entitled attitude. In due time. This jerk had no clue who Dane was or that he'd be fired for that earlier comment as soon as Dane was in charge.

"This is all covered," Dane stated once again. "You and I can both pitch in. This is a nasty storm and every employee here needs to help anywhere they can."

The other guy stood up and turned, his brows drawn in. "I thought Mitch was over maintenance. What's your position?"

Higher than yours, asshole.

"Miss Garcia is waiting on help." Dane gestured toward the doorway. "Let's go."

Dane thought there was going to be an argument, but the guy finally nodded and headed out the door. There was no need to let Stella know about her lazy employee, but Dane wouldn't forget the kid.

By the time they got to the dining area, several employees, all dressed in black, were already bustling around and setting sprigs of evergreen and simple white votives on each of the tables. The lunch decor was quite a bit different than the dinner ambience. For one thing, it was a lot busier. Many couples chose to eat in their room or one of the fantasy rooms during the evening.

There were little changes Dane saw that hadn't been implemented while his mother had been here. The changing of decor being one of them. He liked the touches Stella put on the place—no doubt with her father's permission. The idea of giving the guests a different restaurant feel each time was smart.

The more he saw of Stella—the way she ran this place, the way she actually cared and wasn't just in this for money or recognition—the more he wondered what his mother would've thought of her.

Not that there was any reason to wonder, really. He knew exactly what she'd have thought.

Lara would've loved Stella.

Dane crossed the dining room and cursed himself. What the hell did he care what his mother would've thought of Stella? The thought was absolutely irrelevant. Stella and her father weren't going to be part of Mirage much longer and Lara would be proud of Dane for getting back what belonged to him.

There she was. Across the room against the two-story windows encased with stone. Stella had on another one of those sexy little dresses that stopped at her knee…this one in red that made her look only more exotic with that dark skin and hair.

Instead of her usual brown boots, she had on black. There

were several inches of bare skin between the top of her boot and the hem of her dress. He clenched his fists, aching to touch her.

Soon, he promised himself.

Stella turned to talk to an employee, pointing in the direction of the kitchen, then she nodded and spun back around. He watched for only a minute before she shifted that dark gaze to him. Even from across the room he could read her body language. She was exhausted, but running on pure determination.

She offered him a soft smile and the gesture hit him square in the gut. Out of this crowd of people she focused on him and the unspoken bond that they shared shouldn't have his heart clenching, but damn it…

There was no room for distractions, no matter how tempting and captivating. He wanted her physically, something he hadn't expected. But he could at least control the passion. Desire and sex were easy—as long as he stayed in control, kept himself from getting too attached and kept her away from his ugly scars.

The true problem came from all the other unwanted, unexplained feelings that were flooding in before he had a chance to shut the damn door on his emotions.

Hadn't he locked that once already? How the hell had this woman, in such a short amount of time, managed to kick it down?

Dane made his way across the room, circling the tables and weaving through chairs not quite set in place yet. Once he reached her, Dane used every ounce of his willpower not to reach out and touch her or to pull her out of this room so he could force her to rest.

But resting wasn't Stella's style. They were cut from the

same proverbial cloth in that they didn't rest when there was still work to be done.

"All hands on deck, huh?" he asked when she came to stand right before him.

With a smile and a nod, she replied, "Something like that."

"What do you want?"

Stella quirked her brow. "That's a loaded question."

"It was meant to be."

He might not be able to touch her, but that didn't mean he couldn't let her know exactly what he wanted.

"In that case, I wouldn't mind being away from here, somewhere secluded so I could do anything I wanted for just one day." She closed her eyes and sighed before meeting his gaze again. "But since that's not happening anytime soon, maybe you could check in at the front desk and make sure everything is okay?"

Dane nodded. "Not a problem."

When he started to turn, she called his name. "Be in my room at eight."

Already turned on by her demand, Dane leaned toward her to whisper, "You'd better be ready for me."

Her visual tremble had him whistling on his way out. Damn if she wasn't sexy. She'd been all authoritative, but then when he'd turned the tables, she practically melted to a puddle.

Dane had every intention of doing whatever he could to help her make sure this storm went unnoticed by the guests. But tonight, well, Stella would be his and there was no better recipe for seduction than to be snowbound with a sultry vixen.

Eleven

Stella stared at all the food and the special bottle she'd had brought up just for Dane. Was she a complete and utter fool? How could she feel so strongly for a man when she'd only just met him a few days before?

Yet he'd proved time and time again that he was selfless—both in the bedroom and out. He'd jumped at the chance to help her and pitch in around the resort since some employees couldn't make their shifts. He'd helped work in areas she hadn't even asked, putting in hard labor during what was supposed to be his vacation.

Was that why it was nearly quarter after eight and he still hadn't made it to her penthouse? Perhaps he'd fallen into bed like all the other workers she'd put on sleep rotation.

There had been some serious shuffling of cots and blow-up mattresses in order to fit in the staff members who would be resting while others filled in.

She'd already made a mental note to give each employee a

bonus for all their hard work. She hadn't heard one complaint and anything she'd asked, they'd gotten right to handling.

Yet now she stood with her thoughts and her concerns. Not over Mirage or the raging storm. Those two were easy to manage. But Dane proved to be a much more unpredictable beast.

Stella padded through her penthouse and went to the fire. There was nothing like coming back here at the end of a long day and staring at the flickering red and gold flames. A glass of wine in her hand never hurt, either, but she was waiting on Dane.

"Stupid," she muttered to herself and turned away from the fire. Even that wasn't calming her nerves.

Dane was likely just as worn down as she was. Maybe he'd even had enough of her. Why was he busting his ass so much anyway? What was he getting out of all of this? Nothing here was his responsibility, his future didn't hinge on how well this resort ran if the power went out and the road didn't open for several days.

Jerking the rubber band from her wrist, Stella pulled her hair atop her head and twisted it into a knot. She should eat something since she'd brought leftovers from the kitchen up to her room. She hadn't had much time for eating earlier, between bustling from common rooms to suites to fantasy rooms and thinking about her night with Dane.

Just as she popped a cube of smoked gouda into her mouth, the buzzer on her private elevator echoed through the penthouse. Nerves curled together in her belly, which was so silly. Dane was just a man and he was a temporary man at that. Their time would likely draw to a close as soon as the road opened and he was on his way. He had already overstayed his time here and his reservation was technically up. Not that she cared or would kick him out at first chance.

Was she an even bigger fool because she felt a little sliver of emptiness at the thought of him leaving?

Honestly, she didn't care that she was getting in over her head. Dane had shown her so much compassion and support during these past couple of days. And the things that man could do in the bedroom? Her body tingled just thinking about his talents. Even if she got to keep him for only a short time, it would be worth it. That man would certainly fuel fantasies for years to come.

The elevator door slid aside and there he was. A man in a bespoke suit couldn't have looked more powerful, more confident and in control. He had that whole rugged rancher look down to a perfectly imperfect manner. The plaid shirt, the worn jeans, the scuffed cowboy boots.

And those eyes. Dark as midnight surrounded by inky lashes any woman would envy.

Dane came toward her, but his eyes scanned the room before landing back on her.

"You worked all day and came back here to set up dinner?" he asked, obviously shocked.

Stella shrugged, not sure how to take his tone. Was he surprised in a good way or a bad way?

"I may not be able to escape to that remote location I dream of, but this is close enough."

She took a step toward him, closing the gap. Stella reached up, flicking his top button until it slid through the hole. She glanced from her fingertips on his shirt up to his coal-like gaze.

"And if you're here, I don't really care where I am," she

added. “Maybe for tonight, we can pretend we’re just like any other guest and…”

His hand covered hers. “And what?”

Stella laughed and shook her head. “I’m being silly. You *are* a normal guest.”

Dane tipped her head up, framing her face with those rough, firm hands. “I’m a guest, but nothing about this stay has been normal.”

“No, I guess not.” Stella sighed and took a step back. “I probably shouldn’t throw myself at a man who just came off an engagement.”

The corner of his mouth tipped up. “No, maybe not, but I never asked you to stop.”

“You didn’t,” she agreed. “But before you rip my clothes off—”

“I believe that was you working on my clothes when I’d barely taken a few steps in.”

“Details.” Stella waved her hand in the air. “Anyway. I have something for you, something other than leftovers from the kitchen.”

She turned toward the bar area separating the living room and kitchen. Tucked perfectly on the other side of the domed lids, she pulled out the white bag and presented it to Dane.

He eyed the gift she clutched in her hand, but he didn’t take a step to get it.

“You found time to get me something?” he asked. “In the midst of a raging snowstorm and running a resort full of anxious guests with cabin fever?”

“You’re not the only one with pull,” she stated.

Dane quirked one thick, dark brow and reached for the bag. “You didn’t have to get me anything.”

“I didn’t do it because of the lotions you got me,” she told him. "I did it because I wanted to thank you for everything you've done. You didn't have to be so amazing."

"It's a character trait I can't shake."

Stella couldn't help but laugh at his dry humor as he reached into the bag and pulled out the bottle she had procured from a secret stash that only certain employees knew about.

"Stella." He turned the bottle around and stared at it for a long moment before turning his attention back to her. "This is… I've never had anyone give me a gift like this."

Seriously? He'd been engaged, he had a brother, and a bottle of rare bourbon had him struggling to find words? Even her selfish father gave her gifts—granted, the gifts were given only on birthdays and Christmas and always delivered by his assistant or, in the early years, the nanny. But still…

"It's just bourbon," she muttered, suddenly wondering if she'd gone too far. They were just casually involved and she'd had no clue this would be so emotional for him. "I knew we had a couple bottles of important liquor hidden for special guests or clients who had requests."

He continued clutching the bottle. "I didn't request it."

"It's a gift."

Dane stared down at the bottle, the muscle in his jaw ticked as he remained silent. She'd definitely done something wrong because she'd thought he'd be a bit happier.

"If you'd rather another brand, I know we have several bottles of—"

His eyes snapped to hers. "No. This is… This is more than thanks enough. I'm just surprised since these bottles are hard to come by."

Stella smiled. "Not so difficult."

He raked that dark gaze over her and she knew full well he knew just how powerful that visual caress was.

"I don't need to be paid, or to get lavish gifts," he told her as he set the bottle on the table and closed the distance between them. "I already told you I'm a simple man."

"The way you're looking at me proves how simple you are."

Dane snaked an arm around her waist and hauled her flush against him. Stella flattened her palms against his chest and tipped her head back to meet his hungry gaze.

"You deserve better," he murmured against her lips. "But I can't pull myself away."

Stella threaded her fingers through his coarse hair. "I never asked you to go and I'll decide what I deserve. Right now, I deserve for you to make this ache go away."

Dane's hands slid down the curve of her body, those talented fingers slid beneath the hem of her skirt and teased along the edge of her lacy panties. So close. So, so close. She wanted him, she didn't care about anything else right now. She didn't care about what was happening between them, because she was positive there was more going on here than sex. Though at that moment, sex was all she wanted.

As for the long term, she had her goals and Dane…well, she assumed his were substantial since he'd been so tight-lipped about them.

"I feel a little guilty." She arched into his touch, barely suppressing a moan. "Doing this while everyone is trapped here."

Dane's low chuckle vibrated against her chest. "I assure you, nobody is complaining they're stuck at a couples' resort with fantasy rooms. And they're doing the same thing we are."

"Does that mean I can take a minute off?"

Dane eased back, drew his brows in and gripped her backside. "I assure you, this will take more than a minute."

Stella sure hoped so because she wanted as much of Dane as she could get. She'd never felt more alive, more powerful than when she was with Dane.

The way he held her, looked at her, worshipped her, were all so new, so exhilarating. There was no reason not to just take what she wanted.

Being stranded with a sexy stranger wasn't something that happened every day, right?

Before she could continue her justifications, Dane palmed her backside and lifted her up as he carried her toward the balcony.

"My bedroom is the other way."

Lips trailed down her throat. "I want you out in the open, where I can see everything."

He stepped out onto the glass-enclosed patio. The one-way windows allowed them to see down to the valley below, but nobody could see in. Still, the idea of being exposed was erotic and thrilling. She knew her guests took full advantage of the various hot tubs positioned on the glass balconies, but she'd had no reason to come out here for anything like this before.

Dane eased her to her feet and made quick work of stripping her of her clothes. When she reached for him, she fully expected him to push her away.

And he did, but he grasped her hands in his. Dark eyes held hers and something other than passion looked back at her. There was that heaviness of pain once again. She'd seen that emotion in his eyes before, but never when they'd been on the brink of driving each other out of their minds with want and need.

"I need to tell you something."

His words were coated with a raw, emotional tone she'd never heard from him. Stella turned her hands over beneath his. She might be standing before him completely stripped, but Dane was much more exposed, much more vulnerable.

"I… I have secrets." The muscle in his jaw clenched as he glanced down to their joined hands, then back up to her face. "Before this goes further, you need to know that I never expected this."

"I never expected finding a sexy stranger, either," she countered with a slight smile, hoping to put him at ease. "You don't have to tell me your deepest, darkest secrets. We have no strings."

"I know, but…"

Dane released her hands and stepped back. Stella wished she'd left something on now that she stood there without him so near. But she realized he wasn't staring at her, he was reaching behind his back and gripping his shirt. With a quick jerk, he had it off and then fisted the material in his hands.

"When I was in the army, I lost some buddies." He stared down as he continued to twist his shirt. "There was an accident. Details aren't necessary here, but the scars are—"

"Stop." Stella reached for him and pulled the shirt away. She dropped it to the floor and raked her eyes over his chest. "I don't care about scars and you don't owe me any type of explanation."

The dark hair covering his chest and abdomen, the tattoo curving over his right shoulder…none of that seemed to hide any imperfections that she could see. She ran her hands over him, up his arms to his chest, down toward the top of his jeans.

"You feel fine," she murmured. "You look fine."

Without a word, she moved around to his back. Stella's breath caught in her throat, instant tears burning her eyes. She slid her fingertips over the puckered scars and obvious burns.

"You don't have to—"

"You look and feel fine here, too," she affirmed, not wanting him to offer her an out. She didn't *need* an out. She needed to make him feel that he was worthy of her, that she appreciated the fact he trusted her enough to tell her, show her.

Dane's entire body remained rigid beneath her touch. Ignoring his obvious discomfort, Stella stepped into him, resting her cheek against his back and wrapping her arms around his waist.

"Did you think this would turn me off?" she asked.

"I've never shown anyone," he murmured. "It's not exactly a time I want to talk about."

Stella pressed her lips to his back, then moved on and placed another kiss, then another. "I wasn't in the mood to talk anyway, cowboy."

Her lips traveled all over until she moved to the front and placed them on that ink over his chest and shoulder. Taking his face between her hands, Stella forced him to meet her gaze.

"You're still wearing too many clothes."

He kept that dark, pained gaze locked on her. "You don't deserve this."

Stella threaded her fingers through his hair and pulled his lips to hers. "I know what I want, Dane. Now stop talking."

Dane surprised her by nipping at her lips, then easing back to slide his fingertip down the valley between her breasts. “Have your way with me.”

The low, rumbling words filled the space between them and Stella wasted no time in removing those jeans that hugged his lean hips so deliciously.

Dane may be imperfect in his mind, but to her…well, he was the most perfect, stable, comforting aspect of her entire life.

Now she had to figure out what to do when he chose to leave.

Twelve

"Get down!"

Dane fell to his stomach, using his elbows to crawl away from the knoll. The blast shook the ground. The air was filled with the sound of men screaming in pain. And then something hit his back so hard, the air left his lungs.

One second everything was chaos and hell, then it was quiet and hell. His back burned like nothing he'd ever experienced, but he couldn't lose himself in the pain. He needed to get to his buddies. Reese and Bagger were on the other side of their Humvee. If he could crawl to them, they could somehow get out of here.

With each pull he took to move himself forward with his arms, the pain in his back seemed to intensify. There was something heavy pressing against him. If he could just get to his buddies, maybe they could help each other.

But the quiet seemed to grow. Being out in the open, shouldn't he hear something? Those cries moments ago had stopped, leaving only his own grunts as he dragged himself to the front of the vehicle.

Dane looked around the front, fully expecting to see his comrades, but there was only one person. Stella. She smiled at him.

"Help me," he cried. "Help."

She squatted down and smirked. "Help you? Like you helped me lose everything? You're on your own, Dane. That's how you like it anyway."

"Stella, please." He just needed this weight gone. He couldn't breathe, and the pain had him fading fast. "Stella. Stella."

He kept calling for her. Why wasn't she answering him?

"Stella!"

That weight on his back finally shifted, then something kept pounding against him. Over and over. Dane pushed away, tried to pull in a breath, but he wasn't getting enough oxygen. He was dying and Stella had walked away.

"Dane."

He jerked up, panting. The frantic tone in Stella's voice had him blinking against the darkness. With the sheet pooled around his waist, Dane gripped the edge of the fabric and attempted to regain some normalcy to his breathing.

Her hand went to his back and Dane cringed, still not used to the touch there and not ready to be consoled after the same damn nightmare that had plagued him for years.

No. Not the same. This time the ending was quite different and almost more disturbing than the usual horrendous scene.

He didn't have to be Dr. Freud to understand what the dream meant. In it, she'd obviously found out about his plan.

She'd discovered he'd been lying to her, that he'd stolen her business from her.

But it wasn't hers. Not now, not later. Mirage could never belong to her and he shouldn't feel guilt when he wasn't the one who put her in this position.

Yet guilt still gripped him by the throat and made it damn near impossible to breathe.

He jerked the covers aside and rose from the bed. His eyes adjusted easily to the dark; he'd been living in darkness for years so this wasn't new.

"Dane."

That soft voice, the voice that belonged to a woman who cared for him, who saw his scars and wasn't bothered by them.

"I can't stay." He searched for his clothes and didn't look back at her when the sheets rustled. "I shouldn't have fallen asleep here to begin with. I know what happens."

He scooped up his shirt, but couldn't find his damn pants.

"The nightmares?" she asked. "You weren't dreaming of the war. You were screaming for me to help you. So let me."

Those slender arms came around his chest, pinning him in place before he could put his shirt on. She wanted to help, but if she knew the truth she'd turn away from him, just as she had in the dream.

Dane didn't want to hurt her. Hell, he didn't purposely want to hurt anybody, except for Robert, but he wanted what belonged to him. Why did all the paths leading to his goal get more twists and turns and roadblocks?

"I never stay with a woman," he admitted. "Not since the accident. But you're…different."

"All the more reason for you to quit running." She circled around to the front and gripped his biceps. "I'm here. I'm not asking you to leave, I'm not asking you to talk about anything if you don't want to. But I am asking you to give me a chance. Don't shut me out."

Give her a chance? That's not what he'd come here for, but damn it. He couldn't help himself and now anything they had was based on a foundation of deception.

"I wasn't lying when I said you don't deserve this." He fisted his shirt and wished like hell he'd found some other way to get what he wanted. "I won't be here long and you're dealing with your father—"

Stella's soft laugh filled the room, her warm breath tickled his bare chest. "You know how to ruin a mood. Yes, I'm dealing with my father, but right now, I'm dealing with you."

"I'll go back to my room," he offered. "It's best that way."

"Best? For you?" she asked. "Because the best thing for me is for you to stay. You obviously trusted me enough to show me your scars. Let me see the ones you're hiding on the inside."

There was nothing else he wanted more than to let her in completely. But they were at odds with each other, though she had no idea who he truly was. This seduction had gotten out of hand, his guilt had grown more and more, and damn it, he actually cared about her.

There was no way he could prevent her from being hurt. None. Even if he walked away and gave up on Mirage—which he could never do—she'd still be hurt by her father's callous treatment and failure to keep his bargains. All he could do at this point was either keep going and enjoy this time with her while it lasted, or start to put some distance between them. She would hate him in the end anyway. Did it matter when that started?

"You can't want more," he warned. "I'm leaving when the mountain clears."

Stella's hands fell away. "I know you are. I guess I was just hoping you would stay a little extra time."

If only she knew the irony in her statement.

"I don't want to get too deep," he added. "There's so much we both have going on and this fling…"

"Doesn't have to end."

She reached for the shirt he held on to and dropped it onto the floor. Taking him by the hand, Stella led him toward the bed. He was utterly defenseless. He was also a bastard. Going back to his room was the smart move, but clearly he'd not been making smart decisions since coming to Mirage because now he had a sinking feeling Stella was falling for him.

As she lay next to him, with her arm over his chest and leg over his thighs like she dared him to leave again, all Dane could think of was that he'd been too busy enjoying her to pull out the secrets he'd come here to discover.

Darkness transitioned into light and Dane continued to stare up at the ceiling. Stella had fallen asleep, but now she stirred. He'd been lying here too long with his thoughts, with his damn guilt that gnawed a hole in his gut.

How was lying to this innocent woman honoring his mother? That's not the type of person Lara Anderson had been. She'd been kind and caring and so giving and loyal. She'd been perfect and Dane, well, he was anything but.

"I want to buy Mirage."

The words were out before he could talk himself out of admitting the truth—or at least a partial truth.

Stella's hand pressed against his chest as she lifted slightly to look down at him. Her hair flattened against one side of her head where she'd slept against his side, her heavy lids shielded half her eyes.

"What?"

Dane swallowed and tucked one arm behind his head. "I want to buy Mirage."

"Yeah, I heard you." She shook her head as she sat all the way up and shifted to face him. "But it's not for sale."

"Everything is for sale for the right price."

She stared back at him as if seeing him for the first time—as if she was finally seeing the man beneath the façade. But she still didn't know the truth.

"My father is turning this over to me," she told him as she let out a laugh. "And I'm certainly not selling it."

Dane remained still. "Are you *certain* your father is going to give this place to you?"

A flash of irritation followed by determination crossed her face. Stella tipped her chin and shoved her hair away from her face. "I won't settle for anything less. I know I'm not what he envisioned for this business or any business of his, really. A son would've already had his choice of companies. I ask for one and I'm jumping through damn hoops to secure it."

So her father's issue was that his only child was a girl? What the hell kind of backward thinking was that?

Dane clenched his teeth and eased up onto one elbow. "Your father won't be the one keeping this resort," he vowed.

Stella's brows drew in. "I'm not following you this morning. You didn't get any sleep, did you?"

He reached for her hand and gave it a reassuring squeeze. "This has nothing to do with last night."

A total lie. This had *everything* to do with last night. He'd let her in, deeper than he'd let anyone. He'd seen a side of her he hadn't expected and damn it, he respected her.

None of this was going according to plan and now he was just winging everything and he hoped like hell his goals didn't vanish forever now that they were finally within reach.

"Your father will not be the owner of Mirage for much longer," Dane reiterated. "I promise."

"I still don't get it," she muttered. "Do you know something I don't? And if you say you know my father, that you actually do work for him, I will throw you out into that blizzard—"

"No. I don't know him." Not personally anyway. "And I certainly don't work for him. But I've dealt with men like him before. He won't hold on to this place and he won't turn it over to you because all he cares about is money."

If he cared half as much about his daughter, that would be a nice step in the right direction.

Dane didn't want to ask more questions, didn't want to get more involved emotionally than he already was. But he couldn't stop himself.

"Were you two always at odds?" he asked. "When you were growing up, what was he like?"

Stella shrugged and took her fingertip to the back of his hand. She drew imaginary circles around his knuckles as she seemed to be contemplating her words.

"He wasn't around much. My mom died when I was born, so he hired a nanny." She chewed on her bottom lip as she went around another knuckle. "When he was there, I was never good enough at anything I tried. I loved skiing and would take my thoughts out to the slopes. One lesson turned into another and years later I found myself competing at national levels."

Dane knew that was the extremely shortened version because anyone who competed at that level had worked their ass off for years, giving up most of their social life for the ultimate goal.

"I think he blames me for her death," she went on, emotion lacing her tone. "He's never come right out and said so, but he's hinted enough."

"It wasn't your fault. You know that, right?"

Stella remained silent as she glanced away.

"You're not responsible for her death," he stressed as he sat all the way up. "Listen to me."

Dane took her bare shoulders and turned her to face him before he framed her face and forced her to hold his gaze.

"Whatever you grew up believing, whatever he said or just implied, you know nothing was your fault."

Stella stared back and shrugged. "It was not exactly my fault, but if I hadn't been born maybe she and my dad would still be married. Maybe they would've had other children. Boys—to fulfill all the requirements to be a Garcia heir."

Dane couldn't wait to take this resort back and get Stella out from under her father's ruling thumb. She might hate Dane in the end, but at least she'd be saved from one bastard.

"You don't really believe that." Dane wanted to shake sense into her, but he'd only known her a handful of days and he couldn't exactly reprogram her from over twenty years of dealing with her father. "You're stronger than your father. You wouldn't be here if you were weak. Being a woman is actually your strength. Women think in a different way than men and this resort needs you."

Stella attempted a smile. "Nobody has ever acted like I'm needed here or at any other business, for that matter."

"Then everyone is a damn fool."

He meant every word. She was valuable, and she'd done wonderful work here. The only problem was that he just couldn't have her take his resort.

"You're a sharp businesswoman and if your dad can't see that, then stop beating yourself up and go out and make something of your own without worrying about how he'd react."

"That's easy for you to say," she retorted. "I don't have unlimited means of income. Everything I have is from my salary, but it's not a lot. My father considers room and board enough. This resort, this little piece of his life is all I've ever wanted. I gave up on his love a long time ago, but getting his respect is something I may never give up wanting."

"Why?"

"Because he only deals in business," she explained. "Respect for my business abilities may be the closest thing to love that he can give. I don't know that he's capable of love in the way that I need it."

Not likely, but since Dane didn't know how to love anyone like they needed, he wasn't the person to offer advice on this matter.

His cell rang, breaking the tension and giving him the out he needed.

"I need to take that," Dane explained as he eased off the bed.

He scooped up his jeans and pulled the cell from his pocket. With a quick glance to the screen, he saw it was Ethan.

"I'm just going to step out here." He started for the patio when her words stopped him.

"That's not your ex-fiancée wanting you back, is it?"

Ex-fiancée. Damn it. Dane had gotten so swept away

in this whole charade, he'd forgotten about the fictitious woman.

"I promise, it's nobody wanting me back."

Possessive girlfriends had never been an issue in his life because no one had ever been allowed to get that close. He was fine with that. There was no need to chance having your heart ripped out again. Once was more than enough for him when he lost his mother. The ranch kept him busy and that was all he needed. Well, that and Mirage.

Dane swiped the screen and glanced over his shoulder to see Stella sliding beneath the covers, her hand going to the dent in his pillow.

Swallowing the guilt, he answered. "It's awfully early for you, isn't it?"

"I haven't been to bed, yet," Ethan replied. "I figured being a rancher you're always up at this time anyway."

"I'm not on the ranch."

"I'm aware," Ethan growled. "Shut up and listen. Robert is due to be at Sunset Cove in three days."

Dane gripped his cell. "How do you know? And are you positive?"

"My sources confirmed his travel arrangements. How soon can you get here?"

"You're already there?" Dane shook his head and glanced to the hot tub where hours ago he'd pleasured Stella until she cried out his name.

The memories of her would last him a lifetime, which was good since she'd hate him in the very near future.

"I'm here," Ethan confirmed.

"Just make sure you keep the goal in mind—and I don't mean bikini-clad women."

His brother chuckled. "No reason I can't enjoy myself while I wait."

There was static on the line and Ethan's muffled voice a moment before he said, "I'll text you updates. I gotta go."

The call ended, leaving Dane wondering just how quick he could wrap things up here. Ruiz needed to be dealt with here and now. The next number Dane would have his broker throw out would be impossible to turn down. Maybe he could make things move faster by appealing to Ruiz's male chauvinist side.

Dane stared out the window as the sun started peeking over the mountaintops. The snow had stopped sometime during the night, which was good news for the stranded guests.

With another quick glance over his shoulder, Dane sent a text to his broker with the new offer and stipulations. There was no way this would be turned down. Ruiz was a smart businessman. If all went as planned, this resort would be his in thirty days.

Thirteen

Stella had never taken advantage of a fantasy suite. She had her own penthouse for one thing, but the main reason was she'd never had a need or a man.

Well, now she had both.

Butterflies fluttered in her stomach and she had no clue why she was nervous. It wasn't like she was a virgin or hadn't slept with Dane before. Over the past several days, they'd been all over each other.

The blizzard had calmed down to Montana's usual snow accumulation and guests came and went, still cautious of slippery roads. All was mostly back to normal.

Except Dane stayed. His stay was technically up two days ago and his penthouse had been taken by a couple celebrating their tenth wedding anniversary.

So she moved his stuff into her suite.

Stella jerked on the tie of her shirt. She couldn't believe she had donned this outfit, but she figured Dane would like it. At least, she hoped he went for that whole lumberjack girl vibe. She'd taken one of her plaid flannels and left all buttons undone, simply tying the bottom in a knot just below her breasts. She figured the bright red lacy bra beneath was a nice touch.

Then she'd found an old denim skirt and ended up taking a pair of scissors to it to make it about four inches shorter. Dane would love the present beneath the skirt.

Of course she couldn't exactly parade through her resort looking like she was about to take the stage as a strip club's version of *Twin Peaks* with her boobs on display. That wouldn't be professional at all and her father's minion, whoever that might be, would certainly be all too eager to tattle.

Stella had put a fake name into the computer system to block off the room for the night and she'd sneaked in with her costume in her purse. She still wore her knee boots, but she had pulled her hair from the twist and left it in a wild mess around her shoulders.

She pulled her cell from her back pocket and checked the time. Dane should be here any minute. She'd told him she needed help moving something in the Lumberjack Room and he'd said he'd be right there.

Now she waited.

Stella crossed the hardwood floor and put the cell in her bag in the corner. A click of the door had her spinning back around.

Dane stepped through the door, took in the lanterns all around the room, the hanging tent, and the bourbon bar.

Then his eyes scanned back to her. The dark gaze raked over her, up and down. Then another slow, visual perusal.

"So I'm assuming you don't want to move anything," he said as he reached behind him, flicking the lock into place.

He crossed to the middle of the room and put his hand

on the small wooden steps leading to the tent. He peered inside and back to her.

"This thing hold people?" he asked.

Stella smiled. "It's secure for up to eight hundred pounds."

Dane hooked his thumbs through his belt loops as his gaze took another travel down her body. "Then I guess we're safe."

Safe? She was anything but safe with him. At least not emotionally because she was pretty sure she was falling for him, which was ridiculous considering she'd known him just over a week. The level of feelings she *thought* she had couldn't be developed in such a short time…could it?

"Something is rolling around inside that head of yours," he stated, pulling her from her thoughts. "Maybe you need a distraction."

"Oh, believe me. You've distracted me since you got here."

Dane kept that dark gaze on hers as his mouth kicked up in a grin and he pulled on his belt buckle. "That's the nicest compliment I've ever received."

"You *would* take that as a compliment."

Dane stood before her with his jeans unfastened, belt dangling, and reached for the hem of his shirt. "Why did you go to this trouble? We could've just stayed in your penthouse."

Stella shrugged. "I wanted to change it up a little. I never know when you're going to leave, so I guess I wanted to—"

"Give me a going away present?" he asked.

When he whipped his shirt over his head, she felt a warm glow of satisfaction at the realization that he'd gotten so comfortable with being bare around her he no longer even hesitated to take off his shirt. Everything about being together had become natural and effortless. They'd fallen into an easy pattern of making love at night, and when she worked during the day he would text to check on her or he'd make himself scarce and let her work. He never tried to tell her how to do her job and he'd never mentioned buying Mirage again and she certainly hadn't brought it up.

"Let's not talk about you leaving," she added. "I'd rather focus on you and this fantasy of mine."

Dane quirked a brow. "Did you have any man in mind for this fantasy?"

She took a step toward him and toyed with the tie between her breasts. "I didn't even think of this fantasy until I saw you."

He reached out, easing her hands aside, and slid apart the knot holding her shirt closed. Dane's fingertips grazed over her skin as he pushed the material from her shoulders. Stella shrugged until the shirt fell to the floor.

"I do like this outfit you came up with." He caressed the line on her skin just above the lacy edge of her bra. "I don't think I've seen you wear this around the resort before. Is this special for me?"

"You know it is."

His hand slid down and he curled his fingers inside her waistband, tugging her toward him. "I like knowing you thought of me, of this. Nobody has ever done anything like this before."

Which would explain the lack of fiancée now.

"First the bourbon and now the fantasy room." Stella smiled. "This has been quite the week for you."

"You have no idea," he murmured. "But let's get to this fantasy."

"Well, as much as I'd love to escape to the middle of nowhere and just chill, that's not possible for me now. So, I thought I'd bring you here and we could at least pretend to be somewhere else."

Dane unfastened her skirt and sent it down her legs. She kicked it aside, leaving her in her matching red bra and thong set, and her boots.

"I don't care where I am if that's what you're wearing." Dane finished undressing and wrapped an arm around her waist. "Tell me you've never brought another man in here."

Stella rolled her eyes. "What do you think?"

He dipped his head and feathered his lips over the swell of her breasts. "I think I'm damn lucky and I'm done talking."

She fisted his hair and arched her back as he jerked her bra cups aside and feasted on her. His hands gripped her backside as he lifted her off the ground. She wrapped her legs around his waist and let him take total control.

Dane spun toward the suspended, oversize tent and sat her on the open edge. When he eased back, Stella nearly whimpered. But he didn't go far. He reached down to her boots and slid one, then the other off, letting them thunk to the floor.

Stella spread her legs, making room for him. He stepped up onto the bottom rung of the small ladder and curled his fingers around her waist.

"I want to see and taste every damn inch of you," he told her as he scooted her back into the pile of pillows. "I'll ruin you for another man."

Stella stilled, her eyes darting to his. Ruin her for another man? What was he saying? Did that mean he wanted more? That he wanted to stay and see what happened?

Little did he know, he'd already ruined her for anybody else. There would never be another man like Dane.

But that was something they'd have to discuss later when he wasn't making her toes curl with passionate promises.

Dane trailed his lips over her chest and down to her abdomen. "You're so damn sexy."

He made her feel that way. She never would've taken another man to the fantasy suite. Sex with Dane was, well, indescribable. She wanted to experience everything with him.

Hooking his thumbs in the silky material of her panties across her hips, he didn't tear them off or jerk them down. Instead he drove her out of her mind with sliding those rough, calloused hands over her heated skin as he slowly eased the material down her legs.

His mouth seemed poised to follow the path of his hands and Stella couldn't control her restlessness. She ached, she needed, she craved.

When he held her knees apart with the width of his broad shoulders, Stella couldn't suppress the groan that escaped her. And then his mouth was on her. Those big, firm hands gripped her inner thighs as he pleasured her in a way she'd never known before.

Stella threaded her fingers through his hair and arched her back. Dane's relentless urge to please her had her body spiraling out of control and she didn't even try to hold back her cries.

The climax hit her so fiercely, Stella shook against him for what felt like hours until her tremors began to slow. Before she could fully recover, he was putting on a condom and climbing up to her.

"I'm not nearly done with you."

He gripped the backs of her thighs and slid into her in one slow, delicious thrust. Then he flipped them so she straddled him and he smiled up at her.

"Do what you want, cowgirl."

Why did he have to be so sexy? Was there anything about him that didn't turn her on? The relinquishing of power right when her body still zinged and tingled made her feel dizzy and overwhelmed. She wasn't sure she could even move right now.

Dane playfully smacked her hip. "I'm waiting."

Bracing her hands on his chest, Stella smiled as she started to move. Dane's fingertips dug into her thighs as she rocked against him. From the way his jaw was set, his nostrils flared, and his lids lowered, she'd guess she was doing just fine.

As she quickened her rhythm, her body started climbing again. The pleasure became too intense and she leaned down, capturing his mouth with hers.

Dane palmed her backside and urged her faster while he made love to her mouth. He seemed to touch her everywhere all at once, causing that familiar tingling to build and grow until she exploded all around him.

He tightened his hold as he stilled beneath her. His lips moved over hers almost as if he couldn't get enough.

Yeah, he'd definitely ruined her for any other man.

Stella waited until they both stopped trembling before she sat back up and smiled. "Well, I should book this room more often."

Dane reached up and cupped her breasts. "You'll only be booking it with me."

When he said things like that, she couldn't help but think…

"What do you say we take that bottle of bourbon and go upstairs?" he suggested. "I have a few more things I want to do to you."

Mercy. Was he serious? She wasn't sure she could walk on these shaky legs, let alone head in for round two…or three in her case.

Within minutes, though, they were dressed and heading the private back way toward the elevator exclusively for her.

Dane laced his fingers through hers and Stella couldn't help but smile. She hadn't held hands with a man in, well, years. There was something so innocent, yet so…was *bonding* the right word? After all they'd done together, the fact he led her back to her suite by her hand was so damn adorable.

There was no denying she'd fallen in love with him. What would he do if she actually came out and told him? Would he vanish? Would he tell her he felt the same?

Part of her wanted to be completely honest and open with her feelings. The rest of her wanted to keep her feelings locked away inside her heart where they couldn't be hurt or crushed. She'd never told someone she loved them before.

Maybe she couldn't trust her feelings. What did she know about love? She'd never known her mother, her father was about as loving as a tree stump, and the only other time she'd thought she was in love, the man had been a cheating scumbag who had been using her only to impress her father.

Maybe all this amazing sex had her emotions and thoughts too scattered.

"You're awfully quiet," Dane stated as he punched the code in to take them up to her penthouse. "Maybe I wore you out."

Stella squeezed his hand and rested her head on his shoulder. "I'm not even going to deny that because it's true."

He kissed her forehead. "I'll let you sleep a few hours before I take you again."

Her body stirred. Just those simple words had her imagining them together again. Each time was just as thrilling as the first. She was half-dressed, and they were entirely alone, so he could have her right here and now and nobody would ever know.

But she really needed to figure out what she was going to do about her feelings…how to tell him.

Maybe she should actually put some clothes on to have the talk because it didn't seem appropriate to have a serious conversation when her underwear was gone, her shirt was tied over her bare breasts and her skirt was so short her nether regions were nearly showing.

The elevator door slid open and Stella took in everything all at once. The roaring fire that she hadn't started, the overwhelming scent of a pipe and the robust man wearing a suit at nearly midnight.

"Dad. What are you doing here?"

Fourteen

Dane released Stella's hand and stared at the man across the room. So this was Ruiz Garcia. The businessman was clearly all business. Who the hell stayed dressed up at this time of the night?

"I told you I was coming."

Ruiz turned to face them and his eyes widened at the sight of Stella's outfit. "I don't have to ask what you've been doing. Is this typical behavior at my resort for you?"

"Dad, I just—"

"Decided to take advantage of a fantasy suite," Dane chimed in, earning him a glare from Stella. "She's been working her ass off," Dane went on, ignoring her wide eyes. He stepped around her, mostly to shield her half-naked body, but also to shield her from the proverbial big, bad wolf. "This is an adult resort, and it's beautifully managed and maintained, with everything a couple could want. No reason she can't take advantage of the amenities."

Ruiz narrowed his eyes as he slid aside his suit jacket and slid his hands into his pockets. "And you are?"

"He's with me," Stella answered before Dane could.

Ruiz wouldn't recognize Dane's name because each deal that Dane had his broker send had been listed under a business name. Ruiz had no clue who he was really dealing with. But Dane knew exactly what he was up against, which gave him just another edge he needed.

Stella came to stand beside Dane as she crossed her arms over her chest. "You told me the other day that you were coming in a couple weeks. Why are you here now?"

"I had news I wanted to deliver and didn't want to discuss over the phone." Ruiz glanced to Dane. "Perhaps your friend could give us some privacy and you could put some decent clothes on."

Stella stepped forward and Dane remained rooted in place. This was her fight, but he wanted her to know he had her back. If her father started mansplaining or talking like he had the impression he was above her, she could know Dane was there and was totally on her side.

"Dane is staying here with me, so say whatever you need to say."

Ruiz's brow quirked as he glanced between the two. "Well, whatever you have going on is irrelevant to the news I need to pass on. I'm selling Mirage."

Stella gasped. "Does that mean you're giving me the chance to—"

"No." Ruiz pulled in a deep breath and took a step toward his daughter. "I received an offer just today and I'm accepting it. The terms were too good to pass up."

Dane didn't know what to feel, how to react. Clearly he

couldn't show any sign of knowing about the offer, even though he had no doubt the offer Ruiz spoke of was his.

After all this time, Mirage would be his. Dane swallowed the lump of emotions at the thought of getting his mother's place back where it belonged.

But he glanced at Stella and all of his elation simply vanished. The look on her face, one of betrayal and pain, sliced right through him.

"You—you're just selling this when you've known how much I want to have it?" she asked.

"Business is business," Ruiz stated with a shrug as if that summed up crushing his daughter's entire world. "If you didn't get so emotionally involved, you would know that and you'd already have a plan B instead of investing your entire future here."

"Plan B?" Stella asked, her voice cracking, revealing just how close to the edge she was. "You're my family—I shouldn't need a plan B for how to prove myself worthy of your time or attention. My entire life I've wanted you to notice me, to make a point to acknowledge that I'm your daughter. Your employees and stockholders rank higher on your priority list than I do."

Ruiz's eyes darted to Dane. "You care to give us a minute?"

"Yeah, actually I do care."

Dane folded his arms over his chest and glared back at the man who was used to people jumping at his every command. The muscle in Ruiz's jaw clenched. Clearly he hadn't expected Dane's response.

"Just tell me why?" Stella demanded. "Why would you do this? Why even give me hope when you planned on selling?"

Ruiz focused his attention back to his daughter and Dane

took a step toward her. She stood there not caring about her precarious state of dress as she fought for her future…a future he had stolen from her.

Seeing her pain firsthand was sure as hell nothing he'd planned on. He'd thought he'd be gone before the ramifications of his actions kicked in…and back when he'd made the plan, he honestly hadn't cared enough to even consider how someone else might feel at that moment in time.

Her pain, her obvious anger, couldn't deter him. He still had a goal, he still had to get his mother's resort back where it belonged, and once he had that…well, then he could deal with Stella without her father prying into their business.

Because now Stella was his business. He didn't want her hurt, so all he could do at this point was try to make things less crushing. He had no idea how, but he'd damn well figure out something for her because unlike her bastard father, Dane actually cared about Stella's future.

"What was the offer?" Stella asked.

More than you have, sweetheart.

Yet Mirage was all he'd ever wanted. Money was just paper, not what kept him driven. Revenge and justice kept him pushing forward each and every day of his life.

"The offer was well over what I paid for this resort, so the profit will be a nice chunk in my pocket," Ruiz replied with a smug smile. "I'm sure we can find something else for you to do."

"I don't want anything else," Stella growled. "You know this is what I wanted. I love the story behind it, I love the setting, the idea. I love every aspect. Do you even know that kind of passion?"

Ruiz narrowed his gaze at his daughter. "Don't preach to

me about passion. It's my passion that gave you any opportunity you ever had. Money is the greatest passion of all."

"That's sad if that's truly how you feel," Stella told him.

Dane pressed a hand to the small of her back. Of course Ruiz would hang his black heart on his finances. He probably slept with a bag of money as a security blanket.

"I never cared about money growing up," Stella cried. "I wanted you there. I'd lost my mother and I never really had a father."

"You had opportunities most kids dream of," Ruiz spat back. "So maybe you should be thanking me instead of whining. Without me, you would've been in the foster system and then what would've happened?"

Stella gasped. "Foster care? What are you talking about?"

Ruiz sneered and dread curled through Dane.

"Your mother had an affair. I'm not your father."

Stella reached out for something stationary to hold on to, to help her remain standing. But her knees shook, buckled, and only Dane's strong, familiar arms wrapping around her kept her from collapsing.

She leaned back against him as she stared at her father.

No. Not her father. A man who wanted accolades for his half-hearted efforts in keeping her out of the system.

"You're lying," she accused, not really knowing what else to say. Dane's strength kept her up, but she held on to his forearm for fear he'd let her go.

"I'm not," her father said. "She cheated on me and her lover was your father."

How could he just now be dropping this bomb on her? Why after all of these years did he want to purposely continue hurting her?

"I want his name." She straightened her shoulders and stood straight up, but didn't let go of Dane. "I want to know who my real father is."

"He's dead."

Stella stared at him for a moment before she let out a laugh. "You're such a liar. You're going to great lengths to ensure I hate you forever."

"Fine, if you need to know, then his name was Martin Hernandez. He was killed in a small commuter plane crash when you were two. Look him up if you don't believe me. Use my investigator. I had a paternity test done to prove in case I needed it for future reference, but he died before—"

"What? Before you could blackmail him or hold me over his head?" Stella snarled. "Why did you even keep me? Why not just give me to him when I was born?"

"Because he hit your mother when she told him about the pregnancy." Ruiz might have had a flash of remorse in his eyes if he had a heart. "I might be a bastard, but I don't condone hitting a woman. Besides, I grew up in the foster system and I didn't want that for Maggie's baby."

Stella fisted her hands at her sides and had no clue what to do next. How did anyone react when their entire world was ripped away? First her mother passed, then her father—who wasn't her father—kept her out of some semblance of pity, only to pawn her off on nannies and teachers and coaches. And now? Well, now that she thought she could get somewhere with her life, somewhere that might make her father take notice and maybe see her as a worthy businesswoman, that opportunity was stripped away.

As much as she wanted to scream and shed tears, Stella wouldn't dare show Ruiz any emotion. He didn't deserve to know that he could affect her. All of these years and she'd never gotten anything from him by way of feelings. That's all she'd wanted, but apparently because she hadn't been his by blood, she hadn't deserved even the slightest hint of true affection.

"I want you to leave."

The words slipped through her lips before she realized she was even thinking them. But as soon as they came out, she realized she really did want him gone. Stella didn't want to look at that smug smirk another second.

"Listen to me," he started, taking a step toward her. "I didn't purposely set out to hurt you, but things fell into place, both in the past and now. It's out of my hands."

Stella gritted her teeth and used up every ounce of energy not to haul off and hit him. If he wanted her to truly hate him, he needn't say another word.

"All of this was in your hands," she fired back. "You could've told me about my father, you could've told me you had no intention of ever letting me take over this resort. You spied on me because you didn't think I could handle running this place, and then you went behind my back to sell to the highest bidder. Don't act like you couldn't have done anything about this. You've manipulated my life from the start without a moment of care or concern for me. You never had time for me—well, now I have no more time for you. So get the hell out."

Ruiz smoothed his suit jacket down and cleared his throat. "Actually, this resort belongs to me until the new owners take over. So if anyone is leaving it's you. But, since I'm kind enough, I'll give you two weeks to move your things."

Stella glanced around her space. She'd already gotten so used to being here, in this space she called her own.

Swallowing the lump of pain and remorse, Stella focused her attention back on Ruiz. "Who bought Mirage?"

"My assistant handled most of the details, but I was told Strong L Ranch is going to be the new owner."

Stella chewed on her lip to keep it from quivering. Whoever bought this place couldn't love it near as much as she did. There was no way they had the emotional connection she did. Stella had wanted this place for years and had been so close. So damn close.

"Stella asked you to leave."

Dane's low, commanding tone reminded her he was still here, still supporting her. He'd been quiet, letting her handle things, but she was damn near to the point of breaking. She wanted her father—no, Ruiz—gone. She *needed* him gone.

"I hate that things came to this," Ruiz stated. "You've actually surprised me with your determination and work ethic. I'm sure there's another business that I can—"

"I don't want your businesses and I don't want your pity." Stella pulled in a deep, shaky breath. "I'm done waiting for approval from you. I'm done hoping you'll see me for the woman I am. I'm not a failure, I kick ass at what I do and someone will see that…even if the man who supposedly raised me can't."

Stella turned and crossed to the elevator. She punched the button with more force than necessary, but she had nowhere else to channel all of this anger.

Ruiz stepped into the elevator and Stella forced herself to look at him. She wanted him to see that she wasn't weak, no matter how many times he had continued to knock her down. He may have shown a sliver of nobility by raising another man's kid, but Stella knew he regretted every day he'd been stuck with her. She'd never truly been his daughter, and as much as that hurt, she was glad she knew the truth.

He continued to hold her stare as the doors slid closed.

And then he was gone.

All the energy, all the emotions from the last hour took their toll. Stella flattened her hand over the elevator keypad and dropped her head. Tears burned her eyes, every word she didn't know to say got caught in her throat.

Strong arms wrapped around her. Dane eased her around until she faced him, then he scooped her up without a word. Stella looped her arms around his neck and shut her eyes as he carried her away. As strong as she prided herself on being, there were times she just couldn't hold it together anymore. Everyone had a breaking point and Stella had more than reached hers.

Dane set her on her feet and Stella blinked up at him. He'd carried her to the bed and he started undressing her.

"I don't have the—"

Dane placed his finger over her lips, cutting off her words. "You're going to rest. That's all you need to do right now. Nothing can be done about the resort or Ruiz right this minute. Just let me care for you."

Tears continued to slide down her cheeks. Stella swatted at them. "I'm not weak," she defended.

Dane framed her face with his hands and forced her attention on him. "Baby, I never thought you were. You just got the wind knocked out of you. I'm here and I'm not going anywhere."

Stella lifted one foot, then the other for him to remove her boots. When he straightened back up, Stella rested her head against his chest and inhaled that masculine, woodsy scent she'd come to associate with Dane.

"Why haven't you left yet?" she muttered.

She thought he murmured something about "not being done" but she wasn't sure and she was too tired to ask him to repeat it. All that mattered was that he was there and she knew he would stay for as long as she needed.

Fifteen

"I'll wrap up a few things and then be right there," Dane explained. "I've verbally secured the deal. I need to get back to the ranch and finalize the sale, then I'll pack a bag."

Ethan gripped the cell as he stood on the balcony of his penthouse resort room, overlooking the ocean. He glanced over his shoulder to the owner of the red bikini he'd met on the beach. She'd been in his bed since.

Harper. Her name was Harper and she had been filling his time and keeping him relaxed while he waited on Robert to get to the island. He hadn't planned on finding the distraction, but there was no way in hell he was turning her down.

"Leave the flannels at home," Ethan replied, turning his attention back to the view of the beach. "Do you even own swim trunks?"

"I'm not coming to work on my tan," Dane growled. "We're halfway to our goal. Do you think you can stay focused?"

Memories of the past few days and the curvy woman in his bed flashed through his mind in vivid detail.

"Oh, I'm focused."

Dane let out a sigh. "I'm going to the ranch later today. I'll text you when I'm on my way to Sunset Cove."

Something in his brother's tone had Ethan turning back to make sure the patio door was closed. He crossed the balcony and took a seat on the club chair.

"You don't sound near as thrilled as I thought you'd be."

"I finally have Mirage," Dane muttered. "What more could I want?"

"I don't know. That's why I'm asking."

The line went silent and Ethan waited. He stared out at the horizon as the sun started creeping up. A new day, and another step closer to finalizing their goals.

So why was Dane so…monotone?

"It's the manager, isn't it?" Ethan guessed. "Is there something going on there?"

"Don't worry about me."

Ethan clenched his teeth, but ultimately decided he was done being pushed aside.

"I've worried about you every single day since Mom died," he stated. "You might have dealt with grief your own way, but I needed you. Damn it. Don't push me out now."

More silence and Ethan wondered if he'd gone too far, revealed too much. He was human and sometimes those emotions just came out. He wasn't sorry he'd finally said something, but he was sorry that this conversation was over the phone.

"I'm not pushing you out," Dane finally said. "Not on purpose anyway. I'm just… Let me get things wrapped up here. This isn't all about the resorts. It's about us."

For the first time in nearly two decades, Ethan had a blossom of hope that he and Dane could get back to where they'd been before their world got ripped to shreds.

"I've got a room booked for you," Ethan assured him. "See you soon. And, Dane? Great job getting your resort. Mom would be proud."

The line went dead.

Ethan stared at his phone before dropping it to his lap and raising his gaze to the sky. Maybe he and Dane had further to go in repairing their relationship than he'd thought. Perhaps the mention of their mother triggered something in Dane.

Ethan didn't know. What he did know was that there was a vivacious woman in his bed, more than eager to continue this fling for as long as she was in town, and he was *this close* to securing his future and his legacy…and claiming revenge on Robert Anderson.

Dane had packed his meager bag, touched base with his broker and was all set to head back to his ranch.

But he didn't want to leave Mirage. He'd just acquired it—technically. All that was left was to sign the papers, but this was a done deal.

He wasn't frustrated and cranky because he was leaving Stella. No, they'd decided at the beginning this connection or whatever they had would be temporary. Just because he was leaving her while she happened to be already emotionally crushed and shattered because of Ruiz, well…

Damn it.

Dane ran a hand over his stubbled jaw and glanced around the penthouse. His eyes landed on the note he'd left for Stella. She was working and he didn't want to interrupt.

Even though she had been dismissed by her father, she was downstairs right now making sure each and every guest had what they needed to ensure a getaway they'd never forget.

And Dane was a damn coward for sneaking out without saying goodbye. He could freely admit it, but there was no way in hell he could stay any longer. He'd gotten what he came for and hanging around would only prolong the inevitable. Stella needed to move on, and so did he.

So why was there so much pain? Why did that heaviness on his chest leave him feeling like a complete jerk?

Because he was. At this point, Dane was no better than the man who'd raised her. They'd both lied to her, deceived her, betrayed her.

She was still dealing with learning the truth about Ruiz. He couldn't unload more secrets on her. Leaving was the best option—for both of them.

Keep telling yourself that, buddy. Maybe you'll believe the lies.

Gripping the handle of his suitcase, Dane headed toward the elevator. He'd be back. This would be his suite when he returned, but he knew in his heart things wouldn't be the same.

When he'd first arrived he could see only one woman here—his mother. Now he knew when he returned, he'd see only Stella.

She'd left an imprint on his life and on this place that would never disappear. There was something so permanent about her. They'd forged a bond whether he wanted to admit it or not.

And he didn't want to admit any such thing.

Since he knew the layout of this place better than his own home, Dane slipped out in such a way that he knew Stella would never see him. He could be honest enough with himself to admit that if he saw her and attempted to explain why he was leaving, the guilt would consume him.

Dane had to push that aside. He couldn't allow anything to steal the moment he'd been preparing for. Once this was all officially his, he'd feel better. All he had to do was finalize the sale, and get to Ethan. Working with his brother to bring down Robert would only add to the euphoria of finally reclaiming everything they'd been robbed of.

Once they came in contact with Robert, well, there would be a little surprise waiting for him. Their miserable bastard of a stepfather was done stealing and being deceitful. He wouldn't be free to ruin anybody else's lives or rob futures.

Dane started to head toward the back hallway from another hallway he'd sneaked through, but a familiar voice through the door leading to the back office stopped him.

"Come to me for any specialty needs for the fantasy rooms," Stella stated.

"What about Savannah?" an unfamiliar voice asked.

"Her daughter has her first dance recital tonight and tomorrow. I told her to take the days off. Family is too important."

"You know the staff talks. We like that you're much different than our last manager," the worker said.

"Yeah, well, that was my goal."

Dane heard the hurt in her voice. He knew every moment she spent working here had to be absolutely soul crushing now that she knew the place would never be hers. She was a damn good manager and had compassion for her staff. She truly cared about this place, these employees.

Stella had just been dismissed in the most uncaring of ways only hours ago. But this morning, she went on with the business-as-usual attitude. She had her pride, sure, but she did this because she didn't want the staff or guests to suffer.

How could he just take everything from her? How could he not want her to be part of this once he took over?

But she wanted the resort to be hers and he simply couldn't allow that to happen. Mirage belonged to him.

Damn that guilt. Not only did the guilt threaten to choke hold him, he didn't know what he'd do once he got home and she wasn't there. She'd been the only person in his entire life to know what he fully suffered from. He'd never let anyone in like he had with Stella. She'd been so easy to talk to, so…

He couldn't find the words. She was everything he didn't know he needed. There was something so therapeutic about her, in the way she genuinely cared, in the way she made everyone else feel like they were the top priority in her life.

But when had anyone made her a priority?

Dane clenched his jaw and shoved the door open to the hallway. He needed to get out and get back to his ranch. An evening with his dogs, his horses, and a ride out in the country would help him think more clearly.

There had to be a way to not ruin Stella's life and still keep everything he'd worked so damn hard for. He just needed to find it.

Dane left the resort, left the mountain, and didn't look back in his rearview mirror. He'd learned the hard way that looking back only kept you in the past. Dane knew only one way to go and that was forward.

From this second on, he'd take charge of Mirage, work with Ethan to destroy Robert and find out some way to make things right for Stella.

Sixteen

After three days of riding horses, drinking bourbon on his enclosed back porch with his dogs at night and messaging back and forth with Ethan, Dane still wasn't calm.

His nerves were on edge. He still hadn't come up with a way to make things right with Stella. He had heard from her—she'd texted him, but he'd replied that he'd have to talk later.

Still taking the coward's way out.

He wanted to offer her the manager position, but deep in his gut he knew she'd turn it down and likely tell him exactly where to take his offer once she realized he was the new owner.

But Stella was exactly the type of person who should be running the resort. Dane was in no position to be hands-on every day—not if he wanted to keep his ranch. Moving permanently to the resort was something he'd have to ease into, even though ultimately that was his goal.

Dane relaxed forward in the front porch swing and rested

his elbows on his knees. Buck lay at his feet all curled up, but Bronco sat obediently on the other side waiting on affection.

As he rubbed the soft fur between his dog's ears, Dane ran over and over through his mind what he would say to Stella when he saw her again. There would be no avoiding her, and he didn't want to, but he needed space to sort things out. Even before he left the resort a few days ago, he'd known he needed Stella in the business.

And as much as he wanted to keep thinking of her in that capacity, Dane knew that trail of thoughts barely scratched the surface of everything he remembered when Stella came to mind.

Oh, hell. Who was he kidding? The woman never left his mind. Everything about her clung to his skin even as he dealt with every aspect of daily life. When he'd come home, he'd imagined her here. She'd said more than once that she wanted to escape to the middle of nowhere and unwind. His ranch certainly fit that criteria and now that he was back, he realized just how much he wanted to show her his place.

As the sun set behind the mountain peaks, Dane was glad he was alone. He wasn't in the mood to talk or handle any issues. He just wanted the simplicity of swaying on the swing on his climate-controlled wraparound porch and petting his dogs. His mind was too full of worry and possibilities to consider adding anything else to the mix.

The past few nights since coming home he'd been so damn restless. Sleep hadn't been his friend since returning from the war, but now the dynamics were completely different. He wasn't afraid to go to sleep, he was afraid to wake up without Stella by his side.

When the hell had his heart gotten involved in this charade? That had never been part of his grand plan.

Knowing Stella, as soon as she found out the truth, she'd verbally attack him and make him feel like he wasn't even worthy of being in the same vicinity as her. She had every right to annihilate him, and she would as soon as she learned he was Mirage's new owner. He needed to tell her before she found out some other way.

He needed to be clear where he stood, as the owner, and that he wanted her to remain on board as the manager. Compensating her with a raise and a bonus might go a long way in securing her staying at Mirage. He had to find a way to convince her.

Dane's cell vibrated in his pocket. When he went to grab it, Bronco jerked his head back, giving a glare from the instant lack of attention.

"Hang on, boy."

The alert on his phone was from the gate announcing a visitor. From the video image, he knew who that unexpected guest was and there was no hiding from her anymore.

Dane typed in the code to access the gate and watched as Stella drove her SUV onto his ranch. The drive from the gate to the main house was just over a minute. Not nearly enough time to fine-tune the speech he'd rehearsed because the second she drove through the iron arch with his ranch name, she would know the truth.

A gut-sinking feeling rendered him motionless. His eyes stared off down the driveway, knowing any second he'd see headlights cut through the dusky night.

As dark gray clouds shadowed the sunset, Dane knew another storm was brewing…from all aspects of his life right now.

Dane came to his feet and snapped his fingers, immediately getting his dogs' attention. He opened the front door and put them inside just as those lights cut across his porch.

The knot in his gut tightened, but he remained on the edge of his porch and waited for her to get out of the car. She'd come here for a reason, and had he not deceived her and lied to her face, stealing everything she'd worked for, he might believe that she had come to him to see if there was a chance for them.

Dane wasn't that naive or stupid to think that anything good could come from a fling and a trail of deception. But now that she was here, he had to keep things businesslike and make her understand where he came from. It was time to put all his cards on the table and explain his past with Mirage. Surely she would understand the importance of family, considering that's all she'd wanted for herself.

Sliding his hands into the pockets of his jeans, Dane stared out at the drive as Stella killed the engine. He couldn't see into the windshield that well, but he knew when he looked into her dark eyes, he'd see…

Hell, maybe he didn't know what he'd see. Pain? Regrets? Rage? Likely all of the above.

She didn't get out immediately. Keeping him waiting and wondering was the least that he deserved.

Unable to wait a second longer, Dane made his way down the wide stone steps. The first fat snowflake hit his cheek. His boots scuffed against the concrete drive, but he kept his eyes on that door, waiting.

When he reached the side of her SUV, Dane peered in to see Stella with her head in her hands, her shoulders shaking. Dane jerked on the handle and opened the door. More flakes fell, but he ignored the chill.

"Stella."

Dane started to reach in, but she jerked her head up and slinked back.

"Don't touch me," she commanded as she held him with a watery gaze. "You're nothing but a liar and I'm a damn fool for even coming here."

He didn't know that someone could look so broken, yet so angry at the same time. But Stella was definitely both.

"I *am* a liar, but you're not a fool," he corrected.

Ignoring her plea to leave her alone, Dane reached for her arm and urged her from the vehicle.

"Don't," she cried, tears streaming down her cheeks. "Don't try to make this better. You can't."

No, he couldn't. Stella had taken hit after hit, but this was the first time he'd seen her so broken and completely vulnerable. He'd done this. He'd crushed her more than her father had…which was truly saying something.

The air seemed to turn colder, icier.

"Come inside," he told her. "You can hate me and cry and anything else you want, but we need to get out of this weather."

"I'd rather drive back to Gold Valley through a snowstorm than to be here with you." She pulled her arm away and took a step back. "To think I came here because…"

Dane's heart clenched. There was no way to keep his heart out of this because likely it had been involved from the beginning. Stella drove all this way for him—well, she drove for the man she thought he was.

"You're the new owner," she muttered, then let out a mock laugh. "My father is one hell of an actor because he pretended not to know you."

"He *doesn't* know me," Dane confirmed. "The sale went through my broker and was done in the name of the ranch."

"I'm aware of the ranch name," she scoffed.

The snow came down so thick and fast, the entire area seemed to be blinding white. Dane didn't wait to hear what else she had to say and he didn't ask for permission. She already thought he was a bastard. Might as well go whole hog.

He scooped her up and ran toward the porch. She smacked at his back and cursed him the entire way. Damn she was sexy fired up like this. Not that he'd ever be worthy of having her again. Those memories of their time together were all he'd ever have.

Once he set her down on the porch, Dane kept his hands on her shoulders. He didn't want to force her to do anything, but he didn't want her to bolt before she could hear him out—especially if bolting meant trying to drive in blizzard-like conditions when she was crying and upset. That just sounded like a disaster in the making.

"Why?" she demanded as she stared up at him. She didn't bother swiping at her tears, likely so he'd see the full impact his actions had on her. "Why did you lie to me? Sleeping with me was, what? Just a way to pass the time until you stole my future?"

"No," he defended with a shake of his head. "I… Damn it."

Dane dropped his hands, unable to ignore the agony on her face.

"You came to Mirage purposely to find me," she accused. "Did you laugh when you got me into bed so quickly? I must've made this all so easy on you."

When the wind kicked up and trees cracked outside the window, his dogs started barking their fool heads off. Stella jumped and glanced toward the front door.

"They're not scared," he explained. "When it thunders or gets too windy, they think someone is knocking."

"I can't imagine you get many visitors out here in the middle of nowhere."

He didn't, but his staff would always knock before entering. "Let's get inside," he told her. "You can yell at me all you want there, but I need to get in there before my boys tear up my front door."

"I should leave," she muttered, barely audible over the wind. "I came here thinking we'd see where things went. Now, I want to be anywhere else."

"I get that," he replied. "But it's nasty out there and it's a long drive back to Gold Valley. Might as well stay at least a little longer."

He turned and reached for the door, ready to hold back his dogs so they wouldn't lick Stella to death.

"I don't want to stay," she repeated, but the fight had left her tone and Dane knew she wasn't going anywhere yet.

She'd never admit her vulnerability, and he admired her for that, but he also knew if he was ever going to get through to her to fully understand his side, then now was the time to explain himself. And Stella deserved an explanation.

Dane stepped over the threshold and gripped his dogs' collars as he hustled them back from the door. Two overly excited golden retrievers wasn't something Stella needed to put up with right now.

Once she was inside and had closed the door, Dane let go of the dogs and snapped his fingers. The boys immediately sat at his side.

"You don't have to stay long, but I need you to hear me out." He stared back at her, knowing she could bolt out of that door at any time, knowing he deserved exactly that. "It's not safe to try to drive right now. You know how Montana weather can be."

Stella's eyes darted down to the dogs and back up to him. "You're used to everyone doing exactly what you want, aren't you?" she sneered. "I'm not going to be that person."

Yet here she was, standing in his foyer.

"Mirage was always meant to be mine," he explained, needing to get to the heart of the issue. "My brother and I both have resorts that were stolen from us before we were old enough or had any power to stop it."

Stella narrowed her eyes. "Stolen? That doesn't even make sense."

Dane ran a hand over his jaw, the stubble raked against his palm. "My mother was Lara Anderson. She built Mirage in Gold Valley and Sunset Cove."

Stella's eyes widened. "That's why you were so determined? Because you think this is owed to you?"

"It is owed to me," he demanded. "Robert Anderson was a complete bastard who took advantage of my mother by marrying her when she was vulnerable after her father's death. When she passed, Ethan and I were still in high school and Robert underhandedly gained rights to those properties and left with our money."

Stella stared at him for a minute before shaking her head and pressing her hand to her eyes. "I can't grasp all of this," she muttered. "I can't figure out how any of this is my fault and why I'm being punished when all I wanted was to have a place of my own, to stand on my own."

Dane took a step forward. "I can help you. I just can't give you Mirage."

Taking a step away from him, Stella leveled his gaze. "I don't want your help. I don't want pity and I don't want..."

Her voice cracked as she trailed off and ultimately turned her back. Dane fisted his hands at his sides, knowing she wanted nothing at all from him at this point. The only thing she'd ever wanted had been ripped from her life…just like it had been ripped from his.

They both wanted Mirage. They both had had the resort pulled away from them when they were so close to obtaining it.

"I know how you feel," he stated. "I've been there. I didn't want to hurt you. I never wanted any of this to harm you in any way. I just wanted what belonged to me."

Stella spun around, her eyes full of fury and unshed tears. "Didn't want me hurt? What did you think would happen? Did you think I'd be so totally blown away by your seduction skills that I'd overlook you jerking my life from me?"

"I never thought that." Though the way she worded it made him sound like an even bigger bastard than he already felt. "I just wanted to find a way to get the resort back in my family like my mother always planned."

"You didn't have to lie to me," she threw back.

Dane gritted his teeth as he tried to find words to defend himself. But she was right. Now that he looked back, now that he realized the impact he'd had on her and how much she'd already been through with her father, she was absolutely right.

The wind kicked up so much the windows rattled. Stella jumped and the dogs started barking again.

Dane snapped his fingers and turned to the dogs. "Bed."

The one-word command had them darting toward the wide stairs and they raced each other up to the second floor. Once they were out of sight, Dane turned back to Stella.

"Come into the living room."

She crossed her arms over her chest. “I’m not staying or obeying your commands.”

“You’re being ridiculous right now,” he growled. “Are you just going to stand in my foyer all night?”

“If I want.”

Dane raked a hand over his hair and blew out a sigh. “Don’t be so damn stubborn.”

Stella stared at him for another minute before she turned her attention around the open space and ultimately went in the opposite direction of the living room.

He glanced up to the ceiling and willed himself to remain calm. This woman had been through hell, at the hands of her father and then him. She was strong willed and angry, and totally entitled to all her frustration and rage.

Having her here at his ranch seemed perfect in all the wrong ways. So as she set off, Dane had no choice but to follow.

Seventeen

Stella figured the storm inside was better to deal with than the storm outside…or at least that's what she told herself as she explored the first level of Dane's ranch.

She wasn't actually focusing on anything, more just wandering aimlessly through the oversize rooms. One area seemed to flow to the next and everything looked like something from a magazine. The high beams, the worn wooden floors, the plush leather sofas, and stone fireplace.

Everything about this house reminded her of the resort. The dark wood, the way everything from the furniture to the size of the rooms just screamed power and money. His mother might have built Mirage, but Dane was clearly his mother's son. Stella was not only fighting her father, but she was also up against a family lineage. Dane wasn't just going to let her have the resort, and she wouldn't expect him to if what he told her was true.

Still, that didn't mean he had gone about things the right

way. She wasn't sure what the right way would have been, but she sure as hell knew he'd made the wrong choice.

"Looking for another escape route?" Dane asked as he came up behind her.

Stella turned her attention from the photos lining the mantel to Dane. He stood behind her, just close enough she could reach out and touch him, but far enough to give her a bit of space.

"I'm trying to wrap my head around all of this," she replied honestly. "I mean, what the hell were you thinking coming into all of this? That you deserved Mirage, that you'd get it no matter what and that anything that wasn't your feelings or your end goal simply doesn't matter? Did I sum it all up?"

The muscle clenched in his jaw as he shoved his hands into his pockets. Those dark eyes narrowed.

"Don't even try to be offended," she went on. "You brought all of this upon yourself."

"I had no time," he demanded. "It's not just Mirage in Gold Valley. There's more going on and I had to move when I could."

"More what? More businesses you're trying to steal from unsuspecting women?"

He stared at her for another minute before cursing under his breath and turning to pace toward the wall of windows. The harsh conditions continued to rage outside and honestly, it wasn't much prettier inside. She wished she'd never come. She wished she'd never met Dane Michaels. And she wished like hell she'd never put stock in thinking her father would finally give her something—anything—she truly wanted.

She'd felt so damn isolated for so long. Even training for

the competitions she'd felt alone because not many people understood that willpower and determination.

Now here she was alone. Stella knew she needed to dig deep and find that drive and determination all over again. She would, too. Nothing would keep her down. Life may knock her, but she couldn't let the hits deter her.

Stella stared at Dane across the room. He'd not answered her and from his rigid shoulders and silence, she had a feeling he wasn't planning on it, either.

She turned back to the photos on the mantel. There were only three. There were two on each end and each picture was a teenage version of Dane with another boy who she assumed was his brother, and their mother. The photo in the middle of the mantel was a snapshot of his mother alone. Her head was thrown back as she laughed and there was so much happiness, so much life in that image.

Tears formed once again and Stella wished she didn't feel for this woman, this man. But Lara Anderson was the woman Stella had admired for years. Stella had loved hearing the story about Lara and how she'd started the resorts for couples…yet she was a single mother with two boys.

There was a family here in these photos, a family Stella had always wanted and craved. But this family had been torn apart by an untimely death and Dane just wanted to reclaim what he believed belonged to him.

She turned back to find him staring directly at her. Her stomach tightened. That darkened stare had her nerves on edge. She didn't want to see this side of him. She didn't want to see him as a human with real feelings. From the second she turned into the drive and saw that iron arch with the ranch name, Dane had become a complete stranger. She didn't know where the man was from the resort, but damn if her heart didn't have a hole in it that was just his size.

She could walk away, no matter how much it hurt, if she could convince herself that everything about that man she'd thought he was had been a lie. But the longer she stayed, the more she realized the truth was complicated—and so was Dane.

"I realize we're not that different," she stated. "We both want the same thing for justifiable reasons."

Dane started forward, but Stella held up her hands and kept going. "Your methods are clearly what sets us apart. I never would've used someone, blindsided them, and then stolen their life."

"You really think your dad was just going to turn the resort over to you?"

Stella's heart clenched. "Maybe not, but I had a fighting chance before you came along throwing your money and whatever else at him."

Dane crossed his arms over his chest and clenched his jaw. "I gave him two of my businesses on top of the money."

Part of her admired the lengths he would go to in order to reclaim his mother's legacy. The other part of her, the part that had been manipulated, hated every part of Dane Michaels for going behind her back to steal what she'd thought could be hers.

But damn if she wasn't still attracted to him. Her body still responded to that midnight gaze, those broad shoulders…one glimpse of those talented hands.

Why couldn't there be some switch to turn off emotions and tingly reactions? Sex messed with her head. Great sex somehow managed to mess with her heart because there was no way she'd fallen for him. Stella refused to believe that she could have in such a short time.

"You're thinking."

Dane's words settled between them. That low tone always got to her in ways she'd never been able to explain. How could a voice cause arousal?

But, yes, she was thinking. Thinking how she was stuck here waiting for the storm to pass. Thinking about how she'd been used. Thinking about how the past few weeks had been out of her control and she wanted to take that control back.

Stella took a step toward Dane before she could talk herself out of this. If she thought too much she'd find every reason not to take this leap. But for now, just for this moment, she was in charge and she'd be damned if anyone else would ever take the decisions from her again.

"I hate you," she told him as she started working on the buttons on her dress. "I hate how you stole my world from me. But you're right. You are the same man who stayed in my bed when I was exhausted and alone, who helped me when I didn't even ask. You're the same man my body craves and the man I can't stop wanting."

"Stella—"

"No." She shrugged out of her dress, sending it to the floor in a whisper. "I call the shots now. You used me, right? Well, I'm about to use you. I want you and I'm going to have you."

Dane's eyes widened, his jaw clenched and his nostrils flared. She recognized his signs of arousal and desire. His gaze raked over her nearly bare body. She had on only her knee boots and her matching nude lace bra and panties.

"This isn't a good idea," he told her. "You know it's not. Are you doing this to get back at me?"

Stella shrugged. "Perhaps. But I'm also doing it because I want you. I wish I could turn that off, but I see you and my body responds."

She quickly rid herself of her boots before focusing on him again. "Unless you've decided you've gotten all you wanted from me."

Dane muttered a curse before he was on her. "I should turn you away, but damn if you don't have some power over me."

He scooped her up and started back toward the entryway, back toward the steps.

"Not your bedroom," she commanded.

There was no way she'd go somewhere that personal, that intimate.

"This isn't anything more than sex," she added.

Dane set her back on her feet and backed her against the wide door frame leading from the living room. For a half second, he merely stared, seeming to take in her entire body with one hungry sweep.

Then he thrust his hands through her hair and captured her lips. Stella arched her body and found the edge of his T-shirt. With frantic motions, she jerked it up, pulling her lips away long enough to get the shirt up and over his head. Then he was on her again as she went for his belt and the snap on his jeans.

She'd barely gotten them unzipped when he pulled away. Dane kept his eyes on her while he reached into his pocket and pulled out protection. He covered himself and stepped back toward her.

Stella opened for him, threading her fingers through his hair, and taking everything he gave. Part of her knew this was wrong, but the devil on her shoulder thought it was a great idea. There was nothing wrong with taking charge and allowing pleasure. There was nothing wrong with going into this moment with her eyes wide-open and her heart shut tight.

When Dane gripped her waist and lifted her, Stella's thoughts vanished. All she knew was passion as she wrapped her legs around his waist and sank onto him. Clutching his shoulders, she closed her eyes and pressed her back against the solid door frame. Dane's lips trailed over the column of her neck, over her sensitive breasts. He palmed her backside as he pumped his hips and Stella just let the euphoric sensations wash over her.

Dane muttered something as he traveled back up to the erogenous area just below her ear.

That was all it took for her body to respond and spiral out of control. All of her emotions balled up together and she gave herself over to the climax. This was why she'd decided to surprise him. She'd needed to be with him, needed to feel him.

Stella's entire body shook and all thoughts vanished. She kept her eyes shut, needing to keep her emotions locked inside and not look too closely at him. She just wanted to feel.

Dane murmured something in her ear, she only made out the word "need" but she ignored it as he jerked his hips harder. His body tightened, his fingertips dug into her backside, and Stella dropped her head to his shoulder as he took his own pleasure.

His heated body stuck to hers, and Stella didn't want to lift her head. She didn't want to face reality.

But she knew this was it. She and Dane were done…if they'd ever really started. They'd had a fling, that was all. Though she'd thought there was more, there couldn't be.

He'd deceived her, slept with her under false pretenses and then left without a word. At any time he could've given her the truth, but he'd chosen to keep his true self hidden away.

The same way she'd have to hide away the fact she'd fallen in love with the man she thought he was.

Pulling together all of her strength and resolve, Stella extracted herself from the warmth and strength she'd only experienced from Dane. She hated him for making her hate him. That sounded so messed up in her own thoughts, but he'd damaged something inside her. Something she didn't know if she'd recover from.

He didn't say a word as he stepped from the room. Stella dressed in a hurry, not caring if her buttons were straight or her hair was in knots. She had to go. Staying here, waiting on him to state another defense, would only make her thoughts, her heart, even more muddled.

Just as she zipped up her boot and came to her feet, Dane stepped back into the room.

"You want to talk about this?" he asked.

"Nothing to discuss." Did that even sound convincing? "You used me, I used you."

"Is that what this was?" he asked, crossing his arms over his chest and leaning against the very spot he'd just taken her. "You wanted to retaliate? Doesn't seem like you."

Stella swallowed and tipped her chin. "Seems we didn't know each other as well as we thought."

She crossed to the doorway, easily moving past him in the large opening.

"Where are you going?"

Tossing a look over her shoulder, she replied, "The storm has passed."

"What about us?"

Gripping the doorknob, Stella turned away and whispered, "That's passed, too."

Eighteen

Mirage wasn't near as inviting as it had been.

For the past month, he'd been back and forth between the resort and the ranch. More at the resort, though, since he needed to acclimate the staff to his management style and get up-to-date with the various systems.

Ethan had told Dane to hold off on coming because something had held Robert up and it looked like he wasn't going to be coming for a bit. Dane certainly had things he could be doing here to bide his time.

His first order had been to fire the asshole who'd disrespected Stella. Apparently he'd also been the spy, hence the cockiness since he worked directly with Ruiz.

Dane's second order had been to get his attorney and accountant on-site to see what the hell he could do to get Stella back here—where she belonged.

That had been over three weeks ago and he'd still not heard a word from her. He'd known full well she'd received the employment offer and he didn't know what was taking her so damn long to respond. Though her silence was nothing less than he deserved.

Damn it. Nobody just flat-out ignored him. Never. Not even when he had it coming. He might be a recluse, he might shy away from getting too involved with crowds of people, but that didn't mean he was soft or ready to just give up.

Dane knew he had to give Stella time. Her entire world had been shattered and he'd precipitated it all. Now he was trying to piece all those shards back together and without seeing her, he had no idea if his tactics were even working.

Since she'd walked out of his house after using him, he'd been destroyed. He didn't care that she'd wanted to use his body. Their physical connection couldn't be just ignored or brushed aside. There was no way someone as caring and loving as Stella could just walk away and not think or feel anymore.

And there was love looking back at him when she'd been in his home. He'd seen it, felt it.

And he knew he'd fallen just as hard.

Dane turned the corner heading to his office at Mirage. He nearly ran into one of the receptionists, but quickly put his hands out to stop her from plowing into him.

"Oh, Mr. Michaels," she gasped. "I'm so sorry."

Dane might still be struggling with some names of his new employees, but not Lola. He remembered her quite well.

"I've told you to call me Dane," he reminded her, as he'd done every single day he'd been there. "You worked for my mother."

Lola smiled and smoothed her cropped, gray hair from her forehead. "That may be, and I may remember you as a thirteen-year-old boy, but that doesn't mean anything now. You're my boss and I respect that."

"I appreciate the respect, but Dane will be just fine," he confirmed. "You've been here since the beginning. I hope you'll stay on."

Lola nodded and patted his arm. "I wouldn't dream of leaving. Your mother would be so proud of you."

Guilt threatened to choke him, but so did a rush of warmth at the kind comment. Story of his life lately. He'd destroyed one woman he loved while honoring the other.

"Oh, Stella is in your office," Lola added.

Dane jerked. "Excuse me?"

"Stella Garcia," Lola repeated. "She said she had an appointment, so I let her in. I was getting ready to call you. I hope that was okay."

The worry in her tone had Dane offering a smile. "That was more than okay. Thanks, Lola."

He skirted around the faithful employee in an effort to get to his office. Dane didn't care that he looked like a madman racing down the hall. There was only so much control a guy could have and he'd waited long enough for Stella to get back with him about his offer.

Granted, he'd thought she'd call, but an in-person meeting was sure as hell something he wasn't about to turn down.

Dane opened the door to his office and stepped inside to find Stella in his new leather office chair behind his desk.

She glanced from his computer screen to him as she propped those long bare legs up on the corner of his desk.

Just the sight of her had his gut tightening, his heart pumping faster. He leaned against the door and closed it with his back. She didn't have on boots today like she typically did with her dresses. No, today she had on heels meant for the bedroom and a little red suit that looked like it was made of wrapping paper it was so damn tight…in all the right places.

If he needed to hire someone to torture guests, she'd be the woman for the job. She was killing him.

"Your minion gave me the message," she stated. "Was that some type of a joke?"

Dane hooked his thumbs through his belt loops and shook his head. "Not a joke at all. I just didn't confront you myself because I knew you needed time."

"Time?" Those legs slid off his desk with grace and Stella came to her feet. She smoothed her skirt down to mid-thigh and circled the desk. "You proposed marriage through a damn letter that my attorney delivered from your attorney."

Dane swallowed. "I guess the proposal could use some work, but I figured if I asked in person you'd punch me—and then you'd say no. I can take a punch, but I didn't want you to turn me down."

Stella stared across the room. With her brows drawn in, her hands on her hips, her jacket pulling across pert breasts…she was damn breathtaking.

"Turn you down?" she repeated. "Of course I'm turning you down. You're insane. I'm not marrying you."

"Did you read the entire letter?"

"The part where I'd be part owner of Mirage? Yes." She licked her lips, probably not knowing how arousing that was. Now was certainly not the time to bring it up. "I don't know where this came from, but I'm not marrying you. If you feel guilty for taking all of this from me, that's on you. You can't just ask someone to marry you because your feelings are all out of whack."

Dane took a step toward her, then another, until they stood toe-to-toe. "You could've ripped up the letter and ignored me," he told her, reaching to brush a strand of hair from her cheek. He let his fingertips feather across her jaw as he continued. "You could've texted or even called. Yet here you are."

"I needed to—"

"See me?" he asked, sliding his other hand up to frame her face. "Damn, I've missed you."

Stella closed her eyes. "Don't say that. We are nothing, Dane."

He remained silent, waiting for her to finish the silent war no doubt waging in her head. After a moment, her lids fluttered and she focused on him.

"You don't want to marry me, you want to sleep with me," she told him.

Dane couldn't suppress the smile. "Why can't I do both?"

On a groan, Stella backed away and shook her head. "Because this is reality and the reality is I can't be with someone who lied to and deceived me."

Dane pulled in a shaky breath. He deserved that, but the words still hurt. He reminded himself that she was here, in his office, so not all hope was lost.

"You came to my house and slept with me," he started. "I know you claimed you were using me and it was just physical, but that's not the Stella I know. You love me."

Her eyes widened, her mouth opened, but nothing came out. She quickly snapped her lips shut and set her jaw.

"Even after you realized who I was," he went on, "you still wanted me. That's not ego, that's facts."

Stella shrugged. "So what? Yes, I fell in love with you, but that's not real. I fell in love with the person I thought you were. I don't even know the real you."

"You know me more than anyone else in my life. I've told you things, opened up about my past. I wouldn't do that with someone I didn't care about or someone I was just casually sleeping with."

When she didn't snap back with an answer, Dane hoped there was some part of her that believed him. He couldn't stop this momentum now.

"I fully admit I sought you out as part of my strategy to retake ownership of this place," Dane admitted. "I didn't set out to purposely hurt you and once I got to know you..."

"What?" she demanded. "You magically grew a soul?"

Dane couldn't hide his emotions and quickly realized Stella didn't want him to. She deserved to know exactly how he felt, his every thought on this matter.

"Once I got to know you, I realized deceiving you wasn't how my mom would want me to go about getting the resort back," he explained.

Unable to stand still or to look at that hurt in Stella's dark eyes, Dane started walking around the spacious office. He went to the wall of windows that overlooked the snowy mountain peaks.

"My mom wanted this place to be mine. There was no doubt about that. When I lost it, I knew that one day when I had the money and the power, I'd get it all back. This has been my goal since I was eighteen."

Dane turned back around and leaned against the cool glass. "Now that it's mine, I'm not near as happy as I thought I'd be. Everything is empty without you—the resort, my life. My heart."

Unshed tears swam in her eyes and he couldn't keep this distance between them another second. Dane crossed to her and took her by the shoulders.

"If you believe nothing else, you have to believe that I love you."

Stella reached up and swiped at his cheek and Dane realized he'd let his emotions show a little too well. He hadn't even noticed the tear. His only concern had been getting her to see that he hadn't lied about everything.

"I'll give the entire place to you," he told her. "If you still want it, it's yours."

Stella gasped and jerked back. "What?"

Dane's hands dropped to his sides. He couldn't believe after all of these years, all of this work, he was saying this, but he meant it.

"My mother was proud of this place, she had a goal of passing it to me." Dane raked a hand over the back of his neck and sighed. "But she wouldn't want me ruining lives in order to reclaim it."

"Dane."

"She would've loved you," he murmured, the damn emotions threatening to strangle him. "She would've loved you not only because I love you, but because you're a kick-ass businesswoman."

Stella laughed and closed the distance between them. Those tears swimming in her eyes threatened to spill at any moment.

"Say it again," she demanded.

"I love you, Stella." He smoothed her hair from her face, sliding his thumb along her bottom lip. "I thought I did before you found out who I was, but I was too afraid to admit it—I knew you'd eventually learn the truth and that it would ruin everything between us, so I tried to convince myself it wouldn't wreck me to lose you. I want you to have this place. You may not be ready for marriage, but you deserve this."

Stella fisted his hair and pulled his mouth to hers. Dane didn't miss a chance to wrap his arms around her and pull her in. It had been too damn long.

When she broke the kiss and leaned back, her eyes shone

bright with tears and her smile filled those cracks in his heart.

"I want the resort, but I want you, too," she told him. "Do you think your mother would be on board with both of us running this? I'm not sure that marriage is our next step. We probably should slow down a bit so we don't mess this up again, but that doesn't mean we have to be apart."

"I'll go as slow as you want," he told her, smacking her lips with his. "And I'm the one who messed up before. But I sure as hell won't take you for granted ever again. We're equals, Stella. In business and in life."

"Can I make a confession?" she asked.

"What's that?"

"I don't have anything on under my suit."

Dane's body instantly responded. "Miss Garcia, is this how you plan to conduct all of our business meetings?"

She stepped from his arms and went to the door. With a flick of her wrist, the dead bolt clicked into place. Stella turned back around and started working on the buttons of her jacket.

"I hope that won't be a problem," she asked. "I didn't think my new business partner would mind."

Dane closed the distance between them and finished unwrapping his woman. "Oh, he definitely doesn't mind."

As he pulled her into his arms, he realized that the emptiness in his life that he'd felt ever since losing his mother had healed at last. Here in this place, with this woman beside him, he knew he was exactly where he belonged.

He was finally home.

* * * * *

The Rancher

Joanne Rock

Joanne Rock credits her decision to write romance after a book she picked up during a flight delay engrossed her so thoroughly that she didn't mind at all when her flight was delayed two more times. Giving her readers the chance to escape into another world has motivated her to write over eighty books for a variety of Harlequin series.

Books by Joanne Rock

Dynasties: Mesa Falls

The Rebel
The Rival
Rule Breaker
Heartbreaker
The Rancher

Texas Cattleman's Club: Inheritance

Her Texas Renegade

Visit her Author Profile page at millsandboon.com.au, or joannerock.com for more titles.

You can also find Joanne Rock on Facebook, along with other Harlequin Desire authors, at Facebook.com/harlequindesireauthors!

Dear Reader,

Rancher Miles Rivera seemed like the last man in Montana who would have his head turned by a social media star. So it made me smile that Chiara Campagna is the woman to spin his life upside down when she comes to Mesa Falls looking for answers about her long lost friend who was once Miles's classmate.

Welcome back to Mesa Falls, where old secrets are simmering into new scandals for the friends who own a Montana luxury ranch. Miles and Chiara turn up the heat when he catches her red-handed in his office. She's in town only to uncover his secrets, but soon he's uncovering her instead. When danger threatens her, however, Miles is more determined than ever to keep her close.

I hope you're enjoying the series. Be sure to look for the exciting conclusion next month when *The Heir* comes to town.

Happy reading,

Joanne Rock

To the Rockettes,
for keeping me company
while I write.

One

Chiara Campagna slipped into her host's office and silently closed the heavy oak door, leaving the raucous party behind. Breathing in the scents of good bourbon and leather, she held herself very still in the darkened room while she listened for noise outside in the hallway to indicate if anyone had followed her.

When no sounds came through besides the pop song people danced to in the living room of Miles Rivera's spacious Montana vacation home, Chiara released a pent-up breath and debated whether or not to switch on a lamp. On the one hand, a light showing under the door might signal to someone passing by that the room was occupied when it shouldn't be. On the other, if someone found her by herself snooping around in the dark, she'd be raising significant suspicions that wouldn't be easy to talk her way around.

As a prominent Los Angeles-based social media influencer, Chiara had a legitimate reason to be at the party given by the Mesa Falls Ranch owners to publicize their environmental good works. But she had no legitimate reason to be *here*—in Miles Rivera's private office—snooping for secrets about his past.

She twisted the knob on the wall by the door, and recessed lighting cast a warm glow over the heavy, masculine furnishings. Dialing back the wattage with the dimmer, she left it just bright enough to see her way around the gray leather sofa and glass-topped coffee table to the midcentury modern desk. Her silver metallic dress, a gorgeous gown with an asymmetrical hem and thigh-high slit to show off her legs, moved around her with a soft rustle as she headed toward the sideboard with its decanter full of amber-colored liquid. She set aside her tiny silver handbag, then poured two fingers' worth into one of the glasses beside the decanter. If anyone discovered her, the drink would help explain why she'd lingered where she most definitely did not belong.

"What secrets are you hiding, Miles?" she asked a framed photo of her host, a flattering image of an already handsome man. In the picture, he stood in front of the guest lodge with the five other owners of Mesa Falls Ranch. It was one of the few photos she'd seen of all six of them together.

Each successful in his own right, the owners were former classmates from a West Coast boarding school close to the all-girls' academy Chiara had attended. At least until her junior year, when her father lost his fortune and she'd been booted into public school. It would have been no big deal, really, if not for the fact that the public school had no art program. Her dreams of attending a prestigious art university to foster her skills with collage and acrylic paint faltered and died. Sure, she'd parlayed her limited resources into fame and fortune as a beauty influencer thanks to social media savvy and—in part—to her artistic sensibilities. But being an Instagram star wasn't the same as being an artist.

Not that it mattered now, she reminded herself, lingering on the photograph of Miles's too-handsome face. He stood flanked by casino resort owner Desmond Pierce and game developer Alec Jacobsen. Miles's golden, surfer looks were a contrast to Desmond's European sophistication and Alec's stubbled, devil-may-care style. All six men were wealthy and successful in their own right. Mesa Falls was the only business concern they shared.

A project that had something to do with the ties forged back in their boarding school days. A project that should have included Zach Eldridge, the seventh member of the group, who'd died under mysterious circumstances. The boy she'd secretly loved.

A cheer from the party in the living room reminded Chiara she needed to get a move on if she wanted to accomplish her mission. Steeling herself with a sip of the aged bourbon, she turned away from the built-in shelves toward the desk, then tapped the power button on the desktop computer. Any twinge of guilt she felt over invading Miles's privacy was mitigated by her certainty the Mesa Falls Ranch owners knew more than they were telling about Zach's death fourteen years ago. She hadn't been sure of it until last Christmas, when a celebrity guest of the ranch had revealed a former mentor to the ranch owners had anonymously authored a book that brought the men of Mesa Falls into the public spotlight.

And rekindled Chiara's need to learn the truth about what had happened to Zach while they were all at school together.

When the desktop computer prompted her to type in a passcode, Chiara crossed her fingers, then keyed in the same four numbers she'd seen Miles Rivera code into his phone screen earlier in the evening while ostensibly reaching past him for a glass of champagne. The generic photo of a mountain view on the screen faded into the more businesslike background of Miles's desktop with its neatly organized ranch files.

"Bingo." She quietly celebrated his lack of high tech cyber security on his personal device since she'd just exhausted the extent of her code-cracking abilities.

"Z-A-C-H." She spoke the letters aloud as she typed them into the search function.

A page full of results filled the screen. Her gaze roved over them. Speed-reading file names, she realized most of the files were spreadsheets; they seemed to be earnings reports. None used Zach's name in the title, indicating the references to him were within the files themselves.

Her finger hovered over a promising entry when the doorknob turned on the office door. Scared of getting caught, she jammed the power button off on the computer.

Just in time to look up and see Miles Rivera standing framed in the doorway.

Dressed in a custom-cut tuxedo that suited his lean runner's build perfectly, he held his phone in one hand before silently tucking it back in his jacket pocket. In the low light, his hair looked more brown than dark blond, the groomed bristles around his jaw and upper lip decidedly sexy. He might be a rancher, normally overseeing Rivera Ranch, a huge spread in central California, yet he was always well-dressed anytime the Mesa Falls owners were in the news cycle for their efforts to bring awareness to sustainable ranching practices. His suits were always tailored and masculine at the same time. Her blog followers would approve.

She certainly approved of his blatant sexiness and comfort in his own skin, even though she was scared he was about to have her tossed out of his vacation home on the Mesa Falls property for snooping.

His blue eyes zeroed in on her with laser focus. Missing nothing.

Guilty heart racing, Chiara reached for her bourbon and lifted it to her lips slowly, hoping her host couldn't spot the way her hand shook from his position across the room.

"You caught me red-handed." She sipped too much of the drink, the strong spirit burning her throat the whole way down while she struggled to maintain her composure.

"At what, exactly?" Miles quirked an eyebrow, his expression impossible to read.

Had he seen her shut off the computer? She only had an instant to decide how to play this.

"Helping myself to your private reserves." She lifted the cut-crystal tumbler, as if to admire the amber contents in the light. "I only slipped in here to escape the noise for a few minutes, but when I saw the decanter, I hoped you wouldn't mind if I helped myself."

She waited for him to call her out for the lie. To accuse her of spying on him. Her heartbeat sounded so loud in her ears she thought for sure he must hear it, too.

He inclined his head briefly before shutting the door behind him, then striding closer. "You're my guest. You're welcome to whatever you like, Ms. *Campagna*."

She sensed an undercurrent in the words. Something off in the slight emphasis on her name. Because he knew she was lying? Because he remembered a time when that hadn't been her name? Or maybe due to the simple fact that he didn't seem to like her. She had enough of an empath's sensibilities to recognize when someone looked down on her career. She suspected Miles Rivera was the kind of man to pigeonhole her as frivolous because she posted beauty content online.

As if making women feel good about themselves was a waste of time.

"You're not a fan of mine," she observed lightly, sidling from behind his desk to pace the length of the room, pretending to be interested in the titles of books on the built-in shelves lining the back wall. "Is it because of my profession? Or does it have more to do with me invading your private domain and stealing some bourbon? It's excellent, by the way."

"It's a limited edition." He unbuttoned his jacket as he reached the wet bar, then picked up the decanter to pour a second glass, his diamond cuff-link winking in the overhead lights as he poured. "Twenty-five years old. Single barrel. But I meant what I said. You're welcome to my hospitality. Including my bourbon."

Pivoting on his heel, he took two steps in her direction, then paused in front of his desk to lean against it. For a moment, she panicked that he would be able to feel that the computer was still warm. Or that the internal fan of the machine still spun after she'd shut it off.

But he merely sipped his drink while he observed her. He watched her so intently that she almost wondered if he recognized her from a long-ago past. In the few times they'd met socially, Miles had never made the connection between Chiara Campagna, social media star, and Kara Marsh, the teenager who'd been in love with Miles's roommate at school, Zach Eldridge. The old sense of loss flared inside her, spurring her to turn the conversation in a safer direction.

"I noticed you neatly sidestepped the matter of my profession." She set her tumbler on a granite-topped cabinet beside a heavy wire sculpture of a horse with a golden-yellow eye.

He paused, taking his time to answer. The sounds of the party filtered through to the dim home office. One dance tune blended seamlessly into another thanks to the famous DJ of the moment, and voices were raised to be heard over the music. When Miles met her gaze again, there was something calculating in his expression.

"Maybe I envy you a job that allows you to travel the globe and spend your nights at one party after another." He lifted his glass in a mock salute. "Clearly, you're doing something right."

Irritation flared.

"You wouldn't be the first person to assume I lead a charmed life of leisure, full of yachts and champagne, because of what I choose to show the world on social media." She bristled at his easy dismissal of all the hard work it had taken to carve herself a place in a crowded market.

"And yet, here you are." He gestured expansively, as if to indicate his second home on the exclusive Mesa Falls property. "Spending another evening with Hollywood celebrities, world-class athletes and a few heavyweights from the music industry. Life can't be all bad, can it?"

In her agitation, she took another drink of the bourbon, though she still hadn't learned her lesson to sip carefully. The fire down her throat should have warned her that she was letting this arrogant man get under her skin.

Considering her earlier fears about being caught spying, maybe she should have just laughed off his assumption that she had a shallow lifestyle and excused herself from the room. But resentment burned fast and hot.

"And yet, you're at the same party as me." She took a step

closer to him before realizing it. Before acknowledging her own desire to confront him. To somehow douse the smug look in his blue eyes. "Don't you consider attendance part of your job, not just something you do for fun?"

"I'm the host representing Mesa Falls." His broad shoulders straightened at her approach, though he didn't move from his position leaning his hip against the desk. "Of course it's a work obligation. If I didn't have to take a turn being the face of Mesa Falls tonight, I would be back at my own place, Rivera Ranch."

His voice had a raspy quality to it that teased along her nerve endings in a way that wasn't at all unpleasant. He was nothing like the men who normally populated her world—men who understood the beauty and entertainment industries. There was something earthy and real about Miles Rivera underneath the tailored garments, something that compelled her to get closer to all those masculine, rough edges.

"And I'm representing my brand as well. It's no less a work obligation for me."

"Right." He shook his head, an amused smile playing at his lips, his blue eyes darkening a few shades. "More power to you for creating a brand that revolves around long-wearing lipstick and international fashion shows."

This view of her work seemed so unnecessarily dismissive that she had to wonder if he took potshots as a way to pay her back for invading his office. She couldn't imagine how he could rationalize his behavior any other way, but she forced herself to keep her cool in spite of his obvious desire to get a rise from her.

"I'm surprised a man of your business acumen would hold views so narrow-minded and superficial." She shrugged with deliberate carelessness, though she couldn't stop herself from glaring daggers at him. Or taking another step closer to hammer home her point. "Especially since I'm sure you recognize that work like mine requires me to be a one-woman content creator, marketing manager, finance director and admin. Not to mention committing endless hours to build a brand you write off as fluff."

Maybe what she'd said resonated for him, because the condescension in his expression gave way to something else. Something hotter and more complex. At the same moment, she realized that she'd arrived a foot away from him. Closer than she'd meant to come.

She couldn't have said which was more unnerving: the sudden lifting of a mental barrier between them that made Miles Rivera seem more human, or her physical proximity to a man who…stirred something inside her. Good or bad, she couldn't say, but she most definitely didn't want to deal with magnified emotions right now. Let alone the sudden burst of heat she felt just being near him.

Telling herself the jittery feelings were a combination of justified anger and residual anxiety from her snooping mission, Chiara reached for her silver purse on the desk. Her hand came close to his thigh for an instant before she snatched up the handbag.

She didn't look back as she stalked out the office door.

Still shaken by his unexpected encounter with Chiara Campagna, Miles made a dismal effort to mingle with his guests despite the loud music, the crowd that struck him as too young and entitled, and the text messages from the other Mesa Falls Ranch owners that kept distracting him. Trapped in his oversize great room that took "open concept" to a new level of monstrosity, he leaned against the curved granite-topped cabinetry that provided a low boundary between the dining area and seating around a stone fireplace that took up one entire wall. Open trusswork in the cathedral ceilings added to the sense of space, while the hardwood floor made for easy dancing as the crowd enjoyed the selections of the DJ set up near the open staircase.

Miles nodded absently at whatever the blonde pop singer standing next to him was saying about her reluctance to go back on tour, his thoughts preoccupied by another woman.

A certain raven-haired social media star who seemed to captivate every man in the room.

Miles's gaze followed Chiara as she posed for a photo with two members of a boy band in front of a wall of red flowers brought into the great room for the party. He couldn't take his eyes off her feminine curves draped in that outrageous liquid silver dress she wore. Hugged between the two young men, her gown reflected the flashes of multiple camera phones as several other guests took surreptitious photos. And while the guys around her only touched her in polite and socially acceptable ways, Miles still fought an urge to wrest her away from them. A ludicrous reaction, and totally out of character for him.

Then again, *everything* about his reaction to the wildly sexy Chiara was out of character. Since when was he the kind of guy to disparage what someone else did for a living? He'd regretted his flippant dismissal of her work as soon as he'd said the words, recognizing them as a defense mechanism he had no business articulating. There was something about her blatant appeal that slid past his reserve. The woman was like fingernails down his back, inciting response. Desire, yes. But there was more to it than that. He didn't trust the femme fatale face she presented to the world, or the way she used her femininity in an almost mercenary way to build her name. She reminded him of a woman from his past that he'd rather forget. But that wasn't fair, since Chiara wasn't Brianna. Without a doubt, he owed Chiara an apology before she left tonight.

Even though she'd definitely been on his computer when he'd entered his office earlier. He'd seen the blue glow of the screen reflected on her face before she'd scrambled to shut it down.

"How do you know Chiara Campagna?" the woman beside him asked, inclining her head so he could hear her over the music.

He hadn't been following the conversation, but Chiara's name snagged his focus, and he tore his gaze away from the beauty influencer who'd become a household name to stare down at the earnest young pop singer beside him.

He was only on site at Mesa Falls Ranch to oversee things for the owners for a few weeks. His real life back at Rivera Ranch in central California never brought him into contact with the kind of people on the guest list tonight, but the purpose of this party—to promote the green ranching mission of Mesa Falls by spreading the word among celebrities who could use their platforms to highlight the environmental effort—was a far cry from the routine cattle raising and grain production he was used to. Just like his modern marvel of a home in Mesa Falls bore little resemblance to the historic Spanish-style main house on Rivera Ranch.

"I don't know her at all," Miles returned after a moment. He tried to remember the pop singer's name. She had a powerful voice despite her petite size, her latest single landing in the top ten according to the notes the ranch's publicist had given him about the guests. "But I assume she cares about Mesa Falls's environmental mission. No doubt she has a powerful social media platform that could help our outreach."

The singer laughed as she lifted her phone to take a picture of her own, framing Chiara and the two boy band members in her view screen. "Is that why we're all here tonight? Because of the environment?"

Frowning, he remembered the real reason for this particular party. While the green ranching practices they used were touted every time they hosted an event, tonight's party had a more important agenda. Public interest in Mesa Falls had spiked since the revelations that the owners' high school teacher and friend, Alonzo Salazar, had been the author behind the career-ending tell-all *Hollywood Newlyweds.* In fact, the news story broke at a gala here over Christmas. It had also been revealed that Alonzo had spent a lot of time at Mesa Falls before his death, his association with the ranch owners drawing speculation about his involvement with the business.

Tonight, the partners hoped to put an end to the rumors and tabloid interest by revealing the profits from *Hollywood Newlyweds* had gone toward Alonzo Salazar's humanitarian work around the globe. They'd hoped the announcement would put an end to the media interest in the Mesa Falls owners and discourage newshounds from showing up at the ranch. There'd been a coordinated press release of the news at the start of the party, a toast to the clearing of Alonzo's good name early in the evening, and a media room had been set up off the foyer with information about Alonzo's charitable efforts for reporters.

But there was something the owners weren't saying. While it was true a share of the book profits had benefited a lot of well-deserving people, a larger portion had gone to a secret beneficiary, and no one could figure out why.

"So the threat of global warming didn't bring you here tonight," Miles responded with a self-deprecating smile, trying to get back on track in his host duties. He watched as Chiara left behind the band members for one of the Mesa Falls partners—game developer Alec Jacobsen—who wanted a photo with her. "What did? A need to escape to Montana for a long weekend?"

He ground his teeth together at the friendly way Alec placed his hand on the small of Chiara's back. Miles remembered the generous cutout in her dress that left her completely bare in that spot. Her hair shimmered in the overhead lights as she brushed the long waves over one shoulder.

"Honestly? I hoped to meet Chiara," the singer gushed enthusiastically. "Will you excuse me? Maybe I can get a photo with her, too."

Miles gladly released her from the conversation, chagrined to learn that his companion had been as preoccupied with Chiara as he was. What must life be like for the influencer, who'd achieved a different level of fame from the rest of the crowd—all people who were highly accomplished in their own right?

Pulling out his phone, Miles checked to see if his friend and fellow ranch owner, Gage Striker, had responded to a text he'd sent an hour ago. Gage should have been at the party long ago.

Miles had sent him a text earlier:

How well do you know Chiara Campagna? Found her in my study and I would swear she was riffling through my notes. Looking for something.

Gage had finally answered:

Astrid and Jonah have known her forever. She's cool.

Miles knew fellow partner Jonah Norlander had made an early exit from the party with his wife, Astrid, so Miles would have to wait to check with him. Shoving the phone back in the pocket of his tuxedo, Miles bided his time until he could speak to Chiara again. He would apologize, first and foremost. But then, he needed to learn more about her.

Because she hadn't just been snooping around his computer in his office earlier. She'd been there on a mission. And she hadn't covered her trail when she'd rushed to close down his screen.

Somehow, Chiara Campagna knew about Zach. And Miles wasn't letting her leave Mesa Falls until he figured out how.

Two

Chiara grooved on the dance floor to an old disco tune, surrounded by a dozen other guests and yet—thankfully—all by herself. She'd spent time snapping photos with people earlier, so no one entered her personal dance space while she took a last glance around the party she should have left an hour ago.

Normally, she kept a strict schedule at events like this, making only brief appearances at all but the biggest of social engagements. The Met Gala might get a whole evening, or an Oscar after-party. But a gathering hosted by a Montana rancher in a thinly disguised PR effort to turn attention away from the Alonzo Salazar book scandal?

She should have been in and out in fifty minutes once her spying mission in Miles Rivera's office had proven a bust. Finding out something about Zach had been her real motive for attending, yet she'd lingered long after she'd failed in that regard. And she knew the reason had something to do with her host. She knew because she found herself searching him out in the crowd, her eyes scanning the darkened corners of the huge great room hoping for a glimpse of him.

Entirely foolish of her.

Annoyed with herself for the curiosity about a man who, at best, was keeping secrets about Zach and at worst thought her work shallow and superficial, she was just about to walk off the dance floor when he reentered the room. His sudden presence seemed to rearrange the atoms in the air, making it more charged. Electrified.

For a moment, he didn't notice her as he read something on his phone, and she took the opportunity to look her fill while unobserved. She was curious what it was about him that held her attention. His incredibly fit physique? Certainly with his broad shoulders he cut through the guests easily enough, his size making him visible despite the crowd around him. Or maybe it was the way he held himself, with an enviable confidence and authority that implied he was a man who solved problems and took care of business. But before she could explore other facets of his appeal, his gaze lifted from his device to land squarely on her.

Almost as if he'd known the whole time she'd been watching him.

A keen awareness took hold as she flushed all over. Grateful for the dim lighting in the great room, she took some comfort in the fact that at least he wouldn't see how he affected her. Even if he had caught her staring.

Abruptly, she stepped out of the throng of dancers with brisk efficiency, determined to make her exit. Heels clicking purposefully on the hardwood, she moved toward the foyer, texting her assistant that she was ready to leave. But just as the other woman appeared at her side to gather their entourage, Miles intercepted Chiara.

"Don't go." His words, his serious tone, were almost as much of a surprise as his hand catching hers lightly in his own. "Can we speak privately?"

It might have been satisfying to say something cutting now in return for the way he'd behaved with her earlier. To hold her head high and march out his front door into the night. She looked back and forth between Miles and her assistant, Jules Santor, who was busy on her phone assembling vehicles for the return to their nearby hotel. But the reason Chiara had come here tonight was more important than her pride, and if there was any chance she could still wrest some clue about Zach's death from Miles after all this time, she couldn't afford to indulge the impulse.

"On second thought," she told Jules, a very tall former volleyball player who turned heads everywhere she went, "feel free to take the rest of the evening off. I'm going to stay a bit longer."

Jules bit her lip, her thumbs paused midtext as she glanced around the party. "Are you sure you'll be okay? Do you want me to leave a car for you?"

"I'll be fine. I'll text if I need a ride," Chiara assured her before returning her attention to whatever Miles had in mind.

At her nod, he guided her toward the staircase behind the dining area, one set of steps leading to an upper floor and another to a lower. He took her downstairs, never relinquishing her hand. A social nicety, maybe, because of her sky-high heels, long gown and the open stairs. Yet his touch made her pulse quicken.

When they reached the bottom floor, there was a small bar and a mahogany billiards table with a few guys engaged in a game. He led her past a smaller living area that was dark except for a fire in the hearth, through a set of double doors into a huge room with a pool and floor-to-ceiling windows on three sides. Natural stonework surrounded the entire pool deck, making it look like a grotto complete with a small waterfall from a raised hot tub. The water was illuminated from within, and landscape lights showcased a handful of plantings and small trees.

"This is beautiful." She paused as they reached two easy chairs flanking a cocktail table by the windows that overlooked the backyard and the Bitterroot River beyond.

Withdrawing her hand from his, she took the seat he gestured toward while he made himself comfortable in the other.

"Thank you." He pulled his gaze from her long enough to look over the pool area. "I keep meaning to come here during the summer when I could actually open all the doors and windows and feel the fresh air circulating."

"You've never visited this house during the summer?" She wondered if she misunderstood him. The house where he was hosting tonight's party was at least fourteen thousand square feet.

"I'm rarely ever in Montana." His blue eyes found hers again as he leaned forward in the wingback, elbows propped on his knees. "Normally, my brother oversees Mesa Falls while I maintain Rivera Ranch, but Weston had his hands full this year, so I'm helping out here for the month." His jaw flexed. "I realize I did a poor job in my hosting duties earlier this evening, however."

Surprised he would admit it, she felt her brows lift but waited for him to continue. The sounds of the game at the billiards table drifted through the room now and then, but for the most part, the soft gurgle of the waterfall drowned out the noise of the party. The evening was winding down anyhow.

"I had no right to speak disparagingly of your work, and I apologize." He hung his head for a moment as he shook it, appearing genuinely regretful. "I don't know what I was thinking, but it was completely inappropriate."

"Agreed." She folded her fingers together, hands in her lap, as she watched him. "Apology accepted."

He lifted his head, that amused smile she remembered from earlier flitting around his lips again. "You're an unusual woman, Chiara Campagna."

"How so?" Crossing her legs, she wished she didn't feel a flutter inside at the sound of her name on his lips. She couldn't have walked away from this conversation if she tried.

She was curious why he'd sought her out for a private audience again. Had she been in his thoughts as much as he'd been in hers over the last hour? Not that it should matter. She hadn't decided to stay longer at the party because he made her entire body flush hot with a single look. No, she was here now because Miles knew something about Zach's death, and getting to know Miles might help her find out what had really happened.

"Your candor, for one thing." He slid a finger beneath his bow tie, expertly loosening it a fraction.

Her gaze tracked to his throat, imagining the taste of his skin at the spot just above his collar. It was easier to indulge in a little fantasy about Miles than it was to reply to his opinion of her, which was so very wrong. She'd been anything but truthful with him this evening.

"I appreciated the way you explained your job to me when I made a crack about it," he continued, unbuttoning his tuxedo jacket and giving her a better view of the white shirt stretching taut across his chest and abs. He looked very… fit. "I had no idea how much work was involved."

Her gaze lingered on his chest as she wondered how much more unbuttoning he might do in her presence tonight. She didn't know where all this physical attraction was coming from, but she wished she could put the lid back on it. Normally, she didn't think twice about pursuing relationships, preferring to focus on her work. But then, men didn't usually tempt her to this degree. The awareness was beyond distracting when she needed to be smart about her interaction with him. With an effort, she tried to focus on their conversation.

"I'm sure plenty of jobs look easier from the outside. You're a rancher, for example, and I'm sure that amounts to more than moving cattle from one field to the next, but that's really all I know about it."

"Yet whereas you have the good sense to simply admit that, I made presumptuous wisecracks because I didn't understand your work." He studied her for a long moment before he spoke again. "I appreciate you being here tonight. I do recognize that our ranch party probably wouldn't be on your list of social engagements if not for your friendship with Jonah Norlander's wife, Astrid."

"Astrid is one of my closest friends," she said, wary of going into too much detail about her connections to the Mesa Falls partners and their spouses. But at least she was telling the truth about Astrid. The Finnish former supermodel had caused Chiara's career to skyrocket, simply by posting enthusiastic comments on Chiara's social media content. Because of her friend, she'd gone from an unknown to a full-blown influencer practically overnight. "As someone who doesn't have much family, I don't take for granted the few good friends I have in my life."

Another reason she planned to honor Zach's memory. She counted him among the people who'd given her the creative and emotional boost she'd needed to find her professional passion.

"Wise woman." Miles nodded his agreement. "I guess you could say I'm here tonight because of my good friends, too. I do have family, but I don't mind admitting I like my friends better."

His grin was unrepentant, giving his blue eyes a wicked light.

"What about Weston?" She wondered what he thought of his younger brother, who held a stake in Mesa Falls with him.

"We have our moments," he told her cryptically, his lips compressing into a thin line as some dark thought raced across his expression.

"Does owning the ranch together make you closer with him?"

One eyebrow arched. "It does."

His clipped answer made her hesitate to probe further. But she couldn't stop herself from asking, "If you're close to the other Mesa Falls owners, why don't you spend more time here? I know you said you run Rivera Ranch, but why build this huge, beautiful house if you didn't ever plan on making time to be in Montana?"

She wondered what kept him away. Yes, she was curious if it had anything to do with Zach. But she couldn't deny she wanted to know more about Miles. With luck, that knowledge would help her keep her distance from this far-too-sexy man.

He took so long to answer that she thought maybe he'd tell her it was none of her business. He watched the spillover from the hot tub where it splashed into the pool below, and she realized the sounds had faded from the other room; the billiard game had ended.

"Maybe I was feeling more optimistic when we bought the land." He met her gaze. "Like having this place would bring us together more. But for the most part, it's just another asset we manage."

Puzzled why that would be, she drew in a breath to tease out the reason, but he surprised her into silence when his hand landed on her wrist.

"Isn't it my turn to ask you something?" Mild amusement glinted in his eyes again.

Her belly tightened at his attention, his touch. There was a potent chemistry lurking between them, and she wanted to exercise extreme caution not to stir it any further. But it was incredibly tempting to see what would happen if she acted on those feelings. Too late, she realized that her pulse leaped right underneath the place where his hand rested. His thumb skated over the spot with what might pass for idleness to anyone observing them, but that slow caress felt deliberate to her.

As if he wanted to assess the results of his touch.

"What?" she prodded him, since the suspense of the moment was killing her.

Or maybe it was the awareness. She was nearly brought to her knees by physical attraction.

"I saw you dancing alone upstairs." His voice took on that low, raspy quality that sent her thoughts to sexy places.

She remembered exactly what she'd been thinking about

when he'd caught her eye earlier. She would not lick her lips, even though they suddenly felt dry.

"That's not a question," she managed, willing her pulse to slow down under the stroke of his thumb.

"It made me wonder," he continued as if she hadn't spoken. "Would you like to dance with me instead?"

The question, like his touch, seemed innocuous on the surface. But she knew he wasn't just asking her to dance. She *knew*.

That should have given her pause before she answered. But she gave him the only possible response.

"I'd like that." She pushed the words past the sudden lump in her throat. "Very much."

Even before he'd asked her to be his dance partner, Miles knew the party upstairs had ended and that this would be a private dance.

The Mesa Falls PR team excelled at keeping events on schedule, and the plan had been to move the late-night guests into the media room to distribute gift bags at midnight. His public hosting duties were officially done.

His private guest was now his only concern.

Which was a good thing, since he couldn't have taken his eyes off her if he tried. He needed to figure out what she was up to, after all. What would it hurt to act on the attraction since he had to keep track of what she was doing anyway? Keep your friends close and your enemies closer. Wherever Chiara ended up on the spectrum, he'd have his bases covered.

Helping her to her feet, he kept hold of her hand as he steered her toward the billiards room, now empty. Stopping there, he flipped on the speaker system tucked behind the bar, then dimmed the lights and pressed the switch for the gas fireplace at the opposite end of the room. Her green eyes took in the changes before her gaze returned to him.

"Aren't we going upstairs?" she asked while the opening refrain of a country love song filled the air.

Miles shrugged off his tuxedo jacket and laid it over one of the chairs at the bar. If he was fortunate enough to get to feel her hands on him tonight, he didn't want extraneous layers of clothes between them.

"The DJ is done for the night." He led her to the open floor near the pool table and pulled her closer to him, so they faced one another, still holding hands. He waited to take her into his arms until he was certain she wanted this. "I thought if we stayed down here we'd be out of the way of the catering staff while they clean up."

"I didn't realize the party was over." She didn't seem deterred, however, because she laid her free hand on his shoulder, the soft weight of her touch stirring awareness that grew by the minute. He was glad he'd ditched his jacket, especially when her fingers flexed against the cotton of his shirt, her fingernails lightly scratching the fabric.

"It's just us now." He couldn't help the way his voice lowered, maybe because he wanted to whisper the words into her ear. But he still didn't draw her to him. "Are you sure you want to stay?"

"It's too late to retract your offer, Miles Rivera." She lifted their joined hands, positioning them. "I'll have that dance, please."

Damn, but she fascinated him.

With far more pleasure than a dance had ever inspired in him, he slid his free hand around Chiara's waist. He took his time to savor the feel of her beneath his palm, the temperature of her skin making her dress's lightweight metallic fabric surprisingly warm. Sketching a touch from her hip to her spine, he settled his hand in the small of her back where the skin was bare, then used his palm to draw her within an inch of him.

Her pupils dilated until there was only a dark green ring around them.

"That's what I hoped you'd say." He swayed with her to the mournful, longing sound of steel guitars, breathing in her bright, citrusy scent.

Counting down the seconds until he kissed her.

Because he had to taste her soon.

Not just for the obvious reasons, like that she was the sexiest woman he'd ever seen. But because Chiara had gotten to the heart of the loneliness he felt in this big Montana mansion every time he set foot in the state. With her questions and her perceptive gaze, she'd reminded him that Mesa Falls might be a testament to Zach Eldridge's life, but it remained a hollow tribute without their dead friend among them.

He'd hoped that ache would subside after they'd owned the property for a while. That Mesa Falls could somehow heal the emptiness, the pervasive sense of failure, that remained in him and his partners after they'd lost one of their own. But for Miles, who'd defined his whole life by trying to do the right thing, the consequences of not saving his friend were as jagged and painful as ever.

"Is everything okay?" Chiara asked him, her hand leaving his shoulder to land on his cheek, her words as gentle as her expression.

And damned if that didn't hurt, too.

He didn't want her sympathy. Not when her kiss would feel so much better.

With an effort, he shoved his demons off his back and refocused on this woman's lush mouth. Her petal-soft fingertips skimming along his jaw. Her hips hovering close enough to his to tantalize him with what he wanted most.

"Just wondering how long I can make this dance last without violating social conventions." He let his gaze dip to her lips before meeting her gaze again.

She hesitated, her fingers going still against his cheek. He could tell she didn't buy it. Then her hand drifted from his face to his chest.

"You're worried what I'll think about you?" she asked lightly, her forefinger circling below his collarbone.

The touch was a barely there caress, but it told him she wasn't in any hurry to leave. The knowledge made his heart slug harder.

"A host has certain obligations to the people he invites under his roof." He stopped swaying to the song and looked into her eyes.

He kept one hand on the small of her back, the other still entwined with hers.

"In that case—" Her voice was breathless, but her gaze was steady. Certain. "I think you're obligated to make sure I don't dance alone again tonight."

Three

She needed his kiss.

Craved it.

Chiara watched Miles as he seemed to debate the merits of continuing what he'd started. He was a deliberate, thoughtful man. But she couldn't wait much longer, not when she felt this edgy hunger unlike anything she'd felt before.

She simply knew she wanted him. Even if what was happening between them probably shouldn't.

Maybe the impatience was because she'd had very little romantic experience. In her late teens, she'd mourned Zach and wrestled with the mix of anxiety and depression that had come with his death. Her lifestyle had shifted, too, after her father went bankrupt and she'd been forced to change schools. Giving up her dream of going to an art school had changed her, forging her into a woman of relentless ambition with no time for romance.

Not that it had really mattered to her before, since she hadn't been impressed with the few relationships she'd had in the past. The explosive chemistry other women raved about had been more of a simmer for her, making her feel like she'd only been going through the motions with guys. But tonight, dancing with Miles in this huge, empty house now that all the party guests had gone home, she felt something much different.

Something had shifted between them this evening, taking them from cautiously circling enemies to charged magnets that couldn't stay apart. At least, that's how she felt. Like she was inexorably drawn to him.

Especially with his broad palm splayed across her back, his thumb and forefinger resting on her bare skin through the cutout in the fabric of her gown, the other fingers straying onto the curve of her ass. A touch that made her very aware of his hands and how much she wanted them all over her without the barrier of clothes.

Determined to overcome his scruples, or host obligations, or whatever it was that made him hesitate, Chiara lifted up on her toes. She was going to take this kiss, and whatever else he was offering, because she needed it. She'd worry about the repercussions in the morning. For now, she grazed her mouth over his. Gently. Experimentally.

Hopefully.

She breathed him in, a hint of smoky bourbon enticing her tongue to taste his lower lip.

The contact sparked through her in unexpected ways, leaping from one pulse point to the next until something hot flamed to life. Something new and exciting. And as much as she wanted to explore that, she hesitated, worried about compounding her subterfuge with this man by adding seduction into the mix. Or maybe she just feared she didn't have the necessary skills. Either way, she needed to be sure he wanted this, too.

Just when she was about to pull back, his fingers tangled in her hair, anchoring her to him and deepening the kiss. And every cell in her body cried out a resounding *yes*.

The heat erupted into a full-blown blaze as he took over. With one hand he drew her body against his, sealing them together, while he used the other to angle her face in a way that changed the trajectory of the kiss from sensual to fierce and hungry. She pressed her thighs together against the sudden ache there.

From just a kiss.

Her body thrilled to the new sensations even as her brain struggled to keep up with the onslaught. Her scalp tingled when he ran his fingers through her hair. Her nipples beaded, skin tightening everywhere. A soft, needy sound emanated from the back of her throat, and the noise seemed to spur him on. His arm banded her tighter, creating delicious friction between their bodies as he backed her into the pool table. She wanted to peel off her gown and climb all over him. She simply *wanted*.

Her hands went to his shirt, ready to strip away the barriers between them, her fingers taking in the warm strength of all that delectable male muscle as she worked the fastenings. He lifted her up, seating her on the pool table as he stepped between her knees, never breaking the kiss. The long slit in her silver gown parted, making the fabric slide away as it ceased to cover her. The feel of him against her *there*, his hips pressing into the cradle of her thighs, made her forget everything else. Her fingers fell away from the shirt fastenings as she raked in a gasp, sensation rocking her.

Miles edged back, his blue eyes now a deep, dark ultramarine as his gaze smoked over her, checking in with her.

"I need to be sure you want to stay." His breathing was

harsh as he tipped his forehead to hers, his grip going slack so that his palms simply rested on her hips. "Tell me, Chiara."

She respected his restraint. His concern for her. Things had spiraled out of control in a hurry, but she didn't want to stop now, no matter how it might complicate things down the road. She wanted to know real passion. What it was like to be carried away on that wave of hot, twitchy, need-it-now hunger.

"I've never felt the way you're making me feel tonight," she confided in a low voice, her hands gripping the side rails of the table, her nails sinking into the felt nap. "But I've always wanted to. So yes, I'm staying. I have to see what I've been missing all the years I chose work over…fun."

His lips quirked at that last bit. He straightened enough to look into her eyes again. The flames from the fireplace cast his face half in shadow.

"It's going to be more than fun." His thumbs rubbed lightly where they rested on her hips, the certainty in his tone assuring her he knew how to give her everything she craved.

She resisted the urge to squeeze his hips between her thighs and lock her ankles so he couldn't leave her. "Promise?"

His fingers clenched reflexively, which made her think that she affected him as thoroughly as he was affecting her. "If you make me a promise in return."

"What is it?" She would have agreed to almost anything to put his hands in motion again. To experience another mind-drugging kiss with the power to set her on fire. How did he do that?

"I get a date after this." He pressed his finger to her lips when she'd been about to agree, silencing her for a moment while she battled the urge to lick him there. "One where you'll tell me why you've chosen work over fun for far too long," he continued, removing his finger from her mouth so she could speak.

Her conscience stabbed her as Zach's face floated through her mind. She had no idea how she'd appeal to Miles for information about Zach in the aftermath of this. He'd probably hate her when he found out why she'd come to Montana in the first place. He'd never look at her the same way again—with heat and hunger in his eyes. Was it so wrong to chase the feelings Miles stirred inside her?

"Deal," she told him simply, knowing he'd never follow through on the request once he understood what had brought her here in the first place. Her fingers returned to the studs in his shirt, wanting the barriers between them gone.

He tipped her chin up to meet his gaze before he breathed his agreement over her lips. "Deal."

His kiss seemed to seal the pact, and her fingers forgot how to work. All her thoughts scattered until there was only his tongue stroking hers, teasing wicked sensations that echoed over her skin, dialing up the heat. She shifted closer to him, wanting to be near the source of that warmth. He answered by bracketing her hips and tugging her forward to the edge of the table, pressing her against the rigid length beneath his fly.

She couldn't stifle the needy sound she made at the feel of him, the proof of his hunger pleasing her almost as much as having him right where she wanted him. Almost, anyway. A shiver rippled through her while he tugged the straps of her gown off her shoulders.

"I need to see you," he said as he broke the kiss, watching the metallic silver gown slide down her body.

The material teased her sensitive nipples as it fell, since she hadn't bothered to wear a bra. Miles's eyes locked on her body, and the peaks tightened almost painfully, her breath coming faster.

"And I need to *feel* you." She might not have a ton of romance experience, but she believed in voicing her needs. And damn it, she knew what she wanted. "Your hands, your body, your mouth. You pick."

His blue eyes were full of heat as they lifted to hers again. "Let's find a bed. Now."

He plucked her off the table and set her on her feet while she clutched enough of her gown to keep it from falling off. Holding her hand, Miles tugged her through the bar area and past an office to a bedroom with high wooden ceilings and lots of windows. She guessed it wasn't the master suite in a home like this, given its modest size and single closet, yet she glimpsed a pair of boots near the door and toiletries on the granite vanity of the attached bath.

Miles closed the door behind her, toed off his shoes, then made quick work of his shirt, tossing it on a built-in window seat.

She was about to ask why he was staying in a guest bedroom of his own home when he came toward her. The words dried up on her tongue at the sight of his purposeful stride.

When he reached her, he took the bodice she was clutching and let it fall to the floor, the heavy liquid silver pooling at her feet. Cool air touched her skin now that she was almost naked except for an ice-blue silk thong.

She didn't have long to feel the chill, however, as Miles pressed her body to his. Her breasts molded to his hard chest as his body radiated heat. He took his time wrapping her hair around his hand, lifting the heavy mass off her shoulders and watching it spill down his forearm.

"My hands, my body, my mouth." He parroted the words back to her, the rough sound of his voice letting her know how they'd affected him. "I pick all three."

Oh.

He kissed her throat and the crook behind her ear, then trailed his lips down to her shoulder, letting her feel his tongue and his teeth until she twined her limbs around him, wanting to be closer. He drew her with him to the bed, his hands tracing light touches up her arms, down her sides, under her breasts. When her calf bumped into the mattress, she dropped onto the gray duvet, pulling him down with her into the thick, downy embrace. She wanted to feel the weight of him against her, but he sat beside her on the edge of the bed instead, leaning down to unfasten the strap of her sequined sandal with methodical care.

A shiver went through her that had nothing to do with room temperature. When the first shoe fell away, he slid a warm palm down her other leg, lifting it to undo the tiny buckle on her other ankle. Once that shoe dropped onto the floor, he skimmed his hand back up her leg, circling a light touch behind her knee, then following the line of muscle in her thigh. Higher.

Higher.

She was on fire, desperate for more, by the time he pressed her back onto the bed. He followed her down, combing his fingers through her dark hair and kissing her neck, bracketing her body between his elbows where he propped himself over her. He kissed her jaw and down her neck, tracing a touch down the center of her breastbone, slowing but not stopping as he tracked lower. Lower.

Her pulse rushed as she inhaled sharply. She noticed he was breathing faster, too, his eyes watching the movement of his fingers as he reached the low waist of the ice-blue silk thong that still clung to her hips. As he slipped his fingers beneath the fabric, the brush of his knuckles made her stomach muscles clench, tension tightening as he stroked a touch right where she needed it. His gaze returned to her face as a ripple of pleasure trembled through her. She was already so close, on edge from wondering what would happen between them. Her release hovered as she held her breath.

He must have known. She didn't know how he could tell, but he leaned down to speak into her ear.

"You don't need to hold back." That deep, suggestive voice vibrated along her skin, evaporating any restraint. "There's no limit on how many times you can come."

His fingers stroked harder, and she flew apart. She gripped his wrist, whether to push him away or keep him there, she didn't know, but he didn't let go. Expertly, he coaxed every last shudder from her while waves of pleasure rocked through her. Only when she went still, her breathing slowing a fraction, did he slide off the bed.

She would have mourned the loss, but he shoved off his pants and boxers, reminding her how much more she had to look forward to. He disappeared into the bathroom for a moment but returned a moment later in all his delectable naked glory, condom in hand. Yet even as she tried to memorize the way he looked, to take in all the ways his muscles moved together so that she'd never forget it, she experienced a moment's trepidation. Just because he'd known how to touch her in a way that had made the earth move for her didn't mean she could return the favor.

But when he joined her on the bed, handing her the condom and letting her roll it in place, the worries faded. Having him next to her, covering her with all that warm male muscle as he kneed her legs apart to make room for himself, made it impossible to think about anything but this.

Him.

The most tantalizing encounter she'd ever had with a man.

He kissed her as he eased his way inside her, moving with her as easily as if they'd done this a thousand times before. Closing her eyes, she breathed in his cedarwood scent, letting the heat build between them again, hotter and stronger this time. The connection between them felt so real to her, even though she knew it could only be passion or chemistry, or whatever that nameless X-factor was that made for amazing sex.

Still, when she opened her eyes and found his intense gaze zeroed in on her, she could have sworn he'd seen deep inside her, past all the artifice that was her whole life and right down to the woman underneath. The thought robbed her of breath, stirring a hint of panic until he kissed her again, shifting on top of her in a way that created heart-stopping friction between their bodies.

He thrust again. Once. Twice.

And she lost all her bearings, soaring mindlessly into another release. This time, she brought him with her. She could feel him going still, his shout echoing hers, their bodies utterly in sync. For long moments, all she could do was breathe, dragging in long gulps of air while her heart galloped faster.

Eventually, everything slowed down again. Her skin

cooled as Miles rolled away, but he dragged a cashmere throw up from the base of the bed, covering them both. He pulled her against him, her back tucked against his chest, as he stroked her hair in the darkened room. Words failed her, and she was grateful that he didn't say anything, either. She was out of her depth tonight, but she wasn't ready to leave. The only solace she took was that he didn't seem to want her to go.

In the morning, she'd have to come clean about what she was doing here. She hoped he wouldn't hate her for sleeping with him after she'd tried spying on him. Chances seemed slim that he'd understand the truth—that the two things were entirely unrelated.

Who was she kidding? He'd never believe that.

Guilt and worry tightened in her belly.

"Whatever you're thinking about, stop," came Miles's advice in her ear, a warm reassurance she didn't deserve. "Just enjoy it while we can."

How had he known? Maybe he'd felt her tense. Either way, she didn't feel compelled to wreck what they'd just shared, so she let out a long breath and tucked closer to his warmth.

The morning—and all the consequences of her decision to stay—would come soon enough.

Miles awoke twice in the night.

The first time, he'd reached for the woman in his bed on instinct, losing himself in her all over again. She'd been right there with him, touching him with the urgency of someone who didn't want to waste a second of this time together, as if she knew as well as he did that it wouldn't be repeated. The knowledge gave every kiss, every sigh a desperate need that only heightened how damned good it all felt.

The second time he'd opened his eyes, he'd felt her stirring beside him, her head tipping to his chest as if she belonged there. For some reason, that trust she would have never given him while awake seemed as much a gift as her body had been.

Another moment that he wouldn't be able to repeat.

So when daylight crept over the bed, he couldn't pretend that he felt no regrets. Not about what they'd shared, because Chiara cast a long shadow over every other woman he'd ever been with. No, he didn't regret what had happened. Only that the night was a memory now.

And that's what it had to remain.

He guessed Chiara knew as much, since the pillow next to his was empty. He heard the shower running and left some clothes for her in the dressing room outside the bathroom. The T-shirt and sweats with a drawstring would be huge on her, but a better alternative than her evening gown.

He grabbed cargoes and a Henley for himself before retreating to the pool to swim some laps and hit the shower there. Afterward he retreated to the kitchen to work on breakfast, making good use of the fresh tortillas from a local source his brother, Weston, had mentioned to him. While he and Wes had never been close, they shared a love for the food from growing up with their *abuela* Rosa's incredible cooking on Rivera Ranch. Miles scrambled eggs and browned the sausage, then chopped tomatoes and avocadoes. By the time Chiara appeared in the kitchen to help herself to coffee, the breakfast enchiladas were ready.

"Morning." She pulled down a mug from a hook over the coffee bar and set it on the granite. "I didn't mean to wake you."

At first look, there was something soft and vulnerable about her in the clothes he'd left for her. She'd rolled up the gray sweats to keep them from dragging on the floor; he saw she was wearing his gym socks. The dark blue T-shirt gaped around her shoulders, but she'd tucked a corner of the hem into the cinched waist of the sweats. Memories of their night together blindsided him, the need to pull her to him rising up again as inevitably as high tide.

Then she met his gaze, and any illusion of her vulnerability vanished. Her green eyes reflected a defensiveness that went beyond normal morning-after wariness. She appeared ready to sprint out of there at the first opportunity. Had her spying mission been a success the night before, so that she could afford to walk away from him now? He hadn't been aware that at least a part of him—and yeah, he knew which part—had hoped she'd stick around if she wanted to learn more about Mesa Falls.

Damn it. He needed to be smarter about this if he wanted to remain a step ahead of her.

"You didn't wake me," he finally replied as he grappled with how to put her at ease long enough to have a conversation about where things stood between them. "At home, I'm usually up before now." Gesturing toward the coffee station, he took the skillet off the burner. "Grab your cup and join me for breakfast."

He carried the dishes over to their place settings at the table for eight. The table felt big for two people, but he arranged things so he'd be sitting diagonally from her and could easily gauge her reaction to what he had to say.

Chiara bypassed the single-cup maker for the espresso machine, brewing a double shot. When she finished, she carried her mug over and lowered herself into one of the chairs.

"You didn't have to go to all this trouble." She held herself straight in the chair, her posture as tense as her voice.

What he couldn't figure out was why she was so nervous. Whatever preyed on her mind seemed weightier than next-day second thoughts. Was she thinking about whatever information she'd gleaned from his study during the party?

"It was no trouble." He lifted the top of the skillet to serve her. "Can I interest you in any?" At her hesitation, he continued, "I won't be offended either way."

Her eyes darted to his before she picked up her fork and slid an enchilada onto her plate. "It smells really good. Thank you."

He served himself afterward and dug in, debating how best to convince her to spend more time in Montana. He didn't want to leverage what happened between them unfairly—or twist her arm into keeping that date she'd promised him—but questions remained about what she was doing in his office the night before. If she knew about Zach, he needed to know how and why.

While he puzzled that out, however, Chiara set her fork down after a few bites.

"Miles, I can't in good conscience eat your food—which is delicious, by the way—when I haven't been honest with you." She blurted the words as if they'd been on the tip of her tongue for hours.

He slowly set aside his fork, wondering what she meant. Would she confess what she'd been doing in his office last night? Something else?

"I'm listening." He took in her ramrod-straight posture, the way she flicked a red-painted fingernail along the handle of the mug.

A breath whooshed from her lungs before she spoke again. "I'm an old friend of Zach Eldridge's." The name of his dead friend on her lips sent a chill through him. "I came here last night to learn the truth about what happened to him."

Four

Miles didn't remember standing up from the table, but he must have after Chiara's startling announcement. Because the next thing he knew, he was staring out the kitchen window into a side yard and the Bitterroot River meandering in a bed of slushy ice. He felt ice on the inside, too, since numbing his feelings about his dead friend had always been a hell of a lot easier than letting them burn away inside him.

Snow blanketed the property, coating everything in white. Spring might be around the corner, but western Montana didn't know it today. Staring at the unbroken field of white helped him collect his thoughts enough to face her again.

"You knew Zach?" It had never crossed his mind that she could have had a personal relationship with Zach even though he'd seen the search history on his computer. He'd assumed she'd heard an old rumor. If she'd known him, wouldn't she have come forward before now?

Zachary Eldridge had never talked about his life before his stint in a foster home near Dowdon School on the edge of the Ventana Wilderness in central California where the ranch owners had met. The way Zach had avoided the topic had broadcast all too clearly the subject was off-limits, and Miles had respected that. So he didn't think Chiara could have known him from that time. And he'd never heard rumors of her being in the foster system, making it doubtful she'd met him that way. Zach had been on a scholarship at their all-boys boarding school, a place she obviously hadn't attended.

"Dowdon School did events with Brookfield Academy." She clutched the espresso cup tighter, her gaze sliding toward the river-stone fireplace in the front room, though her expression had the blankness of someone seeing another place and time. Miles was familiar with the prestigious all-girls institution in close proximity to his alma mater. "I met Zach through the art program the summer before my sophomore year."

"You were at Brookfield?" Miles moved back toward the table, struggling to focus on the conversation—on her—no matter how much it hurt to remember the most painful time of his life. And yes, he was drawn to the sound of her voice and a desire to know her better.

He dropped back into his seat, needing to figure out how much she knew about Zach's death and the real motives behind her being in Mesa Falls all these years later.

"Briefly." She nodded her acknowledgment, her green eyes refocusing on him as he returned to the table. "I only attended for two years before my father lost everything in a bad investment and I had to leave Brookfield to go to public school."

Miles wondered why he hadn't heard of her connection to Zach or even to Brookfield. While he'd never sought out information about her, he would have thought her school affiliation would have been noted by the ranch's PR department when she was invited to Mesa Falls events.

Questions raced through his mind. How close had she been to Zach? Close enough to understand his mindset the weekend he'd died?

A hollow ache formed in his chest.

"How well did you know him?" He regretted the demanding sound of the question as soon as it left his lips, unsure how it would come across. "That is, I'm interested how you could make friends during a summer program. The school staff was strict about prohibiting visits between campuses."

Her lips quirked unexpectedly, her eyes lifting to meet his. "Zach wasn't afraid to bend rules when it suited him, though, was he?"

Miles couldn't help a short bark of laughter as the truth of that statement hit home. "'Rules are for people with conventional minds,' he once told me."

Chiara sat back in her chair, some of her rigid tension loosening as warmth and fondness lit her gaze. "He painted over an entire project once, just an hour before a showing, even though I was a wreck about him ruining the beautiful painting he'd done. He just kept slapping oils on the canvas, explaining that an uncommon life demanded an uncommon approach, and that he had all-new inspiration for his work."

The shared reminiscence brought Zach to life in full color for a moment, an experience Miles hadn't had in a long time. The action—and the words—were so completely in keeping with how he remembered his friend.

"He was a bright light," Miles agreed, remembering how often they'd looked up to his fearlessness and, later, stood beside him whenever he got into scrapes with schoolmates who weren't ready for the Zach Eldridges of the world.

"I never met anyone like him," Chiara continued, turning her mug in a slow circle on the table. "Not before, and not since." Halting the distracted movement, she took a sip from her cup before continuing. "I knew him well enough to have a crush on him, to the point that I thought I loved him. And maybe I did. Youthful romances can have a profound impact on us."

Miles searched her face, wondering if Chiara had been aware of Zach's sexual orientation; he'd come out to his friends the summer before sophomore year. Had that been why things hadn't worked out between them?

But another thought quickly crowded that one out. A long-buried memory from the aftermath of that dark time in Miles's life.

"There was a girl who came to Dowdon after Zach's death. Around Christmastime." He remembered her telling Miles the same story. She loved Zach and needed the truth about what had happened to him. But Miles had been in the depths of his own grief, shell-shocked and still in denial about the cliff-jumping accident that had killed his friend.

Chiara studied him now, the long pause drawing his awareness to a clock ticking somewhere in the house.

"So you remember me?" she asked, her words jarring him.

He looked at her face more closely as slow recognition dawned. He couldn't have stopped the soft oath he breathed before he spoke again.

"That was you?"

Chiara watched the subtle play of emotions over Miles's face before he reined them in, regretting the way she'd handled things even more than when she'd first awoken.

But she couldn't back down on her mission. She would have answers about Zach's death.

"Yes." Her stomach clenched at the memory of sneaking onto the Dowdon campus that winter to question Zach's friends. "I spoke to you and to Gage Striker fourteen years ago, but both of you were clearly upset. Gage was openly hostile. You seemed…detached."

"That girl couldn't have been you." Miles's jaw flexed, his broad shoulders tensing as he straightened in his chair. "I would have remembered the name."

Defensiveness flared at the hard look in his blue eyes.

"I was born Kara Marsh, but it was too common for Instagram, so I made up Chiara Campagna when I launched my career." Perhaps it made her sound like she'd hidden something from him, but her brand had taken off years ago, and she no longer thought of herself as Kara. Her family certainly hadn't cared, taking more of an interest in her now that she was famous with a big bank account than they ever had when she was under their roof saving her babysitting money to pay for her own clothes. "I use the name everywhere for consistency's sake. While I don't try to conceal my identity, I also don't promote it."

"Yet you kissed me. Spent the night."

Her gaze lingered on the black Henley he was wearing with a pair of dark brown cargo pants, the fitted shirt calling to mind the feel of his body under her hands.

"That wasn't supposed to happen," she admitted, guilt pinching harder at the accusation in his voice. "What took place between us was completely unexpected."

The defense sounded weak even to her ears. But he'd been there. He had to know how the passion had come out of nowhere, a force of nature.

The furrow in his brow deepened. "So you'll admit you were in my study last night, looking up Zach's name on my computer."

A chill crept through her. "You knew?" She bristled at the realization. "Yet you kissed me. Invited me to spend the night."

She parroted his words, reminding him he'd played a role in their charged encounter.

"You didn't clear the search history. A page of files with Zach's name on them was still open." He didn't address the fact that he'd slept with her anyway.

Because it hadn't mattered to him? Because *she* didn't matter? She stuffed down the hurt she had no business feeling, shoving aside the memories of how good things had been between them. She'd known even then that it couldn't last. She'd told herself as much when Miles had wrested a promise from her that he could have a date afterward. He wouldn't hold her to that now.

Steeling herself, she returned to her agenda. Her real priority.

"Then you know I'm desperate for answers." Regret burned right through all the steeliness. "I'm sorry I invaded your privacy. That was a mistake. But I've been digging for clues about Zach's death for fourteen years. Now that the media spotlight has turned to the Mesa Falls owners thanks to your connection to Alonzo Salazar, I saw a chance to finally learn the truth."

"By using your invitation into my home to spy on me," he clarified.

"Why wasn't Zach's death in the papers? Why didn't the school acknowledge it?" She'd searched for years. His death notice had been a line item weeks after the fact, with nothing about the person he'd been or how he'd died.

"You say you were friends with him, but I only have your word on that." Miles watched her suspiciously. Judging her? She wondered what had happened to the man she'd been with the night before. The lover who'd been so generous. This cold stranger bore him no resemblance. "How do I know this isn't another attempt by the media to unearth a story?"

"Who else even knows about him but me?" she asked, affronted. Indignant. "There was never a public outcry about his death. No demand for answers from the media. Maybe because he was just some foster kid that—"

Her throat was suddenly burning and so were her eyes, the old emotions coming back to surprise her with their force while Miles studied her from across the breakfast table. With an effort, she regained control of herself and backed her chair away from the table.

"I'd better go," she murmured, embarrassed for the ill-timed display of feelings. But damn it, Zach had deserved a better send-off. She'd never even known where to attend a service for him, because as far as she'd known, there hadn't been one.

That broke her heart.

Miles rose with her, covering her hand briefly with his.

"It was a simple question. I meant no offense." He shifted his hand away, but the warmth remained where his fingers had been. "We've safeguarded our friend's memory for a long time, and I won't relax my protection of him now. Not for anyone."

She tilted her chin at him, trying her damnedest to see some hint of warmth in that chilly facade.

"What memory?" she pressed. "He vanished without a trace. Without an opportunity for his friends to mourn him."

"His friends *did* mourn him. They still do." His expression was fierce. "We won't allow his name to be drawn into the public spectacle that Alonzo Salazar brought to the ranch because of that damned tell-all book."

"I would never do that to Zach." She hugged her arms around herself, recalling too late that she wore Miles's clothes. Her fingers rested on the cotton of his sweats. The scent of him. As if she wasn't feeling vulnerable already. "As for his friends mourning him, you weren't the only ones. There were a lot of other people who cared about Zach. People who never got to say goodbye."

For a long minute, they regarded each other warily in the quiet room, the scents of their forgotten breakfast still savory even though no food could possibly tempt her. Her stomach was in knots.

But even now, in the aftermath of the unhappy exchange, awareness of him lingered. Warmth prickled along her skin as they stood facing each other in silent challenge, reminding her of the heat that had propelled her into his arms the night before.

The chime of her cell phone intruded on the charged moment, a welcome distraction from whatever it was that kept pulling her toward a man who was determined to keep his secrets. He was as quick to seize on the reprieve from their exchange as she was. He turned toward the table to begin clearing away their half-finished meal.

She retrieved the device from where it lay on the table, checking the text while she carried her coffee cup to the sink. The message was from her assistant, Jules.

All your platforms hacked. On phone with IG now. Sent help notices to the rest. Some joker who didn't like a post? I'm on it, but knew you'd want heads-up.

She didn't realize she'd gone still until she heard Miles asking, "What's wrong?"

Her brain couldn't quite compute what was wrong. The timing of the attack on all her platforms at once seemed strange. Suddenly feeling a little shaky, she dropped into the closest seat, a bar stool at the island.

"Someone hijacked my social media accounts," she whispered, stunned and not buying that it was the work of a disgruntled commenter. "All of the platforms at once, which seems really unusual."

"Does that happen often?" Miles jammed the food in the huge refrigerator, working quickly to clean up.

"It's never happened before." She gulped back a sick feeling, tapping the tab for Instagram on her phone to see for herself. "I have friends who have had one platform hijacked here or there, but not all at once."

Miles dumped the remaining dishes in the sink and toweled off his hands before tossing the dishcloth aside. He rejoined her, gripping the back of her chair. "That feels like someone has an ax to grind."

The warmth of his nearness was a distraction she couldn't afford. She scooted forward in her seat.

"Someone with enough tech savvy to take over all my properties at once." She checked one profile after another, finding the photos changed, but still of her.

Less flattering images. Older images. But they weren't anything to be embarrassed about. She'd had friends whose profiles were hacked and replaced with digitally altered pictures that were highly compromising.

"Any idea who'd do something like that?" Miles asked, the concern in his voice replacing some of the animosity that had been there before. "Any enemies?"

"I can't think of anyone." She'd had her fair share of trolls on her account, but they tended to stir up trouble with other commenters as opposed to targeting her.

Her phone chimed again. She swiped the screen in a hurry, hopeful Jules had resolved the problem. But the text in her inbox was from a private number. Maybe one of the social media platforms' customer service used that kind of anonymous messaging?

She clicked open the text.

Today's takeover is a warning. Stay out of Zach's business or your accounts will be seriously compromised.

Her grip on the phone tightened. She blinked twice as the threat chilled her inside and out.

"Are you okay?" Miles touched her shoulder, the warmth of his fingers anchoring her as fear trickled through her.

"I've got to go." Shaky with the newfound realization that someone was keeping close tabs on her, she wondered who else could possibly know she was investigating Zach's death besides Miles.

She slid off the bar stool to her feet, needing to get back to her laptop and her assistant to figure out the extent of her cybersecurity problem. This felt like someone was watching her. Or tracking her online activity.

"You're pale as the snow." Miles steadied her by the elbow when she wobbled unsteadily. "What's going on?"

She didn't want to share what she'd just read with him

when he mistrusted her. When she mistrusted him. But his touch overrode everything else, anchoring her in spite of the hollow feeling inside.

"Look." She handed him her phone, unable to articulate all the facets of the new worries wriggling to life. "I just received this." Pausing until he'd had time to absorb the news, she continued, "Who else even knows about Zach, let alone what I came here for?"

His jaw flexed as he stared at the screen, stubble giving his face a texture she remembered well from when he'd kissed her during the night. She fisted her hands in the pockets of the sweatpants to keep herself from doing something foolish, like running an exploratory finger along his chin.

"I didn't think anyone else remembered him outside of my partners and me." He laid her phone on the kitchen island behind her. "As for who else knows why you came here, I can't answer that, as I only found out moments ago."

She hesitated. "You saw my attempt to check your computer last night. So you knew then that I had an interest. Did you share that information with anyone?"

A scowl darkened his expression.

"I texted Gage Striker about an hour into the party to ask how well he knew you, since I thought you'd been going through my files."

She shouldn't be surprised that Miles had as much reason to suspect her of hiding something as she'd had to suspect him. She'd recognized that they'd been circling one another warily the previous night before the heat between them burned everything else away. If anything, maybe it soothed her grated nerves just a little to know he hadn't been any more able to resist the temptation than she had.

"And Gage could have told any one of your other partners. They, in turn, could have confided in friends or significant others." Reaching back to the counter, she retrieved the cell and shoved it in the pocket of Miles's sweats. "So word could have spread to quite a few people by this morning."

"In theory," he acknowledged, though his voice held a begrudging tone. "But Gage didn't even put in an appearance at the party. So he wouldn't have been around anyone else to share the news, and I'm guessing he had something big going on in his personal life that kept him from attending."

"Maybe he needed to hire someone to hack all my accounts." She couldn't rule it out, despite Miles's scoff. Anger ramped up inside her along with a hint of mistrust. "But for now, I need to return to my hotel and do everything I can to protect my brand."

"Wait." He stepped in front of her. Not too close, but definitely in her path.

Her pulse quickened at his nearness. Her gaze dipped to the way the fitted shirt with the Rivera Ranch logo skimmed his broad shoulders and arms. Her mouth dried up.

Maybe he felt the same jolt that she did, because he looked away from her, spearing a hand through his hair.

"Let me drive you back," he told her finally. "Someone might be watching you. And until you know what you're dealing with, you should take extra precautions for your safety."

The thought of spending more time alone with this man was too tempting. Which was why she absolutely had to decline. Things were confused enough between them already.

"I'll be fine. My assistant will send a car and extra security." She withdrew her phone again—a good enough excuse to take her eyes off him—and sent the request. "I just need to get my dress and I'll be on my way."

Still Miles didn't move.

"Where are you staying?" he pressed. "You can't ghost me. You owe me a date."

"I think we both know that's not a good idea in light of how much things have gone awry between us." She couldn't believe he'd even brought it up. But perhaps he only wanted to use that time with her as a way to keep tabs on her while she sought the information he was determined to keep private.

"I still want to see you." He didn't explain why. "Where will you be?"

"I've been in a local hotel, but today I've got a flight to Tahoe to spend time with Astrid. I haven't seen her since she had the baby."

Jonah and Astrid had a house on the lake near a casino resort owned by Desmond Pierce, another Mesa Falls partner. Spending time with Astrid would be a way to keep an eye on two of the ranch owners while removing herself from the temptation that Miles presented just by being in the same town.

Even now, looking into Miles's blue eyes, she couldn't help recalling the ways he'd kissed and touched her. Made her fly apart in his arms.

For now, she needed to regroup. Protect her business until she figured out her next move in the search for answers about Zach.

"I don't suppose it's a coincidence that half of the Mesa Falls partners live around Tahoe," Miles observed drily. "Maybe I should go with you. No doubt we'll be convening soon to figure out who could be threatening you. Zach's legacy is important to us."

She shrugged, averting her eyes because she knew they'd

betray her desire for him. "You can look into it your way. I'll keep looking into it mine. But I don't think it's a good idea for us to spend more time alone together after what happened last night."

Just talking about it sent a small, pleasurable shiver up her spine. She had to hold herself very still to hide it. The least movement from him and she would cave to temptation.

"I disagree. And if we both want answers, maybe we should be working together instead of apart." His voice gentled, taking on that low rasp that had slid right past her defenses last night. "You wouldn't have checked my computer files if you didn't think I had information that could help you. Why not go straight to the source?"

For a moment, the idea of spending another day with him—another night—rolled over her like a seductive wave. But then she forced herself to shake it off.

"If you wanted to share information with me, you could tell me now." She put it out there like a dare, knowing he wouldn't spill any secrets.

He and his friends had never revealed anything about Zach. Not then. And not now. Because Miles was silent. Watchful. Wary.

Her phone chimed again, and she didn't need to check it to know her ride was out front.

"In that case, I'd better be going." She turned on her heel. "Maybe I'll see you in Tahoe."

"Chiara." He called her name before she reached the stairs leading back to the bedroom suite.

Gripping the wood rail in a white-knuckled grip, she looked over her shoulder at him.

"Be careful. We don't know who you're dealing with, but it could be someone dangerous."

The reminder brought the anxiety from earlier churning back. She tightened her hold on the rail to keep from swaying.

"I'll be careful," she conceded before stiffening her spine with resolve. "But I'm not backing down."

Five

Miles began making phone calls as soon as Chiara left. He poured himself a drink and paced circles around the indoor pool, leaving voice messages for Gage and Jonah. Then he tapped the contact button for Desmond Pierce, his friend who owned the casino resort on Lake Tahoe.

For fourteen years, the friends who'd been with Zach Eldridge when he died had kept the circumstances a secret. At first, they'd done so because they were in shock and grieving. Later, they'd remained silent to protect his memory, as a way to honor him in death even though they'd been unable to save him.

But if someone outside the six friends who owned Mesa Falls knew about Zach—about the circumstances that had pushed him over the edge that fateful day—then his secrets weren't safe any longer. They needed to figure out their next steps.

A voice on the other end of the phone pulled him from his thoughts, and he paused his pacing around the pool to listen.

"Hey, Miles," Desmond answered smoothly, the slot machine chirps and muted conversation of the casino floor sounding in the background. "What's up?"

"Problems." As succinctly as possible, he summarized the situation with Chiara and the threat against her if she kept looking for answers about Zach's death.

When Miles was done, Desmond let out a low whistle. The sounds of the casino in the background had faded, meaning he must have sought privacy for the conversation.

"Who else knows about Zach but us?" Desmond asked. "Moreover, who the hell would have known Chiara was asking questions within hours of her showing up at Mesa Falls?"

Miles stared out the glass walls around the enclosed pool, watching the snow fall as he let the question hang there for a moment. He was certain Desmond must have come to the same conclusion as him.

"You know it points to one of us," Miles answered, rattling the last of the ice in his drink. "I texted Gage last night when I thought she was snooping in my office."

He didn't want to think Gage would go to the length of hacking her accounts to protect their secrets, but every one of the partners had his own reasons for not wanting the truth to come to light. Gage, in particular, bore a weight of guilt because his influential politician father had kept the truth of the accident out of the media. Nigel Striker had made a substantial grant to the Dowdon School to ensure the incident was handled the way he chose.

Quietly. Without any reference to Zach's connection to the school. Which explained why Chiara hadn't been able to learn anything about it.

Desmond cleared his throat. "Gage could have shared that information with any one of us."

"I can't believe we're even discussing the possibility of a leak within our group." The idea made everything inside him protest. They'd spent fourteen years trying to protect the truth.

Who would go rogue now and break that trust?

"Just because we're discussing it doesn't prove anything," Desmond pointed out reasonably. "Chiara could have confided her intentions to someone else. Or someone could have tracked her searches online."

"Right. But we need to meet. And this time, no videoconferencing." He remembered the way the last couple of meetings had gone among the partners—once with only four of them showing up in person, and another time with half of them participating remotely. "We need all six of us in the same room."

"You really think it's one of us?" Desmond asked. Despite Desmond's normally controlled facade, Miles could hear the surprise in his friend's tone.

"I'm not sure. But if it's not, we can rule it out faster if we're together in the same room. If one of us is lying, we'll know." Miles might not have spent much time in person with his school friends in the last fourteen years, but their bond ran deep.

They'd all agreed to run the ranch together in the hope of honoring Zach's life. Zach had loved the outdoors and the Ventana Wilderness close to their school. He would have appreciated Mesa Falls's green ranching mission to protect the environment and help native species flourish.

"Do you need help coordinating it?" Desmond asked, the sounds of the casino again intruding from his end of the call.

"No. I think we should meet in Tahoe this time. But I wanted to warn you that Chiara is on her way there even now. She says she's going to see Astrid, but I have the feeling she'll be questioning Jonah, too. She might even show up at your office." Miles couldn't forget the look in her eyes when she'd said she wouldn't back down from her search for answers about Zach.

There'd been a gravity that hinted at the strong stuff she was made of. He understood that kind of commitment. He felt it for Rivera Ranch, the family property he'd inherited and would protect at any cost.

Of course, he felt that way about Zach and Mesa Falls, too. Unfortunately, their strong loyalties to the same person were bound to keep putting them at odds. Unless they worked together. The idea made him uneasy. But did he really have a choice?

The thought of seeing her again—even though she'd only walked out his door an hour ago—sent anticipation shooting through him. He'd never forget the night they'd shared.

"I'll keep an eye out for her," Desmond assured him. "Thanks for the heads-up."

Miles disconnected the call and pocketed his phone. He would hand off the task of scheduling the owners' meeting to his assistant, since coordinating times could be a logistical nightmare. But no matter how busy they were, this had to take priority.

Things were coming to a head for Mesa Falls. And Zach.

And no matter how much Miles didn't trust Chiara Campagna, he was worried for her safety with someone threatening her. Which would have been reason enough for him to fly to Tahoe at the first opportunity. But he also couldn't deny he wanted to see her again.

She'd promised him a date. And he would hold her to her word.

* * *

That night, in her rented villa overlooking Lake Tahoe, Chiara tucked her feet underneath her in the window seat as she opened her tablet. The nine-bedroom home and guesthouse were situated next door to Desmond Pierce's casino resort, assuring her easy access to him. The separate guesthouse allowed her to have her assistant and photo team members nearby while giving all of them enough space. Astrid and Jonah lived just a few miles away, and Chiara would see them as soon as she could. She'd already made plans to meet Astrid for a spin class in the morning.

This was the first moment she'd had to herself all day. First there'd been the morning with Miles, then the flight to Truckee and drive to Tahoe Vista, with most of the travel time spent on efforts to stabilize her social media platforms.

She should probably be researching cybersecurity experts to ensure her social media properties were more secure in the future, even though she'd gotten all of her platforms corrected by dinnertime. It only made good business sense to protect her online presence. But she'd spent so many years making the right decisions for her public image, relentlessly driving her empire to keep growing that she couldn't devote one more minute to work today. Didn't she deserve a few hours to herself now and then? To be a woman instead of a brand?

So instead of working, she thumbed the remote button to turn on the gas fireplace and dimmed the spotlights in the exposed trusswork of the cathedral ceiling. Settling back against the yellow cushions of the window seat, Chiara returned her attention to the tablet and found herself scrolling through a web search about Miles Rivera.

She'd like to think it was all part of her effort to find

out more about Zach. Maybe if she could piece together clues from the lives of his friends during the year of Zach's death, she would find something she'd overlooked. But as she swiped through images of Miles at the historic Rivera Ranch property in the Red Clover Valley of the Sierra Nevada foothills, pausing on a few of him at galas in Mesa Falls and at the casino on Lake Tahoe, she realized she had ulterior motives. Even on the screen he took her breath away.

He looked as at home in his jeans and boots as he did in black tie, and not just because he was a supremely attractive man. There was a comfort in his own skin, a certainty of his place in the world that Chiara envied. She'd been born to privilege as the daughter of wealthy parents, but she'd always been keenly aware she didn't belong. Her mother had never known what to do with her; she'd been awkward and gangly until she grew into her looks. As a girl, she'd been antisocial, preferring books to people. She'd lacked charm and social graces, a failure that confirmed her mother's opinion of her as a hopeless child. So she'd been packed off to boarding school on the opposite coast, where she'd retreated into her art until she met Zach, her lone friend.

Then Zach died, and her parents lost their fortune.

Chiara transferred to public school and made even fewer friends there than she had at Brookfield. She fit in nowhere until she founded her fictional world online. Her Instagram account had started as a way to take photos of beautiful things. That other people liked her view of the world had shocked her, but eventually she'd come to see that she was good at being social on the other side of a keyboard. By the time she gained real traction and popularity, her awkwardness in person didn't matter anymore. Her followers liked her work, so they didn't care if she said very little at public events. Fans seemed to equate her reticence with the aloofness they expected in a star. But inside, Chiara felt like a fraud, wrestling with impostor syndrome that she'd somehow forged an extravagant, envied life she didn't really deserve.

Her finger hovered over an image of Miles with an arm slung around his friend Alec Jacobsen and another around Desmond Pierce. It was an old photo, similar to the one she'd seen in Miles's office at his house. She thought it was taken around the time the six friends had bought Mesa Falls. She'd known even before she'd restarted her search for answers that the men who'd bought the ranch had been Zach's closest friends at Dowdon. One of them knew something. Possibly all of them. What reason would they have to hide the circumstances of his death?

She'd contacted his foster home afterward, and years later, she'd visited the department of social services for information about Zach. The state hadn't been under any legal obligation to release details of his death other than to say it was accidental and that issues of neglect in foster care hadn't been a concern. She'd had no luck tracking down his birth parents. But Miles knew something, or else he wouldn't have been so emphatic about protecting Zach's privacy.

Staring into Miles's eyes in the photograph didn't yield any answers. Just twenty-four hours ago, she'd been convinced he was her enemy in her search. Sleeping with Miles had shown her a different side of him. And reminiscing with him about Zach for those few moments over breakfast had reinforced the idea that he'd shared a powerful bond with their shared friend. What reason did Miles have to push her away?

When she found herself tracing the angles of his face

on the tablet screen, Chiara closed the page in a hurry. She couldn't afford the tenderness of feeling that had crept up on her with regard to Miles Rivera. It clouded her mission. Distorted her perspective when she needed to be clearheaded.

Tomorrow, she'd find a way to talk to Desmond Pierce. Then she'd see if Alec Jacobsen was in town. If she kept pushing, someone would divulge something. Even if they didn't mean to.

Turning her gaze to the moon rising over the lake through the window, she squinted, trying to see beyond her reflection in the glass. She needed to learn something before her anonymous blackmailer discovered she was still asking questions. Because while she was prepared to risk everything—the fame, the following, the income that came from it—to find out the truth of Zach's death, she couldn't help hoping Miles didn't have anything to do with it.

"Dig deep for the next hill!" The spin class instructor kept up her running stream of motivational commentary from a stationary bike at the center of the casino resort's fitness studio. "If you want the reward, you've got to put in the work!"

Chiara hated exercise class in general, and early-morning ones even more, but her friend Astrid had insisted the spin class was the best one her gym offered. So Chiara had pulled herself out of bed at the crack of dawn for the last two mornings. She'd dragged Jules with her, and Astrid met them there to work out in a room that looked more like a dance club than a gym. With neon and black lights, the atmosphere was high energy and the hip-hop music intense. Sweating out her restlessness wasn't fun, but it felt like a way to excise some of the intense emotions being with Miles had stirred up.

"I can't do another hill," Astrid huffed from the cycle to Chiara's right, her blond braid sliding over her shoulder as she turned to talk. A former model from Finland, Astrid had happily traded in her magazine covers for making organic baby food since becoming a mother shortly before Christmas. "You know I love Katja, but being pregnant left me with no muscle tone."

"I would have chosen the yoga class," Chiara managed as she gulped air, her hamstrings burning and her butt numb from the uncomfortable seat. "So I blame this hell on you."

"I would be *sleeping*." Jules leaned over her handlebars from the bike on Chiara's left, her pink tank top clinging to her sweaty shoulders. "So I blame both of you."

"Please," Chiara scoffed, running a skeptical eye over Jules's toned legs. "You were a competitive volleyball player. I've seen you play for hours."

Chiara's family had lived next door to Jules's once upon a time, and the Santors were more like family to her than her own had ever been. When her business had taken off, she'd made it her mission to employ as many of the family members as she could, enjoying the pleasure of having people she genuinely liked close to her. Even now, back in Los Angeles, Jules's mom was in charge of Chiara's house.

"Spiking balls and attacking the net do not require this level of cardio," Jules grumbled, although she dutifully kicked up her speed at their instructor's shouted command to "go hard."

Chiara felt light-headed from the exercise, skipping breakfast, and the swirl of flashing lights as they pedaled.

"We owe ourselves lunch out at least, don't we?" Astrid pleaded, letting go of her handlebars long enough to take a drink from her water bottle. "Jonah got us a sitter tomorrow for the first time since I had Katja, so I've got a couple of hours free."

"This is the first time?" Chiara asked, smiling in spite of the sweat, the aches and the gasping for air.

Astrid had been nervous about being a mom before her daughter was born, but she'd been adorably committed to every aspect of parenting. Chiara couldn't help but compare her friend's efforts with her own mother's role in her life. Kristina Marsh had handed her daughter off to nannies whenever possible, which might not have been a problem if there'd been a good one in the mix. But she tended to hire the cheapest possible household help in order to add to her budget for things like clothes and jewelry.

"I hate leaving her with anyone but Jonah," Astrid admitted, slowing her pedaling in spite of their coach's motivational exhortation to "grind it out."

"But I think it's important to have someone trained in Katja's routine in case something comes up and I need help in a hurry."

"Definitely." Chiara wasn't about to let her friend hover around the babysitter when she could get her out of the house for a little while. "Plus you deserve a break. It's been two months."

"That's what Jonah says." Astrid's soft smile at the thought of her husband gave Chiara an unexpected pang in her chest.

She hadn't realized until that moment how much she envied Astrid's rock-solid relationship with a man she loved and trusted. Chiara hadn't even given a second thought to her single status in years, content to pursue her work instead of romance when she had difficulty trusting people anyhow. And for good reason. Her family was so good at keeping secrets from her she hadn't known they'd lost everything until the headmistress at Brookfield told her they were sending her home because her tuition hadn't been paid in months.

Chiara shoved that thought from her head along with any romance envy. She cheered along with the rest of the class as the instructor blew her whistle to signal the session's end. Jules slumped over her handlebars as she recovered, clicking through the diagnostics to check her stats.

Chiara closed her eyes for a long moment to rest them from the blinking red and green lights. And, no surprise, an image of Miles Rivera appeared on the backs of her eyelids, tantalizing her with memories of their night together.

She could live to be a hundred and still not be able to account for how fast she'd ended up in his bed. The draw between them was like nothing she'd ever experienced.

Astrid's softly accented words broke into Chiara's sensual reverie.

"So where should we meet for lunch tomorrow?" The hint of Finland in Astrid's words folded "where" to sound like "vere," the lilt as attractive as every other thing about her. "Des's casino has a bunch of places."

Chiara's eyes shot open at the mention of Desmond Pierce, one of Miles's partners. She needed to question him and Astrid's husband, Jonah, too. Subtly. And, ideally, close to the same time so neither one had a chance to warn the others about Chiara's interest in the details of Zach's final days.

"The casino is perfect." Chiara slid off her cycle and picked up her towel and water bottle off the floor, locking eyes with another woman who lingered near the cycles—a pretty redhead with freckles she hadn't noticed earlier. Why did she look vaguely familiar? Distracted, she told Astrid, "Pick your favorite place and we'll meet there."

The redhead scurried away, and Chiara guessed she didn't know the woman after all.

"There's an Indo-Mexican fusion spot called Spice Pavilion. I'm addicted to the tikka tacos." Astrid checked her phone as the regular house lights came up and the spin class attendees shuffled out of the room. "Can you do one o'clock? Jonah has a meeting that starts at noon, so I can shop first and then meet you."

A meeting? Chiara's brain chased the possibilities of what that might mean while she followed Jules toward the locker room, with Astrid behind them.

"Perfect," Chiara assured her friend as they reached the lockers and retrieved their bags. "Is Jonah's meeting at the casino, too?"

"Yes. More Mesa Falls business," Astrid answered as she hefted her quilted designer bag onto one shoulder and shut the locker with her knee. "Things have been heating up for the ranch ever since that tell-all book came out."

Didn't she know it. Chiara had plenty of questions of her own about the ranch and its owners, but she'd tried not to involve Astrid in her hunt for answers since she wouldn't use a valued friendship for leverage.

But knowing that Zach's friends would be congregating at the resort tomorrow was welcome information.

"Then you can leave Jonah to his meeting and we'll gorge ourselves on tikka tacos," Chiara promised her, calling the details over her shoulder to Jules, who had a locker on the next row. "Today I'm going to finish my posts for the week, so I can clear the whole day tomorrow. Text me if you're done shopping early or if you want company."

If all the men of Mesa Falls were in town, there was a chance she'd run into one of them at the casino anyhow.

Desmond Pierce had been avoiding her calls, so she hadn't even gotten a chance to meet him. But she needed to speak to all of them.

Although there was one in particular she couldn't wait to see, even though she already knew he had nothing else to say to her on the subject of Zach's death.

Miles might be keeping secrets from her. And he might be the last man she'd ever trust with her heart because of that. But that didn't mean that she'd stopped thinking about his hands, his mouth or his body on hers for more than a few seconds at a time since she'd left Montana.

No doubt about it—she was in deep with this man, and they'd only just met.

Six

Steering his borrowed SUV around a hairpin turn, Miles pulled up to the massive lakefront villa where Chiara was staying for the week. He'd been in town for all of a few hours before seeking her out, but ever since he'd heard from Jonah that the place she'd rented was close to the casino where Miles was staying, he'd needed to see her for himself.

The property was brightly lit even though the sun had just set, the stone turrets and walkways illuminated to highlight the architectural details. Huge pine trees flanked the building, while a second stone guesthouse sat at an angle to the villa with a path linking them.

Stepping out of the casino's Land Rover that he'd commissioned for the evening, Miles hoped all the lights meant that Chiara was taking her security seriously. He'd kept an eye on her social media sites since she'd left Mesa Falls to make sure no one hacked them again, but that hadn't done nearly enough to soothe his anxiety where she was concerned. Someone was threatening her for reasons related to Zach, and that did not sit well with him. He'd messaged her earlier in the day to let her know he would be in town tonight, but she hadn't replied.

Now, walking up the stone path into the central turret that housed the front entrance, he tucked his chin into the collar of his leather jacket against the chill in the wind. He could see into one of the large windows. A fire burned in the stone hearth of a great room, but he didn't notice any movement inside.

He shot a text to Chiara to warn her he was outside, then rang the bell. No sense adding to her unease during a week that had already upset her.

An instant later, he heard a digital chime and the bolt sliding open, then the door swung wide. Chiara stood on the threshold, her long dark hair held off her face with a white cable-knit headband. She wore flannel pajama bottoms in pink-and-white plaid. A V-neck cashmere sweater grazed her hips, the pink hue matching her fuzzy socks.

She looked sweetly delicious, in fact. But his overriding thought was that she shouldn't be answering her own door while someone was watching her movements and threatening her. Fear for her safety made him brusque.

"What happened to taking extra precautions with your safety?" He didn't see anyone else in the house with her. No bodyguard. No assistant.

Tension banded his chest.

"Hello to you, too." She arched a brow at him. "And to answer your question, the door was locked, and the alarm system was activated." She stepped to one side, silently inviting him in. "I gave my head of security the evening off since I had no plans to go out."

Relieved she'd at least thought about her safety, he entered the foyer, which opened into the great room with its incredible views of the lake. He took in the vaulted ceilings and dark wood accents along the pale walls. The scent of popcorn wafted from deeper in the house, the sound of popping ongoing.

"Right. I realize the level of security you use is your own business, I've just been concerned." He noticed a throw blanket on the floor in front of the leather sofa. A nest of pillows had been piled by the fireplace, and there was a glass of red wine on the hearth. "Early night?"

"My job isn't always a party every evening, contrary to popular opinion." She hurried toward the kitchen, a huge light-filled space separated from the great room by a marble-topped island. "Have a seat. I don't want my popcorn to burn."

He followed more slowly, taking in the honey-colored floors and pale cabinets, the row of pendant lamps casting a golden glow over the island counter, where a popcorn popper quickly filled with fluffy white kernels. The excessive size and grandeur of the space reminded him they moved in very different circles. For all of his wealth, Miles spent most of his time on his ranch. His life was quiet. Solitary. Hers was public. Extravagant.

But at least for now, they were alone.

"I didn't mean to intrude on your evening." He had to admit she looked at home in her sprawling rented villa, her down-to-earth pj's and sweater a far cry from the metallic dress she'd worn to the ranch party. She seemed more approachable. "I'm in town to meet with my partners, and I wanted to make sure there have been no new incidents."

He lowered himself onto a backless counter stool, gladder than he should be to see her again. She'd been in his thoughts often enough since their night together, and not just because he'd been concerned about her safety. Her kiss, her touch, the sound of her sighs of pleasure had distracted him day and night.

"Nothing since I left your house. Can I get you a glass of wine?" she asked, turning the bottle on the counter. "It's nothing special, but it's my preferred pairing with popcorn."

Her light tone hinted she wanted to change the subject from the threat she'd received, but he was unwilling to let it go.

"No, thank you. I won't keep you long." He stood again, if only to get closer to her while she leaned a hip on the island.

The urge to pull her against him was so strong he forced himself to plant a palm on the marble countertop instead of reaching for her.

"Well, you don't need to fear for my safety. My assistant's boyfriend is also my bodyguard, and they're both staying in the guesthouse right on the property." She pointed out the window in the direction of the smaller lodge he'd seen close by. "I'm in good hands."

He'd prefer she was in *his* hands. But he ignored the need to touch her; he was just glad to hear she hadn't taken the threat lightly.

"Did you report the incident to the police?" His gaze tracked her emerald eyes before taking in her scrubbed-clean skin and high cheekbones. She smelled like orange blossoms.

"I didn't reach out to them." She frowned, folding her arms. "I was so busy that day trying to get all my social media accounts secured that I never gave it any thought."

He hated to upset her unnecessarily, but her safety was important to him. "You should let the authorities know you're being harassed. Even if they can't do anything to help, it would be good to have the episode on the record in case things escalate."

She mattered to him. Even when he knew that was problematic. She didn't trust him, and he had plenty of reason not to trust her. Yet that didn't stop him from wanting to see her again. He could tell himself all day it was because staying close to her would help him protect Zach's memory. But he wasn't that naive. The truth was far simpler. Their one night together wasn't nearly enough to satisfy his hunger for this woman.

"I'll report it tomorrow," she conceded with a nod, her dark hair shifting along her sweater. "I can head to the local station in the morning, before I have lunch with Astrid."

"Would you like me to go with you?" he offered, his hand leaving the marble counter to rest on top of hers. Briefly. Because if he touched her any longer, it would be damn near impossible to keep his head on straight. "Spending hours at the cop shop is no one's idea of fun."

A hint of a smile curved her lips. "I'll be fine," she insisted.

Refusing his offer, but not moving her fingers out from under his. He shifted fractionally closer.

Her head came up, her gaze wary. Still, he thought there might have been a flash of hot awareness in those beautiful eyes.

"What about the date you promised me?" He tipped up her chin to better see her face, read her expression.

She sucked in a quick breath. Then, as if to hide the reaction, she bit her lip.

He imagined the soft nip of those white teeth on his own flesh, a phantom touch.

"Name the day," he coaxed her as the moment drew out, the desire to taste her getting stronger with each passing breath.

"I told you that it's a bad idea for us to spend more time together," she said finally, not sounding the least bit sure of herself. "Considering how things spiraled out of control after the party at your house."

He skimmed a touch along her jaw, thinking about all the ways he hadn't touched her yet. All the ways he wanted to.

"I've spent so much time thinking about that night, I'm not sure I can regret it." His gaze dipped to the lush softness of her mouth. He trailed his thumb along the seam. "Can you?"

Her lips parted, a soft huff of her breath grazing his knuckle.

"Maybe not." She blinked fast. "But just because you successfully run into and escape from a burning building once doesn't mean you should keep tempting fate with return trips."

"Is that what this is?" He released her, knowing he needed to make his case with his words and not their combustible connection. "A burning building?"

"You know what I mean. We seem destined to be at odds while I search for answers about Zach. There's no point blurring the battle lines." She spoke quickly, as if eager to brush the whole notion aside so she could move on.

He hoped the hectic color in her cheeks was evidence that he affected her even a fraction of how much she tempted him. But he didn't want to press her more tonight for fear she'd run again. For now, he would have to content himself that she'd agreed to speak to the police tomorrow.

"Then we'll have to disagree on that point." He shoved

his hands in the pockets of the leather jacket he'd never removed. "The fact is, you owe me a date, and I'm not letting you off the hook."

Still, he backed up a step, wanting to give her space to think it over.

"You're leaving?" She twisted a dark strand of hair around one finger.

He would not think about how that silky hair had felt wrapped around his hand the night they'd been together. "You deserve an evening to yourself. And while I hope you'll change your mind about a date, I'm not going to twist your arm. I have the feeling we'll run across each other again this week since we have a common interest in Zach's story."

"Maybe we will." Her bottle-green eyes slid over him before she squared her shoulders and picked up her bowl of popcorn. "Good night, Miles."

He would have liked to end the night very differently, but he would settle for her roaming gaze and the memory of her biting her lip when they touched. Those things might not keep him warm tonight, but they suggested the odds were good of her landing in his bed again.

For now, that was enough.

So much for her relaxing evening in front of the fire with popcorn and a book.

Chiara couldn't sit still after Miles left. Unsatisfied desires made her twitchy and restless. After half an hour of reading the same page over and over again in her book, never once making sense of it, she gave up. She replaced the throw blanket and pillows on the sofa, then took her wine and empty popcorn bowl into the kitchen.

Even now, as she opened her laptop and took a seat at the

island countertop, she swore she could feel the place where Miles's thumb had grazed her lip. That, in turn, had her reliving his kisses and the way their bodies had sought one another's that night in Mesa Falls.

Could that kind of electrifying chemistry be wrong? She guessed *yes*, because she and Miles were going to be at odds over Zach. All the sizzling attraction in the world was only going to confuse her real goal—to honor Zach's memory by clearing away the mystery of his death.

But denying that she felt it in the first place, when she wasn't deceiving anyone with her protests, seemed foolish. Miles had surely recognized the attraction she felt for him. And yet he'd walked away tonight, letting her make the next move.

Instead of losing herself in his arms, she opted to search her files on Zach one more time. Checking her inbox, she noticed a retired administrator from Dowdon School had gotten back to her on an email inquiry she'd made long ago. Or, more accurately, the administrator's former assistant had responded to Chiara. She hadn't asked directly about Zach; instead, she'd asked for information about the school year when he'd died under the guise of writing a general retrospective for a class reunion.

Apparently, the assistant hadn't cared that she wasn't a former student. She had simply attached a few files, including some flyers for events around campus, including one for the art fair where Chiara had last seen Zach. There was also a digital version of the small Dowdon yearbook.

After saving all the files, she opened them one by one. The art fair poster brought a sad, nostalgic smile to her face but yielded no clues. Seeing it reminded her how much of an influence Zach had on her life, though, his eye for artistic composition inspiring her long afterward. Other pamphlets advertised an author visit, a homecoming dance in conjunction with Brookfield and a football game. She wrote down the email contact information for the dance and sent a message to the address, using the same pretext as before.

Pausing to sip her wine, Chiara swiped through the yearbook even though she'd seen it twice before. Once, as soon as it came out; she'd made an excuse to visit the Brookfield library to examine a copy since the school kept all the Dowdon yearbooks in a special collection. She only paged through it enough to know Zach hadn't been in there. No photo. No mention.

Like he'd never existed.

Then, a year ago, she'd seen Jonah's copy at Astrid's house and had flipped through. Now, she examined the content more carefully in the hope of finding anything she'd overlooked.

First, however, she searched for Miles's photo. He was there, alphabetized in his class year next to his brother, Weston Rivera. They weren't twins, but they were as close in age as nontwin siblings could be.

The Rivera men had been swoonworthy even then. Wes's hair had been longer and unruly, his hazel eyes mischievous, and his look more surfer than rancher. Miles appeared little changed since the photo was taken, beyond the obvious maturing of his face and the filling out of the very male body she remembered from their night together. But his serious aspect and set jaw were the same even then, his blue eyes hinting at the old soul inside.

Before she could stop herself, her finger ran over his image on the screen.

Catching herself in the midst of fanciful thinking, she dismissed the unfamiliar romantic notions that had somehow attached themselves to Miles. She navigated away from the student photos section to browse the rest of the yearbook while she nibbled a few pieces of cold popcorn.

Half an hour later, a figure caught her eye in the background of one of the candid group shots taken outdoors on the Dowdon soccer field. It was a young woman in a knee-length navy blue skirt and sensible flats, her blond hair in a side part and low ponytail.

An old memory bubbled to the surface of seeing the woman. And she was a woman, not a girl, among the students, looking more mature than those around her.

Chiara had seen her before. Just once. Long ago.

With Zach.

The thrill of discovery buoyed her, sending her mind twirling in twenty directions about what to do with the new information. Funny that the first person who came to mind to share it with was Miles.

Would he know the woman? She picked up her phone, seeing his contact information still on the screen since the last message she'd received had been from him, letting her know he was at her door. The desire to share this with him was strong. Or was it only her desire to see him again? The ache of seeing him walk out her door was still fresh.

With an effort, she set the phone aside.

As much as she wanted to see if Miles recognized the mystery woman, she acknowledged that he might not answer her truthfully. He'd made it clear he planned to keep Zach's secrets. That she couldn't trust someone who could turn her inside out with a look was unsettling.

Tonight, she would research all she could on her own. Tomorrow, she would meet Astrid for lunch and—with a little good luck in the timing department—maybe she could waylay Astrid's husband before he went into his meeting with the Mesa Falls partners.

All she wanted was a real, unfiltered reaction to the image of the woman she'd seen with Zach. Miles was too guarded, and he knew her motives too well. Perhaps Jonah wouldn't be as careful.

Intercepting one of the Mesa Falls partners before the meeting Astrid had mentioned proved challenging. Chiara arrived at the Excelsior early, but with multiple parking areas and valet service, the casino resort didn't have a central location where she could monitor everyone who entered the building. For that matter, having her bodyguard with her made it difficult to blend in, so she'd asked Stefan to remain well behind her while she scoped out the scene.

Chiara decided to surveil the floor with the prominent high-roller suite the group had used for a meeting a month ago when she had first started keeping tabs on them. She hurried up the escalator near a courtyard fountain among the high-end shops. Water bubbled and splashed from the mouth of a sea dragon into a marble pool at the base of the fountain, the sound a soothing murmur when her nerves were wound tight. The resort was already busy with tourists window-shopping and taking photos.

As she reached the second-floor gallery, she spotted Gage Striker entering the suite. The huge, tattooed New Zealander was too far ahead for her to flag his attention, but at least she knew she was in the right place. Maybe Jonah and Astrid would come this way soon. As she darted around a pair of older ladies wearing matching red hats, Chiara pulled her phone from her handbag shaped like a rose, wanting the device ready with the right screen to show Jonah the photo of the mystery woman.

A voice from over her right shoulder startled her.

"Looking for someone?"

The deep rasp that could only belong to Miles skittered along her nerve endings.

Her body responded instantly, thrilled at the prospect of this man's nearness. But she battled back those feelings to turn toward him coolly.

"You're not much for traditional greetings, are you?" She eyed his perfectly tailored blue suit, the jacket unbuttoned over a subtly pinstriped gray shirt with the collar undone. Her attention snagged on the hint of skin visible at the base of his neck before she remembered what she was saying. "Most people open with something like *hello*. Or *nice to see you, Chiara*."

A hint of a smile lifted his lips on one side as he stopped just inches from her. With any other man getting this close, Stefan might have come to her side, but her security guard had been at the party in Mesa Falls the night Chiara stayed with Miles. Stefan didn't intervene now.

"Maybe other people can't appreciate the pleasure I find in catching you off guard." Miles lingered on the word *pleasure*.

Or else she did. She couldn't be certain. She was too distracted by the hint of his aftershave hovering between them.

"I'm joining Astrid for lunch while Jonah attends another super-secret Mesa Falls meeting." She glanced at her nails and pretended to inspect her manicure. She'd far rather he think her superficial than affected by his nearness.

Miles studied her. Keeping her focus on her hands, she felt his gaze more than saw it. She wouldn't have a chance to speak to Jonah now. Not without Miles being present, anyway. While she considered her plan B, a group of women in tiaras and feather boas strolled past, with the one in the center wearing a pink sash that said, "Birthday Girl."

"How did it go at the police station?" Miles asked, his fingers alighting on her forearm to draw her farther from the thoroughfare that led to the second-floor shops.

There were two couches in front of the high-roller suite and a low, clear cocktail table between them. Miles guided her to the area between the couches and the door to the suite, affording them a little more privacy.

"I had some other things to take care of this morning, but I'll call after lunch." She'd been so consumed with finding out the identity of the woman in the yearbook photo, she'd forgotten all about reporting the harassment.

Miles frowned. "I can't in good conscience let you put it off. After the meeting, I'll take you myself."

She bristled at his air of command. "I don't need an escort. I'll take care of it."

He pressed his lips together, as if reining in his emotions for a moment before he spoke. "Remember when you told me you had to be a one-woman content creator, marketing manager and finance director?" He clearly recalled how she'd defended her hard work when he'd been dismissive of her job. "Why don't you let someone else give you a hand?"

His thoughtfulness, underscored by how well he'd listened to her, made her relax a little. "It does sound better when you say it like that," she admitted.

"Good. And this way, you can ask me all the questions you want about the meeting." He nodded as if the matter was settled.

"Any chance you'll actually answer them?" She wasn't

sure it was wise for them to spend more time alone together, but maybe she could find a way to ask him about the photo of the unidentified woman without putting his guard up.

"I've said all along we should be working together." He took her hand in his, holding it between them while he stroked her palm with his thumb. "Where should I look for you after I finish up here?"

Her breath caught from just that smallest of touches. Her heart pounded harder.

"Spice Pavilion," she answered, seeing Astrid and Jonah heading toward them out of the corner of her eye.

"I'll look forward to it." Miles lifted the back of her hand to his lips and kissed it before releasing her.

Skin tingling pleasantly, she watched him disappear into the high-roller suite and wondered what she'd just gotten herself into. She noticed his brother followed him a moment later, while Astrid and Jonah gave each other a lingering goodbye kiss nearby. The blatant public display of affection seemed all the more romantic considering the couple were new parents.

What would it be like to have that kind of closeness with someone day in and day out?

Not that she would be finding out. Although her recent night with Miles reminded her how rewarding it was to share passion, she owed it to Zach not to let the connection distract her from her goal. She would spend time with Miles because he was still her most promising resource for information. And despite the coincidental timing of the threats against her, she'd had time to realize Miles was too honorable a man to resort to those tactics. She was safe with him.

She just had to find a way to get him talking.

Seven

Restless as hell, Miles prowled the perimeter of the high-roller suite, waiting for the meeting to get underway. Weston and Desmond were deep in conversation on a curved leather sofa in the center of the room, while a server passed through the living area with a tray of top-shelf bottles. Gage stared down into the fire burning in a sleek, modern hearth, a glass of his preferred bourbon already in hand. A massive flat-screen television was mounted over the fireplace, but the display was dark. In the past, the group had used the screens to teleconference in the missing Mesa Falls owners, but today all were present in person. Even Jonah, the new father, and Alec Jacobsen, the game developer who spent most of his time globe-hopping to get inspiration for the complex world-building required for his games. The two of them lounged near the pool table.

On either side of the fireplace, windows overlooked Lake Tahoe, the clear sky making the water look impossibly blue. Miles paused by one of them, waving off the offer of a beverage from the bow-tied server. He'd need his wits sharp for his meeting with Chiara afterward.

Hell, maybe he needed to worry more about having his instincts honed for the meeting with his friends. The possibility of a traitor to their shared cause had kept him up at night ever since Chiara had been threatened. He'd never doubted the men in this room before. But who else even knew about Zach to make a threat like the one Chiara had received?

"Are we ready?" Miles stopped pacing to ask the question, his back to a mahogany bookcase. He wasn't usually the one to spearhead discussions like this, but today the need for answers burned hot. "I know you're all busy. The sooner we figure out a plan, the sooner we can all go home."

Desmond gave a nod to the server, who left the room quickly, closing the door to the multilevel suite behind her. As the owner of Excelsior, Desmond commanded the operations of the resort and served as their host when they met on the property.

Weston cleared his throat. "Can you bring us up to speed on what's happening?"

The fact that his brother was the first to respond to him surprised Miles given the enmity between him and Wes that had started when they'd been pitted against one another at an early age by their parents. The tension had escalated years ago when they'd briefly dated the same woman. But they'd made strides to put that behind them over the last year. Miles suspected Wes had mellowed since finding love with April Stephens, the financial investigator who'd discovered where the profits of Alonzo's book were going.

"Chiara Campagna has been digging around to find out how Zach died. She knew him in school," he told them bluntly, fisting his hands in the pockets of his pants as he tried to gauge the reactions of his friends. “She attended Brookfield before she became an internet sensation, and she met Zach through the school’s art program.”

There were no murmurs of reaction. The only sound in the room was the clink of ice cubes in a glass as a drink shifted. But then, they’d known the meeting was called to discuss this issue before walking in the door. So Miles continued.

“She wants to know the circumstances of Zach’s death, suspecting some kind of cover-up since there was no news released about it.” As he explained it, he understood her frustration. And yes, pain.

Just because she’d been a fifteen-year-old with a crush on a friend didn’t diminish their connection. He recognized the power and influence those early relationships could hold over someone.

Near the fireplace, Gage swore and finished his drink. His influential father had been the one to insist the story of Zach’s accident remain private. The gag order surrounding the trauma had been one more complication in an already thorny situation.

“But why now?” Alec asked, spinning a cue ball like a top under one finger while he slouched against the billiard table. He wore a T-shirt printed with shaded outlines of his most iconic game characters, layered under a custom suit jacket. “Zach’s been dead for fourteen years. Doesn’t it seem strange that she’s taken a renewed interest now?”

“No.” Gage stalked over to the tray the server had left on the glass-topped cocktail table and helped himself to another shot of bourbon, tattoos flashing from the cuffs of his shirtsleeves as he poured the drink. “Chiara told Elena that she’d given up searching for answers about Zach until the

Alonzo Salazar story broke at Christmas. With Mesa Falls and all of us in the spotlight, Chiara saw an opportunity to press harder for the truth."

Miles mulled over the new information about Chiara, interested in anything he could gather about the woman who dominated his thoughts. Elena Rollins was a lifestyle blogger who'd visited Mesa Falls to chase a story on Alonzo, but she'd ended up falling for Gage and had backed off. The two women had developed a friendship when Chiara had lent the power of her social media platform to bolster Elena's following.

"But that opportunity is going away now that we've given the public a story about where the profits from Alonzo's book went," Alec chimed in again, using his fingers to shoot the eight ball into a side pocket with a backspin. "Media interest will die out, and we'll go back to living in peace. No one needs to find out anything about Zach."

Even now, it was difficult to talk about the weekend that Zachary Eldridge had jumped to his death off a cliff into the Arroyo Seco River. The men in this room had once argued to the point of violence over whether Zach had planned to take his own life or it had truly been an accident. Eventually, they'd agreed to disagree about that, but they'd made a pact to keep their friend's memory away from public speculation. It had been tough enough for them to deal with the possibility that Zach had jumped to his death on purpose. The thought of dredging all that up again was…unbearable.

"Maybe. Maybe not," Miles returned slowly, turning it over in his head, trying to see what they knew from another angle. "But just because the public doesn't know about the mystery benefactor of the book profits doesn't mean we should just forget about him. We know the boy is thirteen years old puts his conception around the time of the accident. The last time we met, we were going to have a detective track the boy and his guardian."

He didn't remind them of the rest of what they needed to know—if there was a chance any of them had fathered the child.

Around the holidays, a woman had worked briefly at the ranch under the alias Nicole Smith and had claimed that Alonzo's book profits were supporting her dead sister's son—a boy born in a hospital close to Dowdon School seven and a half months after Zach's death. But before any of the ranch owners could speak to her directly, Nicole was abruptly fired. When they'd tried to track down the supervisor responsible for dismissing her, they learned the guy had quit the next day and didn't leave a forwarding address.

All of which raised uncomfortable questions about the integrity of the group in this room. Had one of them ordered the woman's dismissal? Had Nicole been too close to the truth—that Alonzo Salazar had been helping to support Nicole's nephew because he knew who'd fathered the boy? They'd learned that the woman's real name was Nicole Cruz, and they'd obtained some basic information about the boy, Matthew. But they were trying to find her to meet with her in person.

"I'm handling that." Weston sat forward on the couch to flick on the huge wall-mounted television screen controlled by a tablet in front of him. "A detective is following a lead to Nicole and Matthew Cruz in Prince Edward Island. He's supposed to land tonight to check out the address."

Wes flicked through a series of photos on his tablet that then appeared on the TV screen, images of Nicole and Matthew—neither of whom they recognized—followed by grainy security system footage from when Nicole had worked at the ranch, as well as some shots of the boy from his former school. The different angles didn't do anything to help Miles recognize the boy.

"With any luck, the detective finds them." Miles turned his attention back to his colleagues. "And brings them to Mesa Falls so we can speak to the guardian at length and request permission to run a DNA test on the boy."

"Right." Wes clicked to another slide labeled "instructions for obtaining DNA."

"In the meantime, I've sent you all the file and collection kits by courier service. Most of you have already submitted yours, but we still need samples from Gage and Jonah. I've got a shipper ready to take them before you leave the meeting today. Alonzo's sons have already provided samples."

The silence in the room was thick. Did Jonah or Gage have reasons for dragging their feet? It had taken Miles two seconds to put a hair in a vial and ship the thing out.

Jonah blew out a sigh as he shoved away from the pool table and wandered over to a piano in the far corner of the room. He plunked out a few chords while he spoke. "That's fine. But none of us is going to be the father. Alonzo would have never stood by idly and paid for the boy's education if any of us were the dad. He would have demanded we own up to our responsibility once we were old enough to assume that duty."

"Maybe he was a mentor to the boy's mother, and not the father," Gage mused aloud, not sounding convinced. "This kid might not have anything to do with us."

"Possibly," Wes agreed. "But the kid was important to Alonzo, and that makes him important to us. Let's rule out the more obvious connection first."

"Agreed." Miles met his brother's hazel eyes, trying to remember the last time they'd been on the same page about anything. "But the more pressing issue today is that Chiara's social media accounts were hacked and she received an anonymous text threatening more attacks if she kept pursuing answers about Zach's death."

Recalling that morning at his house, Miles felt anger return and redouble that someone had threatened her, a woman who'd gotten under his skin so fast he hasn't seen it coming. That it had happened while she was in his home, as his guest, only added to his sense of responsibility. That it could be one of his friends, or someone close to them, chilled him.

"Anyone remember her from when she attended Brookfield?" Gage asked as Wes switched the image on the screen to show a school yearbook photo of Chiara. "When she was known as Kara Marsh?"

Wariness mingled with suspicion as Miles swung around to face Gage. "You knew?"

He'd texted Gage that night to ask him what he knew about Chiara, and he'd never mentioned it.

"Not until two days ago." Gage held both hands up in a sign of his innocence. "Elena told me. She and Chiara have gotten close in the last month. Apparently Chiara mentioned she used to go by a different name and that none of us remembered her even though she attended a school near Dowdon. If she confided in Elena, she obviously wasn't trying to hide it. And Astrid must be aware."

Miles studied Gage's face but couldn't see any hint of falseness there. Of all of them, Gage was the most plainspoken and direct. The least guarded. So it was tough to envision the big, bluff New Zealander keeping secrets.

From across the room, Alec's voice sliced through his thoughts.

"I remember Kara Marsh." Alec's eyes were on the television screen. "She came to Dowdon that Christmas asking questions about Zach."

Of all the friends, Alec had been closest to Zach. After the accident, he had retreated the most. To the point that Miles had sometimes feared the guy would follow in Zach's footsteps. He'd wondered if they'd wake up one morning to find out Alec had stepped off a cliff's edge in the middle of the night. Alonzo Salazar had shared the concern, speaking privately to all of them about signs to look for when people contemplated suicide. Alec came through it, as they all had. They were good now. Solid. But it had been a rough year.

"Did you talk to her?" Miles asked, needing to learn everything he could about Chiara.

He'd called this meeting out of a need to protect Zach's memory. And yet he felt a need to protect Chiara, too. To find out if any of his partners were the source of the leak that led to Chiara's getting hacked. He'd been watching them all carefully, studying their faces, but he hadn't seen any hint of uneasiness in any one of them.

"No." Alec shook his head as he stroked his jaw, looking lost in thought before his gaze came up to fix on Miles. "But you did. She spoke to you, and then she went to Gage. I was hanging out under the bleachers near the football field with—" he hesitated, a small smile flashing before it disappeared again "—with a girl I knew. Anyway, I was there when I saw Kara sneak onto the campus through the back fence."

"You followed her?" Jonah asked, dropping onto the bench in front of the piano.

Alec shrugged, flicking a white cue ball away from him where he still leaned against the pool table. “I did. The girl I was with was in a snit about it, but I wanted to see what Kara was up to. Besides, in those days, I was more than happy to look for diversions wherever I could find them.”

They had all been emotionally wrecked during those weeks, not sleeping, barely eating, unable to even talk to each other since being together stirred up painful memories. Miles had thrown himself into work, taking a part-time job in the nearest town to get away from school as much as possible.

“Did Chiara see you?” Miles wished like hell he remembered that day more clearly.

“I don’t think so.” He spun the ball under one fingertip, seeming more engaged in the activity than the conversation. But that had always been his way. He had frequently disappeared for days in online realms as a kid and had used that skill as a successful game developer. “She looked nervous. Upset. I had the impression she was afraid of getting caught, because she kept glancing over her shoulder.”

Miles tried to conjure up a better picture of her from that day when she’d cornered him outside the library. Mostly he remembered that her voice had startled him because it was a girl’s, forcing him to look at her more closely since she’d been dressed the same as any of his classmates—jeans, loafers, dark jacket. The clothes must have been borrowed, because they were big on her. Shapeless. Which was probably the point if she wanted to roam freely among them.

Even her hair had been tucked half under a ball cap and half under her coat.

The memory of Chiara’s pale face the morning she’d received the threat returned to his brain, reminding him he needed to figure out who would threaten her. Clenching his fist, he pounded it lightly against the window sash before he spoke.

"Who else even knows about Zach?" he asked the group around him, the friends he thought he knew so well. "Let alone would feel threatened if his story came to light?"

For a long moment, the only sounds were the billiard balls Alec knocked against the rails and the sound of ice rattling in Gage's glass. The silence grated Miles's nerves, so he shared his last piece of important news to see if it got his friends talking.

"I'm taking Chiara to the police station after this to let them know about the threats she's receiving, so there's a chance we'll have to answer questions from the authorities about Zach." He knew it went against their longtime promise to protect their friend's memory. But her safety had to come first.

"You would do that?" Alec shook his head and pushed away from the pool table.

Desmond spoke at the same time. "The negative publicity around Mesa Falls is going to have consequences."

From his seat on the leather sofa, Wes shut down the television screen on the wall before he spoke.

"In answer to your question about who else would remember Zach, he was well-known at Dowdon. Teachers and other students all liked him. As for why someone wouldn't want his story to come out…" Wes hesitated, his hazel eyes flicking from one face to the next. "He had a past. And secrets of his own. Maybe we didn't know Zach as well as we thought we did."

That left the suite even quieter than before. Desmond

broke the silence with a soft oath before he leaned over and poured himself a drink from the tray in front of the couch.

The meeting ended with a resolution to convene the next day in the hope they got word from their investigator about Matthew and Nicole Cruz by then. As they began filing out of the suite, Alec and Jonah were still arguing about the idea that they didn't know Zach after all. Miles didn't stick around, not sure what he thought about the possibility.

For now, he needed to see Chiara.

Stalking out of the meeting room, he ran into a young woman hovering around the door. Dressed in leggings and high-top sneakers paired with a blazer, she didn't have the look of a typical casino guest. A red curl fell in her face as she flushed.

"Sorry. Is the meeting over?" she asked, pushing the curl away from her lightly freckled face. As she shifted, her blazer opened to reveal a T-shirt with the characters from Alec's video game. "I'm waiting for Alec—" She glanced over Miles's shoulder. "Is he here?"

Miles nodded but didn't open the door for her since his partners were still discussing Zach. "Just finishing up. He should be out in a minute. Do you work with Alec?"

She hesitated for the briefest moment, a scowl darkening her features, before she thrust out her hand. "I'm his assistant, Vivian Fraser."

Miles shook it, surprised they hadn't met before. "Miles Rivera. Nice to meet you, Vivian."

Politely, he moved past her, writing off the awkward encounter as his thoughts turned to Chiara.

He'd promised her a date, yes. And the drive to see her was stronger than ever after a meeting that had shaken his foundations. But more importantly, he had questions for her.

Questions that couldn't afford to get sidelined by their attraction, no matter how much he wanted to touch her again.

Chiara sent her bodyguard home for the day when she saw Miles approaching the restaurant. Astrid had departed five minutes before, after seeing Jonah's text to meet him in a private suite he'd taken for the rest of their afternoon together.

The new mother had seemed surprised, flustered and adorably excited to have her husband all to herself for a few hours. Chiara had felt a sharp pang of loneliness once she'd left, recognizing that she'd never felt that way about a man. The lack had never bothered her much. Yet between the incredible night she'd spent with Miles and seeing Astrid's happiness transform her, the universe seemed to be conspiring to make her crave romance.

So when Miles slowed his step near the hostess stand of Spice Pavilion, Chiara bristled with defensiveness before he'd even spoken. It didn't help that he was absurdly handsome, impeccably dressed and only had eyes for her, even though he attracted plenty of feminine attention.

"Hello, Chiara." He spoke the greeting with careful deliberation, no doubt emphasizing his good manners after she'd mentioned his habit of skipping the social niceties. "Did you enjoy your lunch?"

She'd been too preoccupied—and maybe a little nervous—about spending more time with him to eat much of anything, but she didn't share that. She rose from the bench where she'd been waiting, restless and needing to move.

"It's always a treat to see Astrid," she told him instead, her slim-cut skirt hugging her thighs as she moved, her body more keenly aware whenever he was near her. "But what about you? Have you eaten?"

She didn't know what went on behind closed doors during a Mesa Falls owners' meeting, but she couldn't envision some of the country's wealthiest men ordering takeout over a conference table. As they walked through the wide corridor that connected the shops to the casino, Chiara dug in her handbag for a pair of sunglasses and slid them into place, hoping to remain unrecognized. The casino crowd was a bit older than her traditional fan base, but she didn't want to risk getting sidetracked from her goal.

"I'm too keyed up to be hungry." Miles took her hand in his, the warmth of his touch encircling her fingers. "Let's take care of reporting the threats against you, and then we need to talk."

She glanced over at him, but his face revealed nothing of his thoughts.

"We're on the same page then." She kept close to him as he increased his pace, cutting through the crowd of tourists, gamblers and locals who visited the Excelsior for a day of entertainment. "Because I hardly touched my lunch for thinking about how much we needed to speak."

He slowed his step just long enough to slant her a sideways glance. "Good. After we take care of the errand at the police station, we can go to your house or my suite. Whichever you prefer for privacy's sake."

The mention of that kind of privacy made her remember what happened when they'd been alone behind closed doors at his home in Mesa Falls. But she agreed. They needed that kind of security for this conversation.

"You have a suite here?" she asked, her heartbeat picking up speed even though they were already heading toward the parking lot, where she guessed Miles had a car waiting.

She suddenly remembered Astrid's face when Jonah had texted her to meet him in a suite for the afternoon. Her friend had lit up from the inside. Chiara had the feeling she looked the exact same way even though her meeting behind closed doors with Miles had a very different purpose.

"I do." His blue gaze was steady as he stopped in the middle of the corridor to let a small troop of feather-clad dancers in matching costumes and sky-high heels glide past them. "Should we go there afterward?"

A whirlwind of questions circled beneath that deceptively simple one. Would she end up in his bed again? Did he want her there? But first and foremost, she needed to know what had happened at the meeting and if Miles had any ideas about who was threatening her.

So she hoped for the best and gave him the only possible response.

"Yes, please."

Eight

Filing a formal complaint with the proper authorities took more time than Chiara would have guessed, which left her more than a little frustrated and exhausted. She hitched her purse up on her shoulder as she charged through the sliding door of the local police station and into a swirl of late-afternoon snow flurries. The whole process had stretched out as Miles spoke to multiple officers at length, eliciting information on possible precautions to take to protect her.

Each cop they'd spoken to had been courteous and professional but not very encouraging that they would be able to help. With the rise of cybercrime, law enforcement was tapped more and more often for infractions committed online, but most local agencies weren't equipped to provide the necessary investigative work. The FBI handled major cases, but at the local level, the best they could do was point her in the direction of the appropriate federal agency, especially considering the threat had targeted Chiara's livelihood and not her person. Still, the importance of the case was increased by the fact that she was a public figure. She'd worked with the local police to file the complaints with the proper federal agencies, and they'd suggested she keep careful records of any problems in the future.

Bottom line, someone would look into it, but chances were good nothing more would come of it unless the threats against her escalated. And thanks to Miles, she wasn't handling this alone.

Chiara glanced back over her shoulder at him as he rebuttoned his suit jacket on their way out the door.

"Thank you for going with me." Chiara held the handrail as she descended the steps outside the municipal building almost three hours after they'd arrived. Her breath huffed visibly in the chilly mountain air as flurries circled them on a gust of wind. "I know it wasn't as satisfying as we might have hoped, but at least we've laid the groundwork if the hacker follows through on his threats."

"Or *her* threats," Miles added, sliding a hand under her elbow and steering her around a patch of ice as they reached the parking lot. "We haven't ruled out a woman's hand in this."

She pulled her coat tighter around her, glad for Miles's support on the slick pavement. The temperature had dropped while they were inside. Then again, thinking about someone threatening her business empire might have been part of the chill she felt. She'd given up her dream of becoming an artist to build the social media presence that had become a formidable brand. That brand was worth all the more to her considering the sacrifices she'd made for it along the way.

"Did you speculate about who might be behind the threats in your meeting today?" she asked, unwilling to delay her questions any longer as they reached his big black Land

Rover with snow dusting the hood. "You said you'd share with me what you discussed. And I know Zach's legacy is a concern for you and your friends."

Miles opened the passenger door for her, but before he could reply, a woman's voice called from the next row over in the parking lot.

"Chiara Campagna?"

Distracted, Chiara looked up before thinking the better of it. A young woman dressed in black leggings and a bright pink puffer jacket rushed toward them, her phone lifted as if she was taking a video or a picture.

Miles urged Chiara into the SUV with a nudge, his body blocking anyone from reaching her.

"We should have kept your bodyguard with us," he muttered under his breath as other people on the street outside the municipal building turned toward them.

"Can I get a picture with you?" the woman asked her, already stepping into Miles's personal space and thrusting her phone toward him as she levered between the vehicle and the open door. "I'm such a huge fan."

Chiara put a hand on Miles's arm to let him know it was okay, and he took the phone from the stranger. Chiara knew it might be wiser to leave now before the crowd around them grew, but she'd never been good at disappointing fans. She owed them too much. Yet, in her peripheral vision, she could see a few other people heading toward the vehicle. Impromptu interactions like this could be fun, but they could quickly turn uncomfortable and borderline dangerous.

"Sure," Chiara replied, hoping for the best as she tilted her head toward the other woman's, posing with her and looking into the lens of the camera phone. "But I can only do one," she added, as much for Miles's benefit as the fan's.

Miles took the shot and lowered the phone, appearing to understand her meaning as he met her gaze with those steady blue eyes of his. Without ever looking away from her, he passed the woman in the puffer jacket her phone.

"Ms. Campagna is late for a meeting," he explained, inserting himself between Chiara and the fan before shifting his focus to the other woman. "She appreciates your support, but I need to deliver her to her next appointment now."

He backed the other woman away, closing and locking the SUV's passenger door just in time, as two teenaged boys clambered over to bang on the vehicle's hood and shout her name, their phones raised.

The noise made her tense, but Chiara slid her sunglasses onto her nose and kept her head down. She dug in her bag for her own phone, hoping she wouldn't need to call Stefan for assistance. She'd been in situations with crowds that had turned aggressive before, and the experiences had terrified her. She knew all too well how fast things could escalate.

But a moment later, the clamor outside the SUV eased enough for Miles to open the driver's door and slide into his own seat. She peered through the windshield then, spotting a uniformed police officer disbanding the gathering onlookers who had quickly multiplied in number. The teenaged boys were legging it down the street. The woman in the puffer jacket was showing her phone to a group of other ladies, gesturing excitedly with her other hand. People had gathered to see what was happening, stepping out of businesses in a strip mall across the parking lot.

"I'm sorry about that." Miles turned on the engine and backed out of the parking space. He gave a wave to the officer through the windshield. "Does that happen often?"

"Not lately," she admitted, shaken at the close call. "I've

gotten better in the last year about wearing hats and sunglasses, keeping security near me, and having my outings really scripted so that I'm never in public for long."

She'd been so distracted ever since spending the night with Miles that she was forgetting to take precautions. She pressed farther back in her seat, ready to retreat from the world.

"That doesn't sound like a fun way to live." He steered the vehicle out of the parking lot and started driving away from town. "And now that news of your presence here has no doubt been plastered all over the web, I'd like to take you to the villa you rented instead of the resort. It will be quieter there."

"That's fine." She appreciated the suggestion as the snow began falling faster. "I'll message Stefan—he's my head of security—and ask him to bring in some more help for the rest of my stay."

"Good." Miles nodded his approval of the plan, his square jaw flexing. "Until we find out who's been threatening you, it pays to take extra safety measures."

She drew a deep breath, needing to find a way to reroute this conversation. To return to her goal for this time with Miles, which was to learn more about what happened to Zach. But she hadn't quite recovered from the near miss with fans who could turn from warmhearted supporters to angry detractors with little to no warning. It only took a few people in a crowd to change the mood or to start shoving.

"Or…" Miles seemed to muse aloud as he drove, the quiet in the car all the more pronounced as they left the more populated part of the lakeshore behind them.

When he didn't seem inclined to finish his thought, Chiara turned to look at him again, but she couldn't read his expression, which veered between a frown and thoughtful contemplation.

"Or what?" she prodded him, curious what was on his mind.

"I was just going to say that if you decide at any time you would prefer more seclusion, my ranch in the Sierra Nevada foothills is open to you." He glanced her way as he said it.

"Rivera Ranch?" She knew it was his family seat, the property he invested the majority of his time in running.

The invitation surprised her. First of all, because Miles seemed like an intensely private man, the most reserved of the Mesa Falls owners. He didn't strike her as the kind of person to open his home to many people. Secondly, she wouldn't have guessed that she would rank on the short list of people he would welcome.

"Yes." His thumbs drummed softly against the steering wheel. "It's remote. The property is gated and secure. You'd be safe there."

"Alone?" The word slipped out before she could catch it.

"Only if you chose to be. I'm happy to escort you. At least until you got settled in."

The offer was thoughtful, if completely unexpected. Still, it bore consideration if the threats against her kept escalating.

"I hope it doesn't come to that," she told him truthfully. "But thank you."

"Just remember you have options." He turned on the long private drive that led to her villa on the lake. "You're not in this alone."

She was tempted to argue that point. To tell him she felt very much alone in her quest to learn more about Zach since Miles refused to talk about their mutual friend. But he was here with her now. And he'd said they needed to help each other. Maybe he was ready to break his long silence at last.

Yet somehow that seemed less important than the prospect of spending time alone with this man who tempted her far too much.

Miles recognized the couple waiting in front of Chiara's villa as he parked the vehicle. The tall, athletic-looking brunette was Chiara's assistant, and the burly dude dressed all in black had been Chiara's bodyguard the night of the party at Mesa Falls Ranch. The two held hands, wearing matching tense expressions. They broke apart when Miles halted the vehicle but still approached the passenger door as a team.

"They must have seen photos from the police department parking lot online." Chiara sighed in frustration as she unbuckled her seat belt and clutched her handbag. "I'll just need a minute to bring them up to speed."

"Of course." Miles nodded at the muscle-bound man who opened Chiara's door for her. "Take your time. I'll check out your lake view to give you some privacy."

"That's not necessary," she protested, allowing her bodyguard to help her down from the vehicle.

Opening his own door, Miles discovered the tall assistant was waiting on his side of the Land Rover. Meeting her brown eyes, he remembered her name from the party at Mesa Falls.

"Hi, Jules," he greeted the woman, who had to be six feet tall even in her flat-soled running shoes. She wore a sweater and track pants, seemingly unconcerned with the cold. "Nice to see you again."

"You, too." She gave him a quick smile, but it was plain she had other things on her mind. A furrow between her brows deepened before she lowered her voice to speak to him quietly. “I wanted to warn you that while you were out with Chiara today, you attracted the interest of some of her fans.”

“Should I be concerned?” He stepped down to the pavement beside her while, near the rear of the SUV, Chiara related the story of what happened at the police department to her security guard.

“Not necessarily.” Jules hugged her arms around her waist, breathing a white cloud into the cold air. “But since Chiara’s fan base can be vocal and occasionally unpredictable, you should probably alert your PR team to keep an eye on the situation.”

“I’m a rancher,” he clarified, amused. He stuffed his hands in his pockets to ward off the chill of the day. “I don’t have a PR team.”

“Mesa Falls has a dedicated staffer,” she reminded him, switching on the tablet she was holding. A gust of wind caught her long ponytail and blew it all around her. “I remember because I dealt with her directly about the party at your place. Would you like me to contact her about this instead?”

Puzzled, Miles watched the woman swipe through several screens before pausing on an avatar of the Montana ranch.

“Just what do you think could happen?” he asked her, curious about the potential risks of dating someone famous.

If, in fact, what they were doing together could even be called dating. His gaze slanted over to Chiara, who was heading toward the front door of the villa, flashes of her long legs visible from the opening of her coat. He realized he wanted more with her. At very least, he wanted a repeat of their incredible night together. Preferably, he wanted many repeats of that night.

Beside him, Chiara's assistant huffed out a sigh that pulled him back to their conversation.

"Anything could happen," Jules told him flatly as she frowned. "You could become a target for harassment or worse. Your home address could be made public, and you could find yourself or your family surrounded in your own home. Your business could be boycotted if Chiara's fans decide they don't like you. People have no idea how brutal it can be in the public eye."

She sounded upset. Miles wondered what kinds of things Chiara had weathered in the past because of her fame.

He felt his eyebrows rise even as the idea worried him more for Chiara's sake than his own. "I appreciate the warning. If you don't mind sending a message to the Mesa Falls publicity person, I'd appreciate it."

"Of course." She nodded, tapping out some notes on her tablet even as snowflakes fell and melted on the screen. "And you should consider security for yourself once you leave the villa. At least for the next week or so until we know how the story plays out."

"I'll consider it," he assured her, sensing it would be better to placate her for now, or until he had a better handle on the situation for himself. He didn't want to rile Chiara's assistant when the woman already seemed upset. "Did today's incident cause problems for you?"

Jules shoved her tablet under her arm again. "For me personally? Not yet. But having her photographed in front of a police station is already causing speculation that we'll have to figure out how to address."

He nodded, beginning to understand how small missteps like today could have a big impact on Chiara's carefully planned public image. "I should have taken steps to ensure she wasn't recognized."

A wry smile curved the woman's lips. "Bingo."

"I can't fix what already happened today, but I can promise I'll take better care of her in the future," he assured the woman, gesturing her toward the house.

Jules pivoted on the heel of her tennis shoe and walked with him toward the stone steps at the side entrance. "If she keeps you around, I would appreciate that."

Miles chucked softly as he opened the front door for her. "Do you think my days are numbered with her after this?"

"No. Well, not because of today. But Chiara is notoriously choosy when it comes to the men in her life." She lowered her voice as they crossed the threshold of the huge lakefront house.

From the foyer, Miles could see Chiara standing with her bodyguard in the kitchen. Behind her, the setting sun glittered on the lake outside the floor-to-ceiling windows.

"That's a good thing." Miles was damned choosy himself. Until Chiara, he hadn't let any woman close to him for more than a night ever since he'd accidentally ended up dating the same woman as his brother. "I admire a woman with discriminating taste."

Jules laughed. "Then maybe you two have more in common than I would have guessed. I've worked with Chiara for three years, and you're the first man she's ever changed her schedule for."

He wanted to ask her what she meant by that, but as soon as the words were out, Chiara entered the foyer alone. Something about the way she carried herself told him she was upset. Or maybe it was the expression on her face, the worry in her eyes. And damned if he hadn't spent enough time studying her to recognize the subtle shift of her moods.

"Jules." Chiara still wore her long coat, her arms wrapped around herself as if she was chilled. "Stefan went out the back to the guesthouse, but he said he'll meet you out front if you still want to head into town."

Jules looked back and forth between them, but then her attention locked in on Chiara, perhaps seeing the same stress that Miles had noted. Jules stroked her friend's hair where it rested on her shoulder. "I don't want to go anywhere if you need me."

Miles wondered if he'd missed something. If the photos online were a bigger deal than he was understanding. Or was it his presence causing the added stress?

"I can take off if this is a bad time," he offered, unwilling to stay if they needed to take care of other things. He'd come a long way from the guy who'd written off Chiara's job as glorified partying, but no doubt he still didn't understand the nuances of her work, let alone the ramifications of the day's unexpected encounter with her fans.

Chiara's green eyes lifted to his. "No. I'd like to talk." Then she turned to her assistant and squeezed Jules's hand. "I'm fine. But thank you. I want you to have fun tonight. You work too hard."

"It never feels like work for me when we're hanging out," the other woman insisted before she gave a nod. "But if you're sure you don't mind—"

"I insist." Chiara walked toward the oversize door with her. "Stefan already has two guards watching the house tonight, and Miles will be here with me for a few more hours."

He couldn't help but hope that boded well for their evening together. Although maybe Chiara was just trying to soothe her friend's anxiety about leaving her.

In another moment, Jules departed, and the house was vacant except for the two of them. The sound of the door shutting echoed from the cathedral ceiling in the foyer. Chiara took a moment to check that the alarm reset before she turned toward him again.

"May I take your coat?" he asked, moving closer to her.

Wanting to touch her, yes. But wanting to comfort her, too.

She looked down at what she was wearing and shook her head, clearly having forgotten that she'd left her coat on.

"Oh. Thank you." She sucked in a breath as he stepped behind her and rested his hands on her shoulders for a moment. "I think I got a chill while we were out."

"Or maybe it's the combination of dealing with the threats, the police and the work crisis that seems to have snowballed from having our photo taken today." He took hold of the soft wool and cashmere cloak and helped her slide it from her arms.

The movement shifted her dark waves of hair and stirred her citrusy scent. He breathed it in, everything about her affecting him. As much as he wanted to turn her toward him and kiss her, he realized he wanted to ease her worries even more. So after hanging the coat on a wooden peg just inside the mudroom off the foyer, he returned to her side, resting his hand lightly on her spine to steer her toward the living room.

"You're probably right. The police station visit would have been daunting enough without the drama afterward." She shivered and hugged her arms tighter around herself.

Miles led her to the sofa, moving aside a throw pillow to

give her the comfortable corner seat. Then he pulled a plush blanket off the sofa back and draped it around her before finding the fireplace remote and switching on the flames. The blinds in the front room were already drawn, but he pulled the heavy curtains over them, too.

Then he took a seat on the wide ottoman, shoving aside a tray full of design books and coasters to make more room.

"May I take these off for you?" He gestured toward the high leather boots she was still wearing.

Her lips lifted on one side. "Really?" A sparkle returned to her green eyes, a flare of interest or anticipation. At least, he hoped that's what it was. "If you don't mind."

"I want to make you comfortable. And I don't want you to regret sending away your friends tonight." He lowered the zipper on the first boot, reminding himself he was only doing this to help her relax. Not to seduce her.

Although skimming his hand lightly over the back of her calf as he removed the boot was doing a hell of a job of seducing *him*.

"I won't." Her gaze locked on his hands where he touched her. "I've been anxious to talk to you all day."

The reminder that this wasn't a real date came just in time as Miles eased off the second boot. Because he'd been tempted to stroke back up her leg to her knee.

And linger there.

Even now, the hem of her skirt just above her knee was calling to him. But first, they needed to address the topic he'd avoided for fourteen years.

Damn it.

With an effort, he set aside her footwear and released her leg. Then he took the seat next to her on the couch.

"Okay." He braced himself, remembering that his friends

hadn't been any help today. It was time to break the silence. "Let's talk."

"I have a question I've been wanting to ask you." Reaching beneath the blanket, Chiara shifted to gain access to a pocket on the front of her houndstooth skirt. She withdrew a piece of paper and smoothed it out to show him a grainy photo. "Do you know who this is, Miles?"

He glanced down at the photo, and passion faded as suspicion iced everything he'd been feeling. Apparently Chiara wasn't stopping her quest for answers about Zach. Because the face staring back at Miles from the image was someone he and Zach had both known well. And he couldn't begin to guess why Chiara wanted to know about her.

Nine

Chiara didn't miss the flare of recognition in Miles's eyes as he looked at the yearbook photo.

"You're pointing at this woman in the background?" he asked, stabbing the paper with his index finger.

"The one with the side part and the navy blue skirt," she clarified. "She doesn't look like a student."

"She wasn't. That's Miss Allen, one of the student teachers at Dowdon." He met her gaze as he smiled. "Lana Allen. We were all a little in love with her."

"A teacher?" Shock rippled through her, followed by cold, hard dread. "Are you sure? She's not in the yearbook anywhere else. How old do you think she was?"

Miles must have read some of her dismay, because his expression went wary. He tensed beside her on the sofa.

"There was major backlash about her being at our school since she was just nineteen herself. She didn't stay the full year at Dowdon after one of the administrators complained she was a distraction. She worked with Alonzo Salazar briefly during the fall semester and then she was gone—" His jaw flexed as if mulling over how much to say. "Before Christmas break. Why?"

Her stomach knotted at the implications of what this new revelation meant. She hoped it wasn't a mistake to confide in him. But if one of them didn't take the leap and start sharing information, they'd never figure out who was harassing her or what it had to do with Zach.

Taking a deep breath, she sat up straighter and told him. "I saw Zach kissing her. As in a real, no-holds-barred, passionate kiss."

Miles shook his head then gripped his temples between his thumb and forefinger, squeezing. "Impossible. It must have been someone else."

"No." She was certain. How many times had she relived that moment in her mind over the years? "Miles, I had the biggest crush on him. I followed him around like the lovesick teenager I was, just hoping for the chance to talk to him alone. I never would have mistaken him for someone else."

"Then you're confused about her," he insisted. "It was a long time ago, Chiara, how can you be sure—"

"I picked her face out of the background crowd in this photo just like that." She snapped her fingers. "The memory has been burned into my brain for fourteen years, because it broke my heart to see that Zach already had a girlfriend."

"She couldn't have been his girlfriend—"

"His romantic interest, then," she amended, staring into the flames flickering in the fireplace as she tucked her feet beneath her and pulled the plush throw blanket tighter around her legs. "Or hers, I guess, since she was a legal adult by then and he was still technically a kid." The woman had no business touching a student, damn it. The idea made her ill.

"Zach was older than us—seventeen when he died. But obviously that doesn't excuse her. If anything, the relationship gives a probable cause for Zach's unhappiness before he died." His scowl deepened.

A fresh wave of regret wrenched her insides at the thought of Zach hurting that much. "I saw them together at the art show where Zach and I were both exhibiting work. I couldn't find him anywhere, so I finally went outside looking for them, and they were hidden in one of the gardens, arms wound around each other—"

She broke off, the memory still stinging. Not because of the romantic heartbreak—she'd gotten over that in time. But she'd left the art show after that, turning her back on Zach when he'd called after her. Little did she know she'd never see him again. Remembering that part still filled her with guilt.

Miles studied her face, seeming content to wait for her to finish, even as he saw too much. When she didn't speak, he reached between them to thread his fingers through hers. The warmth of his touch—the kindness of it—stole her breath. He'd been an anchor for her on a hard day, and she didn't have a chance of refusing the steadiness he offered.

"Okay. Assuming you're correct, why would Zach tell us he was gay if he wasn't?"

"He might have been confused. Fourteen years ago there wasn't as much discussion about sexuality, so he could have misidentified himself." Although he'd always seemed so sure of himself in other ways… She remembered how mature Zach had been. "Or maybe he thought he was protecting her—misdirecting people so no one suspected their relationship."

Miles seemed to consider this for a moment.

"But he told us over the summer," Miles argued. "We had a group video call before the semester even started, and he told us then."

"Zach and I were both at school all summer," she reminded him. "For our art program. Lana Allen could have been around Dowdon during the summer months, too."

Miles swore softly under his breath, and she wondered if that meant he was conceding her point. He dragged a hand over his face and exhaled as he turned to look her in the eye. His thigh grazed her knee where her legs were folded beneath her, the contact sizzling its way up her hip.

"This is huge." He squeezed her palm, his thumb rubbing lightly over the back of her hand. "It changes everything."

"How so?" She went still, hoping he was finally going to trust her enough to share the truth about Zach's death.

He looked uneasy. Then, taking a deep breath, he said, "For starters, I think Zach might have a son."

The news was so unexpected it took her a moment to absorb what he was saying.

"By this woman?" she wondered aloud, doing the math in her head. Zach had been seventeen at the time, and he'd died fourteen years ago. His son would be at least thirteen by now. "Why? Have you seen her?"

"No." Releasing her hand, Miles rose to his feet as if seized by a new restless energy. He massaged the back of his neck while he paced the great room. When he reached the windows overlooking the mountains, he pivoted hard on the rug and stalked toward her again. "A woman came to Mesa Falls a few months ago claiming to have custody of her sister's child—a thirteen-year-old boy of unknown paternity. The mother died suddenly of an aneurysm and had never told anyone who the father was."

Chiara hugged herself as she focused on his words. "And that's the child you think could be Zach's son?"

He nodded. "The woman claimed the kid's upbringing was being funded by profits from *Hollywood Newlyweds.* At the time, we wondered if the child could have been one of ours, since Alonzo had helped us all through the aftermath of Zach's death. He was a mentor for all of us."

She covered her lips to smother a gasp of surprise as new pieces fell into place. The news that a private school English teacher had been the pseudonymous author behind *Hollywood Newlyweds* had been splashed everywhere over Christmas, sending tabloid journalists scrambling to piece together why the author had never taken credit for the book before his death. It made sense to her that he would keep it a secret if he was using the profits to help Zach's son.

Aloud, she mused, "You think Salazar knew about Zach's son and was trying to funnel some funds to the mother to help raise the baby?"

"Since Lana Allen was his student teacher, maybe he discovered the affair at some point. Although if he knew and didn't report her to the authorities—*hell*. Maybe he felt guilty for not intervening sooner." Miles stopped at the other end of the great room, where Chiara had left her sketchbook. He traced a finger over the open page. "It's all speculation, but you can see where I'm going with this."

Her mind was spinning with the repercussions of the news, and she wasn't sure what it meant for the friends Zach had left behind. For her. For Miles. And all the other owners of Mesa Falls Ranch. Was this the secret her hacker was trying to steer her away from finding? And if so, why?

Needing a break from the revelations coming too fast to process, she slid off her throw blanket and rose to join Miles near the table that held her sketchbook. For the moment, it felt easier to think about something else than to wade through what she'd just learned.

So instead, she wondered what he thought of her drawings. She couldn't seem to give up her love of art even though she'd ended up working in a field that didn't call for many of the skills she wished she was using.

Yet another question about Zach's son bubbled to the surface, and she found herself asking, "Where is the boy now? And the woman who is guarding him—his aunt? She might have the answers we need."

Miles spoke absently as he continued to peruse the sketches. "We have a private detective following a lead on them now. We discussed this at yesterday's meeting, but I don't know if the lead panned out yet." He pulled his attention away from her drawings to meet her gaze. "These are yours?"

She suspected he needed a break from the thoughts about Zach as much as she did.

"Yes." Her gaze followed the familiar lines of pencil drawings from long ago. She'd been carrying around the sketchbook ever since her days at Brookfield, hoping that seeing the drawings now and then would keep her focused on her quest to find out what happened to Zach. Seeing them now helped her to say to Miles, "You're welcome to look at them, but I wish you'd tell me about the day Zach died. I know you were with him."

She'd learned long ago that the Mesa Falls Ranch owners had all been on a horseback riding trip that weekend. She knew seven riders had left Dowdon but only six had returned.

The firelight cast flickering shadows on Miles's face as he flipped a page in the sketchbook, revealing a cartoonish horse in muted charcoals. He must have recognized the image, because his expression changed when he saw it.

"This horse looks like the one in Alec's video game," he noted, the comment so off-topic from what she'd asked that she could only think Miles wasn't ready to talk about it.

Frustrated, she shook her head but let him lead her back to the discussion of the drawings.

"No." She pointed at the image over his shoulder, the warmth of his body making her wish she could lean into him. "That's a favorite image of Zach's. The horse motif was really prevalent in his work over the four months before he died." She thought she'd done a faithful job of copying the sort of figure Zach had sketched so often. He'd inspired her in so many ways. "Why? What does it have to do with a video game?"

Miles's brow furrowed. "Alec Jacobsen—one of my partners—is a game developer. The series he created using this horse as a character is his most popular."

How had she missed that? She made a mental note to look for the game.

"Then Zach's work must have inspired him," she said firmly, knowing that her friend had worked similar images into most of his dreamlike paintings.

"No doubt. Those two were close friends. I think Alec credited Zach somewhere on his debut game." He flipped another page in the book while a grandfather clock in the foyer struck the hour with resonant chimes. "As for how Zach died, it's still disputed among us."

Her nerve endings tingled to hear the words. To realize she was close to finally learning the truth after all this time. She held her breath. Waiting. Hoping he would confide in her.

Miles never took his gaze from the sketchbook as he spoke again. Quietly.

"He jumped off one of the cliffs into the Arroyo Seco River on a day after heavy rainstorms that raised the water level significantly." He dragged in a slow breath for a moment before he continued. "But we were never sure if he jumped for fun, because he was a daredevil who lived on the edge, or if he made that leap with the intent to end his life."

Chiara closed her eyes, picturing the scene. Zach has been a boy of boundless energy. Big dreams. Big emotions. She could see him doing something so reckless, and she hurt all over again to imagine him throwing everything away in one poor decision.

"He drowned?" Her words were so soft, they felt like they'd been spoken by someone else.

"He never surfaced. They found the body later downstream." Miles paused a moment, setting down the sketchbook and dragging in a breath. "Since there were no suspicious circumstances, they didn't do an autopsy. His death certificate lists drowning as the cause of death."

"How could it not be suspicious?" she asked, her heart rate kicking up. She felt incensed that no one had investigated further. "Even now, you don't know what happened for sure."

"The accident was kept quiet since suicide was a possibility. And Zach had no family."

"Meaning there was no one to fight for justice for him,"

she remarked bitterly, knowing from personal experience how difficult it had been to find out anything. "So the school ensured no one found out that a fatal incident occurred involving Dowdon students."

The bleakness in his eyes was impossible to miss. "That's right." His nod was stiff. Unhappy. "On the flip side, there was concern about the rest of us. We were all shell-shocked."

Something in his voice, the smallest hesitation from a man normally so confident, forced her to step back. To really listen to what he was saying and remember that this wasn't just about Zach. What happened on that trip had left its mark on Miles and all of his friends.

"I'm sorry," she offered quietly, threading her fingers through his the way he had earlier. "It must have been awful for you."

"We all went in the water to look for him," he continued, his blue gaze fixed on a moment in the past she couldn't see. "Wes could have died—he jumped right in after him. The rest of us climbed down to the rocks below to see if we could find him."

For a long moment, they didn't speak. She stepped closer, tipping her head to his shoulder in wordless comfort.

"Time gets fuzzy after that. I don't know how we decided to quit looking, but it took a long time. We were all frozen—inside and out. Eventually, we rode back to get help, but by then we knew no one was going to find him. At least—" his chin dropped to rest on the top of her head "—not alive."

Her chest ached at the thought of sixteen-year-old Miles searching a dangerously churning river for his friend and not finding him. She couldn't imagine how harrowing the aftermath had been. She'd grappled with Zach's loss on her own, not knowing the circumstances of his death. But for

Miles to witness his friend's last moments like that, feeling guilt about it no matter how misplaced, had to be an unbearable burden. A lifelong sorrow.

Helpless to know what to say, she stepped into him, wrapping her arms around his waist. She tucked her forehead against his chest, feeling the rhythmic beat of his heart against her ear. She breathed in the scent of him—clean laundry and a hint of spice from his aftershave. Her hands traced the contours of his strong arms, the hard plane of his chest and ridged abs.

At his quick intake of breath, she glanced up in time to see his eyes darken. Her heart rate sped faster.

Miles cupped her chin, bringing her mouth closer to his.

"I never talk about this because it hurts too damned much." His words sounded torn out of him.

"Thank you for trusting me enough to tell me." She'd waited half her life to hear what had happened to her friend. "At least he wasn't alone."

"No. He wasn't." Miles stroked his fingers through her hair, sifting through the strands to cup the back of her head and draw her closer still. "Any one of us would have died to save him. That's how close we were."

She'd never had friendships like that when she was a teen. Only later, once she met Astrid and then Jules, did she feel like she had people in her life who would have her back no matter what. Could she trust what Miles said about his love for Zach? She still wondered at his motives for keeping the details of Zach's death private. But as she drew a breath to ask about that, Miles gently pressed his finger against her mouth.

"I promise we can talk about this more," he told her, dragging the digit along her lower lip. "But first, I need a minute." He wrapped his other arm around her waist, his palm settling into the small of her back to seal their bodies together. "Or maybe I just need you."

Miles tipped his forehead to Chiara's, letting the sensation of having her in his arms override the dark churn of emotions that came from talking about the most traumatic day of his life. He felt on edge. Guilt-ridden. Defensive as hell.

He should have been at Zach's side when he jumped. He knew the guy was on edge that weekend. They'd stayed up half the night talking, and he'd known that something was off. Of course, they'd *all* known something was off since Zach had initiated the unsanctioned horseback riding trip precisely because he was pissed off and wanted to get away from school.

But he'd hinted at something bigger than the usual problems while they'd talked and drank late into the night. Miles had never been able to remember the conversation clearly, since they'd been drinking. The night only came back to him in jumbled bits that left him feeling even guiltier that he hadn't realized Zach was battling big demons.

Miles had still been hungover the morning of the cliff-jumping accident. He hadn't wanted to go in the first place because of that, and he sure as hell hadn't been as clear-headed as he should have been while they'd trekked up the trail. He'd lagged behind the whole way, and by the time he realized that Zach had jumped despite the dangerous conditions, Miles's brother was already throwing himself off the precipice to find him.

His brain stuttered on that image—the very real fear his brother wouldn't surface, either. And it stuck there.

Until Chiara shifted in his arms, her hips swaying against

him in a way that recalibrated everything. His thoughts. His mood. His body. All of his focus narrowed to her. This sexy siren of a woman who fascinated him on every level.

Possessiveness surged through him along with hunger. Need.

A need for her. A need to forget.

He edged back to see her, taking in the spill of dark hair and mossy-green eyes full of empathy and fire, too. When her gaze dipped to his mouth, it was all he could do not to taste her. Lose himself in her.

But damn it, he needed her to acknowledge that she wanted this, too.

"I could kiss you all night long." He stroked along her jaw, fingers straying to the delicate underside of her chin where her skin was impossibly soft.

He trailed a touch down the long column of her throat and felt the gratifying thrum of her pulse racing there. He circled the spot with his thumb and then traced it with his tongue.

"Then why don't you?" she asked, her breathless words sounding dry and choked.

"I can't even talk you into the date you owe me." He angled her head so he could read her expression better in the light of the fire. Her silky hair brushed the back of his hand. "It seems presumptuous of me to seduce you."

"Not really." She tilted her face so that her cheek rubbed against the inside of his wrist, her eyelids falling to half-mast as she did it, as if just that innocent touch brought her pleasure.

Hell, it brought him pleasure, too. But then his brain caught up to her words.

"It wouldn't be presumptuous?" he asked, wanting her

to take ownership of this attraction flaring so hot between them he could feel the flames licking up his legs.

"No." Her breath tickled against his forearm before she kissed him there then nipped his skin lightly between her teeth. "Not when being with you is all I think about every night."

The admission slayed him, torching his reservations, because *damn.* He thought about her that much, too. More.

"Good." He arched her neck back even farther, ready to claim her mouth. "That's…good."

His lips covered hers, and she was even softer than he remembered, sweetly yielding. Her arms slid around him, her body melting into his, breasts molding to his chest. He could feel the tight points of her nipples right through her blouse and the thin fabric of her bra. It felt like forever since he'd seen her. Held her. Stripped off her clothes and buried himself inside her.

He couldn't wait to do all those things, but he wouldn't do them here in the middle of the living room. With someone tracking her activities, he wanted as many locked doors between them and the rest of the world as possible. He needed her safe. Naked and sighing his name as he pleasured her, yes.

But above all, safe.

Breaking the kiss, he spoke into her ear. "Take me to your bedroom. Our night is about to get a whole lot better."

Ten

Chiara didn't hesitate.

She wanted Miles with a fierceness she didn't begin to understand, but ever since their one incredible night together, she'd been longing for a repeat. Maybe a part of her hoped that she'd embellished it in her mind, and that the sizzling passion had been a result of other factors at work that night. That it was a result of her nervousness at being caught in his office. Or her fascination with meeting one of Zach's closest friends.

But based on the way she was already trembling for want of Miles, she knew her memory of their night together was as amazing as she remembered. Wordlessly, she pulled him by the hand through the sprawling villa. At the top of the split staircase, she veered to the right, where the master suite dominated the back of the house.

She drew him into the spacious room, where he paused to close the door and lock it, a gesture that felt symbolic more than anything, since they were the only ones home. The soft *snick* of the lock sent a shiver through her as she flipped on the light switch and dimmed the overhead fixture. A gas fire burned in the stone hearth in the wall opposite the bed, and even though the flames lit the room, she liked to have the overhead light on to see Miles better. She watched him wander deeper into the room to the doors overlooking the lake. He shrugged off his blue suit jacket and laid it over the back of a leather wingback by the French doors. Picking up the control for the blinds, he closed them all and turned to look at her.

With his fitted shirt skimming his shoulders, it was easy to appreciate his very male physique. Her gaze dropped lower, sidetracked by the sight of still *more* maleness. All for her.

She wanted him, but it felt good to know he wanted her every bit as much. She dragged in breath like she'd just run a race. Heat crawled up her spine while desire pooled in her belly.

After a moment, Miles beckoned to her. "You're too far away for us to have as much fun as I was hoping."

The rasp of his voice smoked through her. Anticipation spiked, making her aware of her heartbeat pulsing in unexpected erogenous zones. But she didn't move closer. She lifted her gaze, though, meeting his blue eyes over the king-size bed.

"Give me a moment to take it all in. The first time we were together, I didn't get to appreciate all the details." In her dreams, she'd feverishly recreated every second with him, but there were too many gaps in her memories. How his hair felt in her fingers, for example. Or the texture of his very capable hands. "Tonight, I'm savoring everything."

As soon as she said it, she realized it made her sound like

she was falling for him. She wanted to recant the words. To say what she meant another way. But if Miles noticed, he didn't comment. Instead he turned his attention to unbuttoning his shirt.

"I like the way you think." His lips curved in a half smile. "But if I'm going to show you all my *details* to savor, I hope you plan to do the same."

She knew she should just be grateful for the out—he hadn't taken her words to mean anything serious. And she hadn't meant them that way. But now that the idea was out there in the ether, she had to acknowledge that it rattled her. Worried her. She couldn't fall for Miles.

Could she?

A swish of material jolted her attention back to Miles's shirt falling to the floor. His chest and abs were burnished gold by the firelight, the ripples of muscle highlighted by the shadowed ridges in between them. She wanted to focus on him. On them.

"Chiara." He said her name as he charged toward her. "What's wrong?"

His hands slid around her waist. Bracketed her hips. The warmth of his body rekindled her heat despite her spiraling thoughts.

"Is it crazy for us to indulge this?" She steadied herself by gripping his upper arms, and he felt so good. Solid. Warm.

Like he was hers.

For tonight, at least.

"Why would it be?" He frowned as he planted his feet wider to bring himself closer to her eye level. "What could possibly be wrong with finding pleasure together after the day you've had? Your business has been threatened, but the cops won't help. I'm scared as hell that you could be vulnerable, and yet you don't want to let me get too close to you or take care of you."

The urge to lean into him, to let him do just that, was almost overwhelming. But she had to be honest, even if it doused the flame for him. "Trust comes hard for me."

Her parents hadn't bothered to tell her when they lost their fortune. Zach had kept secrets from her. Miles kept secrets, too. Although he *had* confided more to her tonight.

"Which is why I haven't pushed you to stay with me so I can protect you. But you told me yourself that you thought about being with me every night." His hands flexed against her where he held her hips, a subtle pressure that stirred sweet sensations. "So maybe you could at least trust me to make you feel good."

"I do." She swayed closer, telling herself she could have one more night with him without losing her heart. "I have absolute faith in that."

He gripped the silk of her blouse at her waist and slowly gathered the fabric, untucking the shirttail from her skirt.

"I'm glad. Remember when you told me you chose work over fun for a long time?" he asked, leaning closer to speak into her ear. And to nip her ear with his teeth.

A shiver coursed through her along with surprise that he recalled her words. "Y-yes."

"That ends now."

Miles kissed his way down her neck, smoothing aside her thick, dark hair to taste more of her. She needed this as much as he did. Maybe even more.

It stunned him to think he read her so clearly when they'd spent so little time together, but he recognized how hard she pushed herself. How much she demanded of herself even when her world was caving in around her. The devotion of her staff—all personal friends, apparently—spoke volumes about who she was, and it made him want to take care of her, if only for tonight. He was going to help her forget all about her burdens until she lost herself in this.

In him.

Not that he was being unselfish. Far from it. He craved this woman.

Flicking open the buttons on her blouse, he nudged the thin fabric off her shoulders and let it flutter to the floor before he lifted his head to study her in the glow of the firelight.

"Are you still with me?" He followed the strap of her ivory lace bra with his fingertip.

The dark fringe of her eyelashes wavered before she glanced up at him, green eyes filled with heat. "Definitely."

The answer cranked him higher. He raked the straps from her shoulders and unhooked the lace to free her. The soft swells of her breasts spilled into his waiting hands, stirring the citrus fragrance he'd come to associate with her.

Hauling her into his arms, he lifted her, taking his time so that her body inched slowly up the length of his. He walked her to the bed and settled her in the space between the rows of pillows at the head and the down comforter folded at the foot, her hair spread out behind her like a silky halo. She followed his movements with watchful green eyes as he unfastened the side zipper of her skirt and eased it down her hips, leaving her in nothing but a scrap of ivory lace.

She made an enticing picture on the bed while he removed the rest of his own clothes. When he paused in undressing to find a condom and place it on the bed near her, she kinked a finger into the waistband of his boxers and tugged lightly.

"You're not naked enough." She grazed a touch along his abs, making his muscles jump with the featherlight caress.

"I'm working on it," he assured her, stilling her questing hand before she distracted him from his goal. "But we're taking care of you first."

"We are?" Her breath caught as he leaned over her and kneed her thighs apart to make room for himself.

The mattress dipped beneath them, their bodies swaying together.

"Ladies first." He kissed her hip, and she arched beneath him. "Call me old-fashioned."

He slid his hand beneath the ivory lace and stroked the slick heat waiting for him there. Her only reply was a soft gasp, followed by a needy whimper that told him she was already close.

She sifted her fingers through his hair, wriggling beneath him as he kissed and teased her, taking her higher and then easing back until they were both hot and edgy. The third time he felt her breathing shift, her thighs tensing, he didn't stop. He fastened his lips to her as she arched against him, and with a hard shudder, she flew apart.

He helped her ride out the sensations, relishing every buck of her hips, every soft shiver of her damp flesh. When he kissed his way back up her torso, he stopped at her breasts to pay homage to each in turn. Chiara patted around the bed for the condom and, finding it, rolled it into place. The feel of her hands on him, that efficient stroke of her fingers, nearly cost him his restraint. He closed his eyes against the heat jolting through him.

"Your turn," she whispered huskily in his ear before she gently bit his shoulder. "I'm in charge."

She pushed against his shoulder until he flipped onto his

back. When she straddled him, her dark hair trailed along his chest while she made herself comfortable. Her green eyes seemed to dare him to argue as she arched an eyebrow at him.

But Miles couldn't have denied her a damn thing she wanted. Not now, when her cheeks were flushed with color, her nipples dark and thrusting from his touch. The glow of the chandelier brought out the copper highlights in her raven-colored hair. He caught her hips in his hands, steadying her as she poised herself above him.

Their eyes met, held, as he lowered her onto him. Everything inside him stilled, the sensation of being inside her better than any feeling he'd ever known.

Damn.

He cranked his eyes closed long enough to get command of himself. To grind his teeth against the way this woman was stealing into his life and rewiring his brain. When he opened his eyes again, he sat up, wrapping his arms around her waist to take her to the edge of the bed so she was seated on his lap.

They were even this way. Face-to-face. They had equal amounts of control.

He told himself that with every thrust. Every breath. Every heartbeat. They moved together in sweet, sensual harmony. Their bodies anticipating one another, pushing each other higher. She held on to his shoulders. He gripped her gorgeous round hips.

By the time he saw her head tilt back, her lips part and felt her fingernails dig into his skin, he knew he couldn't hold back when she came this time. He let the force of her orgasm pull him over the edge. They held on to each other tight while the waves of pleasure crashed over them, leaving them wrung out and panting.

Breathless.

Miles found a corner of the folded duvet at the foot of the bed and hauled it around them as he laid them both back down. They were still sideways on the mattress, but it didn't matter. He couldn't move until the world righted. For now, he tucked her close to him, kissing the top of her head, needing her next to him.

He breathed in the scent of her skin and sex, the passion haze behind his eyelids slowly clearing. He'd wanted to make her feel good, and he was pretty sure he'd accomplished that much. What he hadn't counted on was the way being with her had called forth more than a heady release. He'd damned near forgotten his name.

And even worse? After today, he was pretty sure he'd never be able to dig this woman out of his system.

Chiara awoke some hours later, when moonlight filtered through a high transom window over the French doors in the master suite. Even now, Miles's hand rested on her hip as he slept beside her, in just the same position as they'd fallen asleep, her back to his front.

For a moment, she debated making them something to eat since they'd never had dinner, but her body was still too sated sexually to demand any other sustenance. What a decadent pleasure to awake next to this man in her bed.

And yet, no matter how fulfilled her body, her brain already stirred restlessly. After fourteen years, she now knew what had happened to Zach Eldridge. Or at least, she seemed to know as much as Miles did. Miles had insisted he wasn't sure—that none of his friends were sure—whether or not

Zach had jumped to end his life or if he'd jumped in a moment of reckless thrill seeking.

Maybe it didn't matter.

But what if it did? What if one of the Mesa Falls Ranch owners knew more about Zach's motives or mindset than they let on? Was one of them more morally responsible than the others for not stopping Zach's trek up to the top of those cliffs in the first place? Was one of them responsible for Zach's death?

She burrowed deeper into her down pillow, trying to shut out the thoughts. If she didn't get some sleep, she wouldn't be able to solve the mystery. Yet her brain kept reminding her that someone knew she was looking into Zach's death, and whoever it was felt threatened enough by her search that he—or she—had tried blackmailing her into giving up.

"Everything okay?" the warm, sleep-roughened voice behind her asked.

A shiver went through her as Miles stroked his palm along her bare hip under the covers. What might it have been like to meet him under different circumstances? Would she have been able to simply relax and enjoy the incredible chemistry?

"Just thinking about Zach. Trying to reconcile the things you told me with my own understanding of him." That was true enough, even if she had bigger concerns, too. Absently, she traced the piping on the white cotton pillowcase.

Propping himself on his elbow, he said, "If he had an affair with a teacher and she ended up pregnant, it definitely accounts for why he was stressed that weekend. She could have gone to prison for being with him, too, which would have provided another level of stress."

His other hand remained on her hip, his fingers tracing idle patterns that gave her goose bumps.

"She put him in a position no seventeen-year-old should ever be in. Who's to say how he felt about her that weekend? He could have been stressed because she ended things with him. Or because someone found out their secret." She tried to envision what would drive Zach to total despair or to feel reckless enough to make that unwise jump. "Then again, maybe he was stressed because she wanted him to commit to her."

Miles's hand stilled. "What nineteen-year-old woman would want to play house with a seventeen-year-old kid?"

"The same woman who would have had an affair with a student in the first place." Even fourteen years later, she felt angry at the woman for taking advantage of someone she should have been protecting. No matter how much more mature Zach seemed than the other students around him, he was still a kid.

"I should check my phone." Rolling away from her, Miles withdrew his hand from under her body to reach for his device on the nightstand. "I might have heard back from the PI about the stakeout around Nicole Cruz's house."

Instantly alert, Chiara sat up in the bed, dragging a sheet with her. The room was still dark except for the moonlight in the transom window, so Chiara flicked the remote button to turn on the gas fireplace. Flames appeared with a soft whoosh while Miles turned on his phone then scrolled through various screens, his muscles lit by the orange glow.

When his finger stopped swiping, she watched his expression as his blue eyes moved back and forth. Tension threaded through his body. She could see it in his jaw and compressed lips.

"What is it? Did they find her?"

For a moment, when he looked up at her blankly, she wondered if he would go back to shutting her out of news about Zach. Or news about this woman—whether or not she had a direct tie to Zach.

But then his expression cleared, and he nodded.

"According to Desmond's note, Nicole Cruz won't return to Mesa Falls with our private investigator until all the ranch owners submit DNA for paternity testing." His voice was flat. His expression inscrutable. "She's agreed to submit a sample from her sister's son."

"That's good news, right?" she asked, feeling a hunch the child wouldn't be linked to any of them. Her gut told her the mystery boy was Zach's son. "And in the meantime, maybe your detective can see if there's a link between Nicole Cruz and the teacher—Lana Allen. Were they really sisters?"

Miles's fingers hovered over his phone screen. "It would be good to have a concrete lead to give him." He hesitated. "Are you comfortable with me sharing what you told me?"

The fact that he would ask her first said a lot about his ability to be loyal. To keep a confidence. He'd certainly maintained secrecy for Zach's sake for a long, long time. The realization comforted her now that she more clearly understood his reluctance to reveal the truth.

"Would you be sharing the information directly with the investigator, or are you asking for permission to communicate it with all your partners?" She understood that Miles trusted his friends, but her first loyalty had to be to Zach.

A veil of coolness dropped over Miles's features as a chill crept into his voice. "Until now, my partners and I have pooled our knowledge."

She waited for him to elaborate, but he didn't.

She needed to tread carefully, not wanting to alienate him now that he'd finally brought her into his confidence. And yet her feelings for him—her fear of losing him—threatened her objectivity. Hugging the sheet tighter to her chest, she felt goose bumps along her arms. If only it was the room getting cooler and not Miles's mood casting a chill. She weighed how to respond.

"I know you trust your friends." She couldn't help it if she didn't. "But you have to admit that the last time you communicated my interest in Zach to that group, the threats against me came very quickly afterward."

If she'd thought his face was cool before, his blue gaze went glacial now.

"Coincidence," he returned sharply. "I'm not in the habit of keeping secrets from the men I trust most."

A pain shot through her as she realized that the last few hours with Miles hadn't shifted his opinion of her or brought them closer together. If anything, she felt further apart from him than ever. The hurt made her lash out, a safer reaction than revealing vulnerability.

"You realize my entire livelihood rests in the balance?" She couldn't help but draw a second blanket over her shoulders like armor, a barrier, feeling the need to shore up her defenses that had dissolved too fast where he was concerned. "And possibly my safety?"

She thought she spied a thaw in his frosty gaze. He set his phone aside and palmed her shoulder, his fingers a warm, welcome weight.

"I've already told you that I will do everything in my power to keep you safe." The rasp in his voice reminded her of other conversations, other confidences he'd shared with her. She wanted to believe in him.

"I want to find out what drove Zach over that cliff as much as anyone." She swallowed back her anxiety and hoped she wasn't making a huge mistake. "If you think it's best to share what I told you with his other friends in addition to the PI, then you're welcome to tell them what I knew about Zach and the teacher—Miss Allen."

Miles's gaze held hers for a moment before he gave a nod and picked up his phone again to type a text. For a long time afterward, Chiara couldn't help but think his expression showed the same uneasiness she felt inside. But once Miles hit the send button, she knew it was too late to turn back from the course they'd already set.

Eleven

Snow blanketed the Tahoe vacation villa, the world of white momentarily distracting Miles from the tension hanging over his head ever since he'd shared Chiara's insights about Zach with his friends two days ago. A storm had taken the power out the day before, giving them a grace period to watch the weather blow in, make love in every room of that huge villa and not think about their time together coming to an end as they got closer to learning the truth about Zach's death.

Miles had continued to shove his concerns to the back burner this morning, managing to talk Chiara into taking a walk through the woods with him after breakfast. They'd ridden a snowmobile to the casino the day before to retrieve some clothes from his suite.

Now, he held her gloved hand in his as they trudged between sugar pines and white fir trees, the accumulation up to their knees in most places. A dusting clung to her jeans and the fringe of her long red wool jacket. Her cheeks were flushed from the cold and the effort of forging a path through the drifts. Her dark hair was braided in a long tail over one shoulder, a white knitted beanie framing her face as she smiled up at a red-tailed hawk who screeched down at them with its distinctive cry.

For a moment, he saw a different side of her. With no makeup and no fans surrounding her, no couture gown or A-list celebrities clamoring for a photo with her, Chiara looked like a woman who might enjoy the same kind of quiet life he did.

But he knew that was only an illusion. She circulated in a glamorous world of nightlife and parties, far from the ranch where he spent his time.

"I'm glad we got out of the house." She leaned against the rough bark of a Jeffrey pine as they reached an overlook of the lake, where the water reflected the dull gray of the snow clouds. "While having a snow day was fun yesterday, it only delayed the stress fallout from visiting the police station and having it posted online. I feel like I'm still waiting for the other shoe to drop."

Miles leaned back against the trunk near her, still holding her hand. The reminder of those things hanging over them still made him uneasy, and he wished he could distract her. How she felt mattered to him more than it should, considering the very lives they led. And how fast she'd be out of his life again.

He knew her time in Tahoe was bound to her search for answers about Zach, which was why Miles hadn't found a way to tell her yet about the DNA test results he'd received from Desmond earlier that morning. All the Mesa Falls owners had been ruled out, as had Alonzo Salazar through DNA provided by his sons. Which meant there was a strong chance Zach was the father. But Miles hadn't shared that yet, knowing damn well Chiara might leave once she knew. The possibility of her going weighed him down like lead, but he was also still worried about her safety after the anonymous threats. But he ignored his own feelings to try to reassure her.

"It's been two days since the photos of us at the police station started appearing online." He'd checked his phone before driving over to the casino for his clothes, wanting to make sure there'd been no backlash from her fans. "Maybe it won't be a big deal."

Below them on the snowy hill, a few kids dragged snow tubes partway up the incline to sled down to the water, even though the conditions seemed too powdery for a good run. A few vacation cabins dotted the coastline, and he guessed they were staying in one of them. Chiara's gaze followed the kids, too, before she looked up at him.

"Maybe not." She didn't sound convinced. "And my social media accounts are still working." She held up her phone with the other hand. "I successfully posted a photo of the snow-covered trees a moment ago."

While he was glad to hear her accounts hadn't been hacked, he was caught off guard by the idea of her posting nature photos to her profile that was full of fashion. And he was grateful to think about something besides the guilt gnawing at him for not confiding in her about the DNA news.

"Just trees?" He gave her a sideways glance, studying her lovely profile.

Her lips pursed in thought. "I've been posting more artistic images." She shifted against the tree trunk so she faced him, her breath huffing between them in a drift of white in the cold air. "Thinking more about Zach this week has made me question how I could have gotten so far afield from the mixed media art that I used to love making."

Regret rose as he remembered how he'd dismissed her work when they'd first met. "I hope it didn't have anything to do with what I said that night about your job. I had no right—"

She shook her head, laying a hand on his arm. "Absolutely not. I know why I launched my brand and created the blog since I couldn't afford art school. But there's nothing stopping me from doing something different now. From reimagining my future."

While the kids on the hill below them laughed and shouted over their next sled run, Miles shifted toward Chiara, the tree bark scraping his sheepskin jacket as he wondered if she could reimagine a future with him in it. Did he want that? Gazing into her green eyes, he still wrestled with how much they could trust each other. He felt her wariness about his friends. And for his part, he knew she was only here now because of her loyalty to Zach.

So he kept his response carefully focused on her even when he was tempted as hell to ask for more.

"No doubt, you could do anything you wanted now." He brushed a snowflake from her cheek, the feel of her reminding him of all the best highlights from their past two nights together.

Funny that despite seeing stars many times thanks to her, the moments he remembered best were how she'd felt wrapped around him as he fell asleep the last two nights, resulting in the best slumber he'd had in a long time. He'd been totally relaxed, like she was supposed to be right there with him.

She closed her eyes for a moment as he touched her. He'd like to think she relished the feel of him as much he did her. Her long lashes fluttered against her cheeks for a moment before she raised her gaze to meet his again.

"For a long time, I worried that any artistic talent I once had was only because of the inspiration from the year I knew Zach," she confided quietly. "Like I was somehow a fraud without him."

The statement stunned him, coming from someone so obviously talented. "You built your success because of your artistic eye. And hell yes, I know that because I read up on you after we met."

He wasn't about to hide that from her if he could leverage what he'd learned to reassure her. He lifted her chin so she could see his sincerity.

"Thank you." Her gloved fingers wrapped around his wrist where he touched her, the leather creaking softly with the cold. "Oddly, I've been more reassured as I've reconnected with my old sketchbooks. There is a lot more original work in there than I remembered. I think I let Zach's influence magnify in my mind over the years because of the huge hole he left in my life in other ways. I spent at least a year just redrawing old works of his from memory, trying to keep him in my heart."

Tenderness for her loss swamped him. He recognized it. He'd lived it. "I know what you mean. All of us tried to fill the void he left in different ways. Weston took up search and rescue work. Gage disappeared into numbers and investing."

He mused over the way his friends had grown an unbreakable bond, while at the same time venturing decidedly away from the experience they'd shared. Zach's death had brought them together and kept them all isolated at the same time.

"What about you?" Chiara asked as his hand fell from her chin. "What did you do afterward?"

He couldn't help a bitter smile. "I became the model son. I threw myself into ranching work to help my father and prepare for taking over Rivera Ranch."

"That sounds like a good thing, right?" She tipped her head sideways as if not sure what she was hearing. "Very practical."

"Maybe it was. But it only increased the divide between my brother and me." He hated that time in his life for so many reasons. The fact that it had alienated him from the person who knew him best had been a pain that lasted long after. "I could do no wrong in my parents' eyes after that, and it was the beginning of the end for my relationship with Wes."

Her brows knit in confusion as the snow started falling faster. A flake clung briefly to her eyelash before melting.

"Why would your brother resent your efforts to help your family?" she asked with a clarity he could never muster for the situation.

The fact that she saw his life—him—so clearly had him struggling to maintain his distance. The intimacy of the last two days was threatening to pull him under. Needing a breather, he stirred from where he stood.

"He didn't." Miles shrugged as he straightened, gesturing toward the path back to her villa. "But our parents treated us so differently it got uncomfortable for Wes to even come home for holidays. I hated how they treated him, too, but since I spent every second away from school working on Rivera Ranch, I let that take over my life."

For a few minutes, they shuffled back along the paths they'd made through the deep snow on their way out. He, for one, was grateful for the reprieve from a painful topic. But then again, if there was a chance he would be spending more time with Chiara in the future, he owed her an explanation of his family dynamics.

He held his hand out for her to help her over an icy log in the path.

"It seems like the blame rests on your parents' shoulders. Not yours or Weston's," she observed, jumping down from the log to land beside him with a soft thud of her heavy boots.

The sounds from the sledders retreated as they continued through the woods.

"Maybe so. But then, on one of Wes's rare trips home, we ended up dating the same woman without knowing. That didn't help things." It had been a misguided idea to date Brianna in the first place, but Miles had been on the ranch and isolated for too long. So even though Brianna was a rebel and a risk taker, he'd told himself his life needed more adventure.

He'd gotten far more than he'd bargained for when he'd seen Wes in a lip lock with her at a local bar a few weeks later. That betrayal had burned deep.

"That sounds like her fault. Because you may not have known, but she must have." She scowled as she spoke.

Miles couldn't help a laugh. "I appreciate your defense of me. Thank you."

He could see Chiara's villa ahead through the trees and the snow, and his steps slowed. He wasn't ready to return to the real world yet. Didn't want to know what had happened with Nicole Cruz, or with Chiara's anonymous hacker. He wanted more time with her before he lost her to her work and her world where he didn't belong.

Chiara slowed, too, coming to a halt beside him. They

still held hands. And for some reason stepping out of the trees felt like it was bringing them that much closer to the end of their time together.

"I like you, Miles," she admitted, dropping her forehead to rest on his shoulder as if she didn't want to return to the real world yet, either. "In case you haven't guessed."

Her simple words plucked at something inside him. Made him want to take a chance again for the first time in a long time. Or confide in her, at the very least. But long-ingrained habit kept him silent about the deeper things he was feeling. Instead, he focused on the way they connected best.

"I like you a whole lot, too," he growled, winding an arm around her waist to press her more tightly to him. "I'll remind you how much if you take me home with you."

She lifted her eyes to his, and for the briefest of seconds, he thought he saw her hesitate. But then her lids fell shut and she grazed her lips over his, meeting his kiss with a sexy sigh and more than a little heat.

Chiara was half dazed by the time Miles broke the kiss. Heat rose inside her despite the snow, her body responding to everything about him. His scent. His touch. His wicked, wonderful tongue.

Heartbeat skipping, she gladly followed him as he led her back toward the huge stone-and-wood structure, her thoughts racing ahead to where they'd take the next kiss. Her bed? The sauna? In front of the massive fireplace? Sensual thoughts helped keep her worries at bay after the way Miles seemed to pull back from her earlier. Or had that been her imagination?

Sometimes she sensed that he avoided real conversation in favor of touching and kissing. But when his every touch and kiss set her aflame, could she really argue? She'd let her guard down around him in a big way, showing him a side of herself that felt new. Vulnerable. Raw.

Breathless with anticipation, she tripped into the side door behind him, peeling off her snowy boots on the mat. Her hat and gloves followed. He shook off his coat and boots before stripping off her jacket and hanging it on an antique rack for her. He didn't wait to fold her in his arms and kiss her again. He gripped her hips, steadying her as he sealed their bodies together. Heat scrambled her thoughts again, her fingers tunneling impatiently under his cashmere sweater where she warmed them against his back before walking them around to his front, tucking them in the waistband of his jeans.

The ragged sound in his throat expressed the same need she felt, and he pulled away long enough to grip her by the hand and guide her across the polished planked floor toward the stairs.

Her feet were on the first wide step of the formal divided staircase when a knock sounded on the back door.

Miles stopped. His blue gaze swung around to look at her.

Her belly tightened.

"Maybe it's just Jules checking to see how we're faring after the storm." At least, she hoped that was all it was.

Still, her feet didn't move until the knock sounded again. More urgently.

"We'd better check," Miles muttered, frustration punctuating every word. He kept holding her hand as he walked with her through the kitchen.

She sensed the tension in him—something about the way he held himself. Or maybe the way he looked like he was grinding his teeth. But she guessed that was the same sexual frustration she was feeling right now.

Still, her nerves wound tight as she padded through the room in her socks. Through a side window, she could see Jules and Stefan—together—on the back step. Vaguely, she felt Miles give her hand a reassuring squeeze before she pulled open the door.

"What's up?" she started to ask, only to have Jules thrust her phone under Chiara's nose as she stepped into the kitchen, Stefan right behind her.

Miles closed the door.

"Your page is down." Jules's face was white, her expression grim as she waggled the phone in front of Chiara with more emphasis. "We've been hacked."

She could have sworn the floor dropped out from under her feet. Miles's arm wrapped around her. Steadying her.

Chiara stared at Jules's device, afraid to look. Closing her eyes for a moment, she took a deep breath before she accepted the phone. Then, sinking onto the closest counter stool, she tapped the screen back to life.

Miles peered over her shoulder, his warmth not giving her the usual comfort as a shiver racked her. His hand rubbed over her back while her eyes focused on what she was seeing.

Oddly, the image at the top of her profile page—her home screen—was of Miles. Only he wasn't alone. It was a shot of him with his face pressed cheek to cheek with a gorgeous woman—a brown-eyed beauty with dark curling hair and a mischievous smile. A banner inserted across the image read, "Kara Marsh, you'll always be second best."

Miles might have said something in her ear, but she couldn't focus on his words. If she'd thought the floor had shifted out from under her feet before, now her stomach joined the free fall. As images went, it wasn't particularly damaging to her career.

Simply to her heart.

Because the look on Miles's face in that photo was one she'd never seen before. Pressed against that ethereally gorgeous creature, Miles appeared happier than he'd ever been with Chiara. In this image, his blue eyes were unguarded. Joyous. In love.

And that hurt more than anything. In the woods this morning, when she'd tentatively tested out his feelings with a confession that she liked him—not that it was a huge overture, but still, she'd tried—he'd responded with sizzle. Not emotions.

Jules crouched down into her line of vision, making Chiara realize she'd been silent too long. With an effort, she tried to recover herself, knowing full well her hurt must have been etched all over her face in those first moments when she'd seen the picture.

"It could be worse," she managed to say, sliding the phone across the granite countertop to Jules, avoiding pieces from a jigsaw puzzle she'd worked on for a little while with Miles during the snowstorm. "That's hardly a damning shot."

"I agree," Jules said softly, her tone a careful blend of professionalism and caution. "But the banner—coupled with the fact that you were recently photographed with Miles—creates the impression that either Miles or his—" she hesitated, shooting a quick glance at Miles "—um, former girlfriend were the ones to hijack your social media properties. This same image is on your personal blog, too. I'm worried your fans will be defensive of you—"

"I'm sure we'll get it cleared up soon." She wasn't sure

of any such thing as she picked up one of the puzzle pieces and traced the tabs and slots. But the need to confront Miles privately was too strong for her to think about her career. Or whatever else Jules was saying. "Could you give us a minute, Jules? And I'll come over to help you figure out our next steps in a little while?"

Her heartbeat pounded too loudly for her to even be sure what Jules said on her way out. But her friend took Stefan by the arm—even though her bodyguard looked doubtfully from Miles to Chiara and back again—and tugged him out the villa's back door.

Leaving her and Miles alone.

He put his hands on her shoulders, gently swiveling her on the counter stool so that she faced him.

"Are you all right?" He lowered himself into the seat next to her, perching on the edge of the leather cushion. "Would you like me to get you something to drink? You don't look well."

"I'm fine." That wasn't true, but a drink wouldn't help the tumultuous feelings inside her. The hurt deeper than she had a right to feel over a man she'd vowed could only be a fling.

"You don't look fine." His blue eyes were full of concern. Though, she reminded herself, not love. "You can't think for a second I had anything to do with posting that."

"Of course not." That hadn't even occurred to her. She hadn't roused the energy to think about who was behind the post because she was too busy having her heart stepped on. Too consumed with feelings she'd assured herself she wasn't going to develop for this man. But judging by the jealousy and hurt gnawing away at her insides, she couldn't deny she'd been harboring plenty of emotions for this man.

Still, she needed to pull herself together.

"For what it's worth, that's obviously not a recent photo," Miles offered, his hands trailing down her arms to her hands where he found the puzzle piece she was still holding. He set it back on the counter. "I'm not sure where someone would have gotten ahold of it, but—"

"Social media," she supplied, thinking she really needed to get back online and start scouring her pages to see what was happening. Jules had to be wondering why Chiara had only wanted to talk to Miles. "It looks like a selfie. My guess is your old girlfriend has it stored on one of her profiles."

"Makes sense." He nodded, straightening, his touch falling away from her. "But I was going to say that I haven't seen Brianna Billings in years, so I'm sure she wouldn't be sending you anonymous threats."

Not wanting to discuss the woman in the photo, or the feelings it stirred, Chiara stared out the window behind Miles's head and watched the snowfall as she turned the conversation in another direction.

"So if we rule out you and your ex for suspects in hacking the page," she continued, knowing she sounded stiff. Brusque. "Who else should we look at? I'll call the police again, of course, but they'll ask us who we think might be responsible. And personally, I think it's got to be one of your partners at Mesa Falls. One of Zach's former friends."

"No." He shook his head resolutely and stood, then walked over to the double refrigerator doors and pulled out a bottle of water. He set it on the island before retrieving two glasses. "It can't be."

She didn't appreciate how quickly he wrote off her idea. Especially when her feelings were already stirred up disproportionately at seeing a different side of Miles in that photo. She felt Miles pulling away. Sensed it was all plummeting downhill between them, but she didn't have a clue how to stop things from going off the rails.

"Who else would be tracking my efforts to find out what happened to Zach, and would know about your past, too?" she asked him sharply. "I'm not the common denominator in that equation. It's the Mesa Falls group."

"It's someone trying to scare you away from looking into Zach's past. Maybe Nicole Cruz?" he mused aloud as he filled the two glasses of water. Although as soon as he said it, he glanced up at her, and she could have sworn she saw a shadow cross through his eyes.

Then again, she was feeling prickly. She tried to let go of the hurt feelings while he returned the water bottle to the stainless steel refrigerator. Frustration and hurt were going to help her get to the bottom of this.

"It could be whoever fathered the mystery child," she pressed, wondering about the DNA evidence. "Once we know who the father is—"

"It's none of us," Miles answered with a slow shake of his head. He set a glass of water in front of her as he returned to the seat beside her.

His answer sounded certain. As if he knew it for a fact. But she guessed that was just his way of willing it to be the truth.

"We'll only know that for sure once the test results come in," she reminded him before taking a sip of her drink.

"They already have. All of the Mesa Falls partners have been cleared of paternity, along with Alonzo Salazar, courtesy of DNA provided by his sons." Miles's fingers tightened around his glass.

Surprised, Chiara set hers back down with a thud, sloshing some over the rim.

"How long have you known?" she asked, her nerve endings tingling belatedly with uneasiness.

"Desmond texted me early this morning."

"And just when were you going to tell me?" She knew logically that not much time had passed. But she'd been waiting half of a lifetime for answers about Zach. And damn it, she'd spent her whole life being in the dark because of other people's secrets. Her family's. Zach's friends'. Even, she had to admit, Zach's.

Indignation burned. Her heart pounded faster, her body recognizing the physical symptoms of betrayal. Of secrets hidden.

"Soon," Miles started vaguely, not meeting her eyes. "I just didn't want—"

"You know what? It doesn't matter what you did or didn't want." She stood up in a hurry, needing to put distance between herself and this man who'd slid past her defenses without her knowing. She didn't have the resources to argue with him when her heart hurt, and she'd be damned if she'd let him crush more of the feelings she'd never meant to have for him.

She needed to get her coat so she could go talk to Jules and focus on her career instead of a man who would never trust her. More than that, she needed to get out of the same town as him. Out of the same state.

There was no reason to linger here any longer. The time had come to return home, back to her own life in Los Angeles.

"Chiara, wait." Miles cut her off, inserting himself in her path, though he didn't touch her.

"I can't do secrets, Miles," she said tightly, betrayal stinging. And disillusionment. And anger at herself. "I'm sure that sounds hypocritical after the way I searched your computer that night—"

"It doesn't." He looked so damned good in his jeans and soft gray sweater, his jaw bristly and unshaven. "I know trust comes hard for you."

"For you, too, it seems." She folded her arms to keep herself from touching him. If only the want could be so easily held at bay.

"Yes. For me, too," he acknowledged.

She waited for a long moment. Waited. And heaven help her, even hoped. Just a little. But he said nothing more.

Tears burning her eyes, she sidestepped him to reach for her coat.

"I'm going to be working the rest of the day," she informed him, holding herself very straight in an effort to keep herself together. Her heart ached. "I'll head back to LA tomorrow. But for tonight, I think it would be best if you weren't here when I return."

Miles didn't argue. He only nodded. He didn't even bother to fight for her.

Once she had her boots and coat on, she shoved through the door and stepped out into the snow. Some wistful part of her thought she heard a softly spoken, "Don't go" from behind her. But she knew it was just the foolish wish of a heart broken before she'd even realized she'd fallen in love.

Twelve

Three days later, gritty-eyed despite rising late, Miles prowled Desmond's casino floor at noon. Navigating the path to Desmond's office through a maze of roulette wheels, blackjack tables and slot machines, he cursed the marketing wisdom that demanded casino guests walk through the games every time they wanted to access hotel amenities.

No doubt the setup netted Desmond big profits, but the last thing Miles wanted to see after Chiara's defection was a tower of lights blinking "jackpot!" accompanied by a chorus of electronic enthusiasm. A herd of touristy-looking players gathered around the machine to celebrate their good fortune, while Miles suspected he'd never feel lucky again.

Not after losing the most incredible woman he'd ever met just two weeks after finding her. He'd surely set a record for squandering everything in so little time.

He hadn't been able to sleep for thinking about the expression on her face when she'd discovered he hadn't told her about the DNA test results. He'd known—absolutely known—that she would be hurt by that given the trust issues she'd freely admitted. And yet he'd withheld it anyhow, unwilling to share the news that would send her out of his life.

So instead of letting her choose when she should return to her California home once she'd found out all she could about Zach, he'd selfishly clung to the information in the hope of stretching out their time together. And for his selfishness, he'd hurt her. Sure, he'd like to think he would have told her that afternoon. He couldn't possibly have gone to bed by her side that night without sharing the news. But it didn't matter how long he'd kept that secret.

What mattered was that she'd told him how hard it was for her to trust. Something he—of all people—understood only too well. Yeah, he recognized the pain he'd caused when he'd crossed the one line she'd drawn with him about keeping secrets.

When he finally reached the locked door of the back room, a uniformed casino employee entered a code and admitted him. At least the maze of halls here was quiet. The corridors with their unadorned light gray walls led to a variety of offices and maintenance rooms. Miles bypassed all of them until he reached stately double doors in the back.

Another uniformed guard stood outside them. This one rapped his knuckles twice on the oak barrier before admitting Miles.

A stunning view of Lake Tahoe dominated one side of the owner's work suite, with glass walls separating a private office, small conference room and a more intimate meeting space. All were spare and modern in shades of gray and white, with industrial touches like stainless steel work lamps and hammered metal artwork. Desmond sat on a low sofa in front of the windows overlooking Lake Tahoe in the more casual meeting space.

Sunlight reflecting off the water burned right into Miles's eyes until he moved closer to the window, the angle of built-in blinds effectively shading the glare as he reached his friend. Dressed in a sharp gray suit and white collared shirt with no tie, Desmond drank a cup of espresso as he read an honest-to-God newspaper—no electronic devices in sight. The guy had an easy luxury about him that belied a packed professional life.

As far as Miles knew, he did nothing but work 24/7, the same way Gage Striker had when he'd been an investment banker. Gage's wealth had convinced him to start taking it easier as an angel investor the last couple of years, but Desmond still burned the candle at both ends, working constantly.

"Look what the cat dragged in," Desmond greeted him, folding his paper and setting it on a low glass table in front of him. With his posh manners and charm, Desmond looked every inch the worldly sophisticate. And it wasn't just an act, either, as he held dual citizenship in the United States and the UK thanks to a Brit mother.

But Miles remembered him from darker days, when Desmond's father had been a ham-fisted brute, teaching his son to be quick with a punch out of necessity, to protect himself and his mother. It was a skill set Desmond hid well, but Miles knew that a lot of his work efforts still benefited battered women and kids. And he'd channeled his own grief about Zach into something positive, whereas Miles still felt like the old wounds just ate away at his insides. What did he have to show for the past beyond Rivera Ranch? All his toil had gone into the family property. And he hadn't really done anything altruistic.

"I only came to let you know I'm returning to Mesa Falls." Miles dropped onto a leather chair near the sofa, eager to leave the place where his brief relationship with Chiara had imploded. "I'm meeting the pilot this afternoon."

"Coffee?" Desmond offered as he picked up a black espresso cup.

Miles shook his head, knowing caffeine wouldn't make a dent in the wrung-out feeling plaguing his head. He'd barely slept last night for thinking about Chiara's parting words that had been so polite and still so damned cutting.

I think it would be best if you weren't here when I return.

"It's just as well you came in." Desmond set aside his empty cup and leaned back into the sofa cushions. "I was going to message you anyhow to let you know you don't need to return to Mesa Falls."

Miles frowned as he rubbed his eyes to take away some of the gritty feeling. "What do you mean? Someone's got to oversee things."

"Nicole Cruz is flying to Montana tonight," Desmond informed him, brushing some invisible item from the perfectly clean cushion by his thigh. "I assured her I would be there to meet her. Them."

Miles edged forward in his seat, trying to follow.

"You want to be there to meet the guardian of the kid who's most likely Zach's son?" he clarified, knowing something was off about the way Desmond was talking about her.

Was it suspicion?

He'd like to think they were all suspicious of her, though. This seemed like something different.

"I've been her only point of contact so far," Desmond

explained, giving up on the invisible dust. He gave Miles a level gaze. "The only one of us she's communicated with. We can't afford to scare her off when it took us this long to find her."

"Right. Agreed." Miles nodded, needing to rouse himself out of his own misery to focus on their latest discovery about Zach. "If Matthew is Zach's son, we don't want to lose our chance of being a part of his life."

Regret stung as he considered how much Chiara would want to meet the boy. He didn't want to stand in her way, especially when they might not have come this far figuring out Zach's secrets without her help.

Desmond's phone vibrated, and he picked it up briefly.

"I've asked the PI to back off investigating Nicole and Matthew," Desmond continued as he read something and then set the device back on the table. Sun glinted off the sleek black case.

"Why?" Miles picked up his own phone, checking for the thousandth time if there were any developments on who had targeted Chiara's sites. Or, if he was honest, to see if she had messaged him. Disappointment to find nothing stung all over again.

He missed her more than if she'd been out of his life for years and not days. He'd only stuck around Lake Tahoe this long in hopes he'd be able to help the local police, or maybe in the hope she'd return to town to see Astrid. Or him.

But there was only a group message from Alec telling any of the Mesa Falls partners still on site at the casino to meet him at Desmond's office as soon as possible. Miles wondered what that was about.

"Nicole has been dodging our investigators to protect Matthew for weeks. She's exhausted and mistrustful. She asked me to 'call off the dogs' if she agreed to return to Montana, and I have given her my word that I would." Desmond straightened in his seat, appearing ready to move on as he checked his watch. "And, actually, I have a lot to do today to prepare my staff for my absence. Alec agreed to watch over things here, but he's late."

As he spoke, however, a knock sounded at the outer double doors before they opened, and Alec appeared.

Miles only had a second to take in his friend's disheveled clothes that looked slept in—a wrinkled jacket and T-shirt and rumpled jeans. His hair stood up in a few directions, and his face had a look of grim determination as he wound through the office suite to the glassed-in room where Desmond and Miles sat.

"Sorry I'm late." Alec juggled a foam coffee cup in his hand as he plowed through the last door. "I've been at the police station giving my statement. They arrested my personal assistant, Vivian, for threatening Chiara Campagna."

"You're kidding." Miles tensed, half rising to his feet. Then, realizing the woman in question was already in custody, he lowered himself into the chair again. "How did they find out?"

Miles had checked with the local police just the night before but hadn't learned anything other than that they were still looking into the complaint Chiara filed after the second incident.

Alec lowered himself into the chair opposite Miles at the other end of the coffee table. He set his coffee cup on a marble coaster.

"Apparently it wasn't tough to track her once they got a cybercrimes expert to look into it. Vivian and I were working late last night when she got a call from the police asking her to come in so they could ask her some questions." Alec shrugged and then swiped his hand through the hair that was already standing straight up. "I drove her over there, never thinking they already had evidence on her. They arrested her shortly afterward."

"Does Chiara know?" Miles wanted to call her. Check on her. Let her know that the police had done their job.

Hell. What he really wanted was to fold her into his arms.

But holding her wasn't his right anymore.

"I'm not sure if they've contacted her yet." Alec retrieved his coffee cup, a thick silver band around his middle finger catching the light and refracting it all over the room. "I'm still trying to process the news myself."

Before Miles could ask more about it, a knock sounded again on the outer door, and his brother, Weston, ambled in wearing jeans and a T-shirt. With his too-long hair and hazel eyes, he and Miles couldn't be less alike.

"What's up? April and I were going to hit the slopes today. Conditions are incredible." He stopped himself as he looked around at his friends. "What happened?"

As he sank to a seat on the other end of the couch from Desmond, Alec repeated the news about Vivian before adding, "I had no idea Vivian was imagining we had a much deeper relationship than we do, but sometime in the last few years she started crossing the line as my assistant to make sure things went my way—bribing contacts into taking meetings with me, padding the numbers on our financial statements to make the gaming company look stronger for investors, a whole bunch of stuff unrelated to what happened with Chiara."

Miles recalled meeting Vivian lurking outside the high-roller suite that day after the meeting of the Mesa Falls partners. "So why would she hassle Chiara?"

"I guess she intercepted a text on my phone about Chiara's interest in Zach." Alec glanced upward, as if trying to gather his thoughts, or maybe to remember something. "Vivian never liked her. She was a student at Brookfield, too, and I was with her that day at Dowdon that Kara—Chiara—came to school to talk to Miles and Gage."

Miles remembered Alec saying he'd been with a girl under the bleachers that day. Still, fourteen years seemed like a long time to hold a grudge against Chiara. Once again his protective instincts kicked into gear. If he couldn't be with Chiara or make her happy, he owed it to her to at least keep her safe. Which meant getting full disclosure on everything related to Zach's death.

Desmond spoke before Miles had a chance to ask about that.

"So Vivian must have known about Zach if you've been friends that long." Desmond seemed to put the pieces together faster, but maybe it was easier to have more clarity on the situation than Miles, who'd lost objectivity where Chiara was concerned a long time ago. "Maybe she figured it was somehow helping you to keep Chiara from asking too many questions."

Weston whistled softly under his breath. "She sounds like a piece of work."

Alec bristled. "She's smart as hell, actually. Just highly unethical."

The conversation continued, but Miles couldn't focus on it with the urge to see Chiara, to make sure she knew that her hacker was in custody, so strong. He wanted to share the news with her, to give her this much even though he'd failed their fledgling relationship.

"Why did she feel the need to post a picture of me with an old girlfriend on Chiara's page?" he found himself asking, curious not so much for himself, but for Chiara's sake. He'd known that image had bothered her.

And if he was able to see her again—or even just speak to her—he wanted to share answers with her. Answers he owed her after the way he'd withheld information from her before.

Alec took another drink of his coffee before responding. "I wondered about that, too. I guess Vivian was upset about a photo of me with Chiara from that night at your party, Miles. Then, when she saw the pictures of you at the police station with Chiara—looking like a couple—she figured the best way to hurt Chiara would be with an image of you and someone else."

Miles remembered the jealousy that had gone through him when he saw Alec's hand on the small of Chiara's back that night, touching her bare skin through the cutout of her silver gown.

Weston spoke up. "For a smart woman, she definitely made some stupid mistakes. But lucky for us, right? Because now she's behind bars." He stood as if to leave. "I've got to get back to April to meet the car taking us to the mountain."

Miles rose as well, edgy to be out of Tahoe. Now that he'd been relieved of his duties at Mesa Falls, he was free to use the afternoon's flight to see Chiara. To share what he'd learned, at least. "Desmond, if you've got things covered at Mesa Falls, I'm going to head back home."

"You're returning to Rivera Ranch?" Desmond stood and walked to the door with them, though his question was for Miles.

"Eventually." Miles could only think about one destination today, however. "I need to make a stop in Los Angeles first."

After a quick exchange of pleasantries, Miles and Weston left the owner's suite together.

"Los Angeles?" Weston wasted no time in posing the question.

Slowing his step in the long, empty corridor between the casino floor and the offices, Miles couldn't deny the rare impulse to unburden himself. His brother, after all, owed him a listening ear after the way Miles had helped him patch up his relationship with April Stephens, the woman Wes loved beyond reason.

"I messed up with Chiara," he admitted, done with trying to label what happened as anything other than his fault. "I was selfish. Stupid. Shortsighted—"

Weston halted in the middle of the echoing hall, clamping a hand on Miles's shoulder. "What happened?"

Miles explained the way he'd withheld the news about the DNA evidence to give himself more time with her, to try to think of a way to make her stay, even though he'd known about her past and the way her own family had kept secrets from her. Even though she'd told him how hard it was for her to trust. When he finished, Weston looked thoughtful.

"You remember when I screwed up with April, you told me that I needed to be the one to take a risk. To put myself on the line?"

"Yes." Miles remembered that conversation. Of course, taking chances was like breathing to his brother, so it hadn't seemed like too much to ask of him to be the one to tell April he loved her. "I also told you that not everyone can be such a romantic."

Miles knew himself too well. He had two feet on the ground at all times. He was a practical man. Salt of the earth. A rancher. He didn't jump first and ask questions later. That had always been Wes's role. But maybe it was time to take a page from his brother's book, to step up and take a risk when the moment called for it. His gut burned to think he hadn't already done so.

"News flash. What you're feeling doesn't have a thing to do with romance. It has everything to do with love, and you're going to lose it, without question, if you can't get your head on straight and see that." Weston's expression was dire. Grave.

And Miles wasn't too proud to admit it scared the hell of out of him. Especially if what he'd walked away from was love. But by the way the word encapsulated every single aspect of his feelings for Chiara, he knew Weston was right.

"You think I already blew it for good?" He wondered how fast his plane could get to LA.

"It's been three days and you haven't even called? Haven't gone there to tell her how wrong you were?" Weston shook his head. "Why didn't you call me sooner to help you figure this out? I owed you, man. Maybe, with more time, I could have—"

Miles cut his brother off, panic welling up in his chest.

"I've got a plane to catch." He didn't wait to hear any more about how much he'd screwed up. If time was of the essence, he wasn't wasting another second of it to see Chiara and tell her how he felt about her.

That he loved her.

Thirteen

Seated in a low, rolled-arm chair close to her balcony, Chiara sniffed a small vial of fragrance, knowing she'd have a headache soon if she kept testing the samples from her perfumer. Although maybe the impending headache had more to do with all the tears she'd shed for Miles this week. Still, she needed the distraction from her hurt, so she sniffed the floral fumes again, trying to pinpoint what she didn't like about the scent.

The setting sun smudged the western sky with lavender and pink as lights glowed in the valley below her Hollywood Hills home. The glass wall was retracted between her living room and the balcony so that the night air circulated around the seating area where she tested the samples. She'd adored this property once, so modern and elegant, but it felt incredibly lonely to her since she'd returned to it earlier in the week. As for the fragrance vial in her hand, the hint of honeysuckle—so pleasing in nature—was too heavy in the mixture. She handed it back to Mrs. Santor, her housekeeper.

In addition to her regular duties, she was giving her input on developing a signature fragrance for Chiara's brand.

"I didn't like that one, either," Mrs. Santor said from the seat beside her, packing away the vial in a kit Chiara had received from a perfumer. "You should call it a night, honey. You look spent."

Amy Santor was Jules's mother and a former next-door neighbor in Chiara's old life. Mrs. Santor had cleaned houses all her life, and when Chiara's business had taken off, she would have gladly given Mrs. Santor any job she wanted in her company to repay her for kindnesses she'd shown Chiara in her youth. But Jules's mom insisted that she enjoyed keeping house, and Chiara felt fortunate to have a maternal figure in her home a few times a week.

"I shouldn't be. It's still early." She checked her watch, irritated with herself for not being more focused.

She'd given Jules a much-needed night off but hadn't taken one herself, preferring to lose herself in work ever since the heartbreak of leaving Lake Tahoe.

She'd heard from a detective today about arresting the woman who'd hijacked her social media, so it should have felt like she had closure. But that conversation had only made her realize how much more losing Miles had hurt her than any damage a hacker could wreak.

At any rate, she'd *tried* to lose herself in work since that had always been her escape. Her purpose. Her calling. She'd built it up in spite of the grief she'd had for Zach, trusting the job to keep her grounded. But it didn't provide a refuge for her now.

"I'll make you some tea before I go," Mrs. Santor continued, putting away the paperwork from the fragrance kit. "I know you don't want to talk about whatever happened on your travels, but trust me when I tell you that you need to take care of yourself."

And with a gentle squeeze to Chiara's shoulder, Mrs. Santor started the kettle to boil in the kitchen while Chiara tried to pull herself together. Maybe she should have confided in her longtime friend. She hadn't talked to Jules, either, refusing to give the people she loved the chance to comfort her.

For so many years she'd been an island—isolated, independent, and no doubt taking too much pride in the fact. But what good was pride when she felt so empty inside now?

Walking away from Miles was the hardest thing she'd ever done. Second only to the restraint it took every day—every hour—not to call or text him. She wondered if he'd returned to Mesa Falls by now or if he'd gone back to Rivera Ranch. Mostly, she wondered if he ever missed her or regretted the way they'd parted.

A moment later, Mrs. Santor returned with a steaming cup and set it before her. "I'm heading out now, hon. I'll see you Saturday, okay?"

Grateful for the woman's thoughtfulness, Chiara rose and hugged her. "Thank you."

Jules's mother hugged her back with the same warmth she gave her own daughter. "Of course. And don't work too hard."

When Mrs. Santor left, Chiara settled in for the evening. But just as she took a sip of her tea to ward off the loneliness of her empty house, the guard buzzed her phone from the gate downstairs. She picked up her device.

"Ms. Campagna, there's a Miles Rivera to see you."

Everything inside her stilled.

There'd been a time he could have had security toss her out of his home for invading his privacy, but instead, he'd listened to her explanation. For that alone, he deserved an audience now. But more than that, she couldn't resist the chance to see him again. She'd missed him so much.

"You can let him in," she answered, feelings tumbling over each other too fast for her to pick through them.

She'd been thinking about him and wishing she could see him. Now that he was here, was she brave enough to take a chance with him? She didn't want to let Miles go, either. What good did her pride do her if it left her feeling heart-broken and lonely?

Chiara resisted the urge to peek in a mirror, although she may have fluffed her hair a little and smoothed her dress. Who didn't want to look their best in front of the one who got away?

She rose from the seat to stand out on the balcony. Even though she was staring out at the spectacular view with her back to the house, Chiara could tell when Miles was close. The hairs on the back of her neck stood, a shiver of awareness passing over her. She pressed her lips together to ward off the feelings, reminding herself of what had happened to drive them apart.

"I've never seen such a beautiful view." The familiar rasp in his voice warmed her. Stirred her.

Turning on her heel, she faced him as he paced through the living area and out onto the balcony. With his chiseled features and deep blue eyes, his black custom suit that hinted at sculpted muscles and the lightly tanned skin visible at the open collar of his white shirt, he was handsome to behold.

But she remembered so many other things about him that were even more appealing. His thoughtfulness in watching out for her. His insistence she go to the police. His touch.

"Hello to you, too," she greeted him, remembering his

fondness for launching right into conversation. "I'm surprised to see you here."

"I wanted to be sure you heard the news." He stepped closer until he leaned against the balcony rail with her. "That your harasser is behind bars."

She shouldn't be disappointed that this practical man would be here for such a pragmatic purpose, yet she couldn't deny she'd hoped for more than that. Should she tell him how much she'd missed him? How many times she'd thought about calling?

Absently, she drummed her fingernails against the polished railing, trying not to notice how close Miles's hands were to hers. "Yes. A detective called me this morning with some questions about Vivian Fraser from our time together at Brookfield. I didn't realize she worked for Alec now."

"Were you aware she was jealous of you?"

"No. I don't remember her well from Brookfield other than recalling she was a popular girl with a lot of friends. Our paths never crossed much, as she favored chess club and science over the art activities that I liked." She'd been stunned to hear that Alec's personal assistant had intercepted his messages and decided to "protect" Zach's memory for him by attempting to scare Chiara away from her search for answers.

But apparently there was a clear digital trail that led to Vivian's personal computer, and she'd admitted as much to the police. The woman was in love with Alec and would do anything to protect him. She'd also done her best to keep other women away from him since they'd had an on-again, off-again relationship dating all the way back to high school. It was sad to think a promising young woman had gotten so caught up in wanting attention from a man that she'd given up her own dreams and identity in an effort to capture his notice.

"I breathed a whole lot easier once I heard the news," Miles said as he looked over the lights spread out below them now that the pink hues of sunset had faded. "I'm sure you did, too."

She couldn't help but glance over at his profile. The strong jaw and chin. The slash of his cheekbone. His lips that could kiss her with infinite tenderness.

"I guess." She spoke quickly once she realized she'd stared too long. "But the whole business with my blog and Vivian were distractions from my real purpose. I really went there to find out about Zach's final days."

She felt more than saw Miles turn toward her now. His eyes looking over her the way she'd studied him just a moment ago. Her heat beat faster as a soft breeze blew her white dress's hem against her legs, the silk teasing her already too-aware skin.

"I know you did, Chiara. And I'm sorry that I got in the way of what you were doing by not sharing what I knew as soon as I knew it." The regret and sincerity in his voice were unmistakable. "You deserved my full help and attention. And so did Zach."

Drawn by his words, she turned toward him now, and they faced one another eye to eye for the first time tonight. He seemed even closer to her now. Near enough to touch.

"I recognize that I probably should have been more understanding. Especially after the way you overlooked me trying to get into your personal files. I crossed a line more than you did." She hadn't forgotten that, and the unfairness of her response compared to his seemed disproportionate.

"But I didn't know you when I sneaked into your office. Whereas—"

"The situations were completely different." He shook his head, not letting her finish her sentence. "You had every right to think I might have been a bad friend to Zach or even an enemy. But I knew you had his best interests at heart that day I kept quiet about the DNA. My only defense was that I wanted one more day with you."

Startled, she rewound the words in her mind, barely daring to hope she'd heard him right. "You—what?"

"I knew that once I told you the DNA results you'd have no reason to stay in Tahoe any longer." He touched her forearm. "And our time together had been so incredible, Chiara, I couldn't bear for it to end. I told myself that keeping quiet about it for a few more hours wouldn't hurt. I just wanted—" He shook his head. "It was selfish of me. And I'm sorry."

The admission wasn't at all what she'd expected. "I thought you were keeping secrets to hold me at arm's length. It felt like you didn't want to confide in me."

But this? His reason was far more compelling. And it shot right into the tender recesses of her heart.

"Far from it." A breeze ruffled Miles's hair the way she longed to with her fingers. His hand stroked up her arm to her shoulder. "Talking to you was the highlight of my week. And considering everything else that happened, you have to know how much it meant to me."

She melted inside. Absolutely, positively melted.

"Really?" She'd hoped so, until he'd walked away. But she could see the regret in his eyes now, and it gave her renewed hope.

"Yes, really." He stepped closer to her, one hand sliding around her waist while the other skimmed a few wind-tossed strands of hair from her eyes. "Chiara, I got burned so badly the last time I cared about someone that I planned to be a lot more cautious in the future. I figured if I took my time to build a safe, smart relationship, maybe then I could fall in love."

Her pulse skipped a couple of beats. She blinked up at him, hanging on his words. Trying not to sink into the feeling of his hands on her after so many days of missing him. Missing what they'd shared. Aching for more. For a future.

"I don't understand. Are you suggesting we didn't build a safe relationship?"

"I'm suggesting that whatever my intentions were, they didn't matter at all, because you showed up and we had the most amazing connection I've ever felt with anyone." His hold on her tightened, and she might have stepped a tiny bit closer because the hint of his aftershave lured her.

"I felt that, too," she admitted, remembering how that first night she'd felt like the whole world disappeared except for them. "The amazing connection."

"Right. Good." His lips curved upward just a hint at her words. "Because I came here tonight—why I *really* came here tonight—to tell you that I fell in love with you, Chiara. And if there's any way you can give me another chance, I'm going to do everything in my power to make you fall in love with me, too."

Her heart hitched at his words, which were so much more than she'd dared hope for—but everything she wanted. Touched beyond measure, she couldn't find her voice for a moment. And then, even when she did, she bit her lip, wanting to say the right thing.

"Miles, I knew when we were in the woods that day that I loved you." She laid her hand on his chest beside his jacket lapel, just over his heart. She remembered every minute of their time together. "I didn't even want to go back to the house afterward because it felt like our time together was ending, and I didn't want to lose you."

He wrapped her tight in his arms and kissed her. Slowly. Thoroughly. Until she felt a little weak-kneed from it and the promise it held of even more. When he eased back, she was breathing fast and clinging to him.

"You're not going to lose me. Not now. Not ever." His blue eyes were dark as midnight, the promise one she'd never forget.

It filled her with certainty about the future. Their future.

"You won't lose me, either," she vowed before freeing a hand to gesture to the view. "Not even if I have to leave all this behind to live on Rivera Ranch with you."

"You don't have to do that." He tipped his forehead to hers. "We can take all the time you want to talk about what makes most sense. Or hell, just what we want. I know you want to go back to art school one day, so we can always look at living close to a good program for you."

No one had ever put her first before, and it felt incredibly special to have Miles do just that. The possibilities expanded.

"You don't need to be at the ranch?" she asked, curious about his life beyond Mesa Falls. She wanted to learn everything about him.

"I've worked hard to make it a successful operation that runs smoothly. I've hired good people to maintain that, so even if I'm not there, the ranch will continue to prosper." He traced her cheek with his fingers, then followed the line of her mouth.

She sucked in a breath, wanting to seal the promise of their future with a kiss, and much, much more. Lifting her eyes to his, she read the same steamy thoughts in his expression.

"I'll be able to weigh the possibilities more after I show you how much I've missed you," she told him, capturing his thumb between her teeth.

With a growl that thrilled her, he lifted her in his arms and walked her inside the house.

She had a last glimpse of the glittering lights of the Hollywood Hills, but the best view of all was wherever this man was. Miles Rivera, her rancher hero, right here in her arms.

* * * * *

PROLOGUE

London, Summer 2008, a hotel

ANGEL'S EYES HAD adjusted to the dark but from where she was lying the illuminated display of the bedside clock was hidden from her view, blocked by his shoulder. But the thin finger of light that was shining into the room through the chink in the blackout curtains suggested that it was morning.

'The morning after the night before!'

She gave a soft shaken sigh and allowed her glance to drift around the unfamiliar room, the generic but luxurious five-star hotel furnishings familiar, especially to someone who had slept in dozens of similar suites; someone who had imagined at one point that everybody ordered their supper from room service.

Since she'd had the choice Angel had avoided rooms like this as they depressed her. Depressed… Smiling at the past tense, she raised herself slowly up on one elbow. This room was different not because it boasted a special view or had a sumptuously comfortable bed. What was different was that she was not alone.

She froze when the man on the bed beside her murmured in his sleep and her attention immediately returned to him—it had never really left him. She gulped as he threw a hand above his head, the action causing the muscles in his beautiful back to ripple in a way that made her stomach flip over. She couldn't see his face but his breathing remained deep and regular.

Should she wake him up?

The bruised-looking half-moons underneath his spectacular eyes suggested he probably needed his sleep. She'd noticed them the moment she'd looked at him, but then she had noticed pretty much everything about him. Angel had never considered herself a particularly observant person but crazily one glance had indelibly printed his face into her memory.

Mind you, it was a pretty special face, not made any less special by the lines of fatigue etched around his wide, sensual mouth or the dark shadows beneath those totally spectacular eyes. There was a weary cynicism reflected in those electric-blue depths and also in that first instant anger.

He had been furious with her, but it wasn't the incandescent anger that had made her legs feel hollow or even her dramatic brush with death or that he had saved her life. It was him, everything about him. He projected an aura of raw maleness that had a cataclysmic impact on her, like someone thrown in the deep end who from that first moment was treading water, barely able to breathe, throat tight with emotion as if she were submerged by a massive wave of lust.

It wasn't until much later that she had recognised this as a crossroad moment. She didn't see a fork in the road; there was no definable instant when she made a conscious decision. Her universe had narrowed into this total stranger, and she had known with utter and total conviction that she had to be with him. She wanted him and then she had seen in his eyes he wanted her too.

What else mattered?

Did I really just think that?

What else mattered? The defence of the greedy, absurdly needy and just plain stupid! Angel, who was utterly confident she was none of those things, was conscious that this particular inner dialogue was one it would have been more sensible to have had before, not *after*… After she had broken the habit of a lifetime and thrown caution, baby, bath water and the entire package out of the window!

The previous night there had been no inner dialogue, not even any inhibition-lowering alcohol in her bloodstream, no excuses. The words of a novel she had read years before popped into Angel's head. Although at the time they had made her put the gothic romance to one side with a snort of amused disdain, now she couldn't shake them. 'I felt a deep craving, an ache in my body and soul that I had never imagined possible.'

The remembered words no longer made her snigger and translate with a roll of her eyes—*yes, he's hot!*

Which the man in bed beside her was and then some, but Angel had met hot men before, and she had been amused by their macho posturing. She was in charge of her life and she liked it that way. History was littered with countless examples of strong women who had disastrous personal lives, but she was not going to be one of them.

Admittedly the macho men she was able to view with lofty disdain had not just saved her life, but Angel knew what she was feeling hadn't anything to do with gratitude. Beyond this certainty she wasn't sure of anything much. Her life and her belief system had been turned upside down. She had no idea at all why this was happening but she was not going to fight it. In any case, that would have been as futile as fighting the colour of her eyes or her blood type; it just was…and it was exciting!

'*Dio*, you're so beautiful.' Her husky whisper was soft and tinged with awe as she reached out a hand to touch his dark head, allowing her fingers to slide lightly over the sleek short tufts of hair. Her own hair was often called black but his was two shades darker and her skin, though a warm natural olive, looked almost winter pale against his deeply tanned, vibrant-toned, bronzed flesh. It was a contrast that had fascinated her when she'd first seen their limbs entwined—not just skin tone, but the tactile differences of his hard to her soft, his hair-roughened virility to her feminine smoothness. She wanted to touch, taste…

Angel couldn't understand how she felt so wide awake. Why she wasn't tired. She hadn't slept all night, but her senses weren't dulled by exhaustion. Instead they were racing and her body was humming with an almost painful sensory overload.

Languid pleasure twitched the corners of her full, wide mouth up as she lifted her arms above her head, stretching with feline grace, feeling muscles she hadn't known she had. Who wanted to sleep when it had finally happened? The man of her dreams was real and she had found him!

It was fate!

Her smooth brow knitted into a furrowed web. *Fate* again—this sounded so *not* her. When she had once been accused of not having a romantic bone in her body she had taken it as a compliment. She had never thought she was missing out; she'd never wanted to be that person—the one who fell in love at the drop of a hat and out again equally as easily. That was her mother who, despite the fragile appearance that made men want to protect her, had Teflon-coated emotions.

Angel knew she did not inspire a similar reaction in men and neither did she want to; the thought of not being independent was anathema to her. As a kid she had been saved from a life of loneliness and isolation by two things: a brother and an imagination. Not that she ever, even when she was young, confused her secret fantasy world with real life.

Angel had never expected her fantasies to actually come true.

She stretched out her hand, moving her fingers in the air above the curve of his shoulder, fighting the compulsion to touch him, to tug the sheet that was lying low across his hips farther down. She was amazed that she could have these thoughts and feel no sense of embarrassment. It had been the same when she had undressed for him—it had just felt right and heart-stoppingly exciting.

No fantasy had ever matched the fascination she felt for his body. Her stomach muscles quivered in hot, hungry anticipation of exploring every inch of his hard, lean body again.

'Totally beautiful,' she whispered again, staring at the man sharing her bed.

His name was Alex. When he'd asked she'd told him her name was Angelina, but that nobody ever called her that. Apparently when she was born her father had said she looked like a little angel and it had stuck.

She tensed when, as if in response to her voice, he murmured in his sleep before rolling over onto his back, one arm flung over his head, his long fingers brushing the headboard.

Angel felt a strong sensual kick of excitement low and deep in her belly as she stared, the rapt expression on her face a fusion of awe and hunger. She swallowed past the emotional thickening that made her throat ache. He was the most beautiful thing she had ever seen or imagined.

In the half-light that now filled the room his warm olive-toned skin gleamed like gold, its texture like oiled satin. A tactile tingle passed through her fingertips. Perfect might have seemed like an overused term but he was. The length of his legs was balanced by broad shoulders and a deeply muscled chest dusted with dark body hair that narrowed into a directional arrow across his flat belly ridged with muscle. There wasn't an ounce of excess flesh on his lean body to disguise the musculature that had the perfection of an anatomical diagram. But Alex was no diagram. He was a warm, living, earthly male, and he was sharing her bed.

A dazed smile flickered across her face as she felt all the muscles in her abdomen tighten. Last night had been perfect—perfect, but not in the way she had expected. There had been hardly any pain and no embarrassment.

Angel has still failed to grasp the concept of moderation. There is no middle ground—she is all or nothing.

The words on her report card came back to her.

Her form teacher had been referring to her academic record

littered with As and Fs, not to sex, but there had been no middle ground last night either. Angel had held nothing back; she had given him everything without reservation.

'I know this is bad timing, but there's a problem.'

The words had been music to Alex's ears. 'Tell me.'

They had and he had acted. Crisis management was something he excelled at—it was a simple matter of focusing, shutting out all distractions and focusing.

He had gone straight from the funeral to his office, where he'd pretty much lived for the past month. He'd washed, eaten and slept—or at least snatched a few minutes on the sofa—there. It made sense, and it suited him. He had nothing to go home to any longer.

Then the crisis was over and Alex had been unable to think of any reason not to go home, where he had, if anything, less sleep. He did go to bed but by the small hours he was up again, which was why it felt strange and disorientating to wake up after a deep sleep and find light shining through the blinds of…not his room… Where the hell?

He blinked and focused on the beautiful face of the most incredible-looking woman. She was sitting there looking down at him wearing nothing but a mane of glossy dark hair that lay like a silky curtain over her breasts—breasts that had filled his hands perfectly and tasted—

It all came rushing back.

Hell!

'Good morning.'

His body reacted to the slumberous promise in her smile, but, ignoring the urgent messages it was sending and the desire that heated his blood, gritted his teeth and swung his legs over the side of the bed. Guilt rising like a toxic tide to clog his throat, he sat, eyes closed, with his rigid back to her. This was about damage limitation and not repeating a mistake no matter how tempting it might seem.

She was sinful temptation given a throaty voice and a perfect body, but this had been his mistake, not hers, and it was his responsibility to end it.

'I thought you'd never wake up.'

His spine tensed at the touch of her fingers on his skin. He wiped his face of all emotion as he turned back to face her.

'You should have woken me. I hope I haven't made you late for anything…?'

'Late…?' she quavered.

He stood up and looked around for his clothes. 'Can I get you a taxi?'

'I… I don't understand… I thought we'd…' Her voice trailed away. He was looking at her so coldly.

'Look, last night was… Actually it was fantastic but I'm not available.'

Available? Angel still didn't get it.

He felt the guilt tighten in his gut but he had no desire to prolong this scene. He'd made a massive mistake, end of story. A post-mortem was not going to change anything.

'I thought—'

He cut across her. 'Last night was just sex.'

He was speaking slowly as if he were explaining something to a child or a moron. The coldness in his blue eyes as much as his words confused Angel.

'But last night…'

'Like I said, last night was great, but it was a mistake.' A great big mistake, but a man learned by his mistakes and he didn't give in to the temptation to repeat them.

She began to feel sick as she watched him fight his way into his shirt, then he was pulling on his trousers. She responded automatically to pick up the object that fell out of the pocket and landed with a metallic twang on the floor just in front of her toes. She bent to pick it up; her fingers closed around a ring.

'Yours?'

He was meticulously careful not to touch her fingers as he took it from her outstretched hand.

'You're married?'

For a moment he thought of telling the truth, saying that he had been, but no longer, that the ring was in his pocket because friends kept telling him it was time to move on. Alex doubted this was what they'd had in mind.

Then he realised how much easier and less painful a lie would be. It wouldn't ease the guilt that was like a living thing in his gut, but it would make this scene less messy and allow her to say when regaling her friends later that *the bastard was married.*

'I'm sorry.'

Her incredible green eyes flared hot as she rose majestically to her feet and delivered a contemptuous 'You disgusting loser!' followed up by a backhanded slap that made him blink. He opened his watering eyes in time to see her vanish into the bathroom, the door locked audibly behind her.

Angel ran, hand clamped to her mouth, across the room, just making it to the loo before she was violently sick.

By the time she returned to the bedroom he was gone.

Angel found herself hating him with more venom than she thought she was capable of. She hated him even more than her mother's creepy boyfriend, the one who had tried to grope her when she was sixteen. The only person she hated more than Alex was herself. How could she be so stupid? He had treated her like a tramp because that was how she had acted.

By the time she left the hotel room later that morning, her tears had dried and her expression was set. She had decided she would never, ever think of him again, not think of him or last night.

It never happened.

He never existed.

It was a solution.

She could move on.

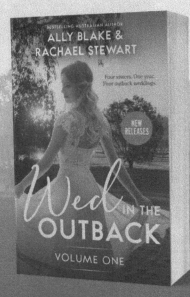

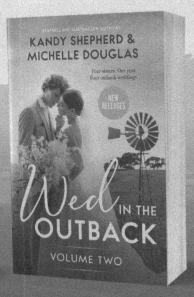